Propositioned by the Playboy

CARA COLTER
FIONA LOWE
BRENDA HARLEN

Published in Great Britain 2014
by Mills & Boon, an imprint of Harlequin (UK) Limited,
Eton House, 18-24 Paradise Road, Richmond, Surrey, TW9 1SR

PROPOSITIONED BY THE PLAYBOY © 2014 Harlequin Books S.A.

Miss Maple and the Playboy, The Playboy Doctor's Marriage Proposal and *The New Girl in Town* were first published in Great Britain by Harlequin (UK) Limited.

Miss Maple and the Playboy © 2009 Cara Colter
The Playboy Doctor's Marriage Proposal © 2008 Fiona Lowe
The New Girl in Town © 2007 Brenda Harlen

ISBN: 978-0-263-91198-5
eBook ISBN: 978-1-472-04493-8

05-0814

Harlequin (UK) Limited's policy is to use papers that are natural, renewable and recyclable products and made from wood grown in sustainable forests. The logging and manufacturing processes conform to the legal environmental regulations of the country of origin.

Printed and bound in Spain
by Blackprint CPI, Barcelona

MISS MAPLE
AND THE PLAYBOY

BY
CARA COLTER

Cara Colter lives on an acreage in British Columbia, with her partner, Rob, and eleven horses. She has three grown children and a grandson. She is a recent recipient of the *RT Book Reviews* Career Achievement Award in the "Love and Laughter" category. Cara loves to hear from readers and you can contact her, or learn more about her, through her website: www.cara-colter.com.

To Chris Bourgeois,
aka riding buddy, drifter, equine therapist

CHAPTER ONE

"IT SUCKS to be you."

Ben Anderson opened his mouth to protest and then closed it again. He contemplated how those few words summed up his life and decided the assessment was not without accuracy. Of course, the truth of those words was closely linked to the fact he had become guardian to the boy who had spoken them, his eleven-year-old nephew, Kyle.

It was a position Ben had held for precisely ten days, the most miserable of his life, which was saying quite a bit since he had spent several years in the Marine Corps, including an eight-month tour of duty in the land of sand and blood and heartbreak.

At least over there, Ben thought, there had been guidelines and rules, a rigid set of operating standards. Becoming Kyle's guardian was like being dropped in the middle of a foreign country with no backup, no map, and only a rudimentary command of the language.

For instance, did he tell Kyle he was sick of the expression *It sucks to be you* or did he let it pass?

While contemplating his options, Ben studied the

envelope in front of him. It was addressed to Mr. Ben Anderson and in careful brackets Kyle's Guardian just so that where was no wriggling out of it. The handwriting was tidy and uptight and told Ben quite a bit about the writer, though Kyle had been filling him in for the past ten days.

Miss Maple, Kyle's new teacher at his new school was old. And mean. Not to mention supremely ugly. "Mugly," Kyle had said, which apparently meant more than ugly.

She was also unfair, shrill-voiced and the female reincarnation of Genghis Khan.

Kyle was a surprising expert on Genghis Khan. He'd informed Ben, in a rare chatty moment, that a quarter of the world's population had Khan blood in them. He'd said it hopefully, but Ben doubted with Kyle's red hair and freckles that his nephew was one of them.

Ben flipped over the envelope, looking for clues. "What does Miss Maple want?" he asked Kyle, not opening the letter.

"She wants to see you," Kyle said, and then repeated, "It sucks to be you."

Then he marched out of his uncle's kitchen as if the fact that his old, mean and ugly teacher wanted to see his uncle had not a single thing to do with *him*.

Ben thought the responsible thing to do would be to call his nephew back and discuss the whole "it sucks" thing. But fresh to the concept of being responsible for anyone other than himself, Ben wasn't quite sure what the *right* thing to do was with Kyle. His nephew had the slouch and street-hardened eyes of a seasoned con, but just below that was a fragility that made Ben debate whether the Marine Corps approach was going to be helpful or damaging.

And God knew he didn't want to do anymore damage. Because the hard truth was if it sucked to be someone in this world, that someone was Kyle O. Anderson.

Ben's parents had been killed in a car accident when he was seventeen. He'd been too old to go into the "system" and too young to look after his sister, who had been fourteen at the time. Ben went to the marines, Carly went to foster care. Ben was well aware that he had gotten the better deal.

By the time she'd been fifteen, Carly had been a boiling cauldron of pain, sixteen she was wild, seventeen she was pregnant, not that that had cured either the pain or the wildness.

She had dragged Kyle through broken relationships and down-and-out neighborhoods. When Ben had been overseas and helpless to do a damn thing about it, she and Kyle had gone through a homeless phase. But even after he'd come back stateside, Ben's efforts to try and help her and his nephew had been rebuffed. Carly saw her brother's joining up as leaving her, and she never forgave him.

But now, only twenty-eight, Carly was dying of too much heartbreak and hard living.

And Ben found himself faced with a tough choice. Except for Carly, his life was in as close to perfect a place as it had ever been. Ben owned his own business, the Garden of Weedin'. He'd found a niche market, building outdoor rooms in the yards of the upscale satellite communities that circled the older, grittier city of Morehaven, New York.

A year ago he'd invested in his own house, which he'd bought brand-new in the well-to-do town of Cranberry Corners, a community that supported his business and was a thirty-minute drive and a whole world away from the mean streets of the inner city that Kyle and Carly had called home.

Ben's personal specialty was in "hardscaping," which was planning and putting in the permanent structures like decks, patios, fireplaces and outdoor kitchens that made the backyards of Cranberry Corners residents superposh. It was devilishly hard work, which suited him to a T because he was high energy and liked being in good shape. The business had taken off beyond his wildest dreams.

Ben also enjoyed a tight network of buddies, some of whom he'd gone to high school with and who enjoyed success and the single lifestyle as much as he did.

Did he disrupt all that and take sucks-to-be-him Kyle O. Anderson, with his elephant-size chip on his shoulder, or surrender him to the same system that had wrecked Carly?

Since Ben considered himself to be a typical male animal, self-centered, insensitive, superficial—and darned proud of it—he astonished himself by not feeling as if it was a choice at all. He felt as if sometimes a man had to do what a man had to do, and for him that meant taking his nephew.

Not that either his nephew or his sister seemed very appreciative.

Not that that was why he had done it.

Ben opened the tidy envelope from Miss Maple. He

The wall contained charts full of shining stars, artwork, reprints of good paintings. This was the space of someone who loved what she did. From Kyle's attitude, Ben had pictured something grimmer and more prisonlike for Miss Maple's lair.

But then, Miss Maple was not the Miss Maple he had imagined, either, and Ben struggled to readjust to the picture in front of him. In fact, the teacher was young, not more than twenty-five. She was concentrating on something on her desk, and her features were fine and flawless, her skin was beautiful, faintly sun-kissed, totally unlined. Her hair, pulled back in a ponytail, was the exact dark golden color of the wildflower honey that Ben kept in a glass jar on his countertop.

Of course, she could still be mean. Ben had known plenty of gorgeous women who were mean straight through. You could tell by their eyes, diamond flint and ice.

But then she lifted her eyes, and he was momentarily lost in their softness and their color, an astounding mix of jade and aqua and copper.

Nothing mean in those eyes, he decided, and tried out his best easygoing boy-next-door grin on her.

An unexpected thing happened. She frowned. It didn't make her look *mean* precisely, but he understood perfectly how an eleven-year-old boy could be intimidated by her.

"Hello," she said, "I think you must be lost." Her voice wasn't screechy at all. It was quite amazing, with the bell-like tone of a church bell ringing on a cold, pure morning. She leaned back in her chair and folded her arms over her chest, as if she had suddenly reached the alarming conclusion she was alone in this end of the building.

Women weren't generally alarmed by him, but the fact she was here at five in the evening probably meant she was sheltered in some way. The atmosphere in the classroom really was a testament to no life. How long did it take to make a tree like that? She'd probably been in here all summer, cloistered away, working on it!

More's the pity, since Ben could clearly see her chest was delicately and deliciously curved, though it occurred to him it was probably some kind of sin to notice that about the grade-five teacher, and the fact that he had noticed probably justified the alarm in her eyes.

Or maybe that was nuns a man was not supposed to think manlike thoughts about.

Which she was dressed like, not that he was an expert on how nuns dressed, but he suspected just like that: high-buttoned blouse in pristine white, frumpy sweater in forgettable beige.

He would have liked a glimpse of her legs, since he was unfortunately curious about whether she was wearing a skirt or slacks, but the desk totally blocked his view.

He moved forward, leaned over the desk and extended his hand. He couldn't think of a way to lean over far enough to see her legs without alarming her more than she already was, so he didn't.

"I'm Ben Anderson, Kyle's uncle." He deliberately turned up the wattage of his smile, found himself wishing he had changed out of his work clothes—torn jeans with the knee out, his company T-shirt with Garden of Weedin' emblazoned across the front of it.

Miss Maple took his hand but did not return his smile. Any idea he had about holding her hand a little too long was dismissed instantly. Her handshake was chilly and brief.

"You are very late," she said. "I was about to leave."

Ben was astounded to find he felt, not like six foot one of hard-muscled fighting machine, but like a chastened schoolboy. Out of the corner of his eye, he saw Kyle slide in the door, and roll his shoulders inward, as if he was expecting a blow. Ben found he didn't have the heart to blame his nephew for not giving him the note.

"Uh, well," he said charmingly, "you know. Life gets in the way."

She was not charmed, and apparently she did not know. "Kyle, will you go down to the library? I had Mrs. Miller order a copy of *The History of Khan* for you. She said she'd leave it on her desk."

"For me?" Kyle squeaked, and Ben, astonished by the squeak glanced at him. The hard mask was gone from his eyes, and his nephew looked like a little boy who was going to cry. A little boy, Ben thought grimly, who had seen far too few kindnesses in his life.

He was aware the teacher watched Kyle go, too, something both troubled and tender in her eyes, though when she looked back at him, her gaze was carefully cool.

"Have a seat, Mr. Anderson."

Miss Maple seemed to realize at about the same time as Ben there really was no place in that entire room where he could possibly sit. The desks were too small, and she had the one adult-size chair.

He watched a faint blush rise up her cheeks and was

reluctantly enchanted. He decided to smile at her again. Maybe she was one of those women who *liked* the real-man look, dirt and muscles. He flexed his forearm just a tiny bit to see if she was paying attention.

She was, because her blush deepened and she took a sudden interest in shuffling some papers on her desk. She apparently forgot she'd invited him to sit down.

"Your nephew is a bit of dilemma, Mr. Anderson," she said in a rush, shuffling frantically to avoid further eye contact with his muscles.

"Ben," he offered smoothly, hoping she might give up her first name in return.

But she didn't. In fact, she stopped shuffling papers and pressed her lips together in a firm line, gazed at him solemnly and sternly, the effect of the sternness somewhat tempered by the fact she picked that moment to tuck a wayward strand of that honey-colored hair behind her ear.

Ben had the unexpected and electrifying thought that he would like to kiss her. He wasn't sure why. Maybe as a shortcut to the woman underneath that uptight outfit and the stern expression.

She was not the kind of woman he usually went for. And he was pretty sure she was not the kind of woman who usually went for him.

She was the kind of woman where there wouldn't be any kind of shortcuts at all. If a guy were to date her, it wasn't going to end in her backyard hot tub after midnight.

Not that Miss Maple would have a hot tub! He regarded her thoughtfully, trying to guess at her after-school activities. Knitting, possibly. Bird-watching, probably. Reading, definitely.

No, she was not his type at all.

Which probably explained why he felt intrigued by her. He wasn't quite sure when he'd become so sick to death of the kind of women who were his type, though that covered a lot of ground from supersophisticated debutantes, to rowdy party-hearty girls, to experienced divorcees, to free-spirited and very independent career women. None of them intrigued him anymore, and hadn't for a long time. For a while nobody had noticed, but lately his buddies were looking at Ben's ability to go home alone as if he had contracted a strange disease that needed to be cured before it became contagious.

The demure little schoolteacher made Ben Anderson feel challenged, the first interest he had felt in what the guys cheerfully called "the hunt" for a long, long time. Or maybe, he told himself wryly, he was looking for a little diversion from his sucks-to-be-you life.

Whatever it was, he now had a secret agenda that was making it very hard to focus on what she was saying about Kyle.

A contract for Kyle to sign. With goals and challenges and rewards.

"Mr. Anderson," she said, ignoring his invitation to call him Ben. "Your nephew has been held back once and has dismal test scores. He won't do his homework, and he doesn't participate in class discussions. But I think he reads at a college level and with complete comprehension.

"If I implement this plan for him," Miss Maple continued sternly, "it is going to take a tremendous amount of work and commitment on my part. I need to know you will be backing me at home, and that you are willing to put in the same kind of time and commitment."

Ben had been around long enough to know he should be very wary of a woman who tossed around the word *commitment* so easily.

He threw caution to the wind. "Why don't we discuss your plan in a little more detail over dinner?" he asked.

Miss Maple looked completely uncharmed. In fact, she looked downright annoyed.

He felt a little annoyed himself. Women didn't generally look annoyed when he asked them out for dinner. Delighted. Intrigued. He thought he should be insulted that the fifth-grade teacher didn't look the least delighted about his invitation or the least intrigued by him.

She was probably trying to be professional, trying to backpedal since he had seen her blush when he'd flexed his muscle. She wasn't as immune as she wanted him to think.

"I'm afraid I don't go for dinner with parents," Miss Maple said snippily.

Despite the fact he was amazed by her rejection, Ben assumed an expression that he hoped was a fair approximation of complete innocence. "Miss Maple," he chided her, "I am not Kyle's parent. I'm his uncle."

There was the little blush again, but Ben was almost positive it was caused by irritation, not the flexing of his forearm.

"I don't date the family members of my students," she said tightly, spelling it out carefully.

"Date?" Ben raised a surprised eyebrow. "You misunderstood me. I wasn't asking you on a date."

Now she had the audacity to look faintly hurt!

The problem with a woman like Miss Maple, Ben thought, was that she would be way more complicated than the women he normally took out. Challenge or not, he knew he should cut his losses and run for the door.

Naturally, he did nothing of the sort.

"I just thought we could get together and go over your plan in more detail." Ben looked at his watch. "Kyle hasn't eaten yet, and I'm trying to get him into regular meals."

That was actually true. His nephew was alarmingly small and skinny for his age, a testament to the Bohemian lifestyle Carly had subjected him to. At first he had resisted Ben's efforts to get him to eat good food at regular intervals, but in the last few days Ben thought he noticed his nephew settling into routines, and maybe even liking them a bit.

He found himself sharing that with Miss Maple, who looked suitably impressed.

"He's had it tough, hasn't he?" she whispered.

Ben could see the softening of the stern line of her face. It made her look very cute. *Time to pounce*. If he asked her for dinner again right now, she'd say yes.

But he was surprised to find he couldn't. Instead he could barely speak over the lump that had developed in his throat. He couldn't even begin to tell her just how tough that kid had had it.

Even though he knew he was capable of being a complete snake, Ben found he could not use Kyle's tragic life to get what he wanted.

Which was a date with Miss Maple. Just to see how it would end. But he'd leave it for now because, whatever else he might be, he had a highly developed sense of what was fair. She genuinely cared about Kyle. That was obvious. And nothing to be played with, either. His nephew had had few enough people care about him without his uncle jeopardizing that in search of something as easy to find as a date with an attractive member of the opposite sex.

Yes, he needed to think the whole thing through a little more carefully.

So, naturally, he didn't. He found himself giving her his cell-phone number, just in case she needed to consult with him during the day. At least that was putting the ball in her court.

She took it, but reluctantly, as if she sensed what he really wanted to consult with her about was her after-school activities.

Kyle came back in the room, clutching his new book to his chest.

"How long can I keep it?" he demanded rudely.

"It's yours," Miss Maple said gently. "I ordered it just for you."

Kyle glared at her. "I've read it before. It's stupid. I don't even want it."

Ben had to bite back a desire to snap at his nephew for being so ungrateful for the kindness offered, but when he looked at Miss Maple, she was looking past the words, to the way Kyle was hugging the book. She said, not the least ruffled, "You keep it anyway. Your uncle might enjoy it."

Ben looked at her sharply, to see if there was a barb buried in the fact Miss Maple thought he might enjoy a stupid book, but nothing in her smooth expression gave her away.

He felt that little flutter of excitement again. He recognized it as a man with a warrior spirit exploring brand-new territory, where there was equal opportunities for success or being shot down.

"I like the tree," Ben said, thinking, *Flattery will get you everywhere.*

"Thank you," she said. "We made it last year as our class project."

It must have shown on his face that he thought that was a slightly frivolous use of school time, because she said haughtily, "We use it as a jumping-off point for all kinds of learning experiences in science, math and English. 'What is learned with delight is never forgotten.' Aristotle."

After they left the school, Ben took Kyle for a burger.

"Your teacher didn't seem that old to me," he said. Of all the things he could have picked to talk about, why her? A woman who quoted Aristotle. With ease. Whoo boy, he should be feeling warned off, not intrigued.

Kyle didn't even look at him, he was so engrossed in his new book. "That's because you're not eleven."

Leave it. There were all kinds of ways to make conversation with an eleven-year-old. *How about those Giants?*

"She didn't seem all that ugly, either."

The burgers had arrived, and Kyle was being so careful not to get stains on his new book that he barely would touch his dinner.

"Well, you haven't seen her face when you don't hand in the homework assignment."

"It would be good if you handed in the homework assignments," Ben said, thinking Kyle was lucky to have a teacher who was so enthusiastic and who actually cared. He remembered "the plan." "If you do it for a month without missing, I'll get us tickets to a Giants game."

Kyle didn't even look up from his book.

On the way home they stopped in at the hospital to see Carly, but she was sleeping, looking worn and fragile and tiny in the hospital bed. Pretty hard to interest a kid whose mom was that sick in a Giants game, Ben thought sadly. Still, he didn't know how to comfort his nephew, and he felt the weight of his own inadequacy when they got home and Kyle went right to his room without saying good-night and slammed his bedroom door hard. Moments later Ben heard the ominous sounds of a musical group shouting incomprehensibly.

He suddenly felt exhausted. His thoughts drifted to Miss Maple and he didn't feel like a warrior or a hunter at all.

He felt like a man who was alone and afraid and who had caught a glimpse of something in the clearness of those eyes that had made him feel as if he could lay his weapons down and fight no more.

The Top-Secret Diary of Kyle O. Anderson

Once, when I was little, my mom told me my uncle Ben was a lady-killer. When she saw the look on my face after she said it, she laughed and said it didn't mean he killed ladies.

It meant women loved him. Now that I live with him, I can see it's true. Whenever we go anywhere, like the burger joint tonight, I see women look at my uncle like he is the main course and they would like to eat him up. They get this funny look in their eyes, the way a little kid looks at a puppy, as if they are already half in love, and they haven't even talked to him.

I know where that look goes, too, because I've seen it on my mom's face, and I'm old enough to know simple problem math. Love plus my mom equals disaster. It probably runs in the family.

I like diaries. I have had one for as long as I can remember after I found one my mom had been given and never used. It had a key and everything. Having a diary is like having a secret friend to tell things to when they get too big to hold inside. I stole the one I am using now because it has a key, too, and I didn't want anyone to laugh at me when I bought it, though afterward I felt bad, and thought I could have said I was buying it for my older sister for her birthday. Which is a lie because I don't have an older sister. I wonder which is a worse bad thing, telling a lie or stealing?

There's lots of things people don't know about me, like I don't really like to do bad things, but it kind of keeps anyone from guessing that I'm so scared all the time that my stomach hurts.

My mom is going to die. She weighs about ninety pounds now, less than me, and I can see bones and blue veins sticking out on her hands. There's a look in her eyes, like she's saying goodbye, even though she still talks tough and as if everything's going to be okay and she's coming home again. Anybody, even a kid, can see that that's not true.

Not that I feel like a kid most of the time. I feel like I've been looking after my mom way longer than she's been looking after me.

Not that I did a very good job of it. Look at her now.

My mom is not like the moms in movies or storybooks. She drinks too much and likes to party, and she falls in with really creepy people. Her boyfriend right now is a loser named Larry. He doesn't even go visit her in the hospital unless her welfare cheque has come and he needs it signed. Uncle Ben moved her to the hospital closer to us, so, gee, Larry would have to take the bus and transfer twice. At least he never hit her or me, which is different than the last one, who was a loser named Barry. That is the sad poem of my mom's life.

Here is another secret: even though I am scared of her dying, I am scared of her living, too. I try not to let my uncle know, but I like it at his house. It's not just that it's nice, even though it is, it's that everything is clean, and he always has food, even if it's dorky stuff like bananas and apples and hardly any cookies or potato chips.

I feel safe here, like I know what's going to happen next, and there aren't going to be any parties in the middle of the night where people start screaming at each other and breaking bottles and pretty soon you hear the sirens coming.

It's weird because one of the things I'm scaredest of is that my uncle won't like me. What will happen to me if he sends me away? And even though that makes me so scared I want to throw up, I am really mean to him. My mom was always mean to him, too. Whenever he turned up, even though he always had groceries for us, she'd yell at him to get lost and it was too late and we didn't need him, and then as soon as he left, she'd slam the door behind him and say, "Why can't he ever say he loves me," and cry for about a week. Which is kind of how I feel after I'm mean to him, too.

He bought all new stuff for my room at his house, and he let me have his supercool TV set and stereo. I never had new stuff before—a brand-new bed and sheets that were so new they felt scratchy the first night I slept in them. It made me want to cry that he bought them just for me, and that he left the television set in there, even though he doesn't even have one in his own bedroom. It kind of made me hope maybe I was staying for good, but I am old enough to know that hope is the most dangerous thing. Maybe that's why I acted mad instead, and told him how lame the cowboy were.

My uncle Ben used to be a marine. He's big as a mountain, and he's probably killed all kinds of people. Maybe with his bare hands. I can't be a crybaby around him.

At my new school everything is new and shiny, and you don't have to go through a metal detector at the front door. The library has lots of books in it, but I'm trying not to care about that too much, either, in case everything changes. You don't want to put too much faith in a place with a corny name like Cranberry Corners. It's not even real. Do you see any cranberries around here?

It is the same with Miss Maple, like she is too good to be true. She does really nice things for me, like the book tonight, but it makes me wish I was little and could just climb on her lap and cry and cry and cry. See? There's that crybaby thing again.

Have you ever seen those movies where people live in a big house on a nice block, with a golden retriever and the kind of yard my uncle builds? All flowers and fountains and that kind of stuff?

Miss Maple is the mom in that movie. You can tell by looking at her, when she gets married and has kids there will be no parties where things get smashed in the night!

No sirree, she will have baked cookies and would serve them warm with milk before bed. And then a nice bath, every single night, whether you are dirty or not, and then I bet she would get right in bed with her kid and read him stories about something lame like turtles that talk.

She would have stupid rules like brushing your teeth, and saying please and thank you and not being *tardy,* and that's why I act like I hate her, because she is the mom I wanted and sure didn't get, and I feel guilty for thinking that when my own mom is going to die.

I told my uncle she was old and mean and ugly because it would have been so much easier for me if that's what she had been. Plus him being a lady-killer and all,

I didn't want him to ever get anywhere near her. Because who knows what would happen next?

I like knowing what is going to happen next. Even though it is supergross to think of your uncle and your teacher *liking* each other, I had an ugly feeling that it was a possibility. I am always thinking of possibilities, trying really hard not to be surprised by life.

I guess I should never have given him the note from her, because it was worse than I imagined when they saw each other. I know *that* look. It usually happens just when my life is getting good, too. Just me and my mom, then *that* look between her and the latest loser and it's a straight downhill slide from there. Not that my uncle or Miss Maple are losers, but I still think if it runs in the family, I'm doomed.

I can probably scare her off my uncle. Sheesh. He comes with a kid. The most rotten kid in her class. She's no dummy. She can do math, too. But what if he decides to have her and get rid of me?

This is the kind of question that makes my stomach hurt. I will just keep her from ever wanting to get mixed up with us.

I wonder if Miss Maple will scream if I put a frog in her desk?

I saw one, a really big one, at Migg's Pond, which is behind the school and out of bounds, except for the science-class field trip. We didn't go on field trips in my old school.

And just thinking about that, how to capture that frog, instead of my mom lying alone in a hospital, and whether or not my uncle is going to keep me, or whether my uncle and Miss Maple are going to progress to the making-eyes-at-each-other stage, eases the ache in my stomach enough that I can go to sleep, finally.

But only if I leave the light on.

CHAPTER TWO

BETH Maple heard a slightly muffled snicker just as she was sliding open her top desk drawer looking for a prize for Mary Kay Narsunchuk, who had just won the weekly spelling bee.

During the whole spelling bee, out of the corner of her eye, Beth had seen Kyle O. Anderson looking absently out the window, seeming not to pay attention, unaware his mouth was silently forming every letter of every word she had challenged the class with, including the one that had finally stumped Mary Kay, *finesse*. But every time she had called on him to spell a word, Kyle had just frowned and ducked his head.

It was an improvement over last week's spelling bee. Whenever she had called on Kyle that time, he had spelled a word, all right, but never the word he'd been given. When the word was *tarry*, he spelled *tarantula*, when she gave him *forte*, he spelled, or started to spell *fornication*. She had cut him off before he'd completed the word. Thankfully, no one in her grade-five class seemed to have any idea what that exchange had been about.

But Kyle was being suspiciously well-behaved for

this spelling bee. At her most optimistic she hoped that meant his uncle had talked to him after their meeting last night about the plan, and had implemented the reward system at home.

It was probably that momentary lapse, thinking about Kyle's uncle, that made Beth react slowly to the snicker as she was opening her desk drawer. Her brain shouting "Beware" did not get to her hand in time. Of course, her brain could just as well have been warning her off the gorgeous, full-of-himself, Ben Anderson, as the contents of her desk drawer!

A blob of green exploded from the desk, and collided with her hand, unbelievably *squishy* and revolting. Beth did what no grade-five teacher should ever do.

She screamed, then caught herself and stuffed her fist in her mouth. She regarded the largest frog she had ever seen, which sat not three feet in front of her on the floor, glaring at her with beady reptilian eyes.

It's only a frog, she told herself sternly, but nevertheless she screamed again when it leaped forward. She could hear Kyle's satisfied chortles above all the other sounds in a classroom that was quickly dissolving into pandemonium.

Twelve economy-size knights rushed to rescue their teacher, aka damsel-in-distress, though she was not naive enough to believe chivalry had trumped the pure temptation of the frog.

Casper Hearn led the charge, a big boy, throwing desks and hysterical girls out of his way as he stampeded around the room in pursuit of the frog.

But somehow, out of the melee, it was Kyle who

emerged, panting, the frog clutched to his chest. Now he faced the other boys, something desperate in his pinched, pale face as they surrounded him. His freckles were standing out in relief he was so white.

"Give me the frog," Casper ordered Kyle with distinct menace.

"I'll warn you once to stay away from me," Kyle said, a warning that might have been more effective if his voice wasn't shaking and Casper didn't outweigh him by a good thirty pounds.

Casper laughed. "Is that so? Then what?"

"Then the aisles will run with the fat melting from your bodies!" Kyle shouted, slipping the frog inside his shirt.

Casper took a startled step back from Kyle. The classroom became eerily silent. Casper stared at Kyle, shook his head and then went and sat down, followed by the other boys.

Kyle gave Beth a look she interpreted as apologetic and darted out the door, Kermit happily ensconced in his shirt.

When he didn't return, she realized with a horrible sense of resignation she was going to have to inform Kyle's uncle she had lost his nephew.

And the truth was, Beth Maple would have been just as happy if she never had to speak to Ben Anderson again.

Or at least the part of her that hadn't nearly swooned from the pure and powerful presence of the man would be happy.

The other part, despicably weak, yearned for just one more peek at him.

Beth thought that Ben Anderson was the type of man who should have a warning label on him. There was that word again. *"Beware."* Followed by *"Contents too potent to handle."*

She did not think she had ever been around a man who was so casually and extraordinarily sexy. When he had walked into her room yesterday, it was as if everything but him had faded to nothing. No wonder she had thought he was in the wrong place, hopelessly lost amongst the welcoming fall leaves that dripped from her ceiling and brushed the top of his head.

Ben Anderson was all masculine power. Every single thing about him, from the ease with which he held that amazing male body, to the cast of features made more mesmerizing by the fact his once-perfect nose had the crook of a break in it, radiated some kind of vital male energy.

He oozed strength and self-assurance, from the ripple of muscle, to the upward quirk of a sexy lip. But somehow all that self-assurance was saved from becoming arrogance by the light that danced in eyes as green as a summer swimming hole. Ben Anderson's eyes were warm and laughter filled. Kyle's propensity for mischief was undoubtedly genetic.

Still, something lurked behind the easy laughter of his eyes, the upward quirk of that sexy mouth. There was an untouchable place in Ben Anderson that was as remote as a mountaintop. But unfortunately, rather than making him less attractive, it intrigued, added to a kind of sizzling sensuality that tingled in the air around him.

Ben Anderson had that certain indefinable something that made women melt.

And he knew it, too, the scoundrel.

Beth, sharing her classroom with him last evening, had been totally aware she was an impossibly unworldly grade-five teacher, with nothing at all in her experience to prepare her for a man like that.

You didn't meet a man like Ben Anderson on the university campus. No, his type went to high, lonely places and battlefields. Even if Kyle had not mentioned to Beth that his uncle had been a marine, she would have known he had *something* other men did not have. It was in the warrior cast in his face, and the calm readiness in the way he carried himself.

He was not the kind of man she met at the parent-teacher conference, the kind who had devoted himself to a wife and children and a dream of picket fences. She met the occasional single dad, attractive in an expensive charcoal-gray suit, but never anything even remotely comparable to Ben Anderson.

Ben's eyes resting on her face had made her feel as if an unwanted trembling, pre-earthquake, had started deep inside of her.

She hated that feeling, of somehow not being in control of herself, which probably explained why she had been driven to explain the educational benefits of her classroom tree to him. And to quote Aristotle! Who did that to a man like him?

But Beth Maple loved being in control, and she especially loved it since her one crazy and totally uncharacteristic trip outside her comfort zone had left her humiliated and ridiculously heartbroken.

She had known better. She was the least likely person to ever make the mistake she had made. She was well educated. Cautious. Conventional. Conservative. But she had been lured into love over the Internet.

Her love, Rock Kildore, had turned out to be a complete fabrication, as if the name shouldn't have warned her. "Rock" was really Ralph Kaminsky, a fifty-two-year-old married postal clerk from Tarpool Springs, Mississippi. What he was not was a single jet-setting computer whiz from Oakland, California, who worked largely in Abu Dhabi and who claimed to have fallen hopelessly in love with a fifth-grade teacher. Even the pictures he'd posted had been fake.

But for a whole year, Beth Maple had believed what she wanted desperately to believe, exchanging increasingly steamy love letters, falling in love with being in love, anticipating that moment each day when she would open her e-mail and find Rock waiting for her. Beth had passed many a dreamy day planning the day all his work and travel obstacles would be overcome and she would meet the love of her life.

She had been so smitten she had *believed* his excuses, and been irritated by the pessimism of her friends and co-workers. Her mother's and father's concern had grated on her, partly because it was a relationship like theirs that she yearned for: stable but still wildly romantic even after forty years!

The youngest in her family, she hated being treated like a baby, as if she couldn't make the right decisions.

After her virtual affair had ended in catastrophe that was anything but virtual, Beth had retreated to her true nature with a vengeance. Most disturbing to her had been that underlying the sympathy of her mom and dad had been their disappointment in her. Well, she was disappointed in herself, too.

Now she had something to prove: that she was mature, rational, professional, quiet and controlled. These were the qualities that had always been hers—before she had been lured into an uncharacteristic loss of her head. They were the qualities that made her an exemplary teacher, and that she returned to with conviction.

Teaching would be enough for her. Her substantial ability to love would be devoted to her students now. Her passion would be turned on making the grade-five learning experience a delight worth remembering. And she was giving up on pleasing her parents, too, since they didn't seem any happier when she announced her choice to be single forever than they had been about Rock.

But looking at Ben Anderson, she had felt rattled, aware that all her control was an illusion, that if a man like that ever touched his lips to hers, she would surrender control with humiliating ease, dive into something hitherto wild and unexplored in herself.

Looking at Ben Anderson, Beth had thought, *No wonder I liked virtual love. The real thing might be too hot too handle!*

But even more humiliating than the fact Beth had recognized this shockingly lustful weakness in herself was the fact that she was almost positive he had recognized it in her, as well! There had been knowing in his eyes, in the little smile that tickled the firm line of his lips, in the fact his hand had touched hers just a trifle too long when he had passed her his business card with his cell-phone number on it.

Ben Anderson had obviously been the conqueror of thousands of hearts.

And all of them left broken, too, Beth was willing to bet.

Not that she had let the smallest iota of any of that creep into her voice when she had spoken to him. She hoped.

When he had handed her his business card, just in case she had needed to *consult* with him, she'd had the ugly feeling he expected her to find some pretext to use it.

And here she was, dialing his number, and hating it, even if this was a true emergency. And at the same time she hated it, a wicked little part of her was completely oblivious to the urgency of this situation, and wanted to hear his voice again, and compare it to her memory. No man could really sound that sexy.

Except he did.

His voice, when he answered, was deep and mesmer-izing. Beth asked herself if she would think it was that sexy if she had never met him in person.

The answer was an unfortunate and emphatic yes.

There was a machine running in the background and Ben sounded faintly impatient, even when Beth said who she was and even though she could have sworn he would be pleased if she called him.

"Mr. Anderson, Kyle has gone missing."

"I can't hear you. Sorry."

"Kyle's gone," she screamed, just as the machine be-hind him shut off.

The silence was deafening, and she rushed to fill it,

which was what a man like that did to a woman like her, took all her calm and measured responses and turned them on their head.

She explained the frog incident. Ben listened without comment. She finished with, "And then he ran off. I checked all the usual hideouts, under the stage in the gym, the last stall in the boy's washroom, the janitorial closet. I'm afraid he's not here."

"Thanks for letting me know," Ben said. "Don't worry."

And then Beth was left holding a dead phone, caught between admiration for his I-can-handle-this attitude when obviously he was fairly new and naive to the trouble little boys could get themselves into, and irritation that somehow, just because he had told her not to worry, she did feel less worried.

He was that kind of man. Ridiculous to plan picket fences around him, and yet if you had your back against the wall, and the enemy rushing at you with knives in their teeth, he was the one you would want to be with you.

Beth told herself, sternly, it was absolutely idiotic to think you could know that about a man from having seen him once, and heard his supersexy voice on the phone. But she knew it all the same. If the ship was sinking, he would be the one who would find the life raft.

And the desert island.

She spent a silly moment contemplating that. Being with Ben Anderson on a desert island. It was enough to make her forget she had lost a child! It was enough to remind her her ability to imagine things had gotten her into trouble before.

An hour later, just as school was letting out and she was watching the children swirl down the hallway in an amazing rainbow of energy and color, the outside doors swung open and Ben Anderson stood there, silhouetted by light. He came through the children, the wave parting around him, looking like Gulliver in the land of little people.

There was something in his face that made Beth feel oddly relieved, even though his expression was grim and Kyle was not with him.

"Did you find him?" she asked.

The hallway was now empty. The absence of little people did not make Ben Anderson seem any smaller. In fact, she was very aware that she felt small as she stood in his shadow.

Small and exquisitely feminine despite the fact she was wearing not a spec of makeup, her hair was pulled back in a no-nonsense bun and she was dressed exactly like the fifth-grade teacher that she was.

"Not yet. I thought he might be at home, but he wasn't." He was very calm, and that made her feel even more as if he was a man you could lean into, be protected by.

Without warning, his finger pressed into her brow. "Hey, don't worry, he's okay."

"How could you possibly know that?" she asked, aware that the certain shrill note in her voice had nothing to do with the loss of a child who had been in her charge, but everything to do with the rough texture of his hand pressed into her forehead.

"Kyle's eleven going on 102. He's been looking after

himself in some pretty mean surroundings for a long, long time. He's okay."

He said that with complete confidence. He withdrew his hand from her forehead, looked at it and frowned, as though it had touched her without his permission. He jammed it in his pocket, and she felt the tiniest little thrill that the contact had apparently rattled him, as well as her.

"If he's not at home, where did he go?" she asked him. The news was full of all the hazards that awaited eleven-year-old boys who were not careful. In the week and a half that Kyle had been in her class, he had shown no sign that he was predisposed to careful behavior.

Of course, his uncle did not look as if he had ever been careful a day in his life, and he seemed to have survived just fine.

Probably to the woe of every female within a hundred miles of him.

"That's what I'm trying to figure out. Kyle's not that familiar with Cranberry Corners yet. Is he hiding somewhere? How much trouble does he think he's in?"

"It's not just about the frog," she told him, and repeated Kyle's awful remark.

"The aisles will run with the fat melting from your bodies?" Ben repeated. She couldn't tell if he was appalled or appreciative. "He said that?"

"Do you think he was threatening to burn down the school?" she whispered.

Ben actually laughed, which shouldn't have made her feel better, but it did. "Naw. He's a scrawny little guy. He used his brains to back down the bully, and it worked. Boy, where would he get a line like that?"

She was oddly relieved that it was not from his uncle!

"The History of Khan?" she guessed.

"Bingo!" he said, with approval for her powers of deduction.

She could not let herself preen under his approval. She couldn't. Wanting a man like him to approve of you could be the beginning of bending over backward to see that appreciative light in his eyes.

"Now if we could use those same powers of deduction to figure out where he is."

"You know him better than me," she said, backing away from the approval game. Besides, she really was drawing a blank about Kyle's whereabouts.

She saw the doubt cross his face, but he regarded her thoughtfully. "You said he still had the frog, right?"

She nodded.

"You said the other boys wanted the frog and he wouldn't give it to them."

Silly to be pleased that he had listened so carefully to what she had said. Troublesome how easily he could nudge down her defenses, even before they were rebuilt from the last collapse!

"So, let's assume he cared about the frog. Maybe he wanted to return it to where he got it from."

That made such perfect sense Beth wished she had thought of it herself.

"We went on a little field trip for science class last week. Migg's Pond," she said. "It's not far from here. We walked."

"I'm sure I can find it."

She was sure he could, too. But she was going with

him. And not to spend time with him, either. Not because just standing beside him made her feel soft, and small and delicate.

She would go because this wasn't really about Ben nor her, nor even about a frog. It was about a child who, despite the fact he was street smart, was still a child. Somehow, someway, somebody needed to let him know that. That they would come for him when he had lost his way.

"I'll just get my jacket," she said. "And my boots." The boots were hideous, proof to herself that she was indifferent to the kind of impression she was making on Ben Anderson. No woman with the least bit of interest in how he perceived her would be seen dead in a skirt and gum boots by him.

"It's wet by the pond," she said, pleased with how rational she was being. She even leveled her grade-five-teacher look at his feet.

And then was sorry she had because her eyes had to travel the very long length of his hard-muscled legs to find the feet at the end of them.

"I'm not worried about getting my feet wet," he said, something flat in his voice letting her know that he had been in places and experienced things that made him scorn small discomforts.

Today Beth was wearing a plaid tartan skirt, which did not seem as pretty to her now as it had when she put it on this morning. The boots, unfashionable black rubbers with dull red toes, were kept in the coatroom for just such educational excursions. They looked hideous with her skirt, but since they were going to a swamp and she was determined to not try and impress him, she thought they were perfect for the occasion.

Still, when she saw the laughter light his eyes as she emerged from the coatroom, she wished she hadn't been quite so intent on appearing indifferent to his opinions. She wished she would have ruined her shoes!

In an effort not to look as rattled as she felt in her gum boot fashion disaster, she said conversationally, "I like the name of your business. Garden of Weedin'. Very original."

He glanced down at his shirt and grinned. A knowing grin, that accused her of studying his chest, which of course she had been.

"Very creative," she said stiffly, keeping on topic with stern determination as he held the door open for her to leave the school.

"Yeah, well, I stole it."

"What?"

"I saw it on a sign in a little town I was passing through a long time ago. It kind of stuck with me."

"I don't think you can steal names," she said. "That would be like saying my mother stole the name Beth from the aunt I was named after."

"Beth," he said, pleased, as if she had given away a secret he longed to know.

The way he said it made a funny tingle go up and down her spine. You could imagine a man saying your name like that, like a benediction, right before he kissed you. Or right before he talked you into his bed, the promise of bliss erasing the fact there had been the lack of a single promise for tomorrow.

She shot him a wary look, but he was looking ahead,

scanning the terrain where the playground of the school met an undeveloped area behind it.

"Migg's Pond is out of bounds," she said. "The children aren't supposed to come back here by themselves."

He grunted. With amusement?

"Are you one of those people who scoffs at rules?" she asked.

"No, ma'am," he said, but his amusement seemed to be deepening.

"You are! I can tell."

"Now, how can you tell that?" he drawled, glancing at her with a lazy, sexy look that made her tingle just the way it had when he had spoken her name.

"I'm afraid I can picture you in fifth grade. Quite easily. Out of bounds would have just made it seem irresistible to you."

"Guilty."

"Frog in the teacher's drawer?" she asked.

"Only if I really liked her."

She contemplated that, and then said, "I don't think Kyle likes me at all."

"I would have, if I was in grade five. Not that I would have ever let on. How uncool would that be? To like the teacher."

How uncool would it be to feel flattered that a man would have liked you in grade five? It didn't mean he liked you now. Only a person without an ounce of pride would even pursue such a thing.

"What makes you think you would have liked me in grade five? I'm very strict. I think some of the kids think I'm mean."

He snorted, and she realized he was trying not to laugh.

"I am! I always start off the year at my most formidable."

"And I bet that's some formidable," he said, ignoring her glare.

"Because, you can't go back if you lose respect from the start. You can soften up later if you have to." She sounded like she was quoting from the teacher's manual, and Ben Anderson did not look convinced by how formidable she was capable of being!

"Well, I would have liked you because you were cute. And relatively young. And obviously you are into the Aristotle school of learning, which would mean really fun things like have everyone making a fall leaf with their name on it to hang from the roof."

He hadn't just used the tree to flatter her, which she had suspected at the time. He'd actually liked it. Why else would he have noticed details? She could not allow herself to feel flattered by that. *Weakened.*

He'd been a marine. He was probably trained to notice all the details of his environment.

They arrived at the pond. As she had tried to tell him, the whole area around it was muddy and damp.

But it wasn't him who nearly slipped and fell, it was her. She found his hand on her elbow, steadying her.

His grip, strong, sure, had the effect, *again,* of making her feel tiny and feminine. A lovely tingling was starting where his fingers dug lightly into her flesh.

She stopped and removed herself from his grip, moved a careful few steps away from him and scanned the small area around the pond with her best professional fifth-grade-teacher look.

As good as her intentions had been in coming here, and even though she had placed Kyle first, she had challenged herself as much as she intended to for one day.

"He's not here," she said. "I should go."

But Ben tilted his head, listening to something she couldn't hear. "He's here," he whispered.

She looked around. Nothing moved. Not even the grass stirred.

"How do you know?"

With his toe, he nudged a small sneaker print in the mud that she would have completely overlooked.

"It's fresh. Within an hour or so. So is this." His hand grazed a broken twig on a shrub near the pathway.

She didn't even want to know how he knew how fresh a print was, or a broken branch. She didn't want to know about the life he had led as a warrior, trained to see things others missed. Trained to shrug off hardship, go where others feared to go. Trained to deal with what came at him with calm and control. She didn't want to know all the multi-faceted layers that went into making such a self-assured man. Or maybe she did. Maybe she wanted to know every single thing about him that there was to know.

"Well," she said brightly, afraid of herself, her curiosity, terrified of the pull of him, "I'm sure you can take it from here. I'll talk to Kyle tomorrow."

"Okay," he said, scanning her face as if she didn't fool him one little bit, as if he knew how uncomfortable he made her feel, how aware of her *needs*.

"Are you going to follow the print?" she asked when he didn't move.

"I'd like him to come to us."

Us? She had clearly said she was leaving.

"Are you going to call him?" she asked.

"No. I'm going to wait for him. He knows we're here."

"He does?"

"Yeah."

She could go. Probably should go. But somehow she needed to put all her self-preserving caution aside, just for the time being. She needed to see this moment. Needed to be with the man who understood instinctively not to chase that frightened child, but to just wait. Or was that the pull of him, overriding her own carefully honed survival skills?

Ben took off his jacket, and put it on the soggy ground, patted it for her to sit on, just as if she had never said she was leaving, and just as if he had never said okay.

Something sighed in her, surrender, and she settled on his jacket, and he went down on his haunches beside her. Ben Anderson was so close she could smell his soap and how late-summer sunshine reacted to his skin.

"So," he said after a bit, "why don't you tell me something interesting about yourself?"

She slid him a look. This whole experience was suffused with an unsettling atmosphere of intimacy, and now he wanted to know something interesting about her? He had actually asked that as if he had not a doubt there was something interesting about her.

"What you consider interesting and what I consider interesting are probably two different things," she hedged.

"Uh-huh," he agreed. "Tell me, anyway."

And she realized he wanted Kyle to hear them talking, to hear that it was just a normal conversation, not about him, not loaded with anger or anxiety.

She suddenly could not think of one interesting thing about herself. Not one. "You first," she said primly.

"I like the ocean and warm weather," he said, almost absently, scanning the marshy ground, the reeds, the tall grass around Migg's Pond, not looking at her. "I like waves, and boats, swimming and surfing and deep-sea fishing. I like the moodiness of the sea, that it's cranky some days and calm others. I was stationed in Hawaii for a while, and I still miss it."

She tried not to gulp visibly. This was a little too close to her desert-island fantasy. She could picture him, with impossible clarity, standing at the water's edge, half-naked, sun and salt kissing his flawless body and his beautiful golden skin, white-foamed waves caressing the hard lines of his legs.

As if that vision had not made her feel weak with some unnamed wanting, he kept talking.

"I used to swim at night sometimes, the water black, and the sky black, and no line between them. It's like swimming in the stars."

"It sounds cold," she said, a pure defensive move against the picture he was painting, against the *wanting* unfurling within her like a limp flag in a gathering breeze.

"No," he said. "It's not cold at all. Even on colder days, the ocean stays about the same temperature year round. It's not warm like a bathtub, but kind of like—"

he paused, thinking "—like silk that's been left outside in a spring breeze."

He did not look like a man who would know silk from flannel. But of course he would. The finest lingerie was made of silk, and no doubt he had worlds of experience with that.

"Parachutes," he said succinctly.

"Excuse me?"

"Made of silk."

As if it was that easy to read her mind! She hoped he wasn't going to ask her about her interesting experiences again. She had nothing at all to offer a man intimately familiar with night swimming, silk and jumping out of airplanes.

"Have you ever gone swimming in the dark, Beth?"

She hoped she was not blushing. This was totally unfair. Totally. She couldn't even sputter out a correction, that she wanted him to call her Miss Maple. Because she didn't. She wanted him to call her Beth, and she wanted to swim in the darkness. And run out and buy silk underwear. And maybe sign up for skydiving lessons while she was at it.

The problem with a man like him was that he could make a person with a perfectly normal, satisfying life feel a kind of restless yearning for something more.

A restless yearning that had made her throw caution to the wind once before, she reminded herself. In her virtual romance with Rock, she had dared to embrace the unknown, the concept of adventure.

It had ended badly, and it would be worse if she let this man past her defenses, defenses which had seemed substantial until an hour ago.

Ben Anderson, conqueror of thousands of hearts, she reminded herself desperately. *Possibly more!*

"No," she managed to choke out. "I've never gone swimming in the dark." It felt like a confession, way too personal, desert-island confidences, not swamp exchanges.

"Too bad," he said, and looked at her, his pity real, as if it was written all over her she'd never swum in the dark.

She wondered, suddenly, horribly, if his nighttime swimming escapades had included swimming trunks.

Another thing she could add to the list of things she had never done, skinny-dipping. And would never do, either, if she had an ounce of self-respect!

Never mind that the thought of silk warm water on naked skin triggered some longing in her that was primal, dangerous and sensual.

"Though, I love to swim," she said. "We always had a pool."

"Ah, a pool," he said, as if that sounded tame indeed.

"Couldn't you have lived there?" she asked, wishing he had stayed there. "In Hawaii?"

"I guess I could have."

"Then why didn't you?" She didn't mean it to come out as an accusation, but it did anyway. She felt as if her whole life could have remained so much safer and so much more predictable if he had made that choice. She certainly wouldn't be sitting here, longing for sensuality!

Buck up, she told herself sternly, *you can have a bubble bath when you get home.*

"I grew up here. My sister was here," he said, softly. "And Kyle."

She saw a nearby patch of rushes rustle, and realized Kyle had been that close all along, listening. He had heard every word. How had she missed that he was there?

Her eyes met the boy's. "Why, Kyle," she said. "There you are! We came here hoping to find you."

She hoped she had not spoken too soon, that he would not get up and bolt away, not ready to be found.

But Kyle stood up awkwardly and made his way over the slippery ground toward them. Which was a relief, not just because he was safe, and found, but because she didn't have to try and come up with something interesting to share with his uncle about herself.

As if she had anything that could compare to swimming in the dark in Hawaii!

Ben stood up then, and if he was affected by the long wait, crouched on his haunches, it did not show. Kyle came with no hesitation. Beth could see he was relieved to have been found, relieved his uncle was not angry with him. He had heard his uncle, and somehow his uncle had said exactly the right thing, exactly what that child needed to hear.

That someone had come back for him.

No man left behind.

Watching him watch his nephew, his gaze calm and measured, she understood Ben Anderson was a man who knew instinctively how to get the job done and, more importantly, how to do the right thing. He was a man who trusted his instincts, and his instincts were good, sharp-honed by the fact that he, unlike most men she had met, had relied on his instinct, his gut, for his survival, and for the survival of his brothers.

If ever there was a child who needed that, it was Kyle.

But the sneaky appalling thought blipped, uninvited and uncensored through Beth Maple's brain, *And if ever a woman needed that, it is me.*

Wrong, she told herself. He was a man who could turn a swamp into a desert island. She was a woman who could turn a nonexistent person into her prince in shining armor.

She wasn't risking herself. She'd learned her lesson. She was sticking to teaching school, giving all her love to the children who came to her year after year.

A rather alarming picture of her in her dotage: alone, white hair in a crisp bun, marking papers with a cat on her lap crowded into her mind. But she pushed it away and jumped to her feet. The damp had seeped through the jacket Ben had set so chivalrously on the ground for her.

"Well," she said brightly, fighting an urge to swipe at her sodden rear end. "Child found. Emergency over. Goodbye." Totally unprofessional. She needed to discuss the events of the day with Kyle. There had to be consequences for putting the frog in her desk. For uttering the threat. For running away from school.

Instead she waggled her fingers ineffectually at Kyle, and made the mistake of looking once more at Ben.

He was looking at her with those sea-green amused eyes, a hint of a smile turning up his way-too-sexy mouth, and she turned briskly away from him and did not look back.

Because she knew his amusement would only deepen when he saw the condition of her dress, and she could not handle his amusement at her expense.

She could not handle him at all. He was a little too

much of everything—too good-looking, too good with his instincts, too charming, even, stunningly, too poetic.

Her world was safe, and a man like that spelled one thing, danger.

"Hey, Beth?" he called after her.

She turned reluctantly, planning to tell him it was Miss Maple, especially in front of children, but somehow she couldn't. Somehow they had progressed beyond that, without her permission, when he had told her about swimming in the warm Pacific Ocean with the stars.

She hoped he wasn't going to remind her of her responsibilities, that they needed to deal with Kyle.

Oh, no, it was so much worse than that.

"You should have a bubble bath when you get home. It will take the chill off."

She was that transparent to him. He probably knew just how his tales of swimming in the dark had tugged at some secret place in her, too. She spun on the heel of her rubber boot so fast she nearly made her exit even more graceless than it already was by falling.

She heard the rumble of his laughter behind her, but she didn't turn to look again.

CHAPTER THREE

The Top-Secret Diary of Kyle O. Anderson

BOY, people are dumb, even Miss Maple, who up until yesterday I thought might be one of the smarter ones. She was waiting for me when I got to school. I got the big lecture about saying things that can be misinterpreted. Is it so hard to figure out a kid who protects a frog isn't likely to burn down the school?

Sheesh. I only said that because I had read it the night before in *The History of Khan*. Genghis Khan used to surround a city, and then he gave them the opportunity to surrender. If they didn't surrender he'd burn it to the ground, until the streets ran with fat melting from bodies. Is that the scariest thing you ever heard? That's where the expression "the wrath of Khan" comes from. Even Casper, who is really dumb, got it.

Miss Maple is dumb in a different way than Casper. Not just that she thought I might burn the school down when I couldn't even hurt a frog, but I saw the look on her face yesterday when she left my uncle. Not much room to misinterpret that. All pink and flustered.

And him talking about bubble baths. If you want to know what embarrassment feels like, try your uncle telling your teacher to have a bubble bath. I didn't miss the fact he's progressed to her first name, either.

Not that I thought about it, but if I had, I could have guessed her name would be something like Beth or Molly or Emily.

I was hoping the frog thing would warn her off us, but it kind of backfired.

She and Uncle Ben, the lady-killer, ended up at Migg's Pond together. Shoot. It's full of mud and mosquitoes, but they were talking away as if they were having a glass of wine over dinner at a five-star hotel.

I didn't know my uncle Ben came back here because of me and my Mom, though it could be a lie. I bet he knows exactly how to worm into the heart of someone as dumb as Miss Maple.

If they get together, I bet I'm out in a blink. Nobody wants a dorky eleven-year-old around when they're getting ready to make kissy-face. Ask me. I've been through it before. With Larry and Barry.

The frog was lame. Well, not totally lame because I still have him. He's not exactly a great pet, like a dog or a horse, but when I got to the pond, I couldn't let him go. The weather's getting colder and I'm not sure what frogs do when it gets cold. I don't want to think about him dying, that's for sure. Where would he go when he dies? I'm not sure about heaven. Even if there is one, I don't know if they let frogs in. I don't know if they'll let my Mom in, either. She never went to church, and she sure swore a lot and stuff.

Miss Maple has the stupidest car you ever saw. It's like a hundred years old, a red VW convertible. She loves that car. You can tell by the way she keeps care of it, all shiny all the time, the way she drives it with her nose in the air.

I guess if I really need her to hate me, I could always do something to the car. It would be just too much to hope that I could make her think my uncle did it. Maybe I better wait and think about this. My uncle will probably take my frog away if I do something that bad to *Beth*. I don't know how somebody who has probably killed people with his bare hands deals with a frog, but whatever he does, I have a feeling it would be better than if Casper Hearn got his big fat mitts on it.

I hope I don't have to do anything to Miss Maple's car. That will be my last resort. And not because of Kermit. I'm not dumb enough to get attached to a frog.

I hope I don't have to make her hate me too bad.

This was looking good, Ben thought, looking at the call display on his cell phone. Miss Beth Maple was calling him again. Two calls in two days.

Though maybe yesterday didn't count, since his nephew had been missing. She was kind of obligated to call about something like that.

But even she couldn't have two emergencies in two days.

He hoped she was calling to tell him about the bubble bath. Though the thought of her telling him such a thing made him want to laugh out loud, because it would be so impossibly not her. Delightful, though, if you were the one she decided to let down her hair for.

Because there was definitely something about her, just beneath the surface. It was as if, as uptight as she seemed to be, she just hadn't had the right guy help her unlock her secrets. He thought of the line of her lips, wondered what it would be like to taste them, and then found he was the one to feel kind of flustered, like he was blushing, which was impossible. No one who spent eight years in the marines had anything like a blush left in them.

Unless what she had, innocence, was contagious.

And why did that make him feel oddly wistful, as if a man could ever be returned to what he had been before?

The truth was that Ben Anderson had had his fill of hard times and heartaches: his parents had died when he was young; he had lost his sister long before a doctor had told him she was going to die; he'd buried men he had shared a brotherhood with.

He could not ever be what he had been before. He could not get back the man who was unguarded, open to life. Long ago, he could remember being a young boy, Kyle's age, and every day ended with the words *"I love you"* to his mom and dad.

He could not be that again.

A memory, unbidden, came to him. His mother getting in the car, blowing him a kiss, and mouthing the words *"I love you"* because at seventeen he didn't want them broadcasted down the street.

Ben had not said those words since then, not ever. Was it insane to see them as a harbinger to disaster, to loss? He did not consider himself a superstitious man, but in this instance he was.

"Hello?" he said, aware that something cautious had entered his tone. He was not what she needed.

He was probably not what any woman needed. Damaged. Commitment-phobic.

"There were problems again today at school," she said wearily.

Considering he had just decided he was not what any woman needed, Ben was inordinately pleased that she had phoned to tell him about her problems! Nice. She probably had a little ache right between her shoulder blades, that he could—

"Kyle put glue on Casper's seat during recess. Not like the kind of glue we use at school for making fall leaves. I've never seen glue like that before."

Construction-site glue, Ben guessed, amazingly glum she wasn't phoning to share her problems with him. No, this was all about *his* problem.

"Casper stuck to the chair. And then he panicked and ripped the seat out of his pants when he tried to get out of the chair." There was a strangled sound from her end of the phone.

"Are you *laughing*?" he asked.

"No." It was a squeak.

"I think you are."

Silence, followed by a snort. And then another, muffled.

"Ah," he said. He could picture her, on the other end of the phone, holding back her laughter, trying desperately to play the role of the strict schoolmarm. He wished he was there to see the light in her eyes. He bet her nose crinkled when she laughed.

After a long time, struggling, she said, "There has to be a consequence. And he can never, *ever* guess I laughed."

"Oh," he teased, "a secret between us. This is even better than I could have hoped."

"If you could be mature, I thought we should talk about the consequence together," she said, her voice all grade-five schoolmistress again.

"I've always thought maturity was a good way to take all the fun out of life, but I will try, just for you."

"I hope you didn't suggest the glue to him!"

The truth was he might have, but his and Kyle's relationship had not progressed to sharing ideas for dealing with the class bully. He decided it was not in his best interest to share that with Miss Maple.

"We have to be on the same page." Sternly.

"Grown-ups against kids. Got it."

Silence. "I wasn't thinking of it that way. As if it's a war."

"A football game, then?"

"It's not really about winning and losing," she said carefully. "It's about finding what motivates Kyle. The class has a swim day coming up. I was going to suggest Kyle not be allowed to go. I hope that doesn't seem too harsh."

"No less than what he deserves. I'll let him know."

"Thank you." And then, hesitating, "You won't tell him—"

"That you laughed? No. I'll keep that to myself. Treasure it. It's something no grade-five boy needs to know about his teacher."

"Thank you for your cooperation," she said formally, and hung up the phone.

Ben went and found Kyle. He didn't have to look far. Kyle was in his room, the music booming. He was trying to get his frog to eat dead flies.

"Ah, Miss Maple just called. I heard about what you did to Casper."

"They can't prove it was me."

"Yeah, well, you're not going on the class swim trip that's coming up because of it."

"Boo-hoo," Kyle said, insincerely. Unless Ben was mistaken, rather than seeing his absence on the class trip as a punishment, Kyle was gleeful about it!

Unremorseful, Kyle went back to feeding his frog. Its long tongue snaked out, and the fly he had thrown in was grabbed from the air and disappeared.

"Wow," Kyle said. "Was that the coolest thing ever?"

Ben thought it was the first time he'd ever seen his nephew look truly happy. Silly to want to call Miss Maple back and tell her about it. Ridiculous to want to hear her laugh again.

If he wanted to hear laughter, he just had to turn on the television.

Except he didn't have one anymore. It was in Kyle's room. And besides, listening to a laugh track was going to seem strangely empty after hearing her trying to choke back her chortles.

"Wanna go for ice cream?" he asked Kyle. Too late, he realized he was letting down the home team. Since swimming had been no kind of consequence at all, he probably shouldn't be taking Kyle for ice cream. It was almost like saying, *Go ahead. Glue Casper to his seat. I think its funny.*

Which, come to think of it, he did.

"Ripped the whole seat out of his pants?" he asked Kyle as they walked down to Friendly's, the best ice cream store in Cranberry Corners.

"Yeah, and he had on blue underwear with cowboys on it."

"Oh, *baby* underwear."

And then he and his nephew were laughing, and despite the fact he was letting down the home team, Ben wouldn't have traded that moment for the whole wide world.

She phoned again the following night.

"I think he was very upset about the swimming being canceled," she confided in Ben. "Everybody else was talking about it all day, especially Casper. And he was left out."

Ben remembered Kyle's gleeful *boo-hoo.*

"He didn't even try to do the class assignment, but I'm remiss to punish him again so soon. Just to punish him will make him feel defeated," she told him. "You have to reward him when he does good things."

"Look, the only thing he does around here is feed his frog. I can't exactly reward him for that."

"I think rewarding him for being responsible for his pet would be good!"

Ben mulled that over. "Okay. I'm going to take him for ice cream." He hesitated. "Want to come?"

She hesitated, too. "I shouldn't."

"Why not? We're on the same team, right? I bet you like vanilla."

"That makes me sound dull."

"Surprise me, then."

And she did surprise him, for showing up at all, and for showing up on her bicycle with her hair down, surprisingly long, past her shoulders, her lovely cheeks pink from exertion.

"I didn't know teachers wore shorts," Kyle said, spotting her first. He frowned. "That should be against the law."

Ben agreed. Even though Beth's shorts would be considered very conservative, ending just above her knee, her legs could cause traffic accidents! They were absolutely gorgeous.

"What's she doing here?" Kyle asked as she came toward them.

"She's going to have ice cream with us."

"Oh," Kyle said, "you *invited* her." He did not sound pleased. He did not sound even a little bit pleased, but what eleven-year-old wanted to have ice cream with his teacher?

She wouldn't let Ben order for her or pay for her, but he watched closely all the same. When she joined them at a small table outside, she had ordered some hellish looking mix of orange and black.

"Tiger," she informed Ben. Then she went on to prove that she could more than surprise him. Who would have guessed that watching that prim little schoolmarm licking an ice cream cone could be the most excruciatingly sensual experience of a somewhat experienced guy's life? When a blob of the quickly melting brackish material fell on her naked thigh, he thought there wasn't enough ice cream in the world to cool down the heat inside of him.

He leaped to his feet, consulted his watch with an astounded frown. "Kyle and I have to go," he announced. "School night. That homework thing."

She should have looked pleased that he was being such a responsible guardian. She *would* have looked pleased to know he was going if she knew what he was thinking about her thighs. And ice cream. In the same sentence.

He'd annoyed her. Actually, he thought she was more than annoyed. Mad. He didn't blame her. He'd invited her for ice cream and then ditched her. She might never know how noble his departure had been. It had been for the protection of both of them.

Kyle seemed mad at him, too. When Ben pressed him about his homework, Kyle said, as regally as a prince who did not toil with the peasants, "I don't do homework."

And instead of thinking of some clever consequence, to go with *the plan,* Ben said, "Well, fail grade five then. See if I care."

Ben Anderson wished his life could go back to being what it had been such a short while ago. Frozen dinners. Guy nights. A home gym in the spare bedroom.

And at the same time he wished it, he missed it when she didn't call him the next night, or the one after that, either. That either meant *the plan* was working, or she was giving up.

Or that his foolish mixing of her professional life with her personal one had left her nearly as confused as it had left him. He doubted he'd been forgiven for leaving her in the lurch with her tiger ice cream. Now she had probably vowed not to speak to Ben Anderson again unless Kyle turned her world upside down.

Should he phone her? And tell her he rewarded Kyle every night for feeding and caring for his frog, trying to make up for the fifth-grade-failure comment. But the reward was ice cream, and Ben didn't think it would be a very good idea to mention ice cream around her for a while.

Besides, after that shared moment of camaraderie over Casper's unfortunate choice of underwear, Kyle had retreated into a sullen silence.

After a week of trying out excuses in his head to phone her, and discarding each one as more lame than the last, the decision was taken out of Ben's hands.

The school's number came up on his cell phone's display. He knew it could be anyone. The principal, the nurse, Kyle himself. But he also knew it was telling him something important that he hoped it was Beth.

And then was reminded to be careful what he hoped for!

He had to hold the phone away—way away—from his ear. Kyle had been right about one thing. She did have kind of a screechy voice—when she was upset, and she was very upset.

She finally paused for breath, a hiccupping sound that made him wonder if she was crying. He did not want to think of Beth Maple crying.

"Let me get this straight," he said uneasily. "While you took the class swimming, somebody took a nail and scratched my company name in the side of your car? Are you kidding me?"

He didn't know why he said that because it was more than obvious she wasn't kidding. He groaned when she told him what else was scratched in there.

"It sucks to be you." And of course, Kyle had not been swimming.

"I'll be there as soon as I can," he said, and hung up the phone. It occurred to him it was totally inappropriate to be whistling. Totally inappropriate to feel happy that he was going to be seeing her again so soon.

She might be able to make eating ice cream look like something out of the Kama Sutra, but he had just been screeched at! He had already deduced he was not the kind of man who could give a woman like that one thing she needed.

Except she did need to be kissed. He could tell by the way she ate ice cream! And he had it on good authority he was very good at that.

But it was not the thought of kissing her that made him happy, because obviously kissing a woman like that would make his life rife with complications that it did not currently have.

As if an eleven-year-old boy armed with a nail was not enough of a complication for him at the moment.

What seemed to be causing the renegade happiness was the thought of the look on her face a long time ago when he had told her about swimming in the dark: a moment of unguarded wonder and yearning, before she had quickly masked whatever she was feeling.

He wanted to make her look like that again.

He supposed it was a guy thing. A challenge.

He reminded himself sternly that his big challenge right now was the person who was vandalizing people's cars.

It was a big deal. A terrible thing for Kyle to have done. A betrayal of the teacher who had been nothing but good to him.

But Ben Anderson still whistled all the way to the school.

Beth Maple's car was about the cutest thing he had ever seen, a perfectly refurbished 1964 Volkswagen Beetle convertible, finished in candy-apple red. The car was kind of like her—sweet and understated, with the surprise element of the candy-apple red, and the unexpected sexiness of a convertible top.

Unfortunately, the car was marred right now. On the driver's side door someone had scratched "THE GARDEN OF WEDDING," an unfortunate misspelling of the name of Ben's business. Like most confirmed bachelors, he did not like weddings. He had never noticed before how close to the word *wedding* that *weedin'* was.

He was startled and horrified that even being in the near vicinity of that word and Beth at the same time, he could picture her as a bride, gliding down an aisle in a sea of virginal white.

Was she a virgin?

He could feel his face getting red, so he frowned hard at the words scratched in the side of her car. What the hell was going on with him? His self-control was legendary, and yet here were these renegade thoughts, just exploding in his mind without warning, as though he had stepped on a land mine. First the naughty thoughts around ice cream and now this.

"There's more," she said.

Yeah, there was, because as hard as he was trying to crowd out the picture of her in a wedding dress from his mind, not to mention that terrible none-of-your-business question, once you had allowed your mind to go somewhere like that, it was very hard to corral the wayward thoughts.

He slid a glance at her face, her smooth forehead marred by a frown, distress in her eyes, as if this was the very worst thing that had ever happened to her.

He would guess she *had* lived a sheltered life.

He followed her around to the passenger side, looked where she pointed. In smaller letters, lower case, was scratched deep into that candy-apple red paint "it sucks to be you."

As if Kyle wasn't the prime suspect anyway, he might as well have signed his handiwork with his own name.

Ben glanced at Beth Maple again. The teacher was looking distressed and pale, as if she was hanging on by a thread and the slightest thing would make her burst into tears.

Which was something Ben Anderson did not want to see at all. The wedding thoughts and *the* question were about as much stress as he wanted for one day. A woman like that, in tears, could be his undoing. It could make a man feel all big and strong and protective. He didn't want to feel like that. He was as unsuited to the role of riding in on his charger to rescue the damsel in distress as he was to the role of standing at the top of that aisle, waiting...

And reacting to tears moved a man toward emotional involvement, and as challenging as he found the prim schoolteacher, he wanted to play with her, that delicious wonderful exhilarating man/woman game where you parted with a kiss and no hard feelings when it was all over.

He did not want to play the game that ended with white dresses, no matter how lovely that vision might be.

He slid a look at her and wondered when he had become so imaginative. Today she was wearing a white sweater and a black skirt and a lavender blouse with lace on it.

Not an outfit that should make a man think of weddings or virginity. Or of bubble baths or swimming in dark ocean waters. At all.

But that is where his unruly male mind went nonetheless.

Her hair was still wet from the class trip, and he wondered what she had worn at the pool. A one-piece, he decided. Matching shorts, that she probably hadn't taken off. Not what she would wear for a midnight swim with him.

He had the sudden, disturbing thought that it might not be exactly ethical to play with Miss Maple. She wasn't the kind of woman who understood the rules he played by. The thought was disturbing because he did not think thoughts like that. She was an adult. He was an adult. Couldn't they just dance around each other a bit and see where it went?

No. It was a whisper. His conscience? Or maybe his bachelor survival instincts. Beware of women who make you think of weddings.

Funny, that of all the women he had gone out with, she, the least threatening, and certainly the least sexy, would be the one who would make him feel as if he needed to be the most wary, the most on guard. Because she had a sneaky kind of sexiness that crept up on you, instead of the kind that hit you over the head.

He slid her another look. No. Not the least sexy. Not at all. No, that wasn't quite it. She wasn't *overtly* sexy. Sneaky sexy in this kind of understated virginal way that could set his blood on fire. If he let it. Which he wasn't going to. He had set his formidable will and sense of discipline against greater obstacles than her.

He turned his focus to his nephew, a welcome diversion, even in these uncomfortable circumstances.

Kyle was also standing off to the side of the car, looking into the distance, as if all this kafuffle had nothing to do with him. He looked pale to Ben, his freckles standing out against the white of his skin. He met his uncle's accusing gaze with nothing even resembling remorse.

But it wasn't quite belligerence, either. Amazingly it reminded Ben of the look on young soldiers' faces when they were scared to death to do something but did what they had to do anyway.

There was a weird kind of bravery in what Kyle had done.

Between her near tears and Kyle's attitude, Ben's happiness was dissipating more rapidly than a snowball in August.

"I *love* this car," Beth said sadly.

And Ben could tell it was true. He could tell by the sparkle shine on the wax, and the buffed white of the convertible top. He could tell by the way her fingers trembled on the scratch marks that she had been hurt and deeply.

A man allergic to love, he should have *approved* of her affection for the car. Why did it seem like a waste to him? Why would a woman like that waste her love on what really was just a hunk of metal and moving parts?

Because it was safe. It was a startling and totally unwanted insight into her. He slid her a look. Ah, yes, he should have seen it before.

The kind of woman who could be least trusted with the kind of man he was. He liked things light and lively and superficial, and he could see, in this moment of vulnerability, that she had already been scarred by someone. Heartbroken. Bruised.

Along with the uncontrolled direction of his own thoughts, it was a back-off insight if he had ever had one. But instead of wanting to back off, he felt a strange desire to fix it. He felt even more like he wanted to see that look on her face again that he had seen when he had told her about swimming in the dark, a look of yearning, of wonder.

"I don't understand," Beth said to Kyle, struggling for composure. "Why would you do this to me? I've been good to you, haven't I?"

Kyle didn't look at her. "What makes you think I did it?" he tried for uncaring, but his voice wavered. "Are you going to get DNA from a scratch mark? It could have been Casper Hearn. He hates me. He would try and make it look like me."

Beth had the bad judgment to look doubtful.

But Ben knew now was the wrong time to let his bewilderment at Kyle's strange bravery, or sympathy for Kyle's past, in any way temper his reaction to this. It was vandalism, and no matter what had motivated it, it couldn't be tolerated or let go. It would be so much easier to let it go, to excuse it in some way, so that he didn't have to tangle any further with a woman who made him think renegade thoughts of weddings and virginity.

But he couldn't. This kid had been entrusted to him, and now he had to do the right thing. Every single time. They had tried Beth's *plan,* her way, but they didn't have time to fool with this any longer, to experiment with the plan that would work for Kyle.

The damage to Beth's car was a terrible movement in the wrong direction for Kyle. If Ben let this slide, how long until the downward spiral of anger and bitterness could not be stopped? It seemed to him he had been here before, watched helplessly and from a distance, as a young person, Carly, had been lost to the swirling vortex of her own negative emotion.

"Kyle," he said sternly. "Stop it. I know it was you."

Beth looked as if she might be going to protest that they didn't have any proof, but Ben silenced her with a faintly lifted finger.

"I don't know why you did it," he continued, "and I don't want to hear excuses for the inexcusable. I do know Miss Maple didn't deserve it. And neither did I. Man up."

Something about those words *man up* hit Kyle. Ben could see them register in his eyes. He was being asked to be more, instead of less. Everything was going to be so much harder if Kyle made the wrong decision right now.

But he didn't. After a brief struggle, he turned to his

teacher. He said quietly, "I'm sorry." The quaver in his voice worsened.

"But why?" she asked, and her voice was quavering, too.

Kyle shrugged, toed the ground with his sneaker, glanced at his uncle with a look so transparent and beseeching Ben thought his heart would break.

Care about me, anyway. Please.

And Ben planned to. But he was so aware of the minefield he was trying to cross.

The wrong kind of caring at this turning point in Kyle's life could destroy him.

Funny. Ben was allergic to that word *love*. He *never* used it. And yet when he looked at his nephew, troubled, so very young, so needy, he knew that's what he felt for him.

And that he could not express it any longer in a way that might be misconstrued as weakness. Kyle needed leadership right now. Strong leadership. Implacable.

Ben folded his arms over his chest and gave his nephew his most steely-eyed look.

"You made this mess," he said quietly. "You're going to have to fix it."

"I don't know how," Kyle said.

"Well, I do. There's probably close to a thousand bucks worth of damage there. Do you have a thousand dollars?"

"I don't have any money," Kyle said. "I didn't even get allowance last week, cuz I didn't take out the garbage."

"Do you have anything worth a thousand dollars?"

"No," Kyle whispered.

This was part of the problem. His nephew was the kid

who perceived he had nothing of value. And he probably didn't have the things the other kids in his class had and took for granted. There had been no fifty-inch TV sets, no designer labels. Ben had bought him a nice bicycle once, and as far as he could tell it had disappeared into the dark folds of that shadowy world his sister lived in before Kyle had ever even ridden it.

"I guess she'll have to call the insurance company, then," Ben said. "They'll want a police report filed."

Beth and Kyle both gasped.

"Unless you can come up with something you have of value."

Kyle's shoulders hunched deeper as he considered a life bereft of value. Beth was looking daggers at Ben.

Didn't she get it? He deserved to be afraid. He *needed* to be afraid. Ben watched, letting the boy flounder in his own misery. He let him nearly drown in it, before he tossed him the life rope.

"Maybe you have something of value," he said slowly.

"I do?"

"You have the ability to sweat, and maybe we can talk Miss Maple into trading some landscaping for what you owe her. But she'll have to agree, and you'll have to do the work. What do you say, Miss Maple?"

"Oh," she breathed, stunned, and then the look of wonder was there, just for a fraction of a second. "Oh, you have no idea. My yard is such a mess. I bought the house last year, after—" She stopped abruptly, but Ben knew. The house was the same as the car. *Safe.* Purchased to fill a life and to take the edge off a heartbreak.

He could see that as clearly in the shadows of her eyes as if she had spoken it out loud.

Move away, marine. But he didn't.

"And you're willing to do the work, Kyle?"

Kyle still seemed to be dazed by the fact he had something of value. "Yeah," he said quickly, and then, in case his quick reply might be mistaken for enthusiasm, shrugged and added, "I guess."

"No guessing," Ben said. "Yes or no."

"Yes."

"Good man."

And as hard as he tried not to show it, Kyle could not hide the fact that small compliment pleased him.

An hour later they pulled up in front of Miss Beth Maple's house. Even if the tiny red car had not been parked in the driveway, Ben would have known it was her house, and his suspicions around her ownership would have been confirmed. It was like a little cottage out of *Snow White*, an antidote for a heartache if he'd ever seen one.

It was the kind of place a woman bought when she'd decided to go it on her own, when she had decided she was creating her own space, and it was going to be safe and cozy, an impregnable female bastion of good taste and white furniture and breakable bric-a-brac.

"It looks like a dollhouse," Kyle said, with male uneasiness that Ben approved of.

It was a tidy house, painted a pale-buttercup yellow, the gingerbread and trim around the windows painted deep midnight blue. Lace curtains blew, white and virginal as a damned wedding dress, out a bedroom window that was open to the September breezes.

It was a reminder, Ben thought, getting out of the truck, that she was not the kind of woman a man could play with, have a casual good time for a couple of weeks or a couple of months and then say goodbye with no hurt feelings on either side.

No, the house spoke of a woman who wanted things, and was afraid of the very things she wanted. Stability. A safe haven. A world that she could trust.

Ben wanted to just drive away from all the things she would be shocked he could see in that neat facade. But he had to do the responsible thing now, for his nephew.

The yard was as neglected as the house was tidy. Yellow climbing roses had gone wild over the arbor over the front gate, and it was nearly falling down under their weight. Inside the yard, the grass was cut, but dead in places, a shrub under the front window had gotten too big and blocked out the front of the house and probably the light to the front room.

Beth Maple came out her door. Ben tried not to stare.

She had gotten home before they had arrived, and she'd had time to change. She was barefoot, and had on a pair of canvas pants, rolled to the knee, with a drawstring waist. Somehow the casual slacks were every bit as sexy as the shorts she had worn the night she had joined them for ice cream, though he was not sure how that was possible, since the delicate lines of her legs were covered.

Imagination was a powerful thing. The casual T-shirt just barely covered her tummy. If he made her stretch up, say to show him those roses, he could catch a glimpse of her belly button.

What would the point of that be, since he had decided

he was not playing the game with her? That he was going to try and fix something for her, not make it worse! Seeing her house had only cemented that decision.

"It's awful, I know," she said ruefully, looking at the yard. "I only bought the place a year ago. I'm afraid there was so much to do inside. Floors refinished, windows reglazed, some plumbing problems." Her voice drifted away in embarrassment.

Ben saw she had an expectation of perfection for herself. She didn't like him seeing a part of her world that was not totally under control.

"I don't imagine a thousand dollars will go very far," she said.

But Ben was going to make it go as far as it needed to go to wear Kyle out, to make him understand the value of a thousand dollars, and the price that had to be paid when you messed with someone else's stuff.

And working at Miss Maple's would be a relatively small price compared to what it could have been if she called the cops.

"You might be surprised how far your thousand dollars will go," he said, and watched as Kyle fixated on the large side yard's nicest feature, a huge mature sugar maple just starting to turn color. It reminded Ben of the tree in her classroom.

His nephew scrambled up the trunk and into the branches. Ben was relieved to see him do such a simple, ordinary, boy thing.

Beth watched Kyle for a moment, too, something in her eyes that Ben tried to interpret and could not, and then turned back to him.

"What should we fix?" she said briskly. "The arbor? The railing up the front stairs? The grass?"

Suddenly Ben did interpret the look in her eyes. It was wistfulness. She wanted to climb that tree! To be impulsive and free, hidden by the leaves, scrambling higher, looking down on the world from a secret perch. Was her affection for the tree the reason she had reproduced it in her classroom? Was she even aware of her own yearnings?

"How do you want this yard to make you feel?" he asked.

"Wow. You can make me feel something for a thousand dollars?"

For some reason his eyes skidded to her lips. He could make her feel something for free. But he wasn't going to.

"I can try," he said gruffly.

"Okay," she said, challenging, as if he'd asked for more than he had bargained for, "I want that summer day feeling. A good book. A hammock in the shade. An ice-cold glass of lemonade. I want to feel lazy and relaxed and like I don't have to do a lick of work."

Low maintenance. He began a list in his head. But when he thought of low maintenance, he wasn't really thinking about her yard. He was thinking about her. He bet she would be one of those low-maintenance girls. She wouldn't need expensive gifts or jewelry or tickets to the best show in town to make her happy.

A picnic blanket. A basket with fried chicken. A bottle of something sparkly, not necessarily wine.

Why did Beth Maple do this to him? Conjure up pictures of things he would be just as happy not thinking about?

Still what people wanted in their yards told him a great deal about them. It was possible that she just didn't know what was available, what was current in outdoor living spaces.

"You know," he said carefully, "lots of people now are making the yard their entertainment area. Outdoor spaces are being converted into outdoor rooms: kitchens with sinks and fridges, BBQ's and bars. Hardscaping is my specialty. Last week I did an outdoor fireplace, copper-faced, and patio where you could easily enter-tain forty or fifty people."

"Hardscaping?" she said. "I've never heard that term."

"It means all the permanent parts of the yard, so walkways and patios, canopies, privacy fences or enclo-sures, ponds. Basically anything that's made out of wood, concrete, brick or stone. I have other people do the greenscaping and the styling."

"Styling?"

"You know. Weather-resistant furniture. Outdoor carpeting."

"Obviously that isn't on a thousand-dollar budget."

"If there was no budget, what would you do?" he asked, having failed to find out how she felt about the posh entertainment area in her backyard.

She snorted. "Why even go there?"

"Landscaping doesn't have to be done all at once. I like to give people a master plan, and then they can do it in sections. Each bit of work puts a building block in place for the next part of the plan. A good yard can take five years to make happen." He smiled, "And a really good yard is a lifetime project."

She folded her arms over her chest. "The plan for a yard, alone, is probably worth more than what Kyle owes me."

"Well, if you don't tell him, I won't. He has nothing to give you right now, except his ability to work. If I take that away from him he has nothing at all."

She nodded, a kind of surrender. Definitely an agreement.

"I want him to have blisters on his hands, and that little ache between his shoulder blades from working in this yard."

"I'm not accepting charity from you," she said, stubbornly.

"And I'm not offering any. You wanted a plan for my nephew, and yours, so far, doesn't seem to be working that well. Now it's my turn. There has to be a price to be paid for what he did to your car, and it has to be substantial. No more rewards for feeding his frog."

"How long are you going to make him work for me?"

"Hopefully until he's eighteen," Ben said dryly. "So, tell me how you'd like to spend time in your yard."

"To be truthful the whole entertainment thing, like an outdoor kitchen and fireplace isn't really me. I mean, it sounds lovely, I'm sure you make wonderful yards for people, but I really do love the idea of simple things out here. A hammock. Lemonade. Book. I'd want a place that felt peaceful. Where you could curl up with a good book on a hot afternoon and listen to water running and birds singing, and glance up every now and then to see butterflies."

It wasn't fair, really. People did not know how easy it was to see their souls. Did he need to know this about her?

That in a world gone wild with bigger and better and more, in a world where materialism was everything, she somehow wanted the things money could not buy.

The miracle of butterfly wings, the song of birds, the sound of water.

She wanted a quiet place.

He imagined her bare feet in lush grass and was nearly blinded with a sense of desire. He was getting sicker by the minute. Now she didn't even need to be eating ice cream for him to be entertaining evil male thoughts.

He saw her gaze move to Kyle in the tree again, wistful, and suddenly he was struck by what he wanted to do for her.

"What would you think about a tree house?" he said softly. And saw it. A flash of that look he had glimpsed twice, and now longed for. Wonder. Hope. Curiosity.

"A tree house?" she breathed. "Really?"

"Not a kid's tree house," he said, finding it taking shape in his mind as he looked at the tree, "an adult retreat. I could build a staircase that wound around the trunk of that tree, onto a platform in the branches. We could put a hammock up there and a table to hold the lemonade."

He thought he would build her a place where the birds could sing sweetly, so close she could touch them. He would put a container garden up there, full of the flowers that attracted butterflies. Below the tree, a simple water feature. She could stand at the rail and look down on it; she would be able to hear the water from her hammock.

"That sounds like way too much," she said, but her protest was weak, overridden by the wonder in her eyes as she gazed at that tree, beginning to see the possibility.

To see her at school, prim and tidy, a person would never guess how her eyes would light up at the thought of her own tree house. But Ben had always known, from the first moment, that she had a secret side to her. The tree in her classroom had held the seeds of this moment.

He was not sure it was wise to uncover it. And he was also not sure if he could stop himself, which was an amazing thought in itself since he considered self-discipline one of his stronger traits.

"We'll take it one step at a time." That way he could back off if he needed to. But then he heard himself committing to a little more, knowing he could not leave this project until he saw the light in her eyes reach full fruition. He did a rough calculation in his head. "We'll come every day for two weeks after school. We'll see if he's learned what he needs to learn by then."

She turned her attention from the tree and he found himself under the gaze of those amazing eyes. He knew, suddenly, he was not the only one who saw things that others did not see.

"There are a lot of ways to be a teacher, aren't there, Ben?"

She said it softly, as if she admired something about him. In anyone else, that would be the flirt, the invitation to start playing the game with a little more intensity, to pick up the tempo.

But from her it was a compliment, straight from her heart. And it went like an arrow to his, and penetrated something he had thought was totally protected in armor.

"Thanks," he said, softly. "We'll be here tomorrow, right after school." He turned and called his nephew.

They watched as he scrambled out of the tree.

"We're going to come, starting tomorrow after school," Ben told him. "We're going to build Miss Maple a tree house."

Kyle's eyes went round. "A tree house?" For the first time since they had laughed together about Casper's underwear, his defensive shield came down. "Awesome," he breathed.

"Awesome," she agreed.

Kyle actually smiled. A real smile. So genuine, and so revealing about who Kyle really was that it nearly hurt Ben's eyes. But then Kyle caught himself and frowned, as if he realized he had revealed way too much about himself.

Ben turned to go, thinking maybe way too much had been revealed about everybody today.

There are lots of ways to be a teacher. As if she saw in him the man he could be, as if she saw the heart that he had kept invisible, unreachable, untouchable, behind its armor. He could teach her a thing or two, too. But he wasn't going to.

CHAPTER FOUR

BETH Maple stood at her kitchen counter and listened to the steady thump of hammers in her yard. She contemplated how it was that her neatly structured life had been wrested so totally from her control.

"Uncle Ben, haven't you ever heard of skin cancer, for cripe's sake? The three *S*s? Slam on a hat, slather on sunscreen and slip on a shirt."

For a moment it only registered how sweet it was that Kyle was so concerned about his uncle.

But then she froze. *Ben Anderson had taken off his shirt? In her backyard?*

"I'll live dangerously," Ben called to his nephew.

Now *there* was a surprise, she thought dryly. *Don't peek,* she told herself, but that was part of having things wrested out of her control. Despite the sternness of the order she had given herself, she peeked anyway.

It was a gorgeous day. September sunshine filtering through yellow-edged leaves with surprising heat and bathing her yard in gold. Her yard actually looked worse than it had a few days ago, with spray-painted lines on her patches of grass, heaps of dirt, sawed-off branches and construction materials stacked up.

But the pure potential shone through the mess and made her feel not just happy but elated. Maybe when a person gave up a bit of control, it left room for life to bring in some surprises, like the one that was unfolding in her yard.

Of course, there was one place she had to keep her control absolute, and where she was failing, the order not to peek being a prime example. She had peeked anyway, and she felt a forbidden little thrill at what she was seeing.

Was it possible that sense of elation that filled her over the past few days had little to do with the yard?

Certainly the forbidden thrill had nothing to do with the landscaping progress in her yard.

No, there was enough heat in that afternoon sun that Ben Anderson had removed his shirt.

It was delicious to spy on him from the safety of her kitchen window, to look her fill, though she was not sure a woman could ever see enough of a sight like Ben Anderson, undressed.

He looked like a poster boy for *sexy*, all lean, hard muscle, taut, flawless skin, a smudge of dirt across the ridged plane of his belly, sweat shining in the deep hollow of his throat, just above the deep, strong expanse of a smooth chest. His jeans, nearly white with age and washing, hung low on the jut of his hips. His stomach was so flat that the jeans were suspended from hip to hip, creating a lip-licking little gap where the waistband was not even touching his skin.

Beth watched his easy swing of the hammer, the corresponding ripple of muscle. It made her feel almost dizzy. She had known from the start Ben Anderson needed a label. *Contents too potent to handle.* She had never gotten a thrill like this over the Internet, that was for sure!

It was embarrassing to be this enamored with his physical being, but he was so *real.* No wonder she had found her Internet romance as delightful as she had. The presence of a real man was anything but; it was disturbing.

It was disturbing to feel so tense around another human being, so aware of them, and so aware of unexplored parts of yourself.

Beth felt she would have been quite content to go through life without knowing that she possessed this *hunger.*

Now that she did know she possessed it, how did she go back to what she had been before? What did she do about it? Surrender? Fight it?

Surely baking cookies was no kind of answer! But it bought her time. Which she should have used wisely. She could have done an Internet search for *defenses against diabolically attractive men* instead of spying from her kitchen window!

This was the third time Ben and Kyle had been here, twice after school, short sessions where his shirt had stayed on. Though for Beth, seeing him deal with that fragile boy with just the right mix of sternness and affection had been attractive in and of itself. She could see that her initial assessment of Ben Anderson—that he could not be domesticated—had been inaccurate. When she saw his patience with Kyle, and the way he guided the child toward making his own decisions, she knew she was looking at a man who would be a wonderful daddy someday, who was growing in confidence in this role of mentor and guardian.

Now it was Saturday and Ben had shown up this morning, way too early, announcing they would spend the whole day.

Saturday was her sleep-in day, and her grocery day, and her laundry day, and her errand day, and she had canceled everything she normally would have done without a second thought. Groceries or hanging out with Ben Anderson. *Duh.*

The buzzer on the oven rang, and Beth moved, reluctantly, from the window and removed the cookies, dripping with melted chocolate chips, from her oven. While she waited for them to cool, she debated, milk or lemonade? Milk would go better with the cookies, lemonade would go better with the day.

That's what having a man like that in your yard did to you. Every decision suddenly seemed momentous. It felt as if her choice would say something about her. To him.

In the end she put milk and lemonade on the tray. To confuse him, just in case her choices were telling him anything about her.

He set down his hammer when he saw her coming, smiled that lazy, sexy smile that was setting her world on edge. Kyle, who was hard at work digging something, set down the shovel eagerly.

She had known Ben was a man with good instincts. This project was not just good for Kyle. The turn-around in his attitude seemed nothing short of spectacular. It was as if he had been uncertain he had any value in the world, and suddenly he saw what hard work—his hard work—could accomplish. He could see how the face of the world could be changed by him in small ways, like her yard. And the possibility of changing the world in big ways opened to him for the first time.

When Ben had unfolded his drawing of the yard, he had included his nephew and consulted with him, listened to him, showed respect for his opinions. And Ben had done the same for her.

The three of them were building something together, and in her most clear moments she was aware it was not just a tree house.

The plan that Ben had drawn for her tree retreat filled some part of her that she did not know had been empty. It was deceptively simple. A staircase spiraled around the tree trunk, though it actually never touched it, because Ben had been concerned about keeping the tree healthy, by not driving nails into the trunk or branches.

The staircase led to a simple railed platform that sat solidly in amongst the strongest branches, but was again supported mostly by the subtle use of posts and beams.

Ben's concern for the health of her tree had surprised her, showed her, again, that there was something more there than rugged appeal and rippling muscle. Ben had a thoughtfulness about him, though if she were to point it out, she was certain he would laugh and deny it.

She soon found out executing such a vision was not that simple. There had been digging, digging and more digging. Then leveling and compacting. She had insisted on having a turn on the compactor, a machine that looked like a lawn mower, only it was heavier and had a mind of its own.

Ben had turned it on, and while under his watchful eye she had tried to guide it around the base of the tree where there would be a concrete pad. The compactor was like handling a jackhammer. The shaking went up her whole body. She felt like a bobble-head doll being hijacked!

"Whoa," she called over and over, but the machine did not listen. Despite all Ben's efforts to be kind to the tree, she banged into the trunk of it three times.

Kyle finally yelled over the noise, begging her to stop, he was laughing so hard. And then she had dared to glance away from her work. Ben was laughing, too.

And then she was laughing, which the unruly machine took advantage of by taking off across her lawn and ripping out a patch of it, until Ben grabbed it and shut it off and gently put her away from it.

"Miss Maple?"

"Yes?"

"You're fired."

When had she last laughed like that? Until her sides hurt? Until everything bad that had ever happened to her was washed away in the golden light of that shared moment? The laughter had made her feel new and alive, and as though life held possibilities that she had never dreamed of.

Possibilities as good as or even better than the tree sanctuary that was becoming a reality in her backyard.

The world she had allowed herself to have suddenly seemed way too rigid, the dreams she had given up on beckoned again. Everything *shimmered*, but was it an illusion of an oasis or was it something real?

Watching Ben work made it harder to see those distinctions, flustered her, and made her feel off balance. When a concrete truck had arrived, she had watched as Ben, so sure of himself, so in charge, so at ease, had directed that spout of creamy cement, pouring concrete footings, a pad for the staircase and a small patio.

It was his world. He was in charge. Competent. Decisive. All business and no nonsense as he showed Kyle what needed to be done. The concrete work seemed so hard, and yet there was nothing in him that shirked from it, he seemed to *enjoy* using his strength to create such lasting structures. That alone was deeply attractive in ways she didn't quite understand, but it was when the concrete was beginning to set that he added the *shimmer*.

The stern expression of absolute concentration fell away. He set down the trowel he'd been using and showing Kyle how to use. "Come on over, Beth, let's show them forever who did this."

Not a man you wanted to use your name in the same sentence that contained the word *forever*. Even if you did dream such things.

And he bent over and put his hands in the setting concrete.

And then he insisted she leave her prints there beside his. Kyle added his handprints happily, writing his name under his handprint, giving her a sideways look.

"Can I write, *it sucks to be you*?"

And then they had all laughed. *Again*. That beautiful from-the-belly laughter that felt as if it had the power to heal everything that was wrong in the world. Her world, anyway.

"Did you know," Ben asked her solemnly, "that your nose crinkles when you laugh?"

She instinctively covered her nose, but he pulled her concrete-covered hand away.

"You don't want to get that stuff on your face," he said, and then added, "It's cute when your nose does that."

She had been blissfully unaware until very recently that there was anything in her world that was wrong, that needed to be healed.

Beth had been convinced she was over all that nonsense with Rock/Ralph. Completely.

But now, as her world got bigger and freshened with new experiences and with laughter, and with a man who noticed her nose crinkled when she laughed and thought it was cute, she saw how her hurt had made her world small. Safe, but small.

Now it was as if something magic was unfolding in her yard, and the three of them were helpless against its enchantment. She had actually considered having Kyle put those words in there, *it sucks to be you*, because with those words this funny, unexpected miracle had been brought to her.

Not just the tree house.

Maybe the tree house was even the least of it. This *feeling* of working toward a common goal with other people, of being part of something. This *feeling* of the tiniest things, like washing the concrete off their hands with the hose, Ben reaching over and scrubbing a spec of stubborn grit off her hand, being washed in light, the ordinary becoming extraordinary.

Who was she kidding? The feeling was of belonging. The feeling was of excitement. It was as if something was unfolding just below the surface, as if the excitement in her life had just begun. As that the yard took shape, her staircase beginning to wind around the tree, it was as if she saw possibility in a brand-new way.

Now, as she came out the door with her tray of goodies and set them on the worn picnic table that once had been the pathetic centerpiece of her yard, she watched Ben stop what he was doing. He walked toward her, scooping up his T-shirt as he came, giving his face and chest a casual swipe with it, before pulling it over that incredible expanse of naked male beauty.

"Milk and lemonade," he said, grinning, eyeing the contents of the tray. "Interesting."

"Why?" she demanded. She had just known he would read something into whatever choice she made! She should have known not making a choice had a meaning, too.

He laughed. "You're trying to make everybody happy."

"No," she said, and put the tray down, stood with her hands on her hips staring at the reality of the staircase starting to gracefully curve around the tree, "you are. And look at my yard." But she wanted to say *Look at me. Can't you tell how happy I am?* Instead she said, "Look at Kyle."

Kyle arrived at the picnic table, smudges of dirt on his face, glowing with something suspiciously like happiness even without the choice between lemonade and milk.

"Look," he crowed, and showed her his hand.

A blister was red across the palm.

"Oh," she said, "that's terrible. I'll get some ointment."

But his uncle nudged her and shook his head. "It's part of being a man," he said.

Just loud enough for Kyle to hear him.

Kyle's chest filled with air, and he grinned happily, dug into the cookies and didn't look up until the plate was nearly emptied. He drank two glasses of milk and one of lemonade, and then leaped up and went back to what he'd been doing.

"Okay, I admit it," she said, watching the boy pick up his shovel. "Your plan is better than mine. He loves this. He is a different boy than he was a few days ago."

"Well, don't say it too loud or he might feel driven to prove you wrong, but, yeah, it's good for him."

"It's really good of you to do this. I'm sure today should have been your day off."

"I don't take much time off at this time of year. It gets slow when the weather changes, and then I take some time."

"And do what?" Was it too personal? Of course it was. She didn't want to know what he did with his spare time. *Yes, she did.*

"Usually I go back to Hawaii for a couple of weeks." His eyes drifted to Kyle. "This year, I'm not sure."

"How is your sister?" She could tell right away that *this* was too personal, by the way his shoulders stiffened, how he swirled lemonade in the bottom of his glass like a fortune-teller looking for an answer.

She could tell this was the part of himself that he didn't want people to know about. It was easy for him to be charming and fun-loving. She almost held her breath waiting to see what he would show her.

And then sighed with relief when he showed her what was real.

He rolled his big shoulders, looked away from the lemonade and held her gaze for one long, hard moment. "She's not going to make it."

Beth had known Kyle's mother was seriously ill. There was no other reason that Ben would have been appointed his guardian. But she was still taken aback at this piece of news.

She touched his arm. Nothing else. Just touched him. And it felt as if it was the most right thing in the world when his hand came and covered hers. Something connected them. Not sympathy, but something bigger, a culmination of something that had started happening in this yard from the first moment he had said he would build a tree house for her.

She could have stayed in that wordless place of connection for a long time. But his reaction was almost the opposite of hers.

He took his hand away as if he could snatch back the feeling that had just passed between them. He smiled at her, that devil-may-care smile, and she realized a smile, even a sexy one—or maybe especially a sexy one—could be a mask.

"I'm going to kiss you one day," he promised.

Was that a mask, too? A way of not feeling? Of not connecting on a *real* level? She looked at his lips.

The terrible truth was she was dying to be kissed by him.

But not like that. Not as part of a pretext, a diversion, a way to stop things from hurting.

"Actually, you're not," she said, and was pleased by his startled expression, as if no one had ever refused him a kiss before.

Probably no one had. And probably she was going to regret it tonight. Today. Seconds from now.

Before that weakness settled in, she got up and gathered up the tray and headed for the house. She pulled open the screen door with her toe and looked over her shoulder.

"You know," she called back to him, "kissing can't solve your problems. They will still be there after you unlock lips."

He sat there, looking as if a bomb had hit him, and then got up and stalked across the yard, stood at the bottom of her steps, glaring up at her.

"How would you know what kissing solves or doesn't solve?" he asked her darkly.

"What are you saying? That I look like I've never been kissed?"

"As a matter of fact, you don't look like any kind of an expert on the subject!"

That exquisite moment when she had felt so connected to him was gone. Completely. Absolutely. The oasis was an illusion, after all.

"You pompous, full-of-yourself Neanderthal," she sputtered.

"Don't call me names over five syllables."

"It was four! But just in case you didn't get it, it's the long version of caveman."

He looked like he was going to come up the stairs and tangle those strong, capable hands in her hair, and kiss her just to prove his point. Or hers. That he was a caveman.

But his point would be stronger; she would probably be such a helpless ninny under his gorgeous lips, just like a thousand helpless ninnies before her, that she would totally forget he was a caveman. Or forgive him for it. Or find it enchanting.

She slid inside the door, let it slap shut behind her and then turned, reached out with her little finger from under the tray and latched it.

"Did you just lock the door?" he asked, stunned.

She said nothing, just stood looking at him through the screen.

"What? Do you think I'd break down the door to kiss *you?*"

"It wouldn't be the first time," she said. Pique made her say it. Not that it was a complete lie. She had spent most of junior high hiding from the overly amorous affections of Harley Houston. Once he had leaped out of a coat closet at her, with his lips all puckered and ready. That was certainly close enough to breaking down a door.

Ben regarded her with ill-concealed temper. "It probably would."

"Look," she said coolly, "I don't understand, if you think I'm so incapable of inspiring great passion, why you're the one, who out of the blue, with no provocation *at all* on my part, said you would kiss me someday. As if it wasn't necessary for me to feel something first. Or you. As if you can just do that kind of thing because you feel like it and without the participation of the other person."

"Believe me, if I ever kissed you, you'd participate."

"I wouldn't," she said stubbornly, though she didn't want to be put to the test. And did want to be put to the test. Which most certainly meant she would fail any kind of participation test that involved his lips. Still, there was no sense feeding his already oversize ego. He was impossible. And aggravating. Irritating.

She had known he would be from the first time he had come into her classroom. And instead of letting good sense reign, what had she done?

She had been swayed by the most superficial of things. By his enormous good looks and by his even greater charm. By the sound of laughter. By a tree house taking shape in her yard.

She, Beth Maple, who really should have had so much more sense, had allowed their lives to tangle together! Given him her address, for God's sake. Allowed him into her yard. Baked him cookies. Fed him milk and lemonade.

She had shamelessly watched him take off his shirt and allowed him to put his big mitt prints in her concrete! Which would be a constant and irritating reminder of the fact that, given a chance, she could make a greater fool of herself for this man than she had for Rock aka Ralph!

She closed the inside door firmly, and locked it with as much noise as she could manage, too. But it wasn't until she was slamming dishes into the dishwasher that she realized he had gotten exactly what he wanted, after all, and it had never really been about a kiss.

He had been feeling something when he had told her his sister was going to die.

Sadness. Vulnerability. Maybe even trust in Beth.

And whether with a kiss or by starting an argument, he had managed to distance himself from his discomfort, move on.

No sense feeling a little soft spot for him because of that. It was a warning. There was no future with a man who was so shut off from his emotional self, who was so frightened of it.

When exactly had some sneaky little part of herself started contemplating some kind of future with *that* man?

"Never," she told herself later, as she watched him load up his tools and his nephew and drive away without saying goodbye, without even glancing at her windows. "I hope he never comes back," she told herself.

But when she wandered out in the yard and saw that the framework for the staircase was nearly completed, she knew he was coming back. If he was a quitter, he would have left right after the argument, and he hadn't.

The argument. She'd had her first argument with Ben Anderson.

And as silly as it seemed, she knew that real people disagreed. They had arguments. It was not like her relationship with Rock, which had unfolded like the fantasy it had turned out to be. Full of love notes and tender promises, not a cross word or a disagreement, only the gentlest of chiding on her part when Rock had been compelled to cancel yet one more rendezvous with his myriad of creative excuses.

"I'm probably not ready for real," she decided out

loud, peering up through the thick leaves to where the platform would be.

But it was like being ready to be kissed by him. He didn't care if she was ready. If she wasn't very careful, he was just going to take her by storm whether she was ready or not.

And just like a storm, her life would be left in a wreckage after he was done blowing through. That's why storms of consequence had names. Hurricane Ben. Batten the hatches or evacuate?

"You're overreacting," she scolded herself. But she bet a lot of people said that when there was a storm brewing on the horizon.

To their peril.

CHAPTER FIVE

The Top Secret Diary of Kyle O. Anderson

I THINK Miss Maple and Uncle Ben had a fight. After she brought us out cookies and drinks—lemonade and milk—she went in the house and didn't come back out. My uncle didn't say goodbye to her when we left. He was pretty quiet on the drive home, but when I asked him if anything was wrong, he looked surprised and said, no everything was great, and how did I enjoy work today.

The truth? I really like working with my uncle. I love Miss Maple's tree house. I never, ever thought about the future before. I'm not one of those kids who always dreamed about being a fireman when I grew up.

Getting through each day seemed like a big enough undertaking to me.

But working with my uncle made me realize I like building things. And he says I'm good at it, too. When I suggested a way to change the steps so that they would work better, he said I was a genius. And one thing about my uncle, you can trust that when he says something like that, he means it.

If he did have a fight with Miss Maple, I'm really glad he didn't tell me about it. My mom always told me everything that was going on in her life, and if you think it feels good knowing all about grown-up problems, think again. Still, it's kind of funny, because I thought I wanted Uncle Ben and Miss Maple not to get along, but now that they aren't I feel worried about that.

When we got home, the phone was ringing and my uncle picked up and gave it to me. The only person I could think of who would call me is my mom, so I nearly dropped the phone when it was Mary Kay Narsunchuk. She said that the planetarium was having a special show called Constellation Prize and would I like to go with her?

At first I thought it was a joke, like if I listened hard enough I would hear her girlfriends laughing in the background, but I didn't hear a sound.

"Why are you asking me?" I said, trying to sound cool and not too suspicious.

"Because you are the smartest person I know," she said, and I liked her saying that, even though we don't really *know* each other. And then she said she liked it that I protected the frog against Casper, even though she doesn't really like frogs.

She told me she hates Casper, which means we have something in common already.

Her mom picked me up at Uncle Ben's house and drove us to the planetarium, which was kind of dorky. I've been taking public transit by myself since I was six, and I don't really think the planetarium is in a rough neighborhood, so I thought the warnings to stand right outside the door when she came back to pick us up were hilarious, though I didn't laugh, just said yes, ma'am.

On the way in, I noticed Mary Kay is at least three inches taller than me, and had on really nice clothes, and that bad feeling started, like I'm not good enough. Then I told myself it wasn't like it was a date or anything, and when she asked what I had done today I told her about building the tree house for Miss Maple, and she thought that was the coolest thing she had ever heard.

The weirdest thing happened when we took our seats. The lights went out and she took my hand.

That was all. But the stars came on in the pitch-blackness, like lighted diamonds piercing black velvet, and I thought, *All of this is because of Kermit*. The tree house, and being with Mary Kay right now, and her thinking I was smart, and not even seeming to notice I was way shorter than her, and not dressed so good, either.

The stars above us made the universe look so immense. That's when I had the weird feeling. That good could come from bad, and that maybe I was being looked after by the same thing that put the stars in the sky, and that maybe everything was going to be okay.

It's the first time in my life I've ever felt that way. Like I didn't have to look after anything at all.

And all that was nothing compared to what happened later. Believe me, my uncle Ben and Miss Maple were about the furthest thing from my mind.

It was the first time Ben Anderson had had an evening to himself since Kyle had become a permanent part of his life. At first, watching his nephew go down the walk in front of the house and get into an upscale SUV, Ben felt heady with freedom.

He cocked his head and listened. No steady thump of the bass beat from down the hall.

"I could rent a movie, with bad language and violence," he said out loud, contemplating his options. "Man stuff." He beat his chest to get in the mood for man stuff, something he'd refrained from doing to avoid being scoffed at by his roomie.

Strangely, he discovered he could feel ridiculous all by himself. It was the influence of the annoying Miss Maple. Somehow, even though he was all alone, he could just picture her eyebrows shooting up at chest beating.

"I'll show her," he decided. "I'll call Samantha." But before he got to the phone he found his steps slowing at the thought of an evening with Samantha, pretty as she was. He'd given up on her even before Miss Maple, so imagine how dumb he'd find her now that he had someone to compare her to. Someone who could quote Aristotle, no less!

"Okay," he said. "Hillary, then." But Hillary hadn't had a moment of wonder for at least twenty-five years, and he didn't feel in the mood for worldliness or cynicism.

Pam had always been light-hearted, but he knew he'd find her giggling grating after the day Miss Maple had been hi-jacked by the compactor and he had heard her laughter. And seen her crinkle her nose.

"Okay," he said, annoyed with himself. "I'll call the guys."

But lately the guys were on a campaign to get him back

in the game, as they called it, and the very thought of that made him feel more tired than a day of pouring concrete.

The truth was, once he stopped talking out loud, Ben thought the house felt oddly empty without Kyle. Ben had become accustomed to the bass boom in the background, the squeak of the refrigerator door, the feeling of being responsible for something other than himself.

For a man who had never even succeeded at looking after a houseplant, the fact that he had taken to his guardian duties was a surprise.

Maybe he was maturing. Becoming a better man.

But then he thought of how he'd behaved this afternoon at Beth Maple's, and he didn't feel the least bit proud of himself.

"I think I will rent a movie," he said out loud, and reached for his jacket. At the movie store he picked up *Jackals of the Desert* a movie with a military theme, and a rating that would have never allowed him to watch it with Kyle, even though Kyle rolled his eyes at his uncle's adherence to the rating system.

But before he got to the cash register, he turned around and put the movie back on the shelf. There, under the bright lights of the video store, Ben faced the truth about himself.

He was trying to run away, fill space, so that he didn't have to look at an ugly fact about himself.

He'd hurt her. He'd hurt Miss Maple.

And he'd done it because telling her his sister was not going to make it, and feeling her hand rest, ever so slightly on his arm, had made him come face-to-face with a deeply uncomfortable feeling of sadness about his sister, and vulnerability toward Beth. He didn't want to face his feelings. He didn't actually even want to *have* feelings, messy, unwieldy things that they were.

So, not facing his feelings was nothing new, but hurting someone else?

Not okay.

Especially not okay because it was her.

By taking on the tree house project, Ben was trying to repair the damage that had been done to her, not cause more.

All she'd done was touch him when he'd told her Carly wasn't going to make it. But something in that touch had made him feel weak instead of strong. As if he could lay his head on her lap, and feel her fingers stroking his hair, and cry until there were no more tears.

No wonder he'd lashed out at her. *Cry?* Ben Anderson did not cry. Still, he could now see that it had been childish to try to get his power back at her expense.

"Man up," he'd said to Kyle when Kyle had been trying to shirk from the damage he had caused.

Now it was his turn.

He went out of the video store, and was nearly swamped by the smell of fresh pizza cooking. He hadn't eaten yet.

And that's how it was that he showed up on Beth Maple's doorstep a half an hour later with a Mama Marietta World-Famous Three-Topping Pizza and a six-pack of soda.

Beth opened the door, which gave him hope, because she'd peeked through the security hole and clearly seen it was him. But then she had folded her arms over her bosom like a grade-five teacher who intended not to be won over by the kid who had played hooky.

She was wearing a baggy white shirt and matching pants, that sagged in all the wrong places. Pajamas?

The outfit of a woman who did not get much company of the male variety by surprise.

And that gave him hope, too, though what he was hoping for he wasn't quite ready to think about.

So he thought about why he had come.

"Peace offering," he said, holding out the pizza box so she could see the name on it. Nobody in Cranberry Corners could resist a Mama's three-topping pizza. "And apology."

"Where's Kyle?" she said, peering into the darkness behind him.

"No Kyle tonight." And lest she think he was an irresponsible guardian, he said, "Kyle's at the planetarium, with Mary Kay somebody."

"Ah. I have to say I didn't see that one coming. Or this one."

She was speaking to him. After he'd been thoughtless and cruel and insinuated no one would break down a door to kiss her.

"Are you going to let me in?"

"I'm going to think about it."

"You know something, Miss Maple? There's such a thing as thinking too much."

"Probably not a problem in your world, Mr. Anderson."

"Not generally."

And then her lips twitched, but she still didn't open the door.

"Okay," he said, "I'm getting the fact that somehow you are finding me resistible, but Mama's pizza? Three-topping? Come on."

"What three toppings?" she said.

"Mushroom, pepperoni and the little spicy sausages." He could see her weakening at the mention of the sausages. Which under different circumstances could be quite insulting to a man like him. She could keep the door shut to him, but not sausages?

"There have to be some rules in place," she said.

"There's such a thing as too many rules, too."

"There's the whole thing about dating family members of my students."

"This isn't a date!" he protested. "It's a pizza."

"Well, there is the complication of the kissing that you brought up earlier." She blushed when she said it.

"Okay," he grumbled. "I won't bring up kissing."

"You can't even think about it. Since we are un-chaperoned this evening."

"Miss Maple, you cannot control what I am thinking about!" Especially now. Because she'd mentioned it, and his male mind had locked in on the delicate curve of that puffy bottom lip.

Suddenly this whole thing seemed like a really stupid idea. What had he come here for?

To make amends or to steal kisses? What did you do with a gal like Miss Maple once the pizza was gone? Play chess? Who on earth used the word *unchaperoned* if they were over the age of twenty-one?

"Look, I'll just leave the pizza. With an apology. I'm sorry if I hurt your feelings this afternoon. By insinuating a man wouldn't break down your door to kiss you. Because the right man probably would." He was making a mess of this somehow.

"You just said you weren't going to bring up kissing!" she said.

"But then you said I couldn't even think about it. Which is ridiculous." What man wouldn't think about it in close proximity to those lips? "Miss Maple, there's an elephant in the middle of the room. We can't just pretend it's not there. Maybe we should just get it over with."

"What?" she squeaked. "Get *what* over with?"

He sighed. He couldn't believe he'd actually said that out loud. "Do you want to share the pizza with me or not? It's getting cold. I'm not asking you if you want to build a cabin in the wilderness with me and have my babies, for God's sake, just because I find your lips, um, provocative."

"I don't think it's wise for you to come in," she said.

"I agree, but let's live dangerously."

She contemplated that, as if inviting him in would rate as the most dangerous thing she had ever done.

He better remember that when he was looking sideways at her damn provocative lips. She didn't know the first thing about how to handle a man like him, despite her claim that her door had been knocked down for kisses before.

He actually wondered if he should do it. Just knock the door down and kiss her, so she could see it was not what she feared.

Except he had a feeling it might be more than he feared. If you kissed someone like her, you'd better not do it lightly, without thinking things all the way through to the end. That was the problem with him, and most men, no impulse control. Act now, pay later.

A little cabin in the woods filled with her and their babies didn't seem like such a terrible consequence.

The thought nearly sent him backward off her step, nearly sent him running for the truck.

Except, the door squeaked open.

"Behave," she told him in her sternest, grade-five-teacher voice.

"Yes, Miss Maple," he said meekly.

He reminded himself as he stepped over her threshold that he had come here to make things better, not worse.

Her inner sanctum was as he had known it would be, and it made him feel big and clumsy and menacingly masculine. There were ceramic vases on the floor, where they could easily be toppled by a wayward size-eleven foot. There was a huge clear-glass bowl with real flowers floating in it right on the coffee table in front of her television. One too-enthusiastic cheer for a touchdown and it would be goodbye flowers. And bowl. Probably coffee table, too, flimsy-looking thing on skinny, intricate legs.

Beth's was clearly a world for one: everything in its place, and everything tidy. Despite the fact the breaka-bility factor made him somewhat nervous, there was nothing sterile or uptight about her home. Her space was warmed by tossed cushions and throw rugs, the walls were bright with beautifully framed artwork from her students.

She cast a look at her white slip-covered sofa, decided against it—whether because pizza and white didn't go together, or because it looked too small to hold two people who were going to behave themselves, he wasn't quite sure.

He did notice on the way through that this house was loved: hardwood reclaimed, moldings painted, windows shining. She led him through to the kitchen. It still smelled of the cookies she had baked that afternoon.

"What were you doing?" he asked, when she hurried over to the stove and shut off the burner.

"Making soup and doing a crossword puzzle. The soup couldn't compete with the pizza."

He stopped himself from asking how he compared to the crossword puzzle. It was still out, on a teeny kitchen table that could barely accommodate one, though there were two fragile chairs at it, with skinny, intricate legs that matched those on her coffee table. There were fresh flowers on that table, as well, and he was willing to bet she had bought them for herself.

The tinyness of the table, the crossword puzzle and the flowers were all stern reminders to him to behave.

She had a life she liked. She was the rarest of things. A person content with her own company and her own life.

"I'll help you with the puzzle," he decided, and took a careful seat. Did the chair groan under his weight?

He handed her the pizza since the table was not big enough to accommodate the box. He didn't miss the fact she raised an eyebrow at him, but took the pizza, and got them plates.

"Knife and fork?" she asked him.

"Get real." He squinted at the crossword puzzle. He should have known. It was one of the really hard ones, not like the sports one that came with the weekly TV guide in the local paper, which had supersimple clues like "Who is the most famous running back of all time?"

Out of the corner of his eye, he saw her setting a knife and fork on one of the plates.

"No utensils or I'll take my pizza and go home. Pizza is food you eat with your hands." *Loosen up*, he wanted to tell her. But then he wasn't so sure he wanted her to loosen up, especially when she complied with his instructions and brought over two plates, no utensils. She picked up her slice gingerly and took a tiny bite, then licked a wayward speck of sauce off her index finger.

He was not so sure he should have encouraged her. Watching Miss Maple eat pizza with her hands was a vaguely erotic experience, nearly as bad as watching her eat tiger ice cream.

He reminded himself they were unchaperoned. He was not even allowed to *think* anything that was vaguely erotic.

So, he concentrated on the crossword book. "A six-letter word for *dumb?*" he asked her, but spelled in his head *B-e-n*.

"*Stupid?*"

He scorned the pencil she handed him and picked up a pen off the table. "Nitwit."

"You can't fill it out in pen!" She didn't look too happy about him touching her book while he was eating, either.

"We're living dangerously," he reminded her. "I'll buy you a new book if I get pizza on it."

"I wasn't worried about my book!" she said huffily.

"Yes, you were. What's a seven-letter word for *hot spot*?"

"*Volcano*? I wasn't worried about the book."

"Yes you were. *Hell*," he said, pleased.

"*Hell* does not have seven letters!"

"*Hellish*, then," he wrote it in, pressing hard on the pen so she wouldn't get any ideas about erasing it later. "Eight-letter word for *aggravation*?"

"*Anderson?*" she said sweetly.

How did she count letters so darn fast? "Perfect," he said approvingly, and wrote it in. "This is too easy for us. Next time the *New York Times*."

Next time. Way to go, nitwit.

But somehow the evening did become easy. As they focused on the puzzle, she lost her shyness. She even was eating the pizza with relish. Her wall of reservation came down around her as she got into the spirit of wrecking the puzzle.

"*Incognito*," she crowed.

"It doesn't fit."

Impatiently she took the pen from him, scowled at the puzzle and then wrote, "*Inkono*."

"Miss Maple, you are getting the hang of this," he said with approval. "That makes *zuntkun* down."

"*Zuntkun*," she said happily, "a seven-letter word for an exotic horned animal in Africa if I'm not mistaken."

"Done," he declared, half an hour later looking down at the mess of scribbles and crossed-out words and wrong words with complete satisfaction. So was most of the pizza. So was his control.

This close to her, he could smell lavender and vanilla over the lingering scent of pizza. He liked the laughter in her eyes, and the crinkle on her nose. He decided to make both deepen. He ripped the puzzle out of the book.

"What are you doing?"

"It's a little something on you. From now on I have this to show your class how their teacher spells *incognito* in a pinch. If you make me happy, I'll never have to use it."

"How would I make you happy?" she asked warily.

"Use your imagination. Any woman who can spell *incognito* like that, and who can invent horned beasts in Africa, has to have a pretty good imagination."

"I have a better idea. Just give it back."

"I'm not one of your fifth-graders. I don't have to do things just because you say so. You come get it," he teased, and at the look on her face he pushed back his chair.

She moved toward him. "Give it!"

"Don't make me run," he said. "You have highly breakable bric-a-brac."

She lunged at him. He turned and ran, holding the puzzle out in front of him. She chased him out of the kitchen and through the living room, around the coffee table and over the couch. The vases on the floor wobbled as he thundered by, but did not break.

She backed him into a corner up the hallway, by her open bedroom door. Decorated in many, many shades of virginal white. Unless he was going to mow her over, or move into her bedroom, which was out of the question, he was trapped. And delightfully so.

"Surrender," she demanded, holding out her hand.

"Surrender? As in nine-letter word for *give up?* Not in the marine vocabulary."

She made a snatch for it.

He held the puzzle over his head. "Come and get it," he said, and laughed when she leaped ineffectually at him.

Her face was glowing. She looked pretty and uninhibited and ferociously determined to have her own way. After several leaps, she tried to climb up him.

With her sock feet on top of his sock feet and her full length pressed against him, she tried to leverage herself for the climb up him. With one arm around his neck, and one toe on his knee, she reached for the paper, laughing breathlessly, her nose as crinkled as a bunny's.

She suddenly realized what she was doing. He wondered if it felt as good for her as it did for him. She went very still.

And then backed off from him so fast she nearly fell over. He resisted the impulse to steady her.

"Hmm," he said quietly. "That made me happy. Your puzzle is safe with me, for now. Unfortunately, I have to go." He looked at his watch. "Kyle will be home soon. I don't want him to come into an empty house. I think there's been a little too much of that in his life."

"You're a good man, Ben Anderson," she said.

He felt the mood changing, softening, moving back to where it had been this afternoon when she had laid her hand on his arm and he had felt oddly undone by it.

So he waggled the puzzle at her, eager to keep it light. Maybe even hoping to tempt her to try and climb up him one more time to retrieve it.

"I'm not really a good man," he said. "I have the puzzle, and I'm not afraid to use this. Don't forget."

"I'll see you to the door," she said, not lured in, and with ridiculous formality, given that she had just tried to climb him like a tree. She preceded him to it, held it open.

"Thank you for the pizza." Again the formal note was in her voice.

"You're welcome."

He stood there for a minute, looking at her. *Don't do it*, he told himself. She wasn't ready to have her world rattled. She wasn't ready for a man like him. There was no sense complicating things between them.

But, as it turned out, she made the choice, not him. Just as he turned to go out the door, he felt her hand, featherlight, on his shoulder. He turned back, and it was she who stood on her tiptoes and brushed her lips against his.

It was like tasting cool, clean water after years of drinking water gone brackish. It was innocence, in a world of cynicism. It was beauty in a world that had been ugly. It was a glimpse of a place he had never been.

So the truth was not that she was not ready for a man like him. The truth was that he was not ready for a woman like her.

Who would require so much of him. Who would require him to learn his whole world all over again. Who would require him to be so much more than he had ever been before.

"Well," she said, stepping back from him, her eyes wide, as if she could not believe her own audacity, "I'm glad we addressed the elephant."

But he wasn't so sure. The elephant had been sleeping contentedly. Now that they had "addressed" it, they couldn't go back to where they had been before. Now that they had "addressed" it, it was going to be hungry.

Now that they'd addressed it, her lips were going to be more an issue for him, not less.

The elephant was now taking up the whole room instead of just a corner in the shadows, swaying sleepily on its feet, not being too obtrusive at all.

She leaned toward him again, and he held his breath. If she kissed him again, he was not going to be responsible for what happened next. Didn't she know the first thing about men?

But then she snatched the paper he'd forgotten all about from his hand, and laughed gleefully. Maybe she knew more about men than she had let on. She had certainly known how to collapse his defenses completely.

"Good night, Ben," she said sweetly.

And all the way home he brooded about whether she had just kissed him to get her hands on that damned puzzle. He was still brooding about it when Kyle came through the front door.

He stopped brooding and stared at his nephew. Kyle was *shining*.

"Uncle Ben," Kyle said breathlessly. "What does it mean when a girl kisses you?" And then, without waiting for an answer, "I guess she likes you *a lot*, huh?"

Ben contemplated that for a minute, and then said, "I guess she does." *Either that or she wants something, like her puzzle back.*

CHAPTER SIX

SHE'D actually kissed Ben Anderson, Beth thought, as she put the leftover pizza in the fridge and the pizza box in the garbage.

Oh, no, not just kissed him, but *instigated* the kiss.

"What's that about?" she asked herself. Well, he'd encouraged her. "Live dangerously," he'd said.

Not wantonly, she chastised herself, *floozy*. And then she laughed at herself. Wantonly? Floozy? In this day and age a kiss like that wouldn't be considered wanton. It wouldn't make a woman a floozy.

She was twenty-five years old and she'd dared to brush lips with a man so attractive he made her heart stand still. She was glad she'd done it. She felt no regret at all. In fact, Beth Maple felt quite pleased with herself. There was something about being around him that made her want to be a different person.

Not reserved. Not shy. Not afraid. Not hiding from life.

She wanted to be a person who did the crossword all wrong and admitted it was so much more fun than doing it right. She uncrumpled her hard-won prize and looked at it, then moved into her kitchen and used a magnet to put it in a place of honor on her fridge.

The new Beth would break rules. The new Beth would not wait for a man to kiss her, but would kiss him if she felt like it.

She contemplated the experience of touching her lips to his and felt a quiver of pure pleasure. Imagine. She had almost gone through life without kissing a man like that! What a loss!

Ben Anderson had tasted even better than she could have hoped. It was as if the walls around her safe and structured little world had crumbled to dust when she had touched her lips to his.

Something was unleashed within her, and she wasn't putting it away. The old Beth would have worried about the awkwardness when she saw him again. But the new Beth couldn't wait.

She was *alive*. She had been sleeping, deliberately, ever since the fiasco with Ralph/Rock. She'd been wounded and had retreated to lick her wounds. She had convinced herself she was retreating for good.

And then, as if the universe had plans for her that she could not even fathom, along had come Kyle, and then his uncle, and then a tree house in her backyard, all the events of the past weeks beckoning to her, calling to her.

Live. She needed to live. Even if it was scary. She needed to embrace the wonderful, unpredictable adventure that was life. Not just live, she thought, but live by Ben's credo: *dangerously*.

Hilarious to have a turning point over a crossword

puzzle, but Ben had shown her that. Have *fun*. Throw out the rules from time to time.

Now it was Sunday morning, and his truck pulled up in front of her house, and he got out. Was his glance toward her window wary? As if he didn't know what to expect?

That was good, because she had a sneaking suspicion that in the past he was the one in control when it came to relationships. He was the one who decided what was happening and when.

Ben Anderson, she said to herself, *you have met your match*. And then she contemplated that with wicked delight.

A week ago she would not have considered herself any kind of match for Ben Anderson.

For a moment caution tried to rear its reasonable head. It tried to tell her there was a reason she had not considered herself any kind of a match for him. Because he was obviously way more experienced than her. She didn't really know him. They were polar opposites in every way.

But below the voice of reason, another voice sang. That it had seen how he was with his nephew, how calm and responsible and willing to sacrifice that he was. And it had seen his vision for her backyard taking shape, his plan, that whimsical tree house speaking to her heart and soul, as if he also saw the things about her that no one else did. Just as she had seen *him*, pure and unvarnished, when he talked about his sister.

And then, when she had kissed him last night she had tasted something on his lips.

Truth. His truth. Strength and loneliness. Playfulness and remoteness. Need and denial of need.

He had already strapped on his tool apron when she came out the door with hot coffee for him and a hot chocolate for Kyle. He took his coffee, said good morning, gruffly, as though they were strangers, but his eyes strayed to her lips before they skittered away.

"Guess what?" Kyle told her. "Mary Kay and I went to the planetarium last night."

"And how was that?" she asked.

"Awesome," he breathed.

She saw in him what she had always wanted for him, a capacity to know excitement, to feel joy, to be just an ordinary kid, a boy moving toward manhood, who could have a crush on a girl and still love tree houses at the very same time.

She glanced at Ben, and knew he saw it, too, and saw the incredible tenderness in his eyes as he looked at Kyle.

And she knew he could say whatever he wanted, but she would always know what was true about him.

"Could I bring her here and show her the tree house?" Kyle asked. "When we're done?"

"Of course," Beth said.

"It's not going to get done if we stand around here, drinking coffee," Ben said, and set his down deliberately. "Kyle, you can start hauling lumber from the truck for the platform. Stack it here."

Ben looked like he intended to ignore Beth, but she had a different idea altogether. She had found an old tool belt in the basement, and she strapped it on, too, picked up some boards and headed for the stairs.

"What are you doing?" he asked.

"I'm helping."

"You don't know anything about building a staircase," he said with a scowl.

"Well, you didn't know anything about crossword puzzles, either."

"We don't want *this* to end like *that*," he said. "Building things isn't like doing a crossword puzzle. There's a purpose to it."

"There's a purpose to crossword puzzles," she told him dangerously.

"Which is?" he said skeptically.

"They build brain power."

"But nobody gets hurt if they're done wrong. If we don't build this right, you could be up there in your hammock on a sunny summer day, sipping lemonade and reading romance novels, and the whole thing could fall down."

"Romance novels?" she sputtered. Had she left one out last night, or was she just that transparent?

"It's just an example."

He saw her as a person who had filled her life with crossword puzzles and fantasies! And annoyingly it wasn't that far off the mark!

But she was changing, but that made her wonder if it was true that nobody was going to get hurt from doing the crossword puzzle wrong. She was open in ways she never had been before, committed to living more dangerously. Rationally, that was a good way to get hurt.

She didn't feel rational. She felt as if she never cared to be rational again!

"Show me how to hammer the damn steps down, and how to do it so that I and my lemonade and my romance novel don't end up in a heap of lumber at the bottom of this tree," she told him.

"Ah, ah, Miss Maple. Grade-five teachers aren't allowed to say *damn*."

"You don't know the first thing about grade-five teachers," she told him.

His eyes went to her lips, and they both knew he might know one thing or two. He hesitated and then surrendered, even though it wasn't the marine way. "Okay, I'll put the stringers and then show you how to put the treads on."

In a very short while, she wondered how rational it had been to ask. Because they were working way too closely. His shoulder kept touching hers. He covered her hand with his own to show her how to grip the hammer. She was so incredibly *aware* of him, and of how sharing the same air with him seemed to heighten all her senses.

Alive. As intensely alive as she had ever been. Over something so simple as working outside, shoulder to shoulder with a man, drinking in his scent and his strength, soaking his presence through her skin as surely as the beautiful late-summer sunshine.

Before she knew it, they were at the top of the staircase.

"It's done," she said.

"Not really. At the moment, it's a staircase that leads to nowhere."

Trust a man to think that! It showed the difference between how men and women thought. He so pragmatic. She so dreamy. Amazing he had thought of the tree house in the first place!

Just to show him the staircase led to somewhere, she stepped carefully off the stair and onto a branch.

"Hey, be careful."

She ignored his warning, dropped down and shinnied out on the branch. From her own backyard was a view she had never seen before.

"I can see all of Cranberry Corners," she said. "This is amazing."

And that's what happened when you took a chance and lived on the edge. You saw things differently. Whole new worlds opened to you.

"You better come back here."

She ignored him, pulled herself to sitting, dangled her feet off the branch, looked out the veil of leaves to her brand-new view of the world and sighed with satisfaction.

"If you fall from there, you're going to be badly hurt," he warned.

She looked back at him. He looked very cross. Too bad.

"In between romance novels, I try and squeeze in a little reading that has purpose. Do you know Joan of Arc's motto?" she asked him.

"Oh, sure, I have Joan of Arc's motto taped to my bathroom mirror. What kind of question is that? Come down from there, Beth. Now is no time to be quoting Joan of Arc."

"'I am not afraid,'" she said, wagging her legs happily into thin air, "'I was born for this.'"

"Hey, in case you don't remember, Joan's story does not have a happily-ever-after ending."

"Like my normal reading?" she asked sweetly.

"It's not attractive to hold a grudge. I'm sorry I insinuated you might just read something relaxing and fun in between studying Aristotle. Get off that branch."

She glanced at him again. He did look sincerely worried. "You're the one who likes to live dangerously," she reminded him.

"Yeah. *Me*."

"You've encouraged me."

"To my eternal regret. Beth, if you don't come back here, I'm going to come get you. I mean it."

"I doubt if the branch is strong enough to hold us both."

"I doubt it, too."

It was a terrible character defect that she liked tormenting him so much. Terrible. It was terrible to enjoy how much he seemed to care about her. Though caring and feeling responsible for someone were two entirely different things.

"Is it lunchtime yet?" Kyle called up the tree. "Hey, that looks fun, Miss Maple. Can I come up?"

"No!" she and Ben called together, and she scrambled in off the branch before Kyle followed her daredevil example. Ben leaned out and put his hands around her waist as soon as she was in reach. He swung her off the branch and set her on the top stair. But his hands stayed around her waist as if he had no intention of letting her go to her own devices.

"I'm safe now," she told him.

But his hands did not move. They both knew that she was not safe and neither was he, and that what was building between them was as dangerous as an electrical storm and every bit as thrilling.

He let her go. "I'll take Kyle and grab a bite to eat."

She knew he was trying to get away from the intensity that was brewing between them.

"No need," she said easily. "There's lots of leftover pizza."

And so even though surrender was not the marine way, she found Ben Anderson in her kitchen for the second time in as many days. The problem with having him in her space was that it was never going to be completely her space again. There would be shadows of him in here long after he'd gone.

And men like that went, she reminded herself. They did not stay.

And right now it didn't seem to matter. At all. It was enough to be alive in this moment. Not to analyze what the future held. Not to live in the prison of the past. Just to enjoy this simple moment.

"Microwave or oven?" she asked of reheating the pizza.

They picked the oven, and while they waited she mixed up a pitcher of lemonade and asked Kyle about the program at the planetarium.

"Hey," she said, catching a movement out of the corner of her eye. "Hey, put that back!"

But Ben had his prize. He held up the puzzle that she had tacked on her fridge the night before.

"Ah," he said with deep satisfaction, and folded it carefully. He put it in his pocket.

"That belongs to me," she said sternly.

"That's a matter of opinion."

"It was on my fridge! It's out of my book."

"My. My. My. I thought by fifth grade you'd learned how to share."

And then she couldn't help it. She was laughing. And he was laughing.

Kyle, giving them a disgusted look, gobbled down the leftover pizza. "Is there any dessert?" he asked.

"Kyle!" Ben said.

But she was glad to see the boy eating with such healthy appetite. Since she didn't have dessert, she said, "Let's not go right back to work. Let's take the bicycles down to Friendly's and have an ice cream."

"How many bikes do you have?" Ben asked, looking adorably and transparently anxious to keep her away from that staircase to nowhere and her perch on the tree branch.

"About half a dozen. I pick up good bikes cheap at the police auctions. Then if there's a kid at school who needs a bike, there's one available."

"You really have made those kids, school, your whole life, haven't you?"

He said it softly. Not an indictment, but as if he saw her, too. "You have a big, big heart, Miss Maple."

And he said that as if a big heart scared him.

"Ice cream," she said, before he thought too hard about their differences.

Kyle made a funny sound in his throat. "I don't want ice cream," he said. "You guys go. Without me."

"Without you?"

They said it together and with such astonishment that some defensiveness that had come into Kyle's face evaporated.

"I don't know how to ride a bike," he said, and his voice was angry even while there was something in his face that was so fragile. "And you know what else? I don't know how to swim, either. Or skate.

"You know what I *do* know how to do? I know how

to stick a whole loaf of bread underneath my jacket and walk out of the supermarket without paying for it. I know they put out the new stuff at the thrift store on Tuesday. I know how to get on the bus without the driver seeing you, and how to make the world's best hangover remedy."

Suddenly Kyle was crying. "I'm eleven years old and I don't know how to ride a bike."

He said a terrible swear word before *bike*.

Beth stared at him in shocked silence. And then her gaze went to Ben. He looked terrified by the tears, but he quickly masked his reaction.

"Big deal," Ben said, with the perfect touch of casualness. Somehow, he was beside his nephew, his strong arm around those thin shoulders. "Riding a bike is not rocket science. I bet I can teach you to ride a bike in ten minutes."

Beth knew if she lived to be 103, she would never forget this moment, Ben's strength and calm giving Kyle a chance to regain his composure.

Ben met her eyes over Kyle's head, and she realized the whole thing was tipping over for her. The look in his eyes: formidable strength mixed with incredible tenderness shook something in her to the very core.

It wasn't about living dangerously.

It was about falling in love. But wasn't that the most dangerous thing of all?

"Ten minutes?" Kyle croaked.

"Give or take," Ben said.

Of course he couldn't teach Kyle to ride a bike in ten minutes.

"Are you in?" Ben asked her.

It wasn't really about teaching Kyle to ride a bike. It

was about so much more. Going deeper out into unknown waters. Going higher up the treacherous mountain.

It was about deciding if she was brave enough to weave her life through the threads of his.

What were her options? Her life before him seemed suddenly like a barren place, for all that she had convinced herself it was satisfying. It had been without that mysterious element that gave life *zing*.

"I'm in," she said. And she meant it. She was *in*. Totally surrendering. She'd never been a marine, anyway. It was perfectly honorable for her to give in to whatever surprises life had in store for her, to be totally open to what happened next.

It was like riding a bike. There was no doing it halfheartedly. You had to commit. And even if you ended up with some scrapes and bruises, wasn't it worth it? Wasn't riding a bike, full force, flat-out, as fast as you could go, like flying? But you couldn't get there without risk.

They selected a bike for Kyle from her garage and took it out on the pavement in front of the house. Soon they were racing along beside him, Ben on one side, she on the other, breathless, shouting instructions and encouragement. Just as in life, they had to let go for him to get it. Kyle wobbled. Kyle fell. Kyle flew. They were so engrossed in the wonder of what was unfolding that no one noticed when ten minutes became an hour.

"I think we're ready for the inaugural ride," Ben finally said. "Let's go to Friendly's for ice cream."

"Really?" Kyle breathed.

"Really?" she asked. Friendly's was too far for a

novice rider. There would be traffic and hills. Try out those brand-new skills in the real world?

Maybe there was a parallel to how she felt about Ben. Try it out in the real world, away from the safety of her yard and her world? She remembered last time she'd been at Friendly's with Ben, too.

He'd gotten up abruptly and left her sitting there, by herself, with a half-eaten ice cream cone!

It reminded her he was complex. That embracing a new world involved a great deal of risk and many unknown factors.

But again she looked at her choices. Go back to what her life had been a few short weeks ago? Where reading an excellent essay full of potential and promise had been the thing that excited her? Or where finishing a really tough crossword had filled her with a sense of satisfaction? Or where building a papier-mâché tree for her classroom had felt like all the fulfillment she would ever need?

Her life was never going to be the same, no matter what she did.

So she might as well do it.

"Let's go," she said.

They rode their three bikes down to Friendly's Ice Cream. And then, after eating their ice cream cones, instead of riding back to her place, they took the bike trail along the river and watched Kyle's confidence grow. He was shooting out further and further ahead of them now, shouting with exuberance when they came to hills, racing up the other side, leaving them in his dust.

"You go ahead," Ben said to him. "You're wearing me out. Me and Miss Maple are going to do the old people thing and lie under this tree until you get back."

There were miles of bike trails here and they watched him go.

"Are you sure he's ready?" she asked, watching Kyle set off.

"Yup."

"How?"

"Look at him. Have you ever seen a kid more ready to fly?"

They sat there, under the tree, enjoying the sunshine and the silence, the lazy drift of the river. They talked of small things: the tree house, the wonder of Friendly's ice cream, bicycles and kids.

Beth was aware of a growing comfort between them. An ease as relaxed as the drift of the river. But just like the river, how smooth it *looked* was deceiving. A current, unseen but strong, was what kept the water moving.

And there was an unseen current between them, too. An awareness. She was *so* aware of the utter maleness of Ben Anderson. She had seen the way the women in the ice cream parlor looked at him, knew the body language of the women who jogged by on the bike path.

The old Beth would have been intimidated by that. The old Beth would have thought, *He's out of my league*. Or *What would a guy like this ever see in me*?

But the new Beth had *played* with him, had done crosswords and eaten pizza with her hands and held a hammer and defied him by sitting way out on the branch of a tree. She liked being with him, and she was pretty sure he liked being with her, too.

"Do you want to kiss me again?" she asked, thrilled at her boldness.

"Miss Maple, do you know what you're playing with?"

"Oh, I think I do, Mr. Anderson. Look at me. Have you ever seen a woman more ready to fly?"

He hesitated, momentarily caught, and then he leaned toward her, and she saw his nostrils flare as he caught the scent of her. His eyes closed, and he came closer.

"Beth," he said, and her name on his lips right before he kissed her sounded exactly as she had known it would, like a benediction.

His lips touched hers, as light as a dragonfly wing. And she touched his back, felt again that delicious sense of coming home, of knowing truth about someone that was so deep it could never be denied.

But then the lightness of the kiss intensified. He took her lips, and she felt his hunger and his urgency, the pure male desire of him.

It occurred to her maybe she didn't know what she was playing with, at all, but the thought was only fleeting, chased away by intensity of feeling such as she had never known.

This was not a picket fence kind of kiss.

It was the kiss of a warrior. The claim. It was fierce and it was demanding, and she knew another truth.

A man like this would take all a woman had to offer. She would have to be as deep and as intense, every bit as strong as he was. With a man like this there would be few quiet moments in the safety of the valleys.

He would take you to the peaks: emotional highs that were as exhilarating as they were terrifying and dangerous.

You would go higher than you had ever been before.

And you could fall further than you had ever fallen.

Unless you could fly. And hadn't she just asked that of him, if he had ever seen a woman more ready to fly?

Only, now that she was here, standing on the precipice of flight or falling, she was not sure she could fly at all.

Was she strong enough? Hadn't she broken a wing?

"Gross."

Ben pulled away from her as if he had been snapped back on a bungee cord. Neither of them had expected Kyle's solo flight be quite so brief.

But there he was, sitting on his bike, glaring at them, looking pale and accusing. Ben jumped up, reached back for her and pulled her to her feet, put her behind him as if he was protecting her from the look on his nephew's face.

"It wasn't gross," he said evenly, and something in the warrior cast of his face warned Kyle not to go further with his commentary, and Kyle didn't.

Still, Beth could clearly see that Ben either regretted the kiss or regretted getting caught, and it was probably some combination of the two. Clearly, unlike Kyle's bike ride, her flight was not going to be solo. And flying with someone who had doubts would be catastrophic. If the choice would be hers to make at all!

"There are some swans on the river down there," Kyle said, obviously sharing his uncle's eagerness to move away from that kiss. "I wanted you two to see them. They're too pretty to see by yourself."

And in that she heard wariness and longing, as if Kyle was showing them all how they felt about this relationship.

There were things too pretty about life to experience it all by yourself.

But trusting another person to share them with you was the scariest journey of all. Things could get *wrecked* by following a simple thing like a kiss to the mountaintop where it wanted to go.

It did feel like you could fly. But realistically, you could fall just as easily.

Kyle was only eleven and he already knew that.

Beth felt her first moment of fear since she had adopted the new her. Ben studiously ignored her as he got back on his bike and followed his nephew down the trail. She followed, even though part of her wanted to ride away from them, back home, to her nice safe place.

Funny it would be swans she thought, gazing at them moments later, the absolute beauty of jet black faces and gracefully curving white necks.

Funny they would be swans when she could feel herself beginning the transformation from ugly duckling. It was a transformation that was unsettling and uncertain.

And being unsettled and uncertain were the two things Beth Maple hated the most.

The Top-Secret Diary of Kyle O. Anderson

When I came down that bike path and saw my uncle and Miss Maple kissing, I felt sick to my stomach. I've seen my mom do this. Along comes the kissing part, and she's looking for a place to put me where no one will know I'm around.

So, I waited. I thought, my uncle will give me ten bucks and tell me to go get some more ice cream, but he didn't.

We went and looked at the swans and then we went back to Miss Maple's house and worked on the tree house some more. They didn't touch each other or kiss in front of me.

Miss Maple gave me the bike to take home, and my uncle and I went riding again after supper.

It's easy to ride a bike. I asked him if it was just as easy to swim and to learn to skate and he said a man could do anything he set his mind to.

As if he thinks of me as a man.

"Is there anything you're scared of?" I asked him.

And he didn't say anything for a long time. And then he said, "There's something everyone is scared of."

But he didn't tell me what it was, and you know what? I didn't want to know, because I bet whatever he's scared of is really, really bad, worse than Genghis Khan being at the gate and telling you to surrender or else.

I wish my uncle Ben wasn't afraid of anything, because it's been really easy, working on Miss Maple's tree house, and eating pizza and ice cream, and going out with Mary Kay to the planetarium, to think maybe

there is a place where I can feel safe and maybe I've
found it.

Ha, ha. It's always when you think you have something that it gets taken away. Always.

CHAPTER SEVEN

BETH Maple had kissed him. Twice. Ben was trying as valiantly as he knew how to be the perfect gentleman, a role he was admittedly not practiced at. That's why he'd gone over there in the first place last night. To do the gentlemanly thing. To apologize.

But he had still planned to keep his distance, treat her like his nephew's teacher. Even doing the crossword had been about teaching her the innocent fun of not being so uptight. Break a few rules, for God's sake.

But the lines had an unpredictable way of blurring around her, and that was without her learning to be less uptight and break some rules. That was without watching her eat ice cream again, or race along a bike trail, shrieking with laughter.

Who would have guessed she would be the one instigating something more, confusing his already beleaguered male mind with kisses?

There was a chance her first kiss had been strictly a ploy to get the puzzle, and considering that would have made his world less complex, he had been strangely wounded by the thought. But kiss number two had erased any suspicion he had about ploys. She hadn't even tried to get the crossword that he had taken from her fridge out of his front pocket when she'd kissed him under the tree by the river.

Thank goodness for that, because things were complicated enough without her getting grabby *there*. Not that she was the type, but twenty-four hours ago he would have laid money she wasn't the instigating-kisses type, either.

This was the problem with kisses: in his experience kisses led to the *R* word, as in a Relationship. And in his experience that never went well for him. Women wanted most what he least wanted to give. Intimacy. Time. Commitment. A chunk of him.

He wanted a good time, a few laughs, nothing too demanding on his schedule, his psyche or his lifestyle. Which probably explained why a relationship for him, beginning to end, first kiss to glass smashing against the door as he said goodbye and made his final exit, was about one month. On a rare occasion, two.

He felt strangely reluctant to follow that pattern with Beth Maple. She'd only been in his life for a few weeks, but when he thought of going back to life without her, no tree house, no crossword puzzles, no bike rides by the river, he felt a strange feeling of emptiness.

"Look," he said, taking the bull by the horns after they had wheeled the bikes back into her garage. Kyle was out of earshot, loading up the tools in Ben's truck. They had made dismally little headway on the tree house today, which was part of why he had to take the bull by the horns. "We have to talk about this kissing thing."

"We do?" She had that mulish look on her face, the same one she'd had as she was dangling her feet off a tree branch thirty feet in the air, the one that clearly said she wasn't having him call the shots for her.

"It's not that I don't like it," he said. He could feel his face getting hot. Hell. Was he blushing? No, too much sun and wind today.

"You don't?" she said sweetly, determined not to help him.

"I like it," he snapped, "but you should know I have a history with relationships that stinks. And that's how a relationship starts. With kissing."

"Thank you for the lecture, Mr. Anderson. Will there be a test?"

"I'm trying to reason with you!"

"You're trying to tell me you don't want to have a relationship with me."

"Only because it would end badly. Based on past history."

"Would you like to know what very important element was probably missing from your past relationships?"

Don't encourage her, he thought. It was obvious to him she was no kind of expert on relationships. Still, he'd come to respect her mind.

"What?" he asked.

"Friendship."

He stared at her. How could she know that? And yet if he reviewed all his many past experiences and failures, it was true.

He had never ever chosen a woman he could have been friends with.

And there was a reason for that.

He'd had his fill of hard times and heartaches. He'd known more loss by the time he was twenty-one than most people would experience in a lifetime.

He'd become determined to have fun, and he'd become just as determined that the easiest way to stop having fun was to start caring about someone other than himself.

"We can be friends or we can be lovers," he said with far more firmness than he felt. "We can't be both."

He could tell by the shocked look on her face she hadn't even considered that's where kisses led.

"Wow," she said. "You know how to go from *A* to *Z* with no stopping in between."

Well put. "Exactly."

She looked at him for a long time. He had the feeling Beth Maple saw things about him that he didn't really want people to see.

She confirmed that by saying, "You know, Ben, you strike me as somebody who needs a friend more than a lover."

He wanted to tell her he had plenty of friends, but that wasn't exactly true. Not *girl* friends. He told himself he'd gotten the answer he wanted, the answer that kept everything nice and safe, especially his lips. He told himself this would be a good place to leave it. But naturally he wasn't smart enough to do that.

"And what do *you* need?" He was surprised that he asked, more surprised by how badly he wanted to hear her answer. What if she said, "I need to have a wild fling where I learn to let down my hair and live up to what my lips are telling you about me"?

He held his breath, but he got the stock Miss Maple answer.

"I need not to get involved with a family member of one of my students. On a lover level."

She blushed when she said it. What a relief. She couldn't even say *lover* let alone invite him to have a wild fling with her.

Her cheeks, staining the color of the beets his mother used to can, told him a truth about her. And about himself.

A man could never take her as a lover. She was the kind of woman who required way more than a recreational romp in the hay, whether she knew that about herself or not. She was the kind of woman who needed commitment. He'd known that from practically their first meeting when she had tossed that word around so lightly!

She was the kind of girl who would never be satisfied with the superficial, who would demand a man leave his self-centered ways behind him.

To be worthy of her. Which he was pretty darn sure he wasn't.

Thank God.

"Well, I'm glad we got that sorted out," he said doubtfully.

"Me, too," she said.

"It's not that I didn't like kissing you."

"I understand."

"So, you won't kiss me again?" What had his life become? He was begging a very pretty woman not to kiss him!

For her own good. Maybe he was becoming a better man, despite himself.

"I'll do my best," she said solemnly. And then, just when he thought she totally got what he was trying to tell her, she giggled, tried to hold it back and snorted in a most un-Miss Maple way.

He scowled at her.

"Rein myself in," she promised, and then snickered again. "Wanton floozy. I didn't mean to throw myself at you."

"Nobody says things like that," he said, irritated. "Wanton floozy."

She was laughing and snorting in an effort to restrain herself. "Oh, you know us readers of romance novels."

"You know, that's another annoying thing about you—" besides the fact that she looked absolutely glorious when she laughed, and her nose wrinkled like that "—you have this mind like a computer, and you store away every single thing a person ever says to you for later use. Against them."

She finally got the laughter under control, thankfully. Though now that he thought about it, he was not sure he liked that thoughtful, stripping way she was looking at him any better.

"You know what else was missing from your past relationships? Besides friendship?"

It was very obvious she planned to tell him, whether he wanted to hear it or not. Which he didn't. At least not very much. He glared at her, folded his arms over his chest.

"Brains," she said, softly. "No wonder you were bored."

"I never said I was bored!" But he realized he had been. Every single time, after the initial thrill, bored beyond belief.

"Well, based on what you said about your past history, *someone* was bored."

"Relationships can end for reasons other than that." She wasn't insinuating the other person had been bored with *him*, was she?

"Yes, that's true. Maybe you're a bad lover."

He opened his mouth to protest, but caught the gleeful twinkle in her eye, and snapped it shut again before he gave her more cause to laugh.

He wasn't sure he even wanted to be friends with her after all, he thought, a trifle sullenly. She saw way too much. And said too much.

But what choice did he have? He had to finish building her tree house. And Kyle was going to be in her class for another nine months or so.

Excuses. Because it really did seem like his life the way it had been before she came along was not what he wanted anymore.

He'd been lonely. He knew that now.

She had been right. He needed a friend. He needed a friend just like her. As long as they didn't go and wreck it all by changing it to something else.

Feeling as if he had just navigated a minefield where he had managed, just barely, not to get himself blown to smithereens, he retreated to his truck and drove home. When they got in the house, Kyle announced he was going to do his homework.

Ben decided it would be counterproductive to remind Kyle he didn't do homework. Instead he contemplated that development, and allowed himself to feel a moment's satisfaction about how *his* plan was working the miracle that hers had not. But maybe it was bike riding that had worked the miracle, and that had been her idea. Turned into a project in cooperation. An outing with a family feeling to it.

Maybe that was at the heart of the miracle. That feeling of family. Ben's wisdom in saying nay to the kisses was confirmed, though there was a sharp and undeniable tingle of regret that went with it every time he thought about it. Or her lips.

He was still contemplating that when the phone rang. Miss Maple's personal number on his call display. He hadn't even been away from the many and varied temptations of her for an hour! Once upon a time, he remembered he had *hoped* she would call him. But that was before he'd known how capable she was of shaking up his world.

Still, it was not reluctance he felt when he answered the phone, much as he knew it *should* be.

"I can call you now that we're friends, right?" she asked. "It's not against your rules, like kissing?"

He hoped she wasn't going to mention kissing at every opportunity, because the whole idea was he didn't want to think about it.

"Of course you can phone me at anytime," he said foolishly. The pathetic truth was he couldn't think of anything he'd like more than talking to her. And the phone was so safe. He didn't even have to see her lips.

"You don't see my calling you as being too forward? Bordering on wanton?"

"No," he said sharply, trying to disguise how much he was liking this. "Are you amusing yourself at my expense?"

"Of course not. Actually, I called about Kyle, so this is definitely not wanton."

"Definitely," he agreed, disappointed that she had called about Kyle, even though he did appreciate her concern for his nephew's well-being. Besides, what could be better? That was a nice and safe topic.

"He told me he was going to do his homework," he whispered into the phone. It occurred to him there was no one else in the world who cared about that except her. It made him feel an unwanted nudge of tenderness for her. "Try not to make too big a fuss when he turns it in tomorrow."

"Don't worry, Ben, I'm not insulted that you think you have to tell me how to conduct myself in my classroom."

"Don't be so prickly." So much for tenderness. Which was good, tender thoughts probably would lead directly back to lip thoughts.

"Don't be so overbearing."

Boy, he was glad he had decided against complicating things!

"I'm not overbearing," he growled.

"Just far too used to calling the shots?"

"I run my own business!"

"You can't run your personal life like your business."

Had he actually been slightly happy to see her number on the call display? Why? She was bossy, opinionated *and* prickly. Who was she to tell him how to run his personal life? As far as he could tell, she didn't have one.

But if he said that, he was probably going to end up on her doorstep with pizza, apologizing again. And that led to lips, too. Instead he said, "Was there a reason you called?"

"I've been thinking about Kyle not knowing how to swim," she said, moving on quickly from the topic of his overbearingness, which he was glad about, even though he might have liked to talk about her prickliness a little more.

"It really bothers me," she said.

And just like that they were beyond the prickliness to that other side of her, so soft it beckoned like a big feather bed on a cold winter's night.

"Me, too," Ben agreed, and then found himself adding, "It's like he hasn't had a childhood."

"It's never too late."

"It isn't?" he said skeptically.

"My mom and dad have an indoor pool. It would be a nice private place to introduce him to the water and give him a few pointers on swimming. Don't you think a public pool might be too humiliating?"

But his mind was stuck on the "her mom and dad" part.

He did not like meeting his female companion's parents. Of course, he had just finished making it clear to her she was not going to be his female companion in the way he generally had female companions. So why not?

It wasn't until the next night, after school, at her parents' very upscale house in the hills, that he realized why not.

Beth met them outside in the curved driveway and led them around to a separate pool building behind the main house, glassed in and spectacular. He was relieved to note there were no parents in sight.

She pointed him and Kyle to a place to change, spa-like and luxurious, and moments later he was in the pool, testing the depth of the water for Kyle, who looked scrawny, goose-bumped and terrified of this new experience.

And then Beth emerged from her own change room. She shuffled up to the edge of the pool, drowning in a too-large pure-white thick terry cloth robe, and then, looking everywhere but at him, she took a deep breath and dropped the covering.

He really hadn't needed to see a woman he had sworn off kissing in a bathing suit. He really hadn't needed to see that at all. Because Beth Maple, out of her school-marm duds was unbelievable. Oh, he'd seen hints of this in the way she dressed at home, casually, but nothing could have prepared him for Beth Maple in the flesh.

Literally.

He wouldn't have ever thought she was a bikini kind of gal. In fact, for the school outing he had guessed she would wear a one-piece *with* matching shorts, not re-moved. Wrong. Though, he had just enough wits about him to see that the shimmery copper-colored hanky she was wearing looked brand-new. It had never been at a school outing! Was she tormenting him, deliberately, with his choice to just be friends?

Surely not! There was nothing conniving about Miss Maple, was there?

Ha. She knew exactly the effect all those scantily covered curves would have on his resolve. Nobody was that innocent!

Proving her own boldness was making her at least as uncomfortable as it was him and that she had no experience with the fact that the kind of swimwear she was wearing was not actually designed for swimming, Beth dove headlong into the water. And came up with one arm crossed firmly across her chest, and the other tugging away at something he couldn't see—but could clearly imagine—below the water.

"Problems?" he purred.

Nope, those little scraps of fabric were definitely not attire designed to get wet. At least her hair made her look like a drowned rat instead of a femme fatale making a play for his soul.

"No," she snapped, but made some tightening adjustments to the little threads holding everything together.

Now satisfied everything was going to stay on, she soon forgot to be self-conscious about her attire. After a few minutes of waiting, hopefully, for things to fall apart, he began to realize the bathing suit proved to be not nearly as revealing as her absolute joy and freedom in the water.

Her enthusiasm was contagious, and soon she had Kyle in the water and doing what she called a "motorboat," blowing bubbles with his mouth to get him over his fear of getting his face wet.

Never once did she make it seem like a swim lesson. Kyle's first time in the pool was all about fun. She never asked him to get out of the three foot end of the pool.

The three of them splashed and played tag. She got out a volleyball for them to throw around. An hour passed in the blink of an eye.

The whole experience made Ben want to get her alone, to swim with her in the Pacific on one of those nights when the sky and the water became one. Was that something someone wanted to do with their friend?

They had no sooner gotten out of the pool than the moment Ben dreaded, meeting her parents, arrived. Her mom provided them all with thick white robes that matched the one Beth had come out on the pool deck in. She got sodas out of the fridge as they all plopped down on the comfy furniture in the poolside lounging area.

Ben didn't miss the way Beth's mother's eyes popped at her daughter's bathing suit before Beth managed to get herself covered up.

So, Miss Maple did have a conniving side! He'd bet his business that her bathing suit was brand-new and carefully chosen to fluster. Though at the moment, trying to tug an uncooperative robe over her wet skin, Ben was pleased to see she seemed to be the flustered one.

After a few minutes her father joined them.

Ben was good at meeting people, and because of his line of work he was not intimidated by wealthy people. Despite his reluctance to meet parents, he realized he didn't have to act like a high school kid picking up his prom date, because he and Beth were not dating.

Her parents were easy people to be with, but Ben became aware he had avoided this kind of gathering since the death of his parents. Mr. And Mrs. Maple were obviously devoted to their youngest child and each other. It soon became evident that family was everything to them, their lives were centered on their children and their grandchildren. It was the main reason they had a pool.

Family.

That thing he had turned his back on so long ago, because it filled him with such an intense sense of yearning for what he could never have back.

But with this family he let himself relax into it, found himself looking at Beth's silver-haired, slender, elegant mother, Rene, thinking, *Beth will look like this one day.* And he hoped she would have the same light in her eyes—the rich contentment of a woman well loved.

But his relaxation faded a bit when he realized he would probably never see her silver-haired. And a bit more when he thought Beth would probably also want this someday. Oh, not necessarily the pool, but what it represented. Family closeness, family gatherings, family having fun together.

Beth's dad, Franklin, thankfully, did not do the interrogation thing. Instead he shared his own memories of his military life, without probing Ben's.

A man used to grandchildren, he included Kyle with ease in the conversation, drawing him out of himself.

"It's good to know how to swim," he told Kyle when Kyle confessed he was just learning. "You never know when you're going to fall out of the fishing boat."

"I've never been fishing," Kyle said.

"Never fishing? That won't do, will it? I'm taking my grandson with me next weekend. He's about your age. Why don't you come?"

"Can I, Uncle Ben?"

Ben looked away from the hope shining in his eyes, tried to control the feeling that came with Beth's world opening up to include them.

Hope. She was steadily hammering a crack into the hard exterior of his cynicism, his protective shell. But she was drawing Kyle into her world, too. Was he going to be hurt in the long run?

Still, he could not say no to the light shining in Kyle's eyes.

Ben had meant for the no-kissing rule to put distance between him and Beth, to erect a much-needed barrier between them, to put ice on that heated flicker of physical attraction they both felt.

Instead, as a week turned into two, he could see it was having the exact opposite effect.

Here was the thing about the no-kissing rule. It gave him room to *know* her. He was falling more for her, not less. He had not been aware how immersion in the throes of passion could actually thwart the process of two people getting to know each other. What he had always foolishly called intimacy was anything but. Physical intimacy, too soon, was actually a barrier to the kind of emotional and spiritual intimacy he was experiencing on a daily basis.

He could talk to her in a way he had never talked to anyone. Not about the weather or football stats or the best pizza, but about things that mattered. Education, politics, local issues. He moved beyond the superficial with her and found their conversations a deeply satisfying place to be. She didn't always agree with him— well, hardly ever, actually—but he loved sparring with her, matching wits, debating. It felt as if she kicked his brain up into a different gear.

After a while, he noticed that in any particular moment he could read how she felt about the day or life or him in the set of her shoulders and the light in her eyes.

Ignoring the signs that something was happening to

him, he got in deeper and deeper as his life seemed to revolve more and more around her. He always seemed to be at her place, working on the tree house or riding bikes after school. Twice a week they went to her parents' to use the pool. Kyle went fishing with her dad and made a new friend in her nephew, Peter.

Even his sister noticed that something was going on in the lives of her brother and her son. On one of their regular visits, her eyes followed Kyle as he went to the hospital cafeteria to get her a soda.

"He seems so happy," she said.

It was probably awful to think it, but his sister was a nicer person since being hospitalized. But without access to drugs and alcohol, she seemed to be becoming a better person every day.

But as her spirit became better, her physical body weakened.

"Who is Miss Maple?" she asked him, turning her attention back to Ben suddenly.

"His teacher."

"No, Ben, who is she to you?"

"Just a friend," he said, defensively.

Something old and knowing and wise was in his younger sister's face.

"I'd like to meet her."

As if their lives weren't tangled enough without Beth meeting his dying sister.

Ben was astonished how strongly he didn't want Beth to meet his sister.

Because he knew as easily as he now read Beth, she also read him with a kind of uncanny accuracy. Beth would know the truth. When it came to Carly, his heart was breaking.

And Beth might try to fix it, knowing Beth.

And the truth was he was not sure he wanted her to. Because a heart shattered beyond repair might be his last remaining defense.

Who is she to you?

It had all been well and good to spend more and more time with her, to pretend that not kissing her meant it wasn't going anywhere that he needed to worry about.

But his sister's question bothered him deeply. Because his heart answered instantly, even though his head refused to give it words.

Who is she to you? Everything.

But there was a problem with making one person everything, with investing too much in them. He left the hospital feeling as if he'd snapped awake after allowing himself to be lulled into a dream. He felt grim and determined. Even the friendship thing wasn't working.

They were going too deep. He was caring too much.

It was time to pull it all back, to gather his badly compromised defenses, to make decisions, rather than just floating along in the flow.

He knew what he had to do. Take back his life. Stop with all the distractions. No more swimming. Or bike riding. In fact, he would finish the tree house.

A nice way to end it. Give her that final gift and bid her adieu.

Though nothing ever quite went as he planned it with her. The kissing thing being a case in point.

* * *

Not everybody would have been as flattered as Beth Maple by a handsome man absolutely resolved not to kiss her. But the situation she was in was different than a man telling a woman he just wanted to be friends because he just wanted to be friends!

With that amazing gift of women's intuition, Beth knew Ben didn't want to kiss her because he had felt her sway over him. What had frightened him had empowered her. Imagine a guy like that being so terrified of a girl like her! It was probably very wicked to find his discomfort as entertaining as she did.

But as the last days of summer shortened into fall, she could see the heady truth every day, deepening around them. Ben Anderson was afraid of how he felt. He was manly enough to be terrified of all his feelings, as if somehow liking a person and coveting their lips gave them the power and made him powerless.

So, she would respect his wishes, but it was only human to torment him, wasn't it? To make him want to kiss her so badly that he would throw his self-control to the wind.

Not that it had happened so far, but she was absolutely confident it was only a matter of time until Ben surrendered to what was sizzling in the air around them.

My goodness, Beth said to herself, astounded at her confidence, *You are a prim little schoolteacher. What makes you think you can bring a man like that to his knees?*

More important, what are you going to do with him once you have him there?

She continued to tangle their lives together as if the only consequences would be good ones.

Her parents adored him and Kyle. Kyle was becoming like a member of her large and loving extended family. If some professional line had been blurred there, it was worth it to see Kyle becoming so sure of himself, flourishing under the attention and care of her family.

This weekend, she thought, watching Ben's truck pull up in front of her yard, will be a turning point. Kyle was gone to spend the weekend at her nephew's house. She and Ben were going to be alone.

She went out to greet him, but faltered when the welcoming grin that she had become so accustomed to was absent. He barely looked at her as he grabbed his tool belt from the back of his truck, strapped it around his waist.

"I'm finishing the tree house tonight."

She froze in her tracks, hearing exactly what he was not saying. It was the thing that linked them together, the tree house was their history.

Some couples had a favorite song.

They had the tree house.

Of course most couples kissed. Of course he was as eager not to be a couple as she was to be one.

That's what finishing the tree house was about, she realized.

Not kissing had not worked. It had not put the distance between them that he had hoped.

He was going to start cutting the ties one by one. She had been confident in her ability to hold him, but now she could see his desire not to be held was fiercely strong. He feared what she longed for.

And she felt devastated by his fear.

But she reminded herself, fiercely, that she had more

power than he wanted her to have. The woman she had been a month ago would have accepted the look on his face, the formidable set of his shoulders, resigned herself to the decision he was making.

But that was not the woman she was today. She was not letting him go, not without a fight.

Too soon, with the last of the daylight leeching from the air, Ben drove home the last nail. The tree house was done.

They stood side by side at the sturdy handrail, close, but not touching. She felt loss rather than accomplishment, and she was almost certain he did, too.

"It's too late to put in the plants that attract butterflies," he said. "I'll get you a list, so you can do it next spring. There's no sense hanging the hammock, either, you'll find it too cold to use it this year."

You. Not *we.* The distinction was not lost on her.

It was true September had somehow drifted into October. There was a chill in the air.

And in his eyes.

"Wait here," she said. "I have something." She went into the house and found a bottle of champagne she had purchased a long time ago, for the weekend that Rock had been supposed to come. The first of many where he had been supposed to come and then never showed up. Why had she saved it? So that she could look at it and pity herself more?

She climbed back up the stairs with the bottle and two fluted glasses and a determination to enjoy every sip. It could be symbolic of letting go of the past.

Looking at him, though, she realized she had already let go of the past.

That was one of the gifts Ben had given her, and even if he went now, he could not take away the woman she had become because of him.

"Are you going to break that over the bow?" he said, but there was no twinkle in his eye the way there usually was when he teased her.

"No, I'm going to get drunk and fall off the platform."

The twinkle flashed through the deep green of his eyes, but it was reluctant. He did not want to get drawn into her world. Normally he would have had some comment, some comeback, but now he remained silent.

She uncorked the champagne with a dramatic pop, but was so aware the atmosphere was not celebratory. It felt like an ending. The end of the season. The end of something that had been growing between them.

She filled the wineglasses, passed him one. He lifted his, held it up to her, his eyes met hers.

"To all your dreams coming true, Beth."

Not *ours*. *Yours*. He was definitely getting ready to say goodbye.

"What do you know of my dreams?" she asked him quietly, taking a sip of her champagne and looking out over her yard and her house, once the only dreams that she had dared to harbor.

He actually laughed, but it had a faintly harsh sound to it, bitter.

"Do you think I could spend this much time with you and not know about your dreams? You dream of having a feeling like your mom and dad have for each other, and a life like the one they have. You dream of a family and swings in the backyard."

"I don't!" she said stunned.

"Yes, you do," he said quietly.

"Maybe I did once," she tilted her chin up proudly. "But I gave it up."

"You thought you did. The lowlife only hurt you temporarily, which is a good thing to remember."

"What do you know about Rock?" she whispered. Had somebody told him? One of her family members? Good grief.

"Rock," he snorted. "The name alone should have sent you running for cover."

"Did somebody tell you?" she demanded.

"Oh, Beth, this told me." He swept the view of her yard, wineglass in hand. "The little house for one, a car babied more than a, well, baby. You told me all about your heartbreak just by being a buttoned-up teacher devoting her life to her students."

"How dare you make me sound pathetic!"

"I don't find you pathetic," he said, quietly and firmly. "Not at all. You just want things, Beth. It's not wrong to want them. But there's no point hanging out with a guy who can't give them to you."

She was stunned by what he was seeing, because she thought that was precisely what she had given up after Rock/Ralph. But now she saw that Ben had clearly seen her truth, maybe before she had completely seen it herself.

She had convinced herself she was just playing a game with Ben, seeing if she could overcome his aver-

sion to caring for another. She had talked herself into
thinking it was all about her reclaiming her power in the
face of having lost it.

But underneath all those things she had been telling
herself, the dream of love had been creeping back into
her life, fueled by his laughter and the green of his eyes
and his fun-loving spirit and his ability to suddenly go
deep in unexpected and delightful ways.

He had seen her more clearly than she saw herself.
And her secret motivations were what was driving him
away, what had brought that look into his eyes, why suddenly he had felt an urgent need to *finish*.

"Well. Whether you think I'm pathetic or not I am.
You know what I did? I fell in love over the Internet.
Conservative, cautious me, taken for a ride. How's that
for pathetic?" She could not believe she was crying, but
she was and she couldn't stop talking, either, despite
the fact her confessions were making her miserable.

Why was she telling him this now, when he had leaving written all over him? She hadn't become one of
those women who would take pity if they couldn't have
love, had she?

"It ended up he wasn't even a real person. He had
stolen pictures from a Web site of a male model. This
fraud was having relationships with dozens of women.
I was contacted by an investigator in his state. Asking
if I'd ever sent him money."

"Had you?" It was a deep growl of ferocious anger.

"I said I hadn't, because I felt so foolish for believing
his stories. An inheritance tangled up in court. His pay
cheque stalled by the bureaucracy in Abu Dhabi. He was

always so sincerely embarrassed. But everyone had tried to tell me. My family. My friends. I wanted so desperately for what I was feeling to be true that I wouldn't listen.

"I told the investigators I hadn't given him money because I just wanted it over. I didn't want revenge, I didn't want my name to appear in lists of women who had been victimized by him."

"You know I'm going to kill him if I ever see him, right?" Somehow his arm was around her shoulder, and she was pulled in hard against the pure strength of him. It seemed like such a safe place. She kept talking, the flood gates refusing to be closed now that everything was gushing out of them.

"The strange thing is for the longest time after, it still felt as if he'd been real. I mourned Rock as though a real person had died."

"And now?"

Now I know real. I have you to thank for that. But out loud she just said, "I can't believe I've wasted one more tear on him."

She found her face cupped in his hand. He dragged the tear away from her cheek with the rough edge of his thumb. Somehow his thumb ended up on her lip, and he was looking deep into her eyes, and she could see his resolve to be on his way melting.

"Come here," he said with a sigh, and he sat down on the planking of the deck and pulled her into him and held her between the vee of his legs. Home.

Wasn't that really what she'd longed for? What she had hoped to find when she had bought that tiny, run-down house?

But the house, in the end, was just sticks and stones. His arms around her felt like a shelter from the hurts of the world. She peeked up at his face. This is what she wanted to come home to.

A real man. Like him.

"I wish I could tell you life won't hurt you anymore," he said finally, quietly. "But I can't. It will. Life stinks sometimes."

"That's why you have to have places like this tree house," she said dreamily. *Places like his arms. Home.*

He said nothing.

"Ben?"

"Uh-huh?"

"Will you tell me? About that hurt inside of you?"

"Trading war stories?" he said. "No, I don't think so."

"Trading trust," she suggested. "Laying down the burden."

"Beth, I don't want to lay my burdens on you."

"You've carried them long enough."

"Beth," he said softly, "why is it you are determined to make me weak? When I am just as determined to be strong?"

"I guess I don't see a man speaking of the forces that shaped him as a weakness. A true form of courage. The ability to be vulnerable. To not be lonely anymore. Tell me."

He was silent; she held her breath. And then he spoke. A surrender.

"My parents were killed in a car accident when I was seventeen. We had a family like your family, only without the financial security. I mean, I didn't know that growing up. We always had everything. Good home, nice clothes, plenty to eat, money to play sports.

"But when my mom and dad died, I found very quickly that there was nothing. A big mortgage on the house, no insurance, no savings."

"Ben, what a terrible burden to add to the grief you must have been feeling."

"Sometimes I think that time was so desperate I postponed grief. I had to figure out quickly how to look after things. There was no question of being able to look after my sister, too.

"The marines took me. A good family for a guy who has just lost everything. Feelings are scorned in the rough camaraderie of men. I was given a new purpose and a new family, and I wasn't allowed to indulge my desire to immerse myself in misery.

"But Carly. Oh, Carly. She was so much younger than me. Fourteen is a hard age without adding the complication of a life unfairly interrupted by tragedy. My parents were gone, and I was going.

"Sometimes I can still hear her howling like a wounded animal when I told her I had to go to the marines. She was a dreamer. Somehow she thought we were going to make it together. She was going to quit school and get a job in a fast-food place, she thought I could get a job, too. Two underage kids on minimum wage, no health care, no safety net. I knew it wasn't going to work, but she hated me for knowing." He shook his head, remembering.

"She went from one foster home to the next, becoming more bitter and more hard and more incensed at the unfairness of her life by the day. She went wild, got pregnant. I don't know if she ever told the father, or if she told him and he just didn't care.

"I'm the last person she ever would confide in. She never ever forgave me for leaving her.

"The truth is I've never really forgiven myself. I look at her and think, Couldn't I have done something? Couldn't I?"

Beth felt the helpless heave of his shoulders.

"Aren't you doing something now?" she asked softly.

"It's too late. I can't save my sister."

"But you're saving Kyle."

"Beth," he said, and there was something tortured in his voice, "don't make me into a man I'm not."

"I think you're the one who wants to make yourself into a man that you're not. I see who you really are, Ben Anderson."

"You do, huh?" And there was that teasing note in his voice again, as if he had decided to stay, after all.

And something in her decided to risk it all.

She spoke the truth that she had just admitted to herself, "And I'm falling in love with who you really are."

She kissed him then, up there in the tree house, with the leaves looking so magnificent in their dying throes.

"That's what I was afraid of," he said against her lips.

"You don't have to be afraid anymore, Ben."

And she felt him surrender to her as he retook her lips with his own.

CHAPTER EIGHT

BEN Anderson had gone to Beth's house planning to *finish*. Everything. It disturbed him that even setting his formidable will to that plan, things had gone seriously awry.

Seriously.

The thing about Beth was that she had seen that he was flawed. She had seen right through his warrior bravado to the fear underneath it.

The fear of loss. He had a terror about caring for people. But Beth clearly saw the cause: the fear of loss.

The thing about Beth was that she saw all that he was, good and bad, strong and weak, and loved him anyway. He saw it in her eyes. That she knew completely who he was, and even knowing that, she was willing to take a risk on him.

The thing about Beth was she took a man worn right out on his own cynicism, a man who had been through the wars, on every level, and made him want to hope again for a better world and a better life, a life with soft places to fall.

Somehow, even though he had gone to her house with every intention of saying farewell to her and to the part of him that *hoped*, he had been unable to leave her. He'd been unable to walk away from that feeling of being connected. He had been seduced by the magic of that place among the leaves, by the look in her eyes, by the way it felt to have her leaning her back against his chest, as if she belonged there, and to him.

She had been right, as she so often was—one of her most annoying qualities. And endearing.

He had felt better after he had spoken of his history. Trusted her with it. He had felt not so alone in the world. Lighter.

Ben had felt connected to another human being in a way that he had lost faith that it was possible to be connected. Destiny had laughed at his resolve to leave her, to finish it. Instead, they had stayed in that tree house all night. Watching the sky turn that purple blue before blackness, watching the stars wink on above them through the filter of leaves that were turning orange and fire red, a reminder that seasons ended.

They had finished the wine, but instead of ending it there, he had acquiesced when she had gone and got blankets and coffee. And then more coffee, and somehow pink had been painting dawn colors in the sky, and they'd both been wrapped in the same blanket, her breath feeling like his breath, her heart beating at one with his heart.

Finally, when he had pulled himself away, it had not been with a feeling of things ending, but of a brand-new day dawning in every possible way.

He'd driven home, the effects of the wine long since worn off, but drunk nonetheless. On exhaustion. And the look in her eyes.

Drunk on the possibility that he loved her, and that maybe he was strong enough and brave enough to say yes to a beginning instead of an end.

But he of all men should have known. What had he said to her? Not very poetic, just truth, unvarnished.

Life stinks.

And wasn't it always when a man forgot that, that life was more than willing to remind him?

He had barely stripped off his clothes and climbed into bed when his phone rang. Who else would call at such a ridiculous hour of the morning? Who else would know he was not asleep? He reached for it eagerly, thinking, *It is her.* Thinking she had thought of one last thing to say to him before she, too, slept.

In that moment before he picked up the phone he had an illuminating vision of what his life could be. He could fall asleep with his nose buried in the perfume of her hair, with her sweet curves pressed into his. His last words at night could be to her, and his first ones in the morning.

She had said she was falling in love with him.

He was falling in love with her. There it was. The admission. And for the first time in a very long time he could see something different for himself.

Not a desire to run. But a desire to have a place to lay his head. A place to put down his armor. A place where he loved and was cherished in return.

"Hello." Everything in his voice greeted her, ready to tell her, ready to see where it all went.

Only, it wasn't her.

"Mr. Anderson?"

His heart plummeted. Something about the official

sound of the voice, the sympathy underlying told him before he heard a single word. That he had hoped too hard for a happy ending.

Carly.

"You'd better come," the nurse told him gently. "It's a matter of hours."

Somehow, in a nightmare of slow motion, he managed to pull on his clothes. He ignored the impulse to call Beth, and instead phoned Peter's house to tell them he was coming for Kyle. His early-morning phone call there had woken the whole family, and when he arrived everybody had that pinched look of distress about them.

Kyle's shoulders were hunched, and he looked bewildered as he followed Ben out to the truck and got in beside him.

Ben wished he had called Beth. She would know what to do. She would, he reminded himself, also trust that he knew what to do.

"Are you okay?" he asked Kyle.

"No."

"Me, neither."

"I'm so scared," Kyle said.

"Me, too."

"Is this what you're scared of?" Kyle asked him, his voice a croak of fear and misery. "You told me once everybody was scared of something. Is this what you're scared of, Uncle Ben?"

Ben could barely speak over the lump in his throat. "Yeah," he finally said, "this is it." He knew his nephew thought he meant death, but he had dealt with more death than most people, and it was not that that scared him.

Love. It was love that scared him the most. Because love always seemed to, in the end, cut a man off at his knees, prove to him how puny his will was against the way of the world.

And he had almost given himself over to the cruel vulnerability of loving again. Almost. Not quite.

Had it been Beth's voice on the phone this morning, his whole life could have been unfolding differently. But he quashed the yearning and vowed not to go there anymore.

Ben and Kyle made their way through the too-bright lights of the hospital hallways to Carly's room.

It was darkened after the hall, and Ben hesitated in the doorway, one hand on Kyle's shoulder as he let his eyes adjust to the light.

Had it been the right thing to bring his nephew here? He wished he had asked Beth. But the privilege of sharing her wisdom, of walking through life sharing his burdens meant he had to make a decision. He had made one in the dawn hours, with her warm in his arms, but with the ringing of the phone this morning he was reneging on it.

Was it right for him to have brought Kyle? He felt the loneliness of having to make these huge decisions alone, but he squared his shoulders, resolved. Ben had seen people die and it was a hard thing to see. But wouldn't it have been harder for his nephew not to have had this opportunity to say goodbye?

In the room his sister was the slightest little bump under a blanket, as if she had begun disappearing long ago. She turned her head to them, and in her face Ben saw no fear and no anguish.

Absolute serenity.

"Kyle," she whispered, "come here."

Kyle went to her, and despite her frailty he climbed on the bed and into her arms. She rocked him and kissed the top of his head. She told him over and over she loved him. She told him she wasn't the mother he deserved. She told him he was a good kid. She told him she was proud of him.

The tears slithering down Kyle's face puddled on her nightgown, soaked it. Ben tiptoed out of the room. This was the moment they needed, the moment Kyle had waited all his life for.

After a long time Kyle came out into the hallway, wiping his face on his sleeve.

"She wants to see you, by yourself."

"Are you okay?"

His nephew gave him a look.

"Sorry, dumb question." He chucked him on the shoulder, changed his mind and pulled him hard into his chest and then released him reluctantly and went into the room.

"You'll look after him, won't you, Ben?" Something so desperate in that, pleading.

"I promise."

She studied his face, seemed satisfied. "Don't tell him I said this, but I'm glad. I'm glad it's over. I missed them so much, Ben."

"I know."

"Could you hold me?" she whispered.

He slid onto her bed, and scooped her up in his arms. It was like holding a baby bird.

"You know what I missed the most? This. Cuddling

with Mom or Dad. Hearing the words *I love you*. You never said them, you know? You'd bring food or toys for Kyle and me, but you never said that."

"I'm sorry."

"Me, too, Ben. So much regret. I've put everyone I ever cared about through hell. Don't let me go," she said, and her hand curled into his shirt, holding him tight to her. Slowly her grip on him relaxed.

Her eyes closed and her breathing rattled laboriously.

He knew what he was hearing. He knew she would not wake up again. At some point Kyle came back into the room, squeezed into the bed with them, laid his head on his mother's breast, allowed his uncle to curl his hand around his shoulder, holding them both.

At six o'clock that night, as normal families sat down to eat their supper and talk about who was driving the kids to Little League, his little sister, as frail as a tiny bird that had fallen from the nest, found peace at last.

But there was no peace for Ben. He realized, even in the end, he had not been able to give her what she needed the most. Shocked, he realized he had let his chance to say the words *I love you* slip away from him.

Now he knew why he had gone to Beth's house to finish it. Not to save himself. But to do the most loving thing of all: to save her from a man who had never been able to give anyone what they needed or wanted.

Three simple words.

I love you. A gift his sister had waited and waited for. And he had never given it. Not even as his chances ran out.

Beth deserved a man who was better than that. So much better.

CHAPTER NINE

BETH tried not to let her shock show when she saw Ben. It was the first time she had seen him since his sister's funeral, which had been over a month ago. She had spoken to him on the phone several times, but there was no mistaking the chill in his voice. She had failed to tempt him back into her world. She could feel the formidable force of his will set against her.

Not her, personally, she reminded herself. His will had become a defense against all the things that had ever hurt him.

She had gotten him here to the school on the pretext of a parent-teacher night, and she knew she had chosen her own outfit—elegant silk blouse, pencil-line black skirt, pearls at her ears and throat—in anticipation of seeing him.

It was that same old thing. Making him try to change his mind. Before about kisses, now about something so much larger.

Trust me. Let me in. Interestingly enough, not *love me*, but *let me love you.* The most incredible thing had happened to her over the last month, even in the face of

Ben's seeming indifference, his rejection of her. She felt better for the fact she loved him, not worse.

Beth felt deeper and more alive and more compassionate than she had ever felt. She felt like a better teacher, a better woman, a better human being. That was what love did. Genuine love didn't rip people apart, it built them up. That's what she wanted to share with Ben, this incredible truth she had discovered.

He was as handsome as ever, seemingly self-assured as he moved up the aisle past desks that seemed impossibly small.

But when he sat down on one of the adult-size chairs she had placed in front of her desk for parents, she could see his face was thinner. He looked gaunt and haunted. The plains of his handsome face were whisker-roughened, and the light had gone out in the green of his eyes.

"Are you all right?" she asked, concerned.

"Let's just keep it about Kyle," he said with rebuff.

"You look like you've been ill," she said quietly.

"Is it so hard for you to listen?" he asked.

"Is it so hard for you to realize you do not make the rules for the whole world?"

For a fraction of a second, a glimmer of a smile. Was he remembering, as she was, those long fall days of sparring with each other, how quickly the sparring could turn to laughter?

And then it was gone.

"Believe me, Beth, I know I don't make the rules for the world. No one knows that better than me."

Of course no one knew it better than him. He had

buried his younger sister. And his parents. And his brothers-in-arms.

At least he'd called her Beth, leaving the door into his terrifyingly lonely world open just a crack?

That was the thing. She was not giving up on him.

"Kyle seems to be doing fairly well," she said carefully.

"Yeah. He does his homework. His report card was good."

"I wasn't talking about his homework or his report card."

"We're muddling through, Beth."

She nodded. "Peter wants him to come stay at their house for the Thanksgiving weekend. My Mom and Dad would like you both to come for Thanksgiving dinner."

"I'll ask Kyle if he wants to go. I'm sure he will. I think your mom and your nephew, Peter, are what's pulling him through this. Would you thank them for me?"

"Meaning you won't be coming for Thanksgiving dinner?"

He shook his head. "I might book a quick trip to Hawaii since Kyle will be gone."

"For four days?" she asked, incredulous.

He shrugged, his facial expressions saying he clearly didn't owe her any explanations.

"You're grieving all of it, aren't you Ben? Not just Carly? All the things that you told me you postponed."

"Don't," he said dangerously.

"Don't tell me don't," she snapped back at him. "Remember when you first came into this classroom? We were losing Kyle, and you wouldn't let it happen. You went back for him. Who's coming for you, Ben, if not me?"

"Don't you have any pride?" he snapped. "Don't waste yourself chasing after a man who doesn't want what you have to give."

The old Beth would have been felled by that arrow, but the new one stepped deftly aside, looked past the arrow to the archer.

Coming for Ben had nothing to do with her own pride, her self-esteem. In fact, it had nothing at all to do with *her*. She sensed his need and his desperation, and love as she now knew it demanded that she hang in there, hold on.

"No man left behind," she said quietly, and she felt a warrior's resolve as she said it. She was not leaving him in this prison he had made for himself. She wasn't.

He stood up so fast the chair fell over. His fists were clenching and unclenching at his sides.

"I don't want it," he said. "Do you get it? I don't want to care about anyone but myself."

"Because it hurts?" she probed softly.

"No! Because I'm self-centered and I plan to stay that way. Don't make me into something I'm not. You already invented a man once. Don't be so stupid again."

Again she watched the arrows flying at her, felt herself step out of their path, focused on him, the archer, the pain and defiance in his face.

"I'm coming for you," she said. "And you can't stop me."

He stared at her.

"I don't know if I'm coming back from Hawaii," he said.

She was sure it was a bluff, but as she contemplated saying that it didn't matter if he went to the ends of the earth, she was still coming for him, she heard the strangled gasp behind him.

When had Kyle come into the room? He stood, staring at his uncle, and then he turned on his heel and ran.

For a moment Ben's shoulders sagged and he looked nothing but defeated. "That's the kind of man I am," he said harshly. "I always seem to hurt people. That's why I don't want you coming after me, Beth."

And he turned and walked away.

The Top-Secret Diary of Kyle O. Anderson

My uncle Ben is going to Hawaii and staying there. I heard him tell Beth. I call her Beth when it's personal and Miss Maple in school. It felt weird at first but it doesn't now.

I knew something was going on with my uncle even before he said that about Hawaii. He's so quiet now. Once I saw him looking through a big book, and when he saw me, he put it away.

But I waited until he went out and went and got it. It was a photo album full of pictures of him and my mom when they were little and my grandma and grandpa when they were alive. I would have liked to look at those pictures with him, and maybe hear some of the stories of the days they were taken, but there was something in his face when he looked at them that made me afraid to ask.

For a while I thought Beth and me and him were going to be a family, but now I see it is stupid to hope for things like that. Little-kid dreams.

For a while I could pretend her family was my family.

Her mom likes me to call her Bubs, just like all the grand-children, and I call her dad Grandpa Ike. Everybody does.

Bubs sent me a card after my mom died. It is the first time I ever got mail just for me, with my name on it. She wrote in it how sorry she was. I still have it, but I think I will rip it up and throw it away.

Because as much as I like them, they aren't my family.

Uncle Ben is. I wonder if he is going to try and leave me with them. If he goes to Hawaii and stays there like I heard him tell Beth. I didn't hear him saying nothing about me going with him.

You know what? He doesn't want to care about any-body or anything.

Probably including me. So I don't want to care about anybody or anything, either. I wonder how old you have to be to join the marines? Probably not eleven.

But maybe I could join the circus.

I always was scared he wouldn't keep me. Now I know he's not going to. But I don't feel as scared as I thought I would. I feel mad.

I'm going to take Kermit and find a new place to live. I heard Australia is nice at this time of year. I bet I could stow away on a boat. Or work off my passage on a steamer.

I'm not waiting to get a postcard from Hawaii, that says, "Nice knowing you kid, have a nice life."

"Kyle?"

The house had that empty feel of when Kyle wasn't in it. Ben wondered if he had forgotten something Kyle had to do after school. Or maybe he was going to a friend's house and had forgotten to say so.

For some reason he went into Kyle's room. And frowned. The closet door was open and most of the clothes were gone. The dresser drawer also hung open, but there was nothing in it.

He looked at the fish tank where Kermit lived.

No frog.

And then he saw a note on Kyle's desk.

"Gone to Australia," it said. "Have fun in Hawaii. Bye." It was signed Kyle O. Anderson. The *O* stood for Oliver. He had been named by an orphan after an orphan. And now he was an orphan, feeling terribly alone in the world, Ben failing him at every turn.

Somehow in those words were all the pain and disappointment he had caused his nephew.

He felt the weight of his total failure. Well, what eleven-year-old didn't run away from home? When Kyle came back, hungry and tired and cold, he would tell him he hadn't really meant it about staying in Hawaii.

But he couldn't tell him the whole truth. That he'd said that just to back off Beth Maple. He didn't want her coming into the darkness to find him, even as a part of him that was weak wondered what her light could do to the darkness.

He had not been able to prepare himself for how hard it had been to see her again, her love for him, so undeserved, shining out of her eyes.

Ben shook away the compellingness of that vision and went to leave Kyle's room. But something caught his eye. Underneath the shelf that housed the empty Kermit quarters, there was a book lying on the floor.

He stooped and picked it up. It was a cheap hardbound

diary with a lock on it. But it wasn't locked. In fact, it looked like it might have fallen, unnoticed, to this place.

Ben opened it to the first page, uncomfortably aware of what a breach of trust it was to read a diary. On the other hand, it might help him find Kyle.

"The Top-Secret Diary of Kyle O. Anderson," he read out loud, and felt a hint of a smile. That was Kyle. Secretive. The secrecy hiding his deep sensitivity.

Ben wasn't good with sensitivity. Another reason to let Beth go. And what about Kyle? Did he deserve something better than what his uncle could give him?

Though Ben could not even imagine giving up Kyle, not for anything. Though it was evident, after reading a few pages of that diary, that he had never managed to impress that message on his nephew.

How had he failed to make it clear to Kyle, right from the beginning, that this would be his home now? That no matter what happened, he wasn't sending him away or giving him up?

Ben had assumed Kyle knew. That stupid cowboy sheets and the surrender of his television and stereo said it all. He'd assumed. Just the way he'd assumed his sister knew he loved her. Had he ever spoken those words to his nephew? No. Here his nephew had been going to bed so scared he would not have a place to belong that his stomach hurt, and Ben had done nothing to reassure him.

No, taken away the one thing that reassured him. The growing feeling of family that they had been enjoying with Beth.

"You know what?" Ben said out loud to himself. "You have a gift for letting people down."

But the more urgent problem was where had Kyle gone? Had he cooled off before he decided to go looking for Australia? He was smarter than most eleven-year-olds, did he know getting to Australia wasn't going to be that easy?

Ben longed for Beth. For someone to turn to. But he decided to go it alone first.

Hours later, having combed every inch of Cranberry Corner, after having talked to all the bus drivers, and gone by the train station, and hiked around Migg's Pond in the dark, there was no Kyle and no sign of Kyle.

What now? Did he call the police?

He had to talk to her. Not because she would know where Kyle was, though she might have some good ideas.

He had to talk to her because she was the one. The one who had crept by his defenses to his heart.

The one he needed to turn to with his strength failing him, when all his strength could not find that boy.

He had fallen in love with Beth Maple.

With any luck she never had to know.

Her voice was sleepy on the other end of the phone, and it warmed some part in him that was too cold. That was so damned cold.

"Beth." He said her name and he heard the way he said it. Like a benediction.

"Ben." She said his name, and he heard the way she said it, with no defenses, open to him, unafraid of the arrows.

"I'm sorry to wake you." He was aware of just how much he was sorry for.

"It's okay. What's wrong? Is it two in the morning?"

As soon as he heard her voice, everything that was

muddled in him became clear. He knew where Kyle was. He knew Kyle, confused and feeling abandoned and unloved would return there.

To that place that love had grown and flourished. To a place where there had been magic in the air.

"Can you see the tree house from your bedroom window?"

"Yes."

"Would you go look at it?"

"Why?" she breathed.

Was she hoping he was inviting her, back to that magic time when they had built something together, something more than wood and concrete?

He could not let her believe that. "Kyle's missing. I think he may be there."

He could hear her moving, wondered what she was wearing, wondered what kind of man wondered something like that at a time like this.

A man unworthy, obviously.

"It's too dark," she whispered. "Do you want me to turn on the porch light?"

"No. I'll be there as soon as I can."

He parked his truck a block away so as not to spook Kyle. He walked through the darkness of inky night feeling the magic of the night, remembering. Surrendering.

She was in the yard, waiting for him, and they went up the stairs to the tree house together.

Kyle had heard them coming, and was squished back in a corner, no place to escape. "Leave me alone," he said.

Ben could clearly see that Kyle had not been prepared for the coldness of the night. His nephew was shaking.

"I'm not leaving you alone," Ben said. "Not ever."

"Yeah, sure." His sneer was forced, a child's fear right underneath it. "What about when you go to Hawaii?"

"If I went to Hawaii, permanently, you would be coming with me. You are my family."

Something relaxed fractionally in Kyle's face. "I don't want to go to Hawaii. I have friends here."

Ben contemplated that. Friends here. How a few months had changed things. And unlike him, Kyle was not damaged enough by life, even though he had every right to be, that he would run away from the gift of friendship instead of toward it.

"Okay," Ben said quietly.

"So, you're not going to Hawaii?"

"I'm not leaving you." *Say it. Tell him you love him.* But he couldn't. Were there ever words that had been spoken that were more misused than those ones? Used to manipulate? Used too casually?

Ben's mother blowing him a kiss, mouthing the words. He could not speak them, superstitious about their use.

"Come on," Beth said. "Let's go inside. I'm freezing. I need some hot chocolate." She held out an arm, and Kyle crept under it, a baby duck under her wing. He ignored Ben.

It was evident at her kitchen table that Kyle was done. His head nodded over the hot drink, his eyes kept closing, then jerking back open. But then they closed, and his head came to rest on the table, a boy utterly and completely exhausted.

"Don't wake him. Put him in the guest room," Beth said, and Ben went over and picked up his nephew.

Who was eleven years old but who felt as frail as a baby in his arms. He took him down the hall the Beth's guest room, she drew back sheets, pristine white, and he hesitated, but she was not worried about her sheets.

Always the children came first for her. Once, he had been able to picture her vividly in a wedding gown.

Now, just as vividly, he could see her like this, leaning over their children, tucking them in.

He rubbed his eyes, trying to clear the vision and the weariness that allowed such vulnerable thoughts.

"I should go," he said.

"No. We need to talk."

"Ah, the words every man dreads hearing." But somehow he didn't dread them. He needed to clear the air with her, once and for all.

"Please don't look at me like that," he said.

"Like?"

"Like you see a knight in shining armor, instead of a man of flesh and blood and bone. I am the furthest thing from that. Look at me tonight."

"What about you tonight? Your nephew was missing and you would not rest until you found him. You allowed your heart to tell you where he was."

He snorted at that. "My heart? Don't kid yourself."

"You're the one kidding yourself. I've always seen your heart. That's what I fell in love with from the very beginning."

"Don't go there."

"I don't have any choice. I feel what I feel."

"Beth," it was a cry of pure anguish, but he could not stop the words from coming. "I will let you down, just like I let down my sister. Just like I let down Kyle to-night. All she ever wanted was for me to tell her I loved her. That's all Kyle needed to hear tonight. I can't say those words. I choke on them."

"Say those words?" she said, astounded, and then she laughed softly. "Oh, you foolish, foolish man. Why would you ever have to? I *see* the love in the way you are with Kyle. Your sister had to be able to see that. I saw it the whole time you were building the tree house. Words only represent the thing. They aren't the thing. Oh, Ben, I have always seen the love pouring out of you. Always."

And then she came to him, something fierce in her face. She took his cheeks between her hands, looked at him hard, sighed with satisfaction and welcome.

"I have always seen you," she said. "And I always will."

And then she kissed him.

And passion did not put a barrier up, because there was too much in place already for it to blur what was real.

Her passion for him took the last barrier down. It told him that she had come back for him. She had not given up until he had found his way home. To her.

The wall around his heart came down like an earthen dam after forty days and forty nights of rain. It collapsed and everything he had been holding back rushed out.

The murky, muddy water of grief, held back, churned out.

And then right behind that the cool, clean water of love. Pure love flowed out of him. And finally, finally, he said the words.

And understood that they represented not a curse but a blessing. That they represented not a prison but freedom.

The Top-Secret Diary of Kyle O. Anderson

I'm still not sure about that heaven stuff, but sometimes lately I feel my mom around me more strongly than I did when she was alive. I guess it's because I'm growing up myself that I can see all the stuff that happened to her when she was just a kid changed her. It's like a blanket got thrown over who she really was. But now the blanket is gone, and I can feel her around me, who she always should have been. I feel her when I least expect it. Like this morning we had frost, and even the weeds were covered in silver and dripped diamond droplets, like chandeliers in a mansion, and I felt her right then, something around me big and pure and sweet.

There is something around Ben and Beth like that, too. The way they look at each other, the way they touch. It's not like they run around kissing each other in front of me, but sometimes I'll just look over and see his hand cover hers and stay there, and it is like everything stops, in awe of what they have.

And they've been married two years, now. That was an awesome day. My uncle Ben asked me to be his best man. And when I saw Beth coming up the aisle looking like an angel in her long white gown, I felt like she was coming for us, not just him. And I guess she was, because me and my uncle Ben are a package deal.

Now the three of us are a package deal. I call Beth Mama B. It could be for Mama Beth, but we both know it isn't. It's for Mama Bear, because she is just like I knew she would be. Warm and fuzzy at times, but a stickler for manners and curfews, and protective of me as a mother bear with a cub. Most thirteen-year-olds would find it super annoying, but I secretly like it. Still, it will be a relief when the baby comes and she has someone else to fuss over.

Most thirteen-year-olds wouldn't like a baby coming, either. Casper and Peter both look at Beth getting rounder like it is something horrible and embarrassing, so I try not to let on how excited I feel, and happy.

This is my world and in it I feel cherished. There is room in a world like mine for a baby. Family makes everything bigger, not smaller.

My uncle is calling me. Casper is on the phone. Casper has done a lot of growing up in the past few years. He is not such a loudmouth anymore, and he never picks on me. Of course, it might help that I am an inch taller than him and outweigh him by ten pounds. Or maybe it's just that Bubs and Grandpa Ike have a swimming pool.

He wants to do our grade-seven project on Genghis Khan. I still like Genghis Khan, but not so much because he conquered the world. It is the secret side to the Khan that intrigues me.

Most people don't know he had a best friend named Jamukha, who became his blood brother. When Jamukha was elected as the universal ruler, instead of Khan, they became enemies. But when he was captured, instead of killing him, Khan, the most ruthless man who ever lived, offered a renewal of their brotherhood, which Jamukha refused.

When I was little, my uncle Ben was the most powerful man in my world. He would come to us over and over, bringing us food and gifts, and my mom was always mean to him, refusing the real gift he was bringing her, family. Love. Forgiveness.

Uncle Ben always came back, always extended the hand of a brother to her. I doubt my uncle would ever use the word *forgive*, just like he hardly ever uses the word *love*, but he forgave my mom, as if he could always see who she really was. There is something in some men that is bigger than words, that does not need words.

I know now that my mom did the best she could. I guess I could be angry at her for all the times she didn't do so great, but I'm going to be like my uncle Ben and forgive her for all the things she did do and didn't do.

I did not have a perfect childhood, but somehow it made me a perfect me. I feel way more grown up than either Peter or Casper and like I can handle things better than them. There are things they just don't get and probably never will.

They don't get the best part of the Khan story and the most powerful part is the love he had for his brother, a love that transcended all the things that happened between them.

They don't get how wondrous toasted bread smells in the morning, or how good it feels to have five bucks in your pocket to spend on anything you like. They don't know what a good thing it is to bring a baby into the world who will have a mom and a dad and a cousin who will do anything to protect it, and who will love it no matter what it does.

Casper and Peter don't really get what it is to be afraid, what a dark place that is, like a prison. They don't really get how wonderful it is to be free, or how good that freedom can make you feel. They are both a little immature. A new TV can make them feel good.

What makes me feel good is to wait for Beth after school and we drive home together. On the way home we talk about what to make for dinner, and after I go visit with Kermit for a bit, I usually help. I'm really good at peeling potatoes, and I make the best Caesar salad.

And then my uncle comes home, and when I see the look on his face when he comes through the door, and sees us, I don't need one other thing. Not even an iPod.

He's usually all dirty and his clothes have tears in them, but Beth looks at him as if a prince has just come through the door. And then his eyes light up, and this smile comes on his face, and he picks Beth up and swings her around as if she is as light as a feather, even though she's not anymore. He swings her around until she is laughing so hard she can't stop. And then he comes and ruffles my hair and asks me about my day, and he really wants to know.

What I see in my uncle's face when he looks at Beth and me is what Genghis never knew, except maybe for one shining moment when he forgave his brother, Jamukha.

And that is that there is only one way to *really* conquer the world.

Love conquers the world. Dumb as it sounds, love really does conquer all.

Not that I'll be putting that in my grade-seven project report.

* * * * *

THE PLAYBOY DOCTOR'S MARRIAGE PROPOSAL

BY
FIONA LOWE

Always an avid reader, **Fiona Lowe** decided to combine her love of romance with her interest in all things medical, so writing Medical™ romance was an obvious choice! She lives in a seaside town in southern Australia, where she juggles writing, reading, working and raising two gorgeous sons, with the support of her own real-life hero! You can visit Fiona's website at www.fionalowe.com.

To Heather—a young woman with a bright future who joins me on philosophical ramblings and enthusiastically provides help with A&E stories plus advice on all things radiological!

And to Alison for her help with deciphering ECGs

CHAPTER ONE

THE med student gagged.

'Out!' Linton Gregory, emergency care specialist, vigorously thrust his left arm toward the door, his frustration rising. Using his right hand, he staunched the flow of blood pouring from the deep gash on his patient's scalp. 'And take deep breaths,' he added as an afterthought, softening his terse tone. The last thing he needed today on top of everything else was a fainting student.

Where was everyone? 'Karen,' he called out, breaking his own enforced rule of no yelling in A and E. 'Room two, please, now!' He ripped open a gauze pack. 'Johnno, stick your hand here.' He lifted his patient's hand to his head. 'Press hard.'

'Right-o, Doc, I know the drill.' Johnno gave a grimace.

Linton shone his penlight into the man's eyes, checking his pupils for reaction to light. The black discs contracted at the bright beam and enlarged when the light source was moved away. 'They look OK. Did you black out?'

'Don't remember.'

Linton sighed and started a head-injury chart. 'This is the fourth Saturday in two months you've been in here. It's time to think about hanging up your rugby boots.'

Johnno cleared his throat. 'Doc, now you're starting to sound like the wife.'

He shot the man an understanding look as the familiar ripple of relief trickled through him that he wasn't tied down, that he was blessedly single again. And he intended to stay that way. He raised his brows. 'And yet this time I agree with Donna. Your scalp is starting to look like a patchwork quilt.' He lifted the gauze gingerly, examining the ragged skin edges. 'You're going to need more stitches.'

'Linton?' A nurse popped her head around the half-open door.

'Karen.' He smiled his winning smile. 'Stellar nurse that you are, can you please organise a suture pack and ring X-Ray? Johnno's got another deep scalp laceration. Oh, and check up on the student—he left looking pretty green.'

Her brows drew together in consternation. 'I'd love to, Linton, but the ambulance service just radioed and they're bringing in a crushed arm, ETA five minutes. I've set up the resus room and now I'm chasing nursing staff. The roster is short and half the town is out at Bungarra Station for Debbie and Cameron's inaugural dune-buggy race.'

He swallowed the curse that rose to his lips. 'Keep pressing on that gauze, Johnno, and I'll send Donna in to sit with you until someone can stitch your head.' Three weeks ago his department had been like a slick, well-oiled machine. Now his charge nurse was on unexpected adoption leave and her second-in-charge was on her honeymoon with *his* registrar. Marriage was a lousy idea, even when it didn't actually involve him.

He stripped off his gloves. 'Ring Maternity, they're quiet, and get a nurse down from there to help us.'

'But we're still short—'

'We've got two medical students. Let's see if they've got what it takes.' He strode into the resus room as the screaming wail of an ambulance siren broke the languid peace of a Warragurra winter's Saturday afternoon, the volume quickly increasing, bringing their patient ever closer.

Linton flicked on the monitors and took a brief moment to savour the quiet of the room. In about thirty seconds organised chaos would explode when their patient arrived.

Anticipatory acid fizzed in his stomach. Emergency medicine meant total patient unpredictability and he usually thrived on every stimulating moment. But today he didn't have his reliable team and the random grouping of today's staff worried him.

Andrew, the senior paramedic, walked quickly into the room, ahead of the stretcher, his mouth a flat, grim line. 'Hey, Linton. If Jeremy Fallon is at the game, you'd better page him now.'

Linton nodded on hearing the orthopaedic surgeon's name. 'We've done that already.' He inclined his head. 'Anyone we know?'

Andrew nodded as a voice sounded behind him.

'Can we triage and talk at the same time? His pressure is lousy.'

A flash of colour accompanied the words and suddenly a petite woman with bright pink hair appeared behind the stretcher, her friendly smile for her colleagues struggling with concern for her patient. 'We need Haemaccel, his BP's seventy on not much.'

'Emily?' Delighted surprise thundered through Linton, unexpectedly warming a usually cold place under his ribs.

She grinned. 'I know, I belong in a Flying Doctors' plane rather than an ambulance, although today I don't belong in either.'

'Ben's lucky Emily was driving into town on her day off.' Andrew's voice wavered before he cleared his throat and spoke in his usual professional tones. 'Ben McCreedy, age twenty-one, right arm crushed by a truck. Analgesia administered in the field, patient conscious but drowsy.'

Linton sucked in his breath as he swung his stethoscope from around his neck and into his ears, checking his patient's heartbeat. Ben McCreedy was Warragurra's rugby union hero. He'd just been accepted into the national league and today was to have been his last local game.

The young man lay pallid and still on the stretcher, his legs and torso covered in a blanket. His right arm lay at a weird angle with a large tourniquet strapped high and close to his right shoulder.

'He's tachycardic. What's his estimated blood loss?' Linton snapped out the words, trying for professional detachment, something he found increasingly difficult the longer he worked in Warragurra.

'Too much.' Emily's almost whispered words held an unjust truth as she assisted Andrew with moving Ben from the stretcher onto the hospital trolley.

Two medical students sidled into the room. 'Um, Dr Gregory, is this where we should be?'

Linton rolled his eyes. *Give me strength.* 'Attach the patient to the cardiac monitor and start a fluid balance chart. Where's Sister Haigh?'

Jason, the student who'd almost fainted, looked nervously around him. 'She said to tell you that Maternity now has, um, three labouring women.'

'And?' Linton's hands tensed as he tried to keep his voice calm against a rising tide of apprehension.

'And…' He stared at his feet for a moment before raising his eyes. 'And she said I wasn't to stuff up because she had a croupy baby to deal with before she could get here.'

Linton suppressed the urge to throttle him. How was he supposed to run an emergency with two wet-behind-the-ears students?

He swung his head around to meet a questioning pair of grey eyes with strands of silver shimmering in their depths. Eyes that remained fixed on him while the rest of her body moved, including her hands which deftly readjusted the female student's misapplied cardiac-monitor dots.

He recognised that look. That 'no nonsense, you've got to be kidding me' look. Twice a year he spent a fortnight with the Flying Doctors, strengthening ties between that organisation and the Warragurra Base Hospital. Both times Emily had been his assigned flight nurse.

'Emily.' The young man on the stretcher lifted his head, his voice wobbly and anxious. 'Can you stay?'

Ben's words rocked through Linton. *What a brilliant idea.* Emily was just who he needed in this emergency. He turned on the full wattage of his trade-mark smile—the smile that melted the resolve of even the most hard-nosed women of the world. 'Emily, can you stay? It would help Ben and it would really help me.'

The faintest tinge of pink started to spread across her cheeks and she quickly ducked her head until she was level with her patient. 'I'm right here, Ben. I'm not going anywhere.'

Then she stood up, squared her shoulders and was instantly all business. 'Catheter to measure urine output and then set up for a central line?'

He grinned at her, nodding his agreement as relief rolled through him. For the first time today he had someone who knew what she was doing. He swung into action and organised the medical students. 'Patti, you take a set of base-line obs, Jason you'll be the runner.'

Andrew's pager sounded. 'I have to go.' He gave Ben's leg a squeeze, an unusual display of emotion from the experienced paramedic. 'You're in good hands, mate. Catch you later.'

The drowsy man didn't respond.

Linton rolled the blanket off Ben. 'Emily, any other injuries besides the arm?'

'Amazingly enough, I don't think so. I did a quick in-the-field check and his pelvis and chest seem to be fine.'

'We'll get him X-rayed just to confirm that. Now, let's see what we're dealing with here.' He removed the gauze from Ben's arm. Despite all his experience in trauma medicine, he involuntarily flinched and his gut recoiled. The young man's arm hung by a thread at mid upper arm. His shoulder was completely intact as was his hand but everything in between was a crushed and mangled mess.

'Exactly what happened here?' Linton forced his voice to sound matter-of-fact.

Ben shuddered. 'I was driving to the game down Ferguson Street.' His voice trailed off.

Emily finished his sentence. 'Ben had the window down and his elbow resting on the car door. A truck tried to squeeze between his car and a parked car.' Her luminous eyes shone with compassion.

'You *have* to save my arm, Linton.' The words flowed out as a desperate plea. 'I need two arms to play rugby.'

I can't save your arm. Linton caught Emily's concerned gaze as her pearly white teeth tugged anxiously at her bottom lip. Concern for Ben—she knew it looked impossible.

Concern for Linton—somehow she knew how tough he found it to end a young man's dream with five small words.

'BP sixty-five on forty, respirations twenty-eight and pulse one hundred and thirty.' Patti's voice interrupted, calling out the worrying numbers.

'The blood bank's sending up three units of packed cells and X-Ray is on its way.' Emily spoke and immediately snapped back to the brisk, in-control nurse she was known to be. 'Jason, go and get more ice so we can repack the arm.'

Linton knew Ben's body had been compensating for half an hour, pumping his limited blood supply to his vital organs. Now they were entering a real danger zone. 'What's his urine output like?'

Emily checked the collection bag that she'd attached to the catheter. 'Extremely low.' Her words held no comfort and were code for 'major risk of kidney failure'.

He immediately prioritised. 'Increase his oxygen. Emily, you take the blood gases and I'll insert a central line.' He flicked the Haemaccel onto full bore, the straw-coloured liquid yellow against the clear plastic tubing. 'Patti, ring the blood bank and tell them to hurry up.'

His pager beeped and he read the message. 'Jeremy's arrived in Theatre so as soon as the central line's in place, we'll transfer Ben upstairs.'

Emily ripped open a syringe and quickly attached the needle. The sharp, clean odour of the alcohol swab dominated the room as she prepared to insert the needle into Ben's groin and his femoral artery. 'Ben, mate, I just have to—'

Suddenly Ben's eyes rolled back in his head and the monitor started blaring.

'He's arrested.' Emily grabbed the bag and mask and thrust them at Patti. 'Hold his chin up and start bagging. I'll do compressions.' She scrambled up onto the trolley, her small hands compressing the broad chest of a man in his athletic prime. A man whose heart quivered, desperate for blood to pump.

'I'm in.' Linton checked the position in the jugular vein with the portable ultrasound then skilfully connected the central line to another bag of plasma expander. 'Now he's getting some circulating volume, let's hope his heart is happier. Stand clear.'

Emily jumped down off the trolley.

The moment her feet hit the floor and her hands went up in the air showing a space between her and the trolley, he pressed the button on the emergency defibrillator. A power surge discharged into Ben's body, along with a surge of hope. It was tragic enough, Ben losing an arm. He didn't need to lose his life as well.

Four sets of eyes fixed on the monitor, intently watching the green flat line slowly start to morph into a wobbly rhythm.

'Adrenaline?' Emily pulled open the drug drawer of the crash cart.

'Draw it up in case we need it but he's in sinus rhythm for the moment. Patti, put the oxygen mask back on. We're moving him up to Theatre *now*. That tourniquet is doing its job but there's a bleeder in there that needs to be tied off.' Linton flicked up the locks on the trolley wheels.

'I've got the ice and the blood.' Jason rushed back into the room.

'Take it with you and summon the lift to Theatre. We're right behind you.' He turned to Emily to give her instructions, but they died on his lips.

She'd already placed the portable defibrillator on the trolley and positioned herself behind Ben's head, the emergency mask and bag in her hand. Small furrows of concentration formed a line of mini-Vs on the bridge on her nose as she caught his gaze. 'Ready?'

It was uncanny how she could pre-empt him. She was on his wavelength every step of the way. 'Ready.'

As they rounded the corner he heard the lift ping. Jason held the doors open as they pushed the trolley inside. The silver-coloured doors slid closed, sealing them into a type of no-man's-land.

Heavy silence pervaded the lift. The medical students watched everything in wide-eyed awe. Emily's gaze stayed welded to the monitor as her fine fingers caressed Ben's hair in an almost unconscious manner.

A stab of something indefinable caught Linton in the solar plexus. He shifted his weight and breathed in deeply. Emily Tippett, with hair that changed colour weekly, her button nose with its smattering of freckles that some might describe as cute, her baggy clothing, which he assumed hid a nondescript figure, and her diminutive height, was so far removed from his image of an ideal woman that it would be almost laughable to find her attractive. He exhaled the un-welcome feeling.

But she's a damn good nurse. The doctor in him could only applaud that attribute.

The lift doors slid open. 'Let's roll.' Linton manoeuvred the stretcher out into the corridor. He spoke to the drowsy Ben, not totally sure the young man could hear him. 'Ben, you're going into Theatre now, mate, and Jeremy Fallon's going to do his best for you. You're in good hands.'

The young man nodded. His expression was hidden behind the oxygen mask but his eyes glowed with fear.

Emily squeezed Ben's left hand and then stepped back from the trolley as the theatre staff took over. A minute later the theatre doors slid shut, locking them on the outside.

'What do you think will happen?' Jason spoke the words no one had been prepared to voice in front of Ben.

'High upper arm amputation.'

They spoke at the same time, Emily's words rolling over his, her voice husky and soft.

An image of a late-night, smoky bar with a curvaceous singer draped in a long, silk dress, its folds clinging to every delicious curve, suddenly branded itself to his brain. He'd never noticed what an incredibly sexy voice she had. It was at odds with the rest of her.

He shook his head, removing the image, and focused squarely on his medical student. Warragurra was a teaching hospital and he had teaching responsibilities. 'The X-ray will determine if the arm can be reattached but due to the violence of the impact it's very unlikely. The humerus, radius and ulna will be pulp rather than bone.'

'So what's next?' For the very first time Jason showed some enthusiasm.

'Cleaning up.' Emily turned and pressed the lift call button.

'Cleaning up?' Jason sounded horrified. 'Don't the nurses do that?'

Linton suppressed a smile and silently counted down from five, anticipating the explosion. Every medical student made the same gaffe, the sensible ones only once.

Emily whirled around so fast she was a blur of pink. 'Actually, it's the nurses who supervise the *medical students* doing the cleaning. How else do you learn what is required in a resus room? How else do you learn where everything is kept so you can find it in an emergency?' She folded her arms. 'And if you're really lucky, if you manage to clean and tidy in a timely manner, you might just be allowed near a patient and graduate from running boy.'

Jason's pale face flushed bright red to the tips of his ears as his mulish expression battled with embarrassment.

Linton started to laugh. A great rolling laugh he couldn't

hold in. His eyes watered and his body ached. Emily was fantastic. Just the sort of nurse he'd welcome with open arms on his staff. *Just the sort of nurse you need.*

He ushered everyone into the lift and this time the silence was contemplative rather than anxiety charged. If Emily came to work in A and E, so many of his problems would be solved. He could go back to worrying about medicine rather than staff politics because she'd organise everyone and everything. She'd always done that during his rotations with the Flying Doctors. With the resident he'd arranged arriving soon, and with Emily on board, he might even get some time away from work. His fifty-two-year-old father, who had just jetted out after one of his unexpected visits, had accused him of being boring!

Yes, this plan would free him up so he could retrieve his badly missed social life.

Emily in charge would make life very easy.

He started to hum. For the first time in two tension-filled weeks he felt almost carefree. *She might say no.*

He instantly dismissed the traitorous thought. When it came to getting what he wanted he usually achieved it with a smile and some charm. The doors opened onto the ground floor. 'Right, you two,' he spoke to the medical students. 'You make a start clearing up the resus room.'

Emily started to follow them.

'Em, got a minute?' His hand automatically reached out to detain her, his fingers suddenly feeling hot as they brushed the surprisingly soft skin close to her elbow.

She spun round, breaking the contact, her expression questioning as she glanced at her watch. 'About one minute. Why?'

He leaned against the wall. 'Still the same Em, always in a hurry.' He smiled. 'I just wanted to say thank you.'

She twisted a strand of hair around her finger in an almost

embarrassed action before flicking her gaze straight at him with her friendly smile. 'Hey, no problem. It was a fun way to spend my day off.' She gave a self-deprecating laugh and shrugged. 'I could hardly walk away and leave you with Jason and Patti, now, could I?'

He spoke sincerely. 'I would have been in deep trouble if you had. You headed off a potential nightmare.'

'Thanks.' He caught a ripple of tiny movement as her shoulders rolled back slightly and her chin tilted a fraction higher as she absorbed his praise.

He flashed her a wide, cheeky smile. 'You said you had fun and we make a great team so how about you come and do it again, say, five days a week?'

The constant motion he associated with Emily suddenly stalled. For one brief and disconcerting moment, every part of her stilled.

Then she laughed, her eyes darkening to the colour of polished iron ore. 'You're such a tease, Linton. Back in February, you spent two weeks bragging to me about your "fabulous team". Where are they now?'

He sighed. 'Love, marriage, babies—the full catastrophe.' The words were supposed to have come out light and ironic. Instead, bitterness cloaked them.

Emily rolled back and forth on the heels of her tan cowboy boots, her brow creased in thought. 'So you're serious?'

He caught the interest reflected in her eyes. He almost had her. 'Absolutely. I'm offering you a twelve-month position of Unit Manager, aka Charge Nurse of A and E.'

Lacing her fingers, she breathed in deeply, her baggy rugby top catching against her breasts.

His gaze overrode his brain, taking control of its focus and sliding from her face to the stripes that hinted at breasts he'd never noticed before. Quickly realising what he was doing, he zoomed his vision back to her face.

Tilting her head to the side, she gave him a long, penetrating look, her eyes a study of diffuse emotion. 'It's an interesting offer.'

Yes! She was tempted to take it on. Life was good. He rubbed his hands together. 'Fantastic. I'll get HR to write up the contract and -'

'I don't think so, Linton.'

Her firm words sliced through his euphoria. 'But—'

'Thanks anyway for the thought.' She rolled her lips inwards and nodded her head slightly. 'So, I guess I'll see you around.' She turned and walked away.

The retreating sound of her cowboy boots on the linoleum vibrated through him. He wasn't used to 'no'. He didn't like 'no' at all.

CHAPTER TWO

THE strong and greasy aroma of shorn wool hung in the air as Emily vigorously swept the ancient floorboards of the shearing shed, the thump and swish of the broom soothing her jangled nerves.

Linton Gregory wanted her to work for him. For a second she hugged the delicious thought close.

No, Linton Gregory wants you to work *in his department for a year.* Note the difference.

Ever since she had been a little girl she'd come out to the shearing shed when she'd needed to think. Or to hide. With four brothers to contend with, that had been reasonably often. She'd come and lie in the softness of the offcuts of wool, stare up at the rough-hewn beams, count the tiny sparkles of sunlight that shone though the pinprick holes in the corrugated-iron roof and find a sense of peace.

Now she was all grown up and far too big to lie in the hessian wool bags, so she swept and quarrelled with herself. For the last hour she'd been caught in an argument loop.

His offer is pure expediency. Nothing personal.

And deep down she knew that. Which was why when he'd asked her to work in A and E, she'd said no. Working side by side with Linton had been hard enough twice a year for two weeks. Working side by side five days a week for a year would completely do her in. She'd be an emotional basket case by the end of that time.

Her subconscious snorted. *And you're not now?*

She thumped the broom hard against the truth. She'd been a basket case from the first moment she'd laid eyes on Linton one year ago.

And she hated herself for it. She was twenty-five, for heaven's sake. A crush at fifteen was normal. At twenty it was forgivable. At twenty-five it was laughable in a tragic and pitying way.

Especially after everything she'd been through with Nathan. After that debacle, she'd promised herself she would never be that foolish again. She needed to keep her heart safe. But some promises seemed impossible to keep.

'Emily? You in there?' Her eldest brother's voice hailed her from outside.

She sighed. Her family knew her too well. If she'd really wanted to hide out she should have gone somewhere else. 'Yes, Mark, I'm here.'

'Thought you would be. You've got a visitor.'

She turned and leaned the broom up against the corrugated-iron wall and called out, 'OK, I'll come back to the house.'

'No need. We can talk here.'

She swung round, her heart pounding wildly like a runaway horse. Her brain immediately recognised that smooth, deep voice which held as many resonant tones as the colours of polished jarrah. Somehow she managed to halt the gasp of astonishment that rocked through her. He was the last person she'd expected. Linton had never visited her at home. In fact, he'd never visited her, full stop.

He leaned casually against the wall, all six feet two of him. His soft-soled Italian leather shoes had been silent against the worn boards more used to the firm tread of boots. His devastating smile hovered on his lips, tinged with the slightest uncertainty. But every other part of him controlled his space with magnetic charisma, from the tips of his blond-brown hair to the hem of his designer trousers.

Emily glanced down at her torn jeans and her brother's old and faded T-shirt, and groaned inwardly. At the best of times she felt frumpy and gauche, but she was usually in her Flying Doctor's uniform rather than her hide-from-the-world, comfort clothes.

She tugged at her hair and pasted a welcoming country smile on her face. 'Linton! What a surprise. What brings you out to Woollara Station?'

He pushed off the wall, toned muscles tensing and relaxing, propelling him forward toward her in one continuous, smooth movement. His lips curved upward into a full smile. 'I came to talk to *you*.'

His words rolled over her like warm caramel sauce—sweet and hot, fanning the bone-deep heat that had smouldered inside her from the first moment she'd met him. The ever-familiar wave of warmth hit her, spinning her round before dumping her against the shore, battering every one of her good intentions to stay immune to him.

She fought her dangerous attraction like she always did, using one of a cache of weapons in her arsenal. She dragged in a long, deep breath. Experience had taught her that men didn't find her attractive, and no way was she going to subject herself to excruciating embarrassment where Linton was concerned. He had *no* idea she had the world's worst crush on him and he *never* would. To him she was just a nurse and a mate—someone to chat to when no tall, gorgeous supermodel types were around.

That wasn't often.

Tall, willowy women flocked to Linton like moths to a flame. They came from all over the town and the region and the rest of the state. Visitors from Sydney often arrived for a weekend so he was never short of company. He dated a different woman every month.

I came to talk to you. Tamping down her reaction to him, she sternly reminded herself that his natural charm and emphasis on the well-placed words wasn't personal. She climbed up onto the post rail of one of the sheep pens and stared straight at him, her chin slightly tilted. 'So, isn't your phone working?'

He rubbed his jaw, his fingertips dipping as they crossed the cute dimple-like cleft that scored his chin. 'My phone's working fine, why?'

She balanced herself with her hands, gripping the rail. 'It's just you've never been out here before and it's a long drive on the off-chance I'd be here.'

He climbed up next to her. 'I wanted to talk to you in person. You raced off so fast this afternoon we didn't have a chance to discuss things fully.'

His familiar and special scent of sunshine, soap and one hundred per cent healthy man enveloped her. She gripped the rail more firmly so she wouldn't move away.

So she wouldn't move closer.

She surreptitiously shot him a sideways glance from under her fringe, taking in how his hair brushed the tips of his ears. Funny, usually his hairstyle was immaculate. 'I didn't think we had anything more to discuss.'

He slapped his thigh, indignation radiating from him. 'Yes we did! I offered you a job.'

'And I said, no, thank you.' Her fingers gripped the wood so hard they started to go numb.

'But why?' Genuine confusion vibrated through his voice. He sounded like a child who couldn't work out why the other kid wouldn't come out to play. 'It would be great experience for you.'

'I'd miss flying.' She tried to keep her tone light. She couldn't tell him the truth. That working with him every day would be delicious yet soul-destroying torture.

'It's *only* for a year.' Lack of understanding stamped itself all over him.

Only for a year. That was so easy for him to say. But for her it was fifty-two weeks, three hundred and sixty-five days, eight thousand, seven hundred and sixty hours. She stared at her feet. 'I don't want to lose my job with the Flying Doctors.'

'You wouldn't.'

She pivoted back to face him, her balance tested. 'How can you be so sure? I can't just leave for a year and expect to return to the same position.'

'What if you could?' His jade eyes usually so full of flirtatious fun, suddenly became serious.

A ripple of apprehension skated through her. Linton Gregory didn't do 'serious' all that often. 'The chief wouldn't be happy. He's already sent Doug Johnston to Muttawindi and now with Kate and Baden married I imagine maternity leave will loom pretty quickly. So me leaving would send the chief into a hypertensive fit.'

She jumped down off the rail, needing to put some more distance between them. 'Besides, this is all hypothetical because we can't even ask him until he gets back from the annual conference. You need help now. An agency from Adelaide or Sydney could supply you with an experienced nurse tomorrow.'

'Oh, come on. Now you're living in fantasyland.' Grumpiness and fatigue rode on the words. 'The Flying

Doctors attract staff because of the history of the organisation, the planes and a sense of adventure.' He sighed and rubbed the back of his neck. 'But Warragurra Base is a little more prosaic.'

She chased a tuft of wool with the point of her boot. 'But it attracted you. You came up from Sydney.'

'I did, but it's part of my career plan. I'm not staying for ever. One more year and I'll be back in the big smoke, sailing on the harbour.'

An irrational jolt of pain shot through her. It was crazy, especially when she knew he didn't really belong in Warragurra.

He jumped down from the rail and walked toward her, his gait relaxed. 'But this conversation's not about me, it's about you. I've spoken to the chief and he sends his regards.'

Her head shot up, taking in the high cheekbones, the smiling lines around his eyes and his cat-that-ate-the-cream grin. Apprehension exploded into full-blown panic. She'd forgotten that Linton thrived on getting his own way.

He leaned one arm against a beam. 'The chief agrees with me that a year in A and E will be a fabulous way to use your health promotion skills and it will hone your emergency skills.'

Her stomach clenched as her tenuous grip on control disappeared from under her. Anger spluttered to life. 'My emergency skills don't need honing.'

'True, but A and E is a different level. The chief thinks you will bring back more than they will lose by letting you go for a year. When you return, you'll return to a promotion.'

She stamped her foot as frustration swamped her. What was it about men just taking over? Her father and brothers did this to her all the time and she hated it. 'And what if I just don't want to work with you?'

His handsome face broke into deep creases and his chest started to heave as deep, reverberating laughter rocked him.

She summoned every angry, indignant fibre of her being and tried to pierce his self-satisfied aura with a withering look. 'I'm glad your self-esteem is so well fortified.'

He wiped a laughter tear from his eye. 'Oh, now, Emily, be fair. The few times we've worked together we've done exceptionally well. Hey, I even let you boss me around sometimes and I can count on half a hand the people I've allowed to do that.'

They *did* work together well. She hated it that he'd recognised that. It gave her one less argument to cement her case. She tried not to slump against the wall as she bent her leg and pressed the sole of her foot into a groove.

He causally leaned over a rail, his chin resting on his fist. 'And then there's your Master's.'

Her mouth went dry. 'What do you know about my Master's?'

His eyes flickered for the briefest moment. 'Don't you remember? Last year when we had to sit out that dust storm you told me you wanted to do your Master's in emergency nursing, but with Kate being away you'd put it on hold.'

Her blood dropped to her feet. He'd actually listened. Listened and remembered. It was completely unexpected— Nathan had never listened, it had always been all about him. She shrugged. 'It was just a pie-in-the-sky idea.'

He clicked his tongue. 'It shouldn't be.' He gave her a sly look. 'Warragurra Base would be the perfect place for you to work while you undertook your Master's.'

Her brain tried to keep up. Every time she had an argument he neatly countered it with almost effortless ease. But right now he was playing dirty pool. He knew she desperately wanted to do her Master's and that as much as the chief and the Flying Doctors supported the idea in principle, with the way staffing had been lately, it hadn't been possible.

Achieving her Master's would mean career security, senior positions and a higher salary. And she'd need that as, unlike her friends, she wouldn't ever be in the position of sharing income with a loving partner. Study leave hovered over her like the devil tempting her into his lair. Was this an opportunity she could really afford to pass up?

Linton pushed off the rail, walking round to lean his back against the wall so he stood next to her.

His heat slammed into her, dissolving all coherent thought. Emily breathed deeply, forcing air into her constricted lungs, in the hope her brain would soon get the much needed oxygen. *Think.*

She tried to fortify her resolution. Working at Warragurra Base meant working with Linton. Unrequited love from a distance had been tormenting enough. Up close and personal it would be torture. But still her words rushed out unchecked. 'How much study leave?'

White, even teeth flashed at her. 'What about you work a nine-day fortnight? The hospital will pay you for two days a month study leave.'

She narrowed her eyes. If she was selling out she should at least get a good deal. 'And one week to attend the "on campus" study component?'

He arched one brown eyebrow and tapped his top lip with his forefinger. 'As long as you can work it so the roster isn't short.'

She hugged her arms across her tightening chest as she committed herself to a path she'd told herself she'd never take. 'I can do that.'

He crossed his arms, his biceps straining against the soft cotton of his sleeves. 'Then we have a deal.'

Deal. The word boomed in her head over and over like the low bass of heavy metal. *What have you just done?* She silenced the words. Her decision was a career move. Linton would eventually leave town and she would get over her crush. Life would go on and she would have extra qualifications. 'A deal? I guess we do.' Somehow she managed to squeak the words out.

He grinned and leaned sideways, nudging her with his shoulder. 'See, that wasn't so hard, was it?'

She looked up into a pair of emerald eyes full of satisfaction. And why not? He'd just solved his staffing problem. All was good in *his* world.

But she'd just taken out a loan on her soul for a chance to study. Unless she was careful, the repayments on the loan would be pieces of her heart.

Emily stared at herself in the mirror in the Warragurra Base Hospital locker room, adjusting to seeing herself in green. Gone were the navy trousers and blue shirt of the Flying Doctors uniform. In their place green scrubs hung baggily revealing nothing of the shape that lay underneath. Hiding the big breasts and the short waist.

You are so ugly. High school had been a nightmare.

University hadn't been much better. *Cover yourself up, you don't want to put people off their dinner.* Nathan's derisive words boomed in her head. The memory of his curled lip and scornful look wormed its way back into her thoughts despite her best intentions to never let him back into her life in any shape or form.

He'd been the one to put the final nails into any delusions she might have had about herself. She now knew for certain that her body wasn't worthy of being on show, so she hid it, avoiding further pain and protecting herself from the glances of men—scrutinising glances that immediately turned to pitying ones.

She tied the string of the shapeless, baggy green pants. It was better this way. Men no longer saw her as a woman and didn't seek her out, which was exactly what she wanted. Her heart, which had loved Nathan and been so badly trampled on, was now well protected.

She turned away from the mirror and spritzed on some perfume, one of the few feminine luxuries she allowed herself. As the only female growing up on a sheep and cattle station, surrounded by men, being a girl hadn't always been easy.

When she was working on the station she generally became 'one of the boys' and fitted in that way. She could shoot a mean game of pool, muster on horseback for a full day without getting saddle-sore and was known for her skill in coaxing difficult engines into life. Her father, brothers and the employees at Woollara had long forgotten she was a woman.

If she was everyone's mate at Woollara, she was all nurse at work. 'Professional, organised and reliable' were the words that always turned up on her performance reviews. At work she had a different 'uniform' from the cowboy boots and jeans she wore at the station. But it was a uniform, and it made her blend in with the other medical professionals and told the community she was a nurse. The role absorbed her and she gave herself to it, enjoying every moment.

The only part of her that really said 'Emily' was her perfume, although most people missed that. They thought the thing that defined her was her dyed hair. But her hair was just a ruse. Bright hair hid her pain. Bright caused people to look up rather than down and distracted them so she could avoid their scrutiny of her lack of attributes.

She ran some hair gel through her hair. She'd worn it spiky short for so long that its current length surprised her. It was still above her shoulders but long enough for the curls to come back and taunt her. She tried to tame them into place with the waxy product.

In celebration or commiseration of the new job—at this point she wasn't exactly certain which one it was—she'd dyed her hair purple. The mirror reflected purple hair and green scrubs. Hmm, the women's movement would be proud of her. Then again, others might think she was going to take up tennis at Wimbledon.

She nervously fingered the hem of her top and then tugged down hard before breathing in deeply. She spoke to the mirror. 'Right, Emily. You're the unit manager and working for Linton for better or worse. Linton only sees you as a nurse so you're safe and your heart is safe. You're a professional and all personal feelings get left on this side of the door.

'This is work. Work is your shield against his charm. Focus on the job. You can *do* this.' She pulled her name tag and security tag over her neck and spun round to face the door.

CHAPTER THREE

PUSHING open the door, Emily walked into her new department. Unlike the last time she'd been in A and E—when it had held an air of panic and unravelling control—today it seemed almost serene.

'Emily!' Karen waved at her, pausing with one hand on the curtains of cubicle two, the other hand holding a dish containing a syringe. 'It's so great to have you here. I'll see you at the desk in a few minutes.'

She waved and smiled at the warmth in the other nurse's greeting. She hoped Karen represented the rest of the nursing staff with her friendliness.

'Emily, you're finally here.' Linton spun round, his freshly starched white coat sitting square across his broad shoulders and his stethoscope draped casually around his neck. Unlike his informal clothes on Saturday, today he wore a blue and white pinstriped business shirt with a silk tie. Everything about him said, 'A doctor in charge of his department'.

Puffs of heat spiralled through her. How could one man look so devastatingly handsome perched casually on the edge of a desk?

'I am, I'm here.' Duh! Of course she was here. What happened to 'lovely to be here' or 'looking forward to working with the team'? So much for wowing him and everyone else with scintillating conversation.

He glanced at her name tag, which snuggled into the indentation under her breasts. 'Survived the admin orientation, I see?'

She laughed, remembering her long and excruciatingly dull morning. 'As long as I remember to fill out every form in triplicate, I should be fine. I sometimes think Admin believes patients should be in triplicate as well.' She glanced up at the patient board. It was pretty empty, only listing two patients in cubicles and no one in the resus room.

'It looks like I've got a nice quiet afternoon to settle in on my first day.'

'Of course. I especially arranged it to welcome you.' His tanned face creased into a sparkling smile, which travelled rapidly up his cheekbones and into his eyes. Twinkling eyes, the same aqua green as the water around the coral cays of the Pacific Ocean.

She wanted to stretch out and float lazily in his gaze, revelling in the emphasis he put on the word 'you'. But that was far too dangerous. *Keep it all business.* She flicked a recalcitrant curl out of her eye. 'Especially for me? Yeah, right, I'll remind you of that when it's frantic and I still don't know where everything is.'

He gave her a long, pensive look, which finished with one brow rising. 'Ah, Emily, for a moment I forgot you don't let me get away with anything.'

A trail of pain pricked her. Surely she hadn't offended him? But there was no way she could flirt with him. He saw flirting as a game. As it was, she was gripping the last vestiges of her self-esteem when it came to Linton, and that was one game she couldn't play.

Before she could speak he slid off the desk, rising to his feet, his height dwarfing her. 'Now, I think you've met almost everyone except for the night staff. You know Karen and you've met Jason and Patti. Our students are with us for three months, and as you worked out the other Saturday, they're in their first weeks. As well as you starting today, we have a new resident, Daniel, and an agency nurse, Jodie. She's on a six-week contract but if she's any good we're hoping she can stay longer.'

'That's a lot of new staff.' A flutter of panic vibrated in her stomach. 'When do Michael and Cathy get back from their honeymoon?'

He drew in a long breath and sighed. 'Another six weeks.'

She did the mental maths of the number of hours in the day over available staff. 'So the roster's still short?'

He grinned. 'Not as short as it was a week ago.'

'And that's supposed to reassure me?' She heard the rising inflection of her voice.

He gave her a playful thump on the shoulder, similar to the ones she received from her brothers on a regular basis. 'I told you I needed you here.' He turned away and started walking as if he knew she would follow.

Irritation at his highhandedness quelled her mounting panic. She cut off a quip and took three quick steps to catch up as he was already talking as if she was standing next to him.

'If I'm out of the department when a patient comes in, I want to be notified. If it's a straightforward case then you and Daniel can deal with it, but page me if you need me or if you believe Daniel needs me.' He gave her a knowing look.

'New resident-itis?'

His shoulders rose and fell. 'It's early days but I don't want him taking on something he can't handle.' He stopped walking as he reached his office door, his face suddenly clearing of the usual fun and flirty expressions that defined him. 'Emily, we're a team. Don't ever feel you have to cope on your own. I'm only ever a page or a phone call away.'

His sincerity washed through her, trickling under her defences like floodwaters squeezing through cracks in a levee. Her mind threatened to leap from work to studying how his eyelashes almost brushed his cheek when he blinked. *Stop reading more into this than exists. He's your boss and he'd be telling all new staff this.*

She forced her attention back to the job. 'What meetings are expected?'

He ushered her into his office and picked up a stack of folders from his desk. 'We have a weekly meeting to discuss medical and nursing issues but I have an open-door policy so, please, don't wait until Tuesdays at two to discuss something important. Honest and open communication is vital in a department like this.'

Honest and open. As long as it only pertained to work, she was off the hook. She couldn't work at Warragurra Base if he knew how she really felt about him. She was embarrassed enough by it. She didn't want to feel this way. She hated it that after everything she'd been through with Nathan, even though she knew she wasn't ready for another relationship, she couldn't control her body's reaction to Linton.

'Right, I promise I won't let anything fester.' She held out her arms. 'Are they for me?'

He winked. 'Just a bit of light reading. We're in the middle of a policy review.'

'Policy review?' A vision of reading long into the night popped into her brain. Not that she slept that well, with Linton always hovering in her dreams. 'Did you just happen to conveniently forget to tell me that when you were twisting my arm in the woolshed?'

His eyes widened in feigned outrage. 'Twisting your arm? I don't coerce my staff, Emily.' He dumped the folders into her outstretched arms. 'By the way, have you enrolled for your Master's?'

'That would be the arm-twisting Master's?' She clutched the folders to her chest.

His mouth twitched smugly. 'All I did was provide you with an opportunity to do something you've wanted to do for a while.' He lowered himself on the corner of his desk, his eyes full of curiosity, appraising her. 'So, which subject are you starting off with?'

Surprise hit her so hard she swayed on her feet. She stared back at his face, so unexpectedly full of genuine interest. She hadn't expected that. 'I, um, I'm starting off with "Interpersonal Relationships in the Clinical Environment".'

Otherwise known as how to survive working closely with a boss whose presence turns your mind to mush and your heart into a quivering mess.

He rubbed his chin in thought. 'That sounds meaty. There's lots of scope there on so many levels—patient-staff, staff-staff, patient-relative, relative-staff.'

His gaze settled back on her, unnerving her with its solicitude. The fun-loving charmer seemed to have taken a back seat. She'd never known him to take such an interest in her before. Her usual approach of friendly mockery didn't seem right. She managed to stammer out, 'I—I thought so.'

'In a high-octane environment like A and E it can be pretty fraught at times, which is why staff wellbeing is high on my agenda.' He walked her to the door. 'Let's do drinks at the end of the shift.'

She almost dropped the folders as blood rushed to her feet, making her fingers numb. *He's inviting you out for a drink.*

Not a good idea, Emily.

But common sense had no chance against the endorphin rush. All thoughts of staying detached and professional got swept away by the sheer joy that exploded inside her. Her feet wanted to happy dance and her hands wanted to high-five.

Stay cool and calm. 'That would—'

'Emily, Linton, you're needed,' Sally, the desk clerk, called them to Reception.

Jodie dashed past, holding two kidney dishes. 'Gastro in cubicles one, two, three and four.'

Emily picked up the histories and noted the patients all had the same surname. 'Looks like it's one family.' She handed out the histories. 'Jason, you and Patti share Mr Peterson and Jodie's in with Mrs Peterson. Get base-line obs and assess for dehydration.'

Linton took the remaining histories. 'You examine the teenager and then join me with the eight-year-old.' He shot her a cheeky grin. 'Your hair colour will convince him you're a clown and he'll relax while I'm inserting an IV.'

She rolled her eyes. 'Ha, ha, very funny. I think I just have my first example for my Master's of interpersonal relationships with staff and harassment.' She jokingly tapped his chest with her forefinger. 'Be nice or I might not help.'

She turned away and pushed open the curtain to see a fourteen-year-old boy heaving into a bowl, his ashen face beaded with sweat. 'David, I'm Emily.'

He fell back against the pillow, exhausted. 'I feel terrible.'

'You don't look too flash.' She picked up his wrist and her fingers quickly located his pulse, which beat thinly and rapidly under her fingertips. She pushed an observation chart under the metal clip of the folder and recorded his pulse, respirations, blood pressure and temperature. 'When did the vomiting start?'

'After lunch.' He flinched and gripped his stomach, pulling his legs up. 'Arrgh, it really hurts.' His quavering voice stripped away the usual teenage façade of bravado.

She hated seeing people in distress. 'I can give you something to help with the spasms but first I have to insert a drip, which means a needle in your arm.'

'Oh, man.'

She stroked his arm. 'It won't hurt as much as the cramps. Tell me, what did you eat for lunch?'

'Sausages and chops.' He grabbed the bowl again, gagging.

'Take long, slow deep breaths, it really helps.' Emily quickly primed the IV. 'When was the meat cooked?'

'Dad and I barbequed it and then we ate it straight away.'

She wrinkled her nose. 'I think I can smell the smoke from the fire on your clothes.'

'Yeah, it was an awesome bonfire. I'd been collecting the wood for a week.'

What was it about men, testosterone and fire? Her brothers loved nothing better than a midwinter bonfire. 'Was it a special occasion?'

He nodded weakly. 'Dad's birthday. Mum even bought coleslaw and potato salad.'

Wrapping the tourniquet around his arm, she kept mental notes of the food. 'Did you have cake?'

'Yeah, one of those mud cakes from the supermarket.'

Swabbing the inner aspect of his left arm she kept talking. 'Sounds like a lovely party.'

'It was, until we all started vomiting.' His arm stiffened as the needle slid into his vein.

'Sorry.' She whipped the trocar out of the cannula and attached the Hartmann's solution. 'Now I can get you something to lessen the nausea.'

David stiffened on the trolley, his eyes suddenly wide and large.

'What's wrong?'

He flushed bright pink. 'I need to go…now.'

'Right.' She grabbed a bedpan from under the trolley and helped him into position. 'Here's the bell, ring when you're done.' She backed out of the cubicle, feeling sorry for the boy who had left his dignity at the door.

'Emily, how's your patient?' Linton stood at the desk, writing up a drug chart.

'I've inserted a Hartmann's drip. Can I have a Maxalon order, please?' She slid her chart next to his.

'No problem.' His lean fingers gripped his silver pen as his almost illegible scrawl raced across the paper. 'So does he have diarrhoea, vomiting and stomach cramps?'

'Yes, all three, poor guy. He's pretty miserable. It sounds like a birthday party gone wrong.' She opened a syringe and assembled it, attaching it to the needle. 'David said his mum bought coleslaw and potato salad. Mayonnaise can harbour *E. coli* so I'm wondering if we should ring the health inspector to check out the deli.' She snapped open the ampoule of Maxalon.

'Good idea, and worth a phone call.' Linton rubbed his creased forehead. 'But if it was the deli we should have other people in with the same symptoms.'

'Unless the Petersons left their food out of the fridge and in the sun.' She confirmed the dose of the injection with Linton.

'It could be the meat.' He walked with her back toward the cubicle, his hands deep in his pockets.

'True, except that a dad and his son were barbequing.'

He arched a brow and stared down at her. 'Meaning?'

She ignored his supercilious look. 'Meaning most of the blokes I know tend to char the meat rather than undercooking it.'

'Now, there's a sexist statement for you. I'm sure you have to be on the lookout for those in your assignment of interpersonal relationships in the clinical environment.' He flashed her a challenging grin. 'I can shoot your gross generalisation down in flames. I happen to be a brilliant barbeque cook and one day I will prove it.'

The dizzy dancing that had been spinning inside her since his invitation to drinks expanded. She couldn't be imagining this. No, the signals were definitely there. He'd asked about her Master's, he'd mentioned drinks, and now a barbeque. There was no doubt about it, he wanted to spend some time with her.

She ducked around the corner and helped her patient off the bedpan before inviting Linton in with the injection. 'David, this is Dr Gergory.'

'Hey, David.' Linton extended his hand, treating the teenager like a young adult.

The patient put his hand out to grasp Linton's and suddenly stopped. He flicked his wrist, shaking his fingers.

'Is there a problem with your hand?' Linton turned David's palm over.

'My fingers feel numb and tingly, like my hands have gone to sleep.'

'Hands? Are both of them feeling like that?' Emily caught Linton's concerned gaze as her own unease increased a notch.

David nodded. 'Yeah, it feels really weird.'

Linton placed David's hand by his side. 'It could be from

all the vomiting. We're replacing the electrolytes you've lost and we're slowing down the vomiting with the medication. This should fix the tingling.' He adjusted the drip flow. 'We need to check on the rest of your family but ring the buzzer if you start to feel any more tingling, OK?'

David nodded wearily, not even raising his head from the pillow.

Emily tucked the blanket around him, made sure he could reach his buzzer and then followed Linton. 'I'll organise for bloods to be taken.'

'Good, but let's get everyone together and review the rest of the family first.'

Jason, Patti and Jodie all reported that their patients had similar symptoms after eating the same food.

'So it's an open and shut case of gastro, right?' Jason recorded some notes in his spiral bound notebook.

'Perhaps.' Linton tugged at his hair, his fingers trailing a path, making his blond tips almost stand on end as he walked back to check on the eight-year-old.

'Something's not quite right, is it?' Emily shared his niggling feeling of doubt.

His eyes reflected his apprehension. 'I just get the feeling that if I call it gastro, then that's just too easy. I think I'm missing something.' He ushered her through the curtain ahead of him.

Little Jade Peterson lay quietly sobbing, her chest rising and falling in shuddering grunts.

'Honey, does it hurt somewhere new?' Emily ducked down so she was at eye level with the little girl.

'No, but who's going to look after Towzer?'

Emily exchanged a questioning look with Linton.

He shrugged his shoulders, his expression blank.

'Who's Towzer, Jade?'

'My dog.' She sniffed violently.

Emily stroked the little girl's hair back behind her ear. 'I'm sure your dog will be fine and waiting for you when you go home.'

She shook her head sadly. 'But his tummy hurt too and he was sick.'

Linton bent down next to Emily, his vivid green eyes fixed on Jade's face. 'What did Towzwer eat?

She clutched her hospital teddy bear. 'He loves sausages but he stole a chop too and Dad got cross.'

The meat. The buzzer sounded. 'That's David.' Emily rose and walked quickly back to the cubicle.

Terror shone in the boy's eyes. 'My face feels all funny now. It's like pins and needles and it's really scary.'

'We're working on what's causing these symptoms. I'm going to take some blood and hopefully that will tell us something.' She gave him a reassuring smile and hoped her face didn't show how worried she really was.

Something weird and neurological was going on. She checked his pupils with her penlight. Both were equal and reacting. 'Can you squeeze my hands, David?'

He put his hands out toward her. Fear shot through her, making her gut lurch. His palms, which had been white before, now looked red and blistered, with flaking skin. If he'd burned himself, they would have known on arrival. Linton would have seen it earlier.

None of this made sense. 'I'll be right back, David.'

She stepped out of the cubicle, her mind racing, trying desperately to work out what was going on. She rushed back to Jade and almost collided with Linton as he opened the curtain. 'Oh, thank goodness you're here.'

He put his hands out to steady her. 'What's wrong? You're

white.' He gently steered her to one side. 'You haven't got gastro too, have you?'

She shook her head. 'I'm fine but David's palms are peeling as if they've come in contact with a corrosive substance. Everyone is getting sicker and sicker in front of our eyes. What do you think this is?'

He clicked his pen up and down, the sound reflecting his agitation before he shoved it back in his pocket. 'I wish I knew. We've got nausea, vomiting, stomach cramps, and the father has blood in his stools.' His forefinger flicked off the tip of each finger on his other hand as he listed each symptom.

'And facial numbness and tingling fingers.' A horrible thought speared her brain. 'It sounds like poison.'

He nodded, his expression grim. 'That is the conclusion I've come to. It matches up that it must have been the meat that was poisoned because the dog was sick as well. I'll call the police. Forget taking blood. Organise for a urine tox screen on everyone and get it to Pathology with an urgent request on it.' He spun round, abruptly calling over his shoulder as he walked away, 'Then organise for the whole family to be in one space. I want to talk to everyone together.'

She gave her staff their orders and ten minutes later, with the tests sent off to the lab, Jason and Patti soon had the trolleys in a square. Each family member lay on their trolley in the foetal position, legs drawn up against the severe stomach cramps, and groaning as each spasm hit.

'I know you're all feeling really ill, but I need you to concentrate on what we're saying.' Emily stood between the trolleys where Christine and Brian Peterson lay. 'Everyone, including the dog, ate the meat and everyone has similar symptoms. David and Brian are the most unwell but I'm guessing that's because they ate the most meat.'

She touched Christine's hand. 'Where did you buy the meat from, Mrs Peterson?'

The sick woman trembled. 'It was one of ours. Brian slaughtered it a month ago.'

'Have you eaten meat from that beast before?' Linton asked, his voice quiet and nonjudgmental.

'Yes, we have, and we've never been sick.' She twisted a hankie in her fingers. 'I defrosted it in the fridge, I did everything the same as normal.'

'The symptoms are leaning very strongly toward poisoning.' Linton's matter-of-fact voice broke the almost surreal news. 'We'll know as soon as the urine tests comes back but in the meantime would there be anyone who might want to hurt you in any way?'

The father of two gasped. 'No, no, no one we know would do such a thing.'

'I don't understand.' Christine gripped the side of the trolley for support, her voice trembling. 'It was supposed to be a special day for Brian. David did such a great job getting the bonfire ready.'

Dad and I barbequed. It was an awesome bonfire, I'd been collecting the wood for a week. Emily's hand shot out, gripping Linton's white, starched sleeve as the thought struck her. 'David, what sort of things were you burning on the fire?'

The teenager replied listlessly. 'Just wood and stuff that I found.'

Linton's eyes flashed his understanding as he immediately picked up on her line of thought. 'Was any of the wood stained green, like the pine they use in the car parks down by the river?'

'Maybe.' He gripped his stomach as another spasm hit.

Emily spoke softly. 'This is really, really important, David. We need you to think. Had any of the wood been treated?'

The boy looked anxiously between Emily and Linton. 'I…I did get some from the building site next door.'

Linton thumped his fist against his forehead. 'Copper-chrome-arsenate. You've barbequed your meat in arsenic vapours. That's what's causing all these symptoms.'

Stunned silence and shocked disbelief scored everyone's faces.

'Arsenic. Hell of a birthday present, son.' Brian grimaced in pain.

'I'm s-s-sorry, Dad.' David's voice quavered as tears filled his eyes. 'Are we going to die?'

'Not now that we know what we're treating.' Linton gave the boy's shoulder a reassuring squeeze.' He turned to Emily. 'We need dimercaprol up to five milligrams per kilogram by intramuscular injection. It acts as a chelator and the arsenic will bind with the drug so it can be removed from the system.'

'I'll ring Pharmacy now.' Emily turned to her staff. 'Jodie, Patti and Jason, attach everyone to a cardiac monitor and monitor urine output. You'll need to weigh each family member so we can work out the dose of dimercaprol. The rest of the nursing care plan is to provide symptomatic care. A cool sponge will help, as well as some refreshing mouth-wash.'

Her staff nodded their agreement and everyone attended to their tasks. By the end of the shift the Petersons had been transferred into the high dependency unit for close monitoring. Emily stifled a yawn as she wished the night staff a good shift.

'You can't say we didn't welcome you with a bang. Who would have thought of arsenic poisoning?' Linton leaned back on his chair, his hands clasped behind his head, his broad chest straining at his now rumpled shirt. 'Fabulous call, by the way. What made you associate the bonfire?'

His praise sent streaks of happiness though her. 'At the risk of being called sexist, I have four brothers. When they were younger they'd burn just about anything, and David reminded me of them. Lucky for us, Dad taught us what was toxic and what was safe so we avoided potential tragedies like today.'

'The Petersons are one lucky family.' He rose to his feet and gazed down at her. 'Ready for that drink?'

I've been ready for you to notice me for over a year. 'Sure, I'll just get changed and meet you in the foyer.' She walked to the locker room, somehow managing to control her feet which wanted to spin, twirl and tap their way there.

It had been an incredible first shift. From the moment she'd stepped into the department Linton had seemed different, as if he was interested in her as a person, not just as a nurse. And he'd asked her out for a drink. She hummed to herself as she quickly changed into her jeans and loose-fitting top. She sprayed some perfume onto her neck and wrists, and almost skipped down the corridor.

As she stepped into the foyer she heard Linton's deliciously deep, rumbling voice. 'It was a huge first day for you, Jodie, but you did a fantastic job. Are you up for A and E's traditional welcome drinks?'

'I think I deserve them.' Her girlish laugh tinkled in the quiet foyer. 'I hope every day isn't going to be like today.'

Emily stopped so fast her boots squeaked on the lino floor.

Jason and Patti pushed through the door on the opposite side of the foyer, both dressed in city black. 'We're ready.'

Emily's stomach rolled. She swallowed hard against the rising bile. *Drinks for new staff.*

Her blood pounded in her head, drowning out all coherent

thought. How could she have been so stupid? How could she have got it so very wrong?

You always get it wrong with men.

This wasn't 'drinks' as in 'I finally noticed you and let's go for drinks'. This was a general invitation for all new staff.

Staff wellbeing is high on my agenda. Linton's words sounded clearly in her head. Welcome drinks. A 'getting to know you' session—team bonding.

She wanted to curl up in a ball and hide. She'd misinterpreted professional team building for personal interest. She'd let her crazy and out-of-control feelings for Linton colour her judgement so much that she'd heard only what she'd wanted to hear. An image of her jabbing his chest with her finger came into her head. She'd even let her guard down and flirted with him.

Linton turned on hearing the squeal of her boots, his smile wide and welcoming. 'Emily, I thought I recognised the sound of your boots.'

Like a rabbit caught in a spotlight, she had nowhere to run and nowhere to hide. *Be the friendly colleague and hide the pain.* Tossing her head, she forced down every particle of disappointment and embarrassment, and summoned up, from the aching depths of her soul, 'bright and breezy, Emily, everyone's best friend'. The public Emily that shielded the real her.

She walked toward the group, smiling. 'Come on, you lot. It's not often Linton opens his wallet so let's take advantage while we can.'

She linked arms with the med students and tugged them forward. 'Linton, I hope you've been to the bank. I'm not only thirsty, but I'm completely starving.' She flashed him a wide, friendly grin as she walked past. A grin that hid more than it displayed. A grin that made her cheeks ache. It was going to be a long evening.

And an impossibly difficult year.

CHAPTER FOUR

LINTON gazed out at the brilliant winter sunset lighting up the rich red soil of the outback and silhouetting the now still windmill against the backdrop of an orange sky. The beams of light caressed the earth, deepening and enhancing the already vivid colours. Nature's slideshow was a lot more interesting than the slideshow he was preparing for the hospital board meeting.

A flash of pink, white and grey swooped past, accompanied by a cacophony of raucous sound. The flock of galahs settled into the huge gumtree on the edge of his garden for their nightly rest. He hadn't used his alarm since arriving in Warragurra. The birds woke him daily at dawn. Somehow their early morning song seemed more acceptable than the grinding and bumps of the rubbish trucks and the antics of the late-night drunks that had woken him in Sydney.

He'd miss the birds when he left Warragurra.

Still, that wasn't for while yet. He headed back inside to his laptop. He'd ducked home to get some uninterrupted time to work on his report. Amazingly, his pager had stayed quiet and he really should have achieved more than he had.

Actually, the quiet pager wasn't all that amazing. Emily had been on duty today. In two short weeks she'd put the wheels back on A and E and his department was running even better than before.

Warm and cosy smugness cuddled up to him, stroking his ego. Talking Emily into taking the unit manager position had been a stroke of pure brilliance. She was the most amazing nurse he'd ever worked with. She only called him in when it was absolutely necessary and if it wasn't an emergency case, but a consult for Daniel, then by the time he arrived all the preliminary tests had been done and everything was waiting for him.

Somehow she'd even managed to whip some enthusiasm into Jason, who no longer sat back but showed signs of being proactive. She'd also cracked the cone of silence that had initially surrounded Patti. The department positively purred.

He had what he wanted—a reliable and dependable team and a department that met every challenge ably and well prepared. Life was good.

He stared back at the computer screen, rereading the same words he'd written over half an hour ago.

So if he had everything sorted at work, why the hell was he constantly thinking about Emily instead of this report? All afternoon she'd slipped in and out of his mind, which was crazy because he'd employed her so he didn't have to think about work twenty-four seven. But snapshot images of her would catch him unawares, like her teasing smile, the way her hips rolled and swayed when she walked quickly through the department, and the floaty trail of her very feminine floral perfume, which had an unexpected kick of sensual spice.

Emily and *sensual* didn't belong in the same sentence. Emily was a colleague and a friend. Yet just lately he'd noticed things about her he'd never seen before. Like yesterday, when she'd bent over to pick up a pen and her scrubs had pulled across pert and curved buttocks he hadn't known existed. He'd found himself wondering what else lay hidden beneath her baggy clothing.

It was ridiculous. Emily was the exact opposite of what he looked for in a woman. Tall, long-legged women caught his eye. Not short women with psychedelic hair. It must be a delayed reaction to his recent lack of a social life. Work had been frantic and he hadn't been out much lately.

The bold ringtone of a 1950s telephone severed the thought. He punched the answer button on his mobile. 'Linton Gregory.'

'Lin, darling. I'm here to rescue you from small-town life and small-town people. Let's fly to Sydney for dinner.'

His mouth curved into a smile at the breathy and cajoling voice at the other end of the line. Tall, blonde and beautiful, Penelope Grainger divided her time between her parents' enormous cattle station and the bright lights of Sydney, doing not much else other than enjoying life. He'd met her at a charity polo match a few months ago and had quickly discovered she was the female version of himself. No strings, all fun, and a well-honed 'don't call me, I'll call you policy'.

It suited him perfectly.

Since the nightmare of Tamara he'd been vigilant and had adhered like superglue to that same policy. He didn't need another I-told-you-so lecture from his father. *Date and move on, son. Don't get trapped again.* Hell, he should have listened better in the first place. It would have saved his heart from being ripped out, pulverised and returned to him on a platter, just like his father had predicted.

'Penelope, I would love to have dinner at Doyle's but I can't actually leave town this weekend as I'm on call.'

The pout of her mouth sounded in her voice. 'That's just

too boring. Well, I guess it will have to be dinner at the Royal, then. Can you meet me there at eight?'

'Eight it is.' He whistled softly as he hung up the phone. Work was sorted and his social life was returning to normal. A night with Penelope would put everything back into perspective and these strange and unsettling thoughts about Emily would recede.

Linton was early. He'd given up completely on the report, rationalising that a fresh mind tomorrow would be more efficient than trying to work on it tonight. Rather than pacing around the house like a caged lion, he'd showered and headed to the Royal.

The meticulously renovated Royal Hotel was Warragurra's tribute to the wealth that had once come out of the soil and had ridden on the sheep's back. One hundred years ago it would have been one of many similar establishments. But the mining boom had faded, wool no longer brought in the money it had and the other hotels had gone. With its intricate wrought-iron 'lace' veranda, the detailed mosaic floor in the foyer and the magnificent carved wooden staircase, the Royal had become *the* place to be seen and the social centre of Warragurra.

Its management had the happy knack of catering to all tastes, from the easy ambiance of the public bar to the rarefied atmosphere of the dining room. In the summer months there was casual dining on the heritage-listed veranda but tonight's cool and crisp winter outback evening had forced people inside.

He pushed open the door to the public bar. On a Friday night he was sure to meet someone he knew for a drink, which would pass the time until he had to meet Penelope in the dining room at eight.

'Linton.' A familiar voice and a waving arm hailed him as he stepped over the threshold.

'Baden, good to see you. But why are you in a bar, alone on a Friday night? Married bliss worn off already?' He shook the flying doctor's hand and signalled to the barman for a glass of merlot.

Baden shook his head, laughing. 'No fear, mate. Married life is pretty good. You might want to consider it one day.'

'I don't think so, Baden.' The familiar irritation chafed him. What was it about married couples that blinkered them to the idea that there *was* life outside being part of a couple? If they'd met his parents and seen their divorce carnage, they might not be quite so enthusiastic.

If they'd experienced Tamara's complete personality change once the wedding ring had slid onto her finger, they'd be rethinking the entire tradition. Words he'd thought he'd left behind trickled through his mind. *I hate you, Linton.*

Looking for a way to change the topic, he spied a gift-wrapped box with an enormous gold bow tied on the top, sitting on a stool next to Baden. 'Special day?'

Baden's blue eyes sparkled with enthusiasm. 'It's Kate's birthday week and Sasha has organised a surprise party for her. I have strict instructions to be in the dining room at seven-thirty with this present. Kate thinks I'm at the usual Flying Doctors' Friday night drinks and fundraising pool match. She's calling in to collect me after picking up Sash from swimming.'

Baden sipped his beer and chatted cheerfully. 'You might want to keep a low profile tonight. Most of the base is here and I'm not sure I should be seen talking to you, seeing as you poached our Emily.'

Linton grinned. 'You guys need to learn how to look after

your staff. All I did was offer her an opportunity to do her Master's. Besides, she'll be back with you in a year.' An unforeseen jag of discomfort suddenly snagged him under his ribs. He automatically rubbed the spot with his hand.

'Baden, you're up.'

Despite the noise of the crowd, the clink of the glasses and the pop and hiss of the open fire, Linton instantly recognised that mellow, husky voice.

He turned toward Emily and caught the moment she recognised him. Her hand gripped a pool cue, which she casually leaned on. Surely he imagined that ripple of tension whipping across her shoulders and down her arm before she gave him her usual broad, welcoming smile?

He didn't associate Emily with tension. She was a friendly, country girl through and through. She had no pretensions and was at ease with everyone, no matter who they were or where they came from. She was everybody's mate. His mate. The sister you could depend on.

She moved closer and her perfume encircled him, tempting his nostrils to breathe in more deeply. Making his gut kick as the sensual spice curled through him, sending heat spiralling. *Sisters don't wear perfume like that.*

'Hi, Linton.' She gave him a casual, cursory greeting and turned her attention back to Baden. 'It's your turn. The kitty's up to ten dollars.'

Baden's expression became apologetic. 'Sorry, Emily, I don't have time tonight, I'm meeting Kate in a minute.' He slid off the barstool and picked up the gift. 'Hey, Linton, how about you play for me?' A teasing smile streaked across his face. 'It gives you a chance to redeem yourself after the whipping Emily gave you at the pool table last time you were on rotation.'

He caught the shared laughing glance between Emily and Baden. He reacted in high dudgeon. 'I was being polite the last time I played.'

The glint of challenge sparked silver in Emily's grey eyes and she rolled her lush lips inward, as if she was stopping herself from laughing out loud. 'Polite? OK, if that's how you want to remember it.'

He caught the time on his watch. He still had half an hour before he had to meet Penelope. Half an hour to best Emily at pool and put her in her place. 'You're on.'

Baden's hand clapped his shoulder. 'Good luck.'

Emily sauntered to the pool table, chalked her cue and hooked his gaze with a shimmering dare-fuelled look. She then blew gently over the tip of the cue, sending a light smattering of blue powder fluttering into the air, like a nineteenth-century cowboy blowing powder from his gun. 'Seeing as you let me win last time, I'll let you break.'

He chalked his cue and stared straight back her while he blew the excess powder off the tip. 'Fair enough.' He grinned as her eyes widened and the cute freckles on her nose wrinkled. She'd expected him to be a gentleman and refuse. *Ah Emily, I hate to lose as much as you do.*

He lined the cue up with the triangle of balls. Bringing the cue smoothly through the L of his left hand, it connected firmly and precisely with the white ball, sending it cleanly into the centre of the pack. A loud clack echoed as the balls scattered, skimming across the green felt.

'Nice job.' Emily walked around the table, winding a strand of hair around her finger as she studied the lie of the scattered balls.

He bent over in a mock bow. 'Thank you.'

'Actually, I think I should be thanking you.' She smiled a

quiet, knowing smile laced with devilish glee before leaning over the table. She shot two balls into the right pocket.

He couldn't believe his eyes. 'Where did you learn how to do that?'

She spun around and grinned. 'I spent hours watching the shearers and my brothers. As the only girl growing up on a sheep and cattle station, there wasn't a lot of choice in the re-creation. It was learn to play pool or spend even more time on my horse.'

'But you didn't just learn how to play, you perfected it into an art form.'

She had the decency to blush. 'Well, why play if you're not playing to win?'

He leaned in close, ready to tease her, and dropped his voice. 'Exactly.'

Her head snapped around so fast that her hair caressed his cheek, trailing her scent across his skin and tantalising his nostrils. He looked down into staring eyes as wide as pools of liquid silver.

Staring up at him. Staring into him.

His heart thumped hard in his chest, pounding blood into unexpected places. Disconcerted, he stepped back fast and turned toward the table, lining up the ball too quickly. Without pausing for breath, he took his turn and fluffed the shot completely. Frustration and disappointment collided and he steeled himself against the urge to thump his fist on the table. What had got into him?

'Bad luck.' Her tone of voice and expression held no sarcasm, only understanding from another sportsman who knew the frustrations of the game.

She bobbed down and squinted at the ball then stood and leaned over the table, supporting the cue. Her top rode up as she stretched out, exposing a taut behind hugged closely by blue denim.

His palms suddenly became damp and he gripped the cue. *Sportsman?* There was *nothing* manly about that derrière. Unlike the loose scrubs, the denim outlined with precision the perfect form that wiggled in front of him, screaming to be cupped by warm hands. His hands.

'Yes!' She squealed happily as another ball clattered into a pocket.

He groaned. What the hell was going on? He was being whipped at pool and he couldn't shift the image of her behind from his head. He gritted his teeth and swung his attention back to the green felt.

Emily walked to the other side of the table and faced him. As she leaned over again her shirt fell forward, exposing the rise of creamy skin and a touch of lace.

Both declared treasure below for the taking.

He breathed in way too fast and coughed.

Laughing, she glanced up from under her fringe. 'Old ploy, Gregory. You'll need to do better than that to distract me.' She hooked her gold necklace between her teeth, out of the way, and returned to the ball.

Hell, she had no idea that he'd caught his breath on a tantalising glimpse of breast and a hint of lace. Had he regressed to sixteen?

He rubbed the tension from his shoulder.

Her cue wobbled, hitting the ball on the side, missing its target but lining up the high balls for him.

'Damn!' She stood up and her baggy shirt resumed its normal place and all signs of treasure were hidden again.

Damn is right. He chalked his cue and threw her a superior 'big brother' type of look. The one he knew she hated because she'd told him once or ten times. 'Now let me show you how it's done.' He strode past her and took aim. 'That's one.' He moved to the end of the table and lined up again. 'That's two.' He glanced over at her to see how she was taking it.

She leaned casually against the side of the table with one hand in her back pocket, which pulled her shirt tight across her chest. He'd stake a bet she had no idea how sexy it made her look.

Sexy? This is Emily. Get a grip.

She rocked back and forth on her boot heels. 'Enjoying yourself?'

'Yep.' He grinned at her.

Her mouth twitched. 'You don't think you're celebrating just a tad too soon?'

'Nope.' He lined up the third ball.

He felt her warmth as she stepped up next to him and moved in close. 'You really think that will work for you?' The whispered words feather-stroked his ear.

He turned, laughing, his gaze fused with hers, catching a streak of pure good-natured banter. Pleasure unfurled deep within, streaming out to all parts of him, visiting uncharted places. 'Attempting to cast doubt in the mind of your competitor, are you? I thought you were better than that.'

She gave him a brazen smile. 'A girl has to try.'

But she had no idea how to try. Not a clue. If she did she'd be using her body the way most women did to get what they wanted. She'd waggle that cute behind and wear a low-cut shirt and distract him that way.

Just like Tamara had. She'd used her body as bait and reeled him in, hook, line and sinker. Then she'd had him for dinner, emotionally and financially.

But Emily wasn't Tamara. Far from it.

He'd only ever seen Emily in overly big uniforms or baggy casual gear. Tonight, for the first time, he'd more than glimpsed the surprisingly curvaceous body that nestled beneath. A body that deserved to be on show instead of hidden away under questionable clothing choices.

He'd always imagined she would have a dumpy body—the clothes she wore certainly gave that impression. But, truth be told, he'd never really imagined anything much about her until recently. Emily was Emily—great nurse, great fun, a mate, just like one of the boys.

The memory of her cleavage and cute behind lit up in his mind. *One of the boys? I don't think so.*

Emily, it seemed, was all woman. So why was she hiding herself?

'Hurry up!' She nudged him gently in the ribs with her elbow. 'A quick game's a good game.'

He peered down at her, using his height to humorously intimidate her. 'You want to be beaten quickly, do you? Get the pain over with sooner?'

'You are *so* dreaming.' Amusement danced across her cheeks.

He pocketed another ball. 'Is that so?'

She took a long look at the table and spun her forefinger around her necklace. 'I think your dream run is just about over, mate.'

He studied the lie of the balls. He hated to admit it, but she might be right. All the low balls had rolled close to the pockets. He picked up the cue bridge and put it in position.

'Tricky shot, that one.' She grinned unashamedly.

At a high angle he tapped the white ball gently. It clipped one of Emily's balls and tumbled into the pocket. 'Blast.' But the word lacked conviction. For some strange reason his usual desire to win had ebbed, and he didn't really mind that he'd missed the shot.

Now you get to watch her play. He shook away the foolish thought. 'Over to you.'

'Now let me show *you* how it's done.' She spun her cue in her hands and chuckled, a husky, vibrato sound that whipped around him, searing and sultry.

Heat slammed through him.

She put away ball after ball, looking up after each success, tossing him merciless smiles as her eyes sent silver lights cascading over him. The black eight disappeared with a thud.

He'd never enjoyed being beaten so much.

He got the balls ready for another game. 'This time you won't be so lucky.'

'Lin, darling, here you are.' Penelope wrinkled her nose as she picked her way through the crowd. 'I thought we were meeting in the dining room?' She tilted her cheek toward him for an expected kiss.

Hell. He'd completely forgotten about Penelope. He gave her a perfunctory kiss. 'Sorry, Pen. I was helping out Baden Tremont.'

She glanced around. 'Really?'

'Yes, and he did such a good job.' Emily's eyebrows shot to her hairline as her eyes crinkled in a smile. 'He just lost at pool.'

Penelope frowned and glanced between the two of them as if she was missing something. 'How is that doing well?'

'Ah, well, the loser has to donate twenty dollars to the Flying Doctors.'

Linton pulled out his wallet. 'Hey, you told Baden the kitty was ten dollars.'

Emily laid her cue on the table. 'True, but that's 'cos he's on staff. You're not and foreigners pay more.' Her stare challenged him to dispute her.

He knew she was making this up on the spot, but he was hardly going to complain seeing as the money was for a worthy cause. He tilted his head toward hers. 'Don't forget, you're a foreigner too now you've crossed to the dark side of Warragurra Base.' He pressed the orange bill into her hand.

She stilled for a brief moment and then laughed. 'Ah, but I'm on loan, remember. I'm not exclusively yours.'

Her fingers trailed along his palm as she curled her fingers around the note. A spark of tingling heat shot along his arm.

Penelope tugged at his sleeve. 'We need to go.' Her voice sounded unusually sharp.

'Enjoy your dinner.' Emily's friendly wishes sent Linton on his way.

'We will.' Penelope hooked her arm through his, her voice almost purring.

He glanced over his shoulder as they left the bar and saw Emily chatting vivaciously with Jason. His gut clenched. What the hell was going on with him tonight? He had a beautiful woman on his arm and an entertaining night ahead of him.

So why did he feel like he was walking away from something he'd miss?

CHAPTER FIVE

EMILY vigorously rubbed the whiteboard clean. 'Top job, everyone. We've cleared the place quickly today.' She smiled at Jason and Patti, who were starting to exhibit signs that one day they really would be good doctors. 'You can go for tea as soon as Jodie gets back.'

'Great.' Jason exchanged a look with Patti and turned back to face Emily. 'When we get back, will you have time to help us with suturing? We're in a bit of a mess with our foam arm.'

'Sure, give me a shout when you get back and we'll run over it. It can be confusing at first.'

'What can?' Linton appeared as if out of the blue, a pile of folders in his arms.

Emily turned and focused on smiling. At the same time she tried to settle the run of funny beats that her heart whipped off whenever she heard his voice. He had this habit of 'just appearing', and each time her already frayed nerves unravelled a bit more.

'Suturing can be tricky. Jason and Patti are after another demo. You're not looking too frantic.'

He tapped his folders. 'Sorry, I've got a meeting. Besides, they're better off with you.' He glanced over her head at the students. 'Emily's stitches are so neat she probably won cross-stitch awards at the Warragurra Show.'

Her adolescence flashed before her, absent of all girlish pursuits, no matter how much she might have longed for them. Her mother's death had left her in a male world, making being a girly-girl almost impossible. 'Now, that would be a snap gender judgement, Dr Gregory.' She neatened up a pile of notepads, lining up the corners and tapping the sides together. 'As a teenager I was too busy branding cattle and drenching sheep to be crocheting doilies.'

She shook her head and caught a glimpse of emerald eyes watching her carefully, their gaze questioning. She instantly realised that, instead of her tone being flippant and dismissive, the words had come out full of regret.

'My mother died when I was ten and Dad wasn't into crafts.' The words rushed out before she could stop them. Why had she felt the need to tell him that? She quickly cleared her throat and turned back to Jason and Patti. 'Right, then. I can see Jodie just walking in so you two shoo to tea.'

The students walked off and Emily continued to tidy up around Linton, who had perched himself in the middle of the desk. She could feel his stare on her.

He spoke softly. 'I'm sorry, I didn't realise you'd lost your mum at such a young age.'

She bit her lip and gave a brief nod, acknowledging that she'd heard him. She really didn't want to talk about this—not now in the middle of the A and E. She pulled open the filing cabinet. 'It's almost two o'clock, you'll be late for your meeting.'

'Are you pushing me out of my own department?' He grinned his easy, bone-melting smile.

Rivers of yearning rolled through her, pulling at every barricade she'd erected in her attempt to stay immune to him. *Immune.* What a joke.

But joking was part of her repertoire to stay strong. 'Yes, I'm pushing you out. Surely you knew when you hired me that I didn't like doctors cluttering up the place? We've no patients so you're not needed.'

He gave her a hangdog look. 'That's a bit harsh.'

She laughed. 'You should have thought of that before you bribed me to work here. Go to your meeting or you might just end up dusted and filed.'

His eyes darkened to a deep jade. 'That could be fun.'

The phone rang as her cheeks burned at his blatant flirting. She'd promised herself she wasn't going down that path but Linton made it all too easy to take the wrong road. As she picked up the phone she mouthed, 'Go,' and pointed to the door.

He tugged his forelock and walked out, whistling.

'A and E. Emily Tippett speaking.'

'Em, it's Trix Baxter.' The school nurse from Warragurra High School spoke down the line. 'I'm just pulling up outside now with Samantha Joseph. She sort of collapsed at netball and went over on her ankle. She might have blacked out but she needs to be checked out. Can you bring out a wheelchair?'

'Be there in a sec, Trix.' Emily hung up the phone and walked toward the doors with a wheelchair.

She met a tall teenager coming toward her, hopping and leaning heavily on Trix's arm.

'I guess you must be Samantha. I'm Emily. Take a seat.' She put the brakes on the wheelchair.

Breathless and pale, Samantha grimaced and then lowered herself into the chair with Emily's help. 'Thanks.'

Trix frowned. 'Sorry, Emily, but I have to get back to school and we haven't been able to contact Sam's mother.'

Emily swung the wheelchair around. 'Don't worry. Leave all the contact details with Reception and they'll keep trying.'

'Thanks.' Trix bent down next to Samantha. 'Sam, they'll look after you here. I'm sure it's just a bad sprain but it's best to get it X-rayed.' She patted her arm.

'Thanks, Mrs Baxter.' The girl closed her eyes as if the effort to speak was almost too much.

'Let's get you inside and have a good look at this ankle.' Emily briskly pushed the wheelchair into A and E. 'What position were you playing?'

'Goal defence.' The girl's hands fidgeted in her lap.

Emily helped her up onto the trolley. 'We'll have to put you into one of those totally gorgeous hospital gowns for the X-ray.' She smiled, trying to relax the girl. 'But first of all we'll get you some ice for the ankle and some pain relief so that it won't hurt so much to get undressed.'

'OK.' She suddenly looked a lot younger than her fifteen years.

Emily quickly grabbed the blue sports-injury ice pack from the fridge, wrapped it in a towel and came back into the cubicle. 'I'll just put this on your ankle.' She rested her hand on the bottom of Sam's tracksuit pants and went to pull them up.

'Leave them, I'm cold.' Sam leaned forward, her hands sitting firmly on the hems of her pants, as if she didn't want the material slid up her leg. 'Can't the ice pack just sit on the top of my ankle?'

'Sure.' Emily put it in place, surprised at the sudden energy the previously lethargic girl showed.

'OK, now I need to do some observations. First your pulse.' She pulled her fob watch out of her pocket.

The girl stuck out her arm, her fine wrist looking ludicrously tiny peeking out of an oversized rugby top.

A rapid beat pulsed under Emily's fingers. She started counting. The fast throb jumped against her fingers. She frowned and continued counting. It jumped again. 'Sam, did you black out on the netball court?'

'Dunno.' She stared at the wall, avoiding Emily's eyes.

She probed gently, needing information but not wanting to upset the girl. 'Did you feel dizzy or light-headed?'

Sam spoke quickly. 'I think I just got bumped too hard.' Her left hand started to finger the edge of the blanket, a red rash on her fingertips obvious against the pale wool.

Emily's radar went on alert. Something odd was going on. She flicked on the cardiac monitor and sorted out the leads. 'We're going to have to put that hospital gown on a bit earlier than I thought, Sam.' She held up a packet of dots. 'I need to put these on your chest so I can see your heartbeat on the monitor.'

'I want to keep my own clothes on.' Sam's mouth pouted in displeasure.

'You can put your rugby top back on over the gown.' She helped the girl lean forward and assisted her in pulling the top over her head. The netball top came off with it.

Shock reverberated through every part of Emily as she worked to stall the gasp in her throat. Every rib of Sam's body pushed her thin skin out and her scapulas protruded. Not a trace of covering fat existed.

Acting as if she hadn't noticed, she quickly helped the girl's stick-like arms into the sleeves of the gown.

'I'm cold,' Sam complained.

'I'll have you warm in a minute and you can wear your jacket over the gown as well as being tucked up in a blanket.'

She quickly attached the dots, connected the leads and plugged in the monitor.

The ECG blipped reassuringly as each beat of the heart traced across the screen in bright green waves, showing a normal sinus rhythm.

Perhaps she'd imagined the irregular pulse. 'You can put your top back on now.' Emily turned the sleeves the right way round and passed it to her. The machine suddenly beeped rapidly.

'What's that?' Sam glanced anxiously at the monitor.

'Your heart just gave off an odd beat. 'Do you feel funny?'

'No.' Fear lit the young girl's eyes.

'Well, that's good, but I'm just going to get Dr Gregory to have a look at you.' She passed the buzzer. 'Call me if you need me but I'll be back in a minute.'

She strode quickly to the desk, picked up the phone and punched the number of Linton's mobile into the keypad.

He answered immediately, his crisp, professional voice reassuring her as well as giving her own heart some funny beats. She tried to sound equally crisp and professional. 'Linton, I've got a fifteen-year-old throwing off ectopic beats.'

He didn't hesitate. 'I'm on my way.'

Instantly, the phone went dead in her ear. She phoned Reception. 'Tracey, I need Samantha Joseph's history asap and have you got onto her parents yet?'

'I'm bringing the history round and we've left messages for the mother.' Tracey's efficiency made life in A and E much easier.

'Thanks, Trace.' She dropped the phone into the cradle and jogged into the supply room, picking up a saline drip and setting up an IV trolley.

'So you got rid of me too early, then?'

She swung around and caught Linton's teasing smile and flash of white teeth. 'So it seems. Samantha Joseph came in with a sprained ankle after collapsing at netball, but my concern is that she's throwing off a few extra heartbeats.' She pushed the trolley toward the door. 'Come and see what you think.'

Linton ushered her into the cubicle and greeted their patient. 'Hi, Samantha, I'm Linton Gregory, and I'm the doctor on duty today. Emily tells me you've been in the wars.' He smiled his golden smile. 'Tough game, netball.'

Samantha giggled and batted her eyelashes while her heart rate visibly leapt on the monitor.

Emily silently groaned. She knew her own heart rate did a similar thing when Linton smiled at her—the man charmed every woman in sight. It was what he did with effortless ease. She'd had to work so hard being casual and friendly to get Samantha to co-operate and all Linton had to do was smile.

'I just want to listen to your lungs so if you can pull up your top, I'll make sure the stethoscope's warmed up.'

'OK.'

Sam leaned forward with such unexpected compliance that Emily hardly recognised her as she helped her lift her top.

Shock, frustration and pity scored Linton's normal urbane face as he caught sight of Sam's desperately thin frame. He listened intently to her air entry, which Emily knew was really an excuse to examine her back and view the evidence that this girl was indeed starving.

He swung his stethoscope around his neck. 'That sounds fine. Now, what about this ankle?' He pushed up her track-suit pants and placed his large, tanned hands around her ankle, feeling for broken bones. But again Emily knew it was also a chance to examine her legs for signs of self-harm. 'I don't think you've broken it.'

He leaned his arms casually against the cot-side of the trolley and stared intently at the monitor.

'Coupled premature ventricular complex?' Emily wanted confirmation that she was actually seeing the paired abnormal beats, as there had been a long period since that last couplet.

Linton nodded slowly, his brow furrowed in thought. 'They're just occasional so we'll monitor her for now.'

He turned back to Sam. 'Your ankle will be fine. I'm actually more worried about the funny little beats of your heart.'

'Why would it be doing that?'

He breathed in deeply. 'That's what we want to find out. Emily's going to take some blood and put a drip in your arm.'

'Oh, are you going?' Sam's crestfallen expression radiated dismay.

'You can't get rid of me that easily.' He gave her an easy smile and pressed a button to print a readout from the monitor.

Sam caught sight of Emily opening the IV cannula onto the sterile field of the dressing pack. 'Will it hurt?'

He ripped the printout off the monitor. 'Nah, I'll keep my questions as painless as possible.'

Sam laughed and Emily slipped the tourniquet onto the girl's arm, tightening it to find a vein. Linton would keep Sam distracted while she took the blood.

Linton focused his attention back onto Sam. 'Have you been feeling sick lately?'

'A bit. I feel sick when I eat.' She glanced at Emily, who was swabbing her arm.

Linton nodded, his expression one of understanding. 'In the mornings or all day?'

'All day.'

'Have you been feeling sick for a long time?'

'A few months. Ouch!'

Emily released the tourniquet as she withdrew the trocar from the cannula. 'Sorry, but that's it. I've taken the blood and the IV is in.' She passed the blood vial to Jodie, who had arrived to run the specimen to the lab.

'Have you been eating much at all?' Linton stayed on task, chipping away.

The clack of high heels sounded on the floor. 'I want to see her now!'

Jodie's placating voice sounded in the distance and then the curtains moved and a well-dressed woman in a black suit appeared.

'Darling, are you all right?' The woman rushed to Sam's side and picked up her hand. Then she took in Emily and Linton. 'I'm Rachel, Sam's mum. What's wrong with her?'

'That's what we're trying to work out.' Linton continued smoothly, 'I was just wondering if Sam had been eating enough.'

Rachel sighed. 'She's like every teenage girl. She won't eat breakfast but she eats a good lunch and dinner, don't you, darling?' She stroked Sam's hair.

For the first time Sam dropped her gaze from Linton's but she didn't look at her mother. She mumbled, 'I eat enough.'

The monitor screeched as Sam's heart threw off a series of arrhythmias, the high line dipping low rather than soaring high. 'Ventricular tachycardia?' Anxiety fluttered in Emily's gut.

Linton's brow creased in a worried frown. 'Bigeminal PVCs. Give her two grams of potassium chloride in one hundred millilitres of saline over an hour through an infusion pump. Let's try and head ventricular tachycardia off at the pass.'

'What about lignocaine to soothe vein irritation?' Emily snapped open the ampoule of KCL.

'Good idea.' Linton wrote up the drug order.

'What's happening?' Rachel's distressed voice sounded loud in the small area.

'We think that Sam's very low on potassium and that's affecting her heart. It's causing the large chamber of her heart, the ventricle, to have these funny beats.' He pointed to the monitor showing the wider beats with the negative drops.

The mother's eyes widened in disbelief. 'Potassium? I don't understand. She's never had anything wrong with her heart.'

Emily injected the KCL into the burette and titrated the drip flow through the pump. She shot Linton a knowing look. Rachel had no idea about Sam's anorexia.

Linton put his hand on the scared girl's arm. 'I believe you when you say you eat enough.'

Sam's shoulders relaxed and she gave Linton a coy smile.

Linton's tone stayed gentle but firm. 'But your body is missing a lot of nutrients and you're very, very thin. So for us to help you, I need you to be honest with me. Have you been using laxatives so that what you eat gets quickly out of your body?'

Sam looked down, pulling at a loose thread on the blanket and unravelling the blanket stitch.

Rachel slumped into the chair by the trolley, still holding her daughter's hand. 'Honey, please, tell us. No one is going to get cross.'

Tears formed slowly and spilled down Sam's cheeks. 'I had to. You made me eat. I'm fat and this is the only way for me to be pretty.'

Emily's heart contracted in pain. Being pretty was everything at fifteen. The taunting voices of high school echoed in her mind. *Hey, Ranga! With that hair and those freckles, no guy will ever think you're hot.*

And they hadn't. She'd never dated until she'd gone to university and even then the only person to beat a path to her door had been Nathan.

He'd reinforced every taunt she'd tried to put behind her. A sigh shuddered through as the memory of Nathan's sarcastic eyes seared her soul, his snarling voice booming in her head. *You're not exactly model material, are you?*

She caught Linton staring at her, his gaze too intent for comfort and his frown disapproving. She immediately covered her reaction by checking the drip.

Linton blinked and turned toward Rachel. 'We're going to admit Samantha and get her electrolytes sorted out. Then we can discuss her ongoing care with regard to her anorexia, which will probably involve a transfer to Sydney.'

Rachel shook her head, as if the action would help her take in the situation. 'I didn't realise...'

Linton's sympathetic glance took in mother and daughter. 'I'll go and arrange for admittance and be back to talk to you soon.'

'Jodie will be here, monitoring you, and ring the bell any time.' Emily squeezed Rachel's shoulder and followed Linton toward the desk, but he kept going to his office. Surprised, she followed him.

'Close the door.' He threw the command over his shoulder as he slammed Sam's history down onto the desk. 'Damn it, the kid's skeletal.'

His anger and frustration buffeted Emily. She understood his sense of hopelessness that in a country where food existed in overabundance this girl had chosen to starve. 'She must have been purging herself for months.'

He sat down hard, his hand raking through his hair. 'How could she possibly think that to be that thin is beautiful? I blame this celebrity culture and obsession with perfection.'

She sat on the edge of his desk. 'That's a bit too simplistic, don't you think? I think it starts a lot closer to home.' The words sounded overly definite and loud in the small room.

Linton's gaze swung around and centred exclusively on her—his green eyes penetrating way too deeply. 'How so?'

Her heart started to pound. Hell, somehow she'd just sparked his attention. No way was she going to tell Linton about Nathan. She tried to sound detached, as if she was giving an academic and professional opinion on any medical topic and not one that related to her.

'Teenagers are vulnerable as they try and work out who they are and how they fit into the world. Take someone who feels they have little control over their life. Combine that with being unhappy at how they look and add in a thoughtless, throw-away comment by someone in the family or a friend, constant teasing at school, and that can result in anorexia or bulimia.'

'Surely one comment wouldn't do it? It would have to be a bullying-type thing.' His brow creased in confusion, as if he was having problems accepting her statement.

She twisted a strand of hair around her finger as visions of her mid to late teenage years assaulted her. 'Studies have shown one comment can do it. A person can latch onto that comment and never let it go, never really see it in perspective. Or it could be a collection of random comments, building up on top of each other.'

Suddenly sympathy radiated from his eyes. 'Did that happen to you?'

His unexpected question suddenly made her academic

musings seem personal. Personal would lead to Nathan and that sent fear spiralling through her. She didn't want to see the same pity in his eyes for herself that she'd just seen reflected for Sam.

Her head whirled, trying to come up with the best way to deflect his question. Perhaps, if she gave him a snippet of her life at fifteen, that would satisfy him and he'd stop asking questions. She lifted her chin and tossed her head, her curls bouncing into her eyes. 'At fifteen I was voted least likely to be kissed by my peers, and my dad confiscated my make-up.'

Linton stiffened, as if his hand had just brushed a hot iron, and gave a tight smile. 'That sounds like the standard behaviour of some teenage girls and the normal behaviour of an over-protective father freaking out when he realised his only daughter was growing up.' His brow furrowed. 'I think you know that.'

A niggle of guilt pulled at her gut that she'd flippantly disregarded the sympathy in his original question. But she ignored it by speaking to his shoulder and avoiding his eyes. 'Let's add on my eldest brother covering my bikini and me in a woolsack. He marched me out of the dam and back to the house, hiding me from every shearer and cowboy on the station.' She crossed her arms. 'It's these sorts of things that add up.'

He narrowed his eyes, which sparked like jade. 'I think that now as an adult you know that your brothers were protecting you from the prying eyes of older, single men. Both your examples tell me you have a loving family.'

Her heart started to hammer as he sliced through her examples. She hated it that he was so perceptive. 'But it's things like this that for some kids spark off anorexia and bulimia.' The words hung defiantly between them.

'True.' He reached out his hand and lightly touched her arm. 'But I think you've told me those two stories to avoid telling me the real story.'

Her breath seemed solidify in her lungs, refusing to move in or out as the caring caress of his hand jumbled her emotions, tugging at her resolve. Memories of Nathan—vicious and soul destroying—oozed out of the deep, dark place she'd thought she successfully contained them. Beads of sweat clung to her hairline as the recollections she'd thought she'd dealt with and accepted hammered her, delivering the same sharp sting as when they'd first been inflicted.

She stood up abruptly, needing to break the contact. Needing to distance herself from the siren call of his touch. 'There is no real story.'

'I don't believe you.' He spoke softly, but the words rained down on her like hailstones, hard and painful.

She swung round, angry that he wouldn't let the topic go. 'I am *not* anorexic.'

He raised his brows. 'But you have been?'

'No.' She flung the word at him laden with hurt. 'I have never been anorexic or bulimic, and why is this conversation suddenly all about me rather than Sam?'

'Because you're hiding your body behind baggy clothes just like that fifteen-year-old, and I want to know why.'

'I dress for comfort!' She marched toward the door, needing to leave and put an end to this conversation. Her hand reached for the handle.

'You dress to bury any signs of being a woman.'

She breathed in sharply, the accuracy of his words slicing into her like a scalpel dividing skin. *Nathan's legacy.* No one else had ever deduced that she hid her body behind shapeless clothes.

Humiliation clawed at her and she wanted to sink through the floor. But she couldn't. She summoned up righteous anger, the only thing that could save her.

How dared he talk to her like that? He had no right at all. She welcomed the surge of fury that rocked through her as it numbed the pain. She spun around, her hands on her hips. 'That is complete nonsense and I need to get back to my patient.'

He checked his watch. 'Jodie is with her and technically you're off duty. But you can leave when you tell me that what I said was incorrect.'

Resentment fizzed in her veins. 'What you said was way out of line. You're my boss and you're out of order with this.'

'I'm also your friend, Emily.'

His earnest look and tone hit her like a medicine ball to the belly. Gone was every sign of the flirting, fun-loving doctor.

He splayed his fingers, palms upward in supplication. 'I get the strongest feeling something has happened to you, only I'm not sure it happened at fifteen. But whatever it is, it's trapping you.' His head moved slightly, the blond tips of his hair shining in the light. 'I want to help.'

She'd never told anyone about her year with Nathan—not her darling father or her teasing but supportive brothers. She'd been too embarrassed, too ashamed. And they'd never asked—at least, not with words. She'd been able to ignore their looks of concern when she'd returned home from uni and as she'd thrown herself into work, life had gone on. It was as if there'd been a tacit agreement that no one spoke about her time in Dubbo.

But Linton's concerned gaze bored into her. She could withstand his teasing, she could mock his flirting behaviour, but this sincerity eroded all her resolve to keep everything to herself.

Her legs suddenly gave way and she abruptly sat down, every part of her aching that he'd seen through her. She hated it that he was the *one* person who had. Now she had nowhere to hide and the galling truth had to be told. 'I accepted a while ago it was best to hide what was offensive.'

The raw pain in her voice stabbed Linton in the chest. 'What are you talking about?'

'Me.' She kept her eyes staring down as she twisted open a paperclip, straightening the wire.

'What about you?' A thousand thoughts whizzed through his mind. What was she hiding? Was she scarred from burns? Did she have a florid birthmark?

'I... Not everyone is blessed with an attractive body.'

He shook his head in disbelief, trying to shake her words into coherence. 'You think you don't have an attractive body?'

'I *know* that I don't.' Her head snapped up, her eyes glittering with daring and defiance. 'So now you've dragged that out of me and completely mortified me, you can let the subject drop, right?'

A streak of remorse twinged but he knew he had to ignore it. He couldn't stop now—he had to get to the bottom of this. The image of creamy breasts and pert buttocks that he'd glimpsed at the Royal rolled out in his mind. 'No, sorry, I can't let the subject drop. Why on earth do you think your body is unattractive?'

A shuddering sigh resonated around the room. 'You get told something often enough, you can't ignore it.'

'Who told you?' The words came out on a growl despite his intentions to sound neutral.

She dropped her gaze and her body started to shiver.

He spoke softly this time. 'Emily?'

Her hands fisted in her lap. 'A boyfriend at uni found me lacking in many attributes.'

Anger curled in his gut at the unknown man. 'This guy sounds like a complete jerk.'

For a moment her lips curved up slightly and the Emily he knew so well almost surfaced. 'I see you've met him.'

He wanted to open her eyes to this guy. 'But he was just *one* guy with *one* opinion.'

She dropped her chin, her hair falling forward, masking her expression, but he caught a glimpse of pearly white teeth nibbling her plump bottom lip.

Heat slammed into him. Hell, what was wrong with him? He pulled his concentration back. He was supposed to be helping her, not imagining what her lips would taste like. 'Other boyfriends must have cancelled out his attitude.'

'He was the *only* guy.' The mumbled words were barely audible.

Her pain rocked through him and he worried he might have pushed her too hard. He suddenly realised she might not have told anyone about this. 'I know it seems tough right now but talking about it will help.'

A moment later she raised her head, her eyes filled with a mixture of defiance and shame. 'I guess starting at the beginning works best.' She hauled in a deep breath. 'I left home at eighteen to study nursing. I was pretty naïve and definitely inexperienced, and I met Nathan toward the end of my second year. He was the first man who had ever shown any interest in me and...' She shrugged and swallowed hard. 'I guess he swept me off my feet. I remember it all happened very fast and we suddenly went from two dates a week apart to being together most of the time.'

His radar went on full alert. 'Did he pay you a lot of attention and shower you with gifts?'

'At the start, yes. He used to text me on the hour, he took me out to dinner, bought me flowers and chocolates. Then he started buying me clothes and no one had ever done anything like that for me. At first it was intoxicating to be the centre of attention when I'd always felt overlooked by men.' She looked straight at him, surprise on her face. 'How did you know he did that? Do you have a crystal ball?'

His gut turned over, aching for her. 'No, but I've met guys like that.' *Treated the women they've left emotionally damaged.*

She jabbed the paperclip onto the edge of the desk. 'By Christmas we were a couple and I was head over heels in love. He visited the station during my summer holidays. When I returned for my final year of study he suggested I move in. He said the rent would be less and I could give up my part-time job and focus on uni. Final year is pretty full on with study and practicals and he convinced me it would be a solution to make my life easier. He even turned the third bedroom into a study for me.'

'I could see how that would be tempting,' Linton murmured encouragingly. He worried she might not want to continue.

She blew out a long breath. 'That was when things started to change. He insisted on picking me up from the hospital, driving me to uni, basically not letting me be alone. He bought me clothes, suggested what I should wear. At first it seemed special, that a man would take such an interest. But then his behaviour started to be unpredictable especially if I didn't wear what he had bought.'

A shudder vibrated through her. 'There were times when

everything was as wonderful as when we first met, but they got further apart and more times than not I didn't recognise him. Like the day he cut up the dress I'd bought to wear to a friend's twenty-first.'

Anger, raw and primitive, blasted through him so hard that had he been standing he would have been knocked off his feet. This low-life had used vicious verbal abuse to crush a young woman who should have been blossoming into womanhood and discovering her own brand of sexuality.

Somehow he managed to sound calm. 'And when he acted irrationally he always blamed you. Men like that don't love, they only want to control.'

Her grey eyes filmed over and she blinked rapidly, nodding her head 'Pretty much. It was so confusing. I wanted to be attractive for him, I wanted to make him happy—I loved him—but no matter what I did, it was wrong. I was never pretty enough, I was never appreciative enough and…'

Her head shot up, her face suddenly full of strength. 'The day I found him in our bed with another student, I left.'

He reached out and picked up her hand. 'Good for you. You're far too good for a worm like him.' But although she'd walked away from this low-life, he could tell she still had the scars.

Emily smiled a wobbly smile. 'Thanks, but I'm OK. You don't have to try and make me feel better.'

I think I do. He had to make her realise she was attractive. Had to try and undo some of the low-life's conditioning. Sure, she wasn't his type of woman but she needed to know that she had qualities that deserved to be showcased. 'What he said about you not being attractive is wrong. Don't you think that four years is long enough to hold onto false impressions?'

A thousand different emotions swirled in her eyes and marched across her face, but fear dominated. She pulled her hand out from under his.

'You're twenty-five now, Emily. It's time to come out of the shadows.'

She twisted on her chair and flung him a derisive look. 'I'll put it on my "to do" list.'

If he let her leave now, nothing would be sorted out. She'd never take the risk. He had to force her to take that step. An idea suddenly exploded in his head. Sure, it wasn't quite what he'd planned but an evening with Emily wouldn't be hard. And he knew Emily never walked away from a dare.

He pulled open his top drawer and plucked out an envelope. 'The Red Cross Desperate and Dateless Ball is on this weekend.'

Her shoulders shot back, her scrubs pulling against her breasts, and her eyes widened, indignation flashing brightly. 'I am not desperate.'

He ignored the zip of sensation that zeroed in on his groin. She had no idea how sexy she looked when she got all fired up. He forced himself to lean back, to act casually. 'You're not dateless either. I dare you to come with me in a little black dress.'

Her hand immediately fisted in her hair, her forefinger tugging at a curl, winding the purple strands around it.

He glimpsed panic before it receded, quickly replaced by a spark of defiance.

Silently, she rose to her feet and walked to the door. She turned as her hand clasped the handle. 'I'll think about it and be in touch.'

She disappeared behind the door, the only evidence that she'd been in the room was the waft of perfume she'd left behind.

He couldn't believe he'd misread her, that she wouldn't rise to his dare. The axis of his world shifted slightly as disappointment, sharp and unexpected, churned his gut.

CHAPTER SIX

'So how's the new job with Linton working out?' Emily's friend and Flying Doctors nurse Kate Tremont put a cup of steaming hot Earl Grey tea down on a coaster.

Emily groaned and buried her head in her arms, leaning against Kate's large jarrah kitchen table.

'That good, huh?'

She looked up into smiling brown eyes and forced herself to sit up. 'The work part is fine.'

Kate shot her a calculating look. 'Is there actually some truth to Baden's theory, then, that you fancy Linton?'

She almost choked on her tea. What on earth had happened to her? For years she'd kept everything to herself but just lately she'd said things that opened her up to difficult questions. Her embarrassing yet strangely cathartic conversation with Linton had rolled through her head almost continuously for three days straight. Now Kate was onto her.

'Emily?' Kate's expression had changed from calculating to concerned. 'Is everything OK?'

Emily sighed. 'Do you have any chocolate-coated teddy-bear biscuits? If I have to tell you this story I'm going to need chocolate.'

Kate rose gracefully and rummaged through the pantry.

'Even better, I have Florentines from the bakery.' She quickly put them on a square white dish and placed them in front of Emily. 'Will three be enough?'

Emily grinned. 'Plenty.' Kate was a good friend and Emily had been thrilled when she'd married Baden Tremont, finding happiness after such a dark time in her life. She wished she'd known such a friend when she'd been younger, when she'd been in Dubbo.

'So?' Kate nibbled on a Florentine.

She took a deep breath. 'So, Linton asked me to the Desperate and Dateless Ball.'

Kate leaned forward. 'Excellent. And you're going?'

Emily ran her finger around the rim of the teacup. 'I told him I'd think about it but really I meant no.'

'And the reason for that would be…?'

She bit her lip and pushed on. 'Because he dared me to wear a dress.'

Kate's forehead creased in a frown. 'But isn't that the sort of thing you'd be wearing anyway?'

Panic swished through her stomach. 'This is *me* we're talking about, Kate. Jeans, jumpers and boots, the occasional voluminous dress—practical clothes.'

'And that's fine for the farm, Em, but not for a ball.' Kate folded her arms and fixed her with a penetrating look. 'What are you really worried about?'

Her fear rushed out, tumbling over the words. 'That I'll look ridiculous. I've never done anything like this before and I'm not designed for elegance, I'm—'

'Nonsense.' Kate's hand hit the table with a loud slap. 'We just need to find you the right dress to show off what you've got.'

I don't have anything. Part of her wanted to believe Kate

but most of her didn't. 'Oh, right, and Warragurra's one dress shop is going to have that dress? I don't think so, which is why I have to say no.' She glared at Kate. 'I will *not* make a fool of myself.'

'I won't let you do that.' The quiet words were delivered with feeling.

And she knew Kate spoke the truth. Tall and graceful, she had an innate sense of style and Emily knew she'd be in good hands. For a moment the sincerity in Kate's voice reassured her, but then the terrors instilled by Nathan rose again. *Cover yourself up, you don't want to put people off their dinner.*

Linton's warm voice vibrated inside her. *Men like that don't love, they only want to control.* She tried to hold onto that thought, pushing Nathan's legacy out.

'Do you want to snag Linton's attention and have him see you in a new way, not as Unit Manager, not as a friend, but as a woman?'

Her stomach churned, driving acid to the back of her throat. 'I… Well, part of me does.' *But what if I'm a disappointment?* That fear had plagued her since high school and more so since she'd left Nathan. It had held her back from ever thinking about another relationship.

Kate smiled. 'Then the solution is easy. We're going to Sydney and we're buying a dress.'

The sensation of being on a runaway train exploded inside her and she scrambled for some control. 'I can't just go to Sydney.' Her voice rose a little higher on each word.

'Sure you can. We've both got days off. I'll book the flights now. Sasha can come with us, she'll love an excuse to shop in Sydney.' Kate clapped in delight. 'It will be a girls' day out, and as Linton dared you to wear the dress, he can pay.'

Kate handed Emily the phone. 'Ring him now and tell him you're going to the ball.'

Kate's eyes glinted with determination and Emily knew right there and then that there was no way out. She'd never realised Cinderella's fairy godmother must have doubled as a bulldozer.

Emily stood shaking in black, lacy underwear, sheer stockings and high heels, staring at the little black dress she'd gone to Sydney to buy. She wished Kate and Sasha Tremont were standing with her right now. Kate had insisted this was *the* dress. Sasha, at twelve, had wanted her to buy the one with the large pink bow.

When she'd baulked at the dress Kate had run roughshod over every excuse and had declared this to be the dress to impress. A traitorous part of her *so* wanted to impress that she'd given in entirely and gone with Kate's choice.

Linton's comments about Nathan had bolstered her confidence into a shaky self-belief. Perhaps Nathan had been wrong. His words still played in her head but the volume was low and the sound quality buzzed with static.

But now with Linton about to arrive, panic clawed at her. What had she let Kate and Linton talk her into? She stared at her reflection, not recognising the person staring back. Her carefully styled hair curved around her face and her make-up looked straight out of a magazine, courtesy of the beautician who had written down detailed instructions for her.

The dress was the last piece of the puzzle.

Putting it on was technically the easy part. Facing her father and her brothers, facing Linton, had her stomach doing continuous somersaults.

Her fingers fumbled as she fastened her mother's pearls

around her neck. It didn't matter that she was twenty-five, didn't matter that she was an experienced nurse—she couldn't walk out there. What if she got the same reaction that Nathan had given her?

Her legs wobbled like jelly.

I dare you to come with me. Linton's teasing words echoed in her head again, just like they'd been doing for the last week.

'Hey, sis, there's a car coming up the drive.' Mark rapped on her door.

Her heart pounded so hard that she glanced down, expecting to see it moving against her chest. She couldn't do this. She couldn't go out there.

Her mouth dried at the alternative. Her father and brothers would demand to know why. Telling Linton about Nathan had been bad enough. She had to go out in this dress.

'Em, you OK?' Mark's muffled voice came under the door.

'Yes, fine.' She forced the words out against her constricted throat and reached for the dress.

With shaking fingers she slipped it over her head.

Linton bounded up the farmhouse steps, pulling on his dinner jacket at the same time. He'd been late getting away and he really regretted it. He had a niggling feeling that being ten minutes late could be enough to make Emily bail on him.

He'd been pleasantly surprised when he'd taken her phone call saying she'd come to the ball. And he'd laughed when she'd matched his dare by telling him he was paying for the dress. Parting with a few hundred dollars for a dress was a small price to pay if he could help her redefine herself.

He knew she'd bought a dress because he'd received a phone call from the exclusive Sydney Double Bay boutique.

But would she wear it? All day he'd half expected a text saying she wasn't coming.

The front door opened as he approached and a solid, middle-aged man extended his hand in greeting. 'Jim Tippett.'

'Linton Gregory.' He returned the strong handshake.

'Come in.' Jim stretched out his arm. 'Have you met Mark, Stuart and Eric, three of Emily's brothers?'

The men stood in a semi-circle, their wide-legged stance declaring this was their territory. They all nodded in silent greeting and shook his hand. Time rolled back to what he imagined life would have been like forty years ago. Linton had the distinct impression he was being assessed for suitability to date their sister.

'We thought you might have missed the turn-off in the dark.' Jim raised one reddish brow.

Linton read the code encrypted in the statement. *You're late—never make a woman wait.*

'Dad, ten minutes late means Linton is actually on time.'

All the men spun around toward the slightly husky voice. Emily stood at the edge of the room, clutching a tiny beaded evening bag, her eyes silver and hesitant.

Linton's breath stalled in his chest as a wave of heat thudded through him.

Her purple hair had vanished. Now Titian curls hovered around her cheeks, softening her face the way natural hair colour did. But her hair was only one change.

A fitted black lace bodice clung to more curves than he could ever have imagined existed under the sack-like clothes she normally wore. Bare, creamy shoulders teased the eye but the bombshell was the drop pearl necklace that nestled in the dip between her breasts, hinting at the generous softness that hid behind the dress.

A froth of tulle fell from a tiny waist, the layers finishing just below her knees. Shapely legs narrowed down to small feet, which were clad in strappy sandals, giving her extra height and an aura of elegance that he'd never associated with Emily.

The transformation stole all coherent thought.

'Who are you and what have you done with my sister?' Mark broke the stunned silence with a cheeky grin.

Jim beamed proudly. 'Don't listen to your brother. You're all grown up and you look as beautiful as your mother did the first time I met her.'

'Really?' Emily's tongue darted out and flicked at her glossy bottom lip.

Silver lights flashed danced in Linton's head as his blood pounded south.

'Of course you do.' Jim kissed her on the cheek and spoke again, this time his voice full of emotion. 'I probably should have told you that more often.' He turned abruptly to Linton, a chuckle on his lips. 'You all right, son?'

The words penetrated the inert haze of Linton's brain and he realised he'd been standing silently, staring like a fourteen-year-old. He propelled himself into action. He presented his arm to Emily. 'Your chariot awaits, Ms Tippett.'

She grinned and slid her arm through his, the slight weight of her arm fitting against his as if it had been made to sit there. As if it belonged there.

He immediately shrugged the feeling away.

Tonight was just an extension of work and Emily was his partner just for the evening.

The Royal's ballroom was almost unrecognisable. Red velvet fabric draped the furniture and red chiffon covered the walls, the filmy material softening the large area. Pearly red helium balloons filled the enormous ceiling space, their silver curling ribbon tails sparkling in the faux candlelight. Even the huge cherub ice statue was backlit by a red spotlight.

Linton took a break and drank some non-alcoholic fruit punch, which was, of course, red. He'd danced with almost every attractive woman at the ball, but he'd battled to get a passing glance from his partner for the evening. Far too many attentive cowboys were dancing with her. Ben McCreedy had held her very tightly with his good arm and Daniel and Jason had been acting like lust-struck puppies all night.

Oh, right, and you haven't?

The image of Emily standing hesitantly in her father's lounge room with the naked need of approval hovering in her eyes and a body that could have modelled swimwear had branded itself deeply in his mind. And it kept playing over and over and over.

He tugged at his collar, suddenly finding the bow-tie constricting. Funny, in Sydney he wore black tie once a fortnight and the tie had never bothered him. Usually he enjoyed these gala events where everyone dressed up and raised money for a worthwhile cause. Even though he hadn't been short of company tonight, his usual sense of freedom that came from numerous dance partners and plenty of conversation seemed to have deserted him. He rolled his shoulders back. It was like he had an unscratchable itch, making him prickly and out of sorts.

He scanned the room again for Emily, but without her signature bright hair she was harder to spot. He batted away some red helium balloons, which had started to hover lower, their tails hitting him across his face. He finally found her dancing with Baden.

He moved in, tapping the Flying Doctor's shoulder. 'Shouldn't you be dancing with your wife?'

Baden laughed. 'Well, I suppose as you paid for the dress, you should get at least one dance.' He spun Emily out of his arms and into Linton's.

Sparkling eyes appraised him with a familiar mocking glint as they swayed to a rock and roll tune. 'You've been busy tonight.'

A sliver of umbrage caught him. 'Hey, I could say the same thing about you.'

She laughed, the tone flirting and wicked. 'I was just keeping busy until there was a break in the queue of women wanting to dance with you. After all, I wouldn't want your reputation as Warragurra's resident playboy to be ruined by you dancing with me twice.' She spun out in a twirl.

He brought her back, his arm firm against her waist, her breasts brushing his chest. A tingle of sensation burned through him. 'My reputation will survive me dancing more than two dances.' *But will you?*

The voice in his head was forgotten as he caught a flash of surprise in her eyes. Hell, did she really think he hadn't wanted to dance with her? He'd tried many times to, but the line for her had been as constant as his own. Surely after the success of tonight she no longer thought she was unattractive?

He dropped his head close to hers, his chin almost resting on her shoulder, and whispered, 'And who knew you had red hair?'

She twirled out laughing and came back facing him, wrinkling her decidedly cute nose. 'Yeah, well, don't even think about going there. That was another torment in my life. Red hair *and* freckles.'

The music slowed and he felt her back stiffen as if she was

about to walk away. He tightened his arm and drew her fractionally closer. Even in heels her head would fit neatly under his chin if she wasn't holding her neck rigid with her chin pointed upward in that, oh, so familiar position.

Her perfume circled him, its sensual spice now so in tune with its wearer. 'You look completely sensational tonight.'

She stared up at him, her eyes like platinum pools. 'Thank you. And thanks for the dress.'

'My pleasure.' It was a standard response—one he used many times a day when he received thanks. Except the wave of uncomplicated happiness that rolled through him, followed by a trailing alien sense of wellbeing, was far from standard. Nothing about this night was standard.

Emily's brain struggled to keep up with everything that had happened from the moment she had stepped into the Royal's ballroom. It was like her world had been turned upside down and she was dizzy, trying to adjust to all the changes. Granted, she'd avoided social functions like this but even so she'd been stunned by the response she'd received from both men and women.

The men had wanted to dance with her. The woman had wanted to gossip about the dress. Kate had been right—the dress had impressed.

And Linton's gaze had been fixed on her for most of the evening. She wasn't a disappointment. A thrill of joy raced through her as she gave herself up to savouring the sensation of being held firmly in his arms.

He danced her out toward the veranda, away from the crowd, the music and the noise of two hundred people talking. The cool evening air washed over them as they twirled through the French doors.

He spun her around and she came to rest against him, her back against his chest, feeling his warmth radiating into her, the pressure of his arm across her waist. Feeling protected. Safe.

With sudden clarity she realised she'd felt that way with him ever since she'd told him about Nathan. He'd accepted her, had not judged her.

She turned in his arms and looked up into his smiling face, his scent of soap and citrus aftershave tingling in her nostrils as she breathed in. 'I almost didn't come tonight.'

He nodded, complete understanding radiating from his eyes. 'I know what a huge step this has been for you. Keep telling yourself this—Nathan is pond scum. Don't let his warped view taint you.' He tucked a stray curl behind her ear.

The light touch sent ribbons of wonder through her, both his actions and words bolstering her fledgling confidence. She realised that, despite her misgivings, telling Linton her story had actually helped her. Trusting him had been the best thing she'd done in four long years.

He was right—she had been hiding. She'd been holding back, holding back from life and keeping her attraction to him a secret. Scared of being a disappointment. But perhaps she didn't have to hide any more.

She gazed up at him, glorying in the look of undisguised desire in his eyes. At that very moment she knew he wanted to kiss her.

And she had no objection at all.

Linton gazed down into her upturned face. Her cheeks glowed pink, luminous grey eyes sparkled with silver, and slightly parted red lips shone like a beacon, daring him to taste.

He never could walk away from a dare.

She moved her palm flat against his chest, her heat scorching him.

Silver lights fired in his head as sensation exploded inside him, knocking hard against his resolve that this was all part of work.

He lowered his lips to hers, tasting strawberries, champagne and fresh air. Feeling lush softness that yielded to his touch and yet returned a pressure that gently demanded more.

Her mouth slowly opened under his, the action full of tentative reserve but overlaid with an invitation to come in and explore. The innocence of the action, so amazingly sexy, drove out all rational thought.

The noise, the music, all sounds of the evening faded as he slid his right hand up along her back, gently cradling her neck and firmly holding her mouth to his.

Blood pounded loudly in his ears as every part of him urged him to deepen the kiss, to taste the ambrosia of her mouth.

But an unfamiliar yet delicious lassitude stole through him, unexpectedly powerful, slowing him down and making him savour this moment.

Lips explored lips. Small nibbling bites, long caressing licks—a millimetre-by-millimetre journey, leaving no space untouched.

Her mouth traversed his lips, each stroke sparking a trail of glorious sensation, each trail spiralling down deeper than the last until all trails merged, coursing through him and energising him like no other kiss ever had.

As if reading his mind, she suddenly leaned in.

Now more than lips touched. Her breasts flattened against his chest as her arms slid around his neck. A soft sigh—half sated, half demanding—tumbled from her mouth as her tongue flicked across his teeth, seeking entry, all hesitancy gone.

A wall of fiery heat exploded in his chest, his need for her burning quickly through the restraint he'd happily welcomed a few minutes ago. His left hand slid from her hip to her bottom, clamping her against him, moulding her to him from ankle to lips, until no space between them existed.

She tilted her head back and he plundered her mouth. Sweetness meshed with experience, heat danced with fire, need collided with need, the explosion unleashing a carefully contained yearning that wound through him, softening years of resolve.

An edge of panic moved into place. *Spend the night but not a lifetime. Don't let a woman trap you.* His father's voice boomed in his head.

'Supper's served,' a voice called out into the dark of the veranda.

He felt a shudder against him and then cool night air caressed his lips and quickly stole down his body. Emily stepped back. 'Great. I'm starving.'

She stood in the shadows, her expression unreadable. An irrational sense of loss lingered, tinged with aggravation that her desire for food sounded stronger than her desire for him.

She caught his hand in a friendly gesture. 'Come on, or the queue for the chocolate fountain will be a mile long.'

She tugged him back into the ballroom, the bright lights and noise making him blink. Nothing looked quite the same. He shook his head. What the hell was wrong with him?

He'd kissed a hundred women at dances over the years. Tall women, stylish women, socialites, divas, blondes and brunettes—all his type of women. All of whom he'd kissed and forgotten. Kissed and moved on.

This was *no* different. If anything, it should be more easily forgotten. Emily, at barely five feet three and free of urban sophistication, was not his type of woman at all.

They reached the chocolate fountain, and she turned, smiling up at him, her lips red, soft and enticing.

His mouth tingled and the need to kiss her again surged inside him like an addiction, jolting him down to his toes.

Emily sat cuddled up next to Linton on the outdoor rattan couch, a soft blanket draped around them warding off the chill of the early morning air. Dappled moonlight lit the usually dark corner of the veranda and the crickets' song serenaded them. Two black and white dogs lay curled up close by, dreaming of chasing sheep.

It had been the most amazing evening of her life and the euphoria of the ball still bubbled in her veins. From the moment Linton had cut in on her dance with Baden, he hadn't left her side.

And he'd kissed her—gloriously, deliciously and wonderfully—until her body had been molten and her brain had been unable to assemble a single coherent thought.

Linton's mouth nibbled her ear. Need, hot and raw, speared down deep inside her. She'd imagined his kisses but no amount of daydreaming had prepared her for the reality.

He trailed kisses down her neck and across her collarbone, lingering in the hollow at her throat, his tongue doing wicked things, stirring up such a strong response she risked losing complete control.

It's happening too fast. Somewhere from deep inside her a warning voice sounded faintly. She placed her hands on his solid chest, gaining some space between their bodies. But her palms revelled in the touch of his smooth, hot skin and she gave in to the tempting sensation to run her fingers down his ribs, tickling him under the last one.

His head shot up, laughter on his lips and danger in his eyes. 'Hey. You want to play a different game, do you?'

He reached under the blanket but his hands got tangled in the layers of tulle. 'What on earth...?'

She started to giggle and put her fingers to her lips. 'Shh, we don't want to wake anyone up.'

'Yeah, your brothers might turn up with a shotgun.' He pulled her close and whispered. 'Your family is very protective of you.'

She laid her head on his shoulder, enjoying the sensation of the fine soft cotton of his shirt under her cheek. 'No, they're not.'

'Yes, they are. Your dad was giving me "take care of my little girl" signals from the moment I arrived and your brothers gave me *the look*.'

She raised her head and stared into green eyes that reflected the moon. 'What look?'

'The look that said, "Put one foot wrong and we'll beat you to a pulp".'

She sighed and laid her head back down. 'Sorry about that.'

His fingers tightened at her waist. 'No need to be sorry. You're really lucky.'

'Lucky?' Her finger fiddled with one of his shirt buttons. 'How is it lucky to have five men organising your life for you?'

His hand gently captured hers and held it against his chest. 'At least they care. I get the impression your brothers would walk through fire for you.'

She shrugged. 'I suppose, but that's what family is all

about. For better or worse, they're there for you even if half the time they're frustrating the life out of you.' She wriggled against him as she brought her feet up under the blanket. 'How do you get along with your brothers?'

He stiffened. 'I don't have any brothers.'

His tension and the tone of voice made her study him closely. Shadows moved in his eyes but that could have been the moonlight. 'Sisters? I bet you're a protective big brother, just like Mark.'

'Nope, no sisters.' The words shot out brisk and abrupt. 'I'm an only child.'

Sadness skittered through her at the bald statement. Her brothers might sometimes drive her crazy but she had plenty of fond memories of riotous games of Monopoly, stories around the campfire when they had been out mustering and even fun times doing mundane chores like drying the dishes at night. She had a strong urge to make him feel better about this. 'At least you didn't have to fight for your parents' attention—that has to be a bonus.'

He grimaced. 'For many years they were too busy fighting each other. They divorced when I was twelve.'

The chill in his words made her shiver. 'Oh, that would have been tough. Was not being able to have more children part of the problem?'

'No, having me *was* the problem.' Acrimony filled his voice. 'I was the accident, the reason for their ill-conceived marriage. At eighteen neither of them was ready for that sort of responsibility.' He sighed. 'Their divorce was inevitable from day one.'

Pain, raw and jagged, slugged her. 'At least they tried to make it work.'

'I suppose.' He sounded unconvinced. 'All I remember is

the bitterness and rancour. It was a relief when they divorced. They still hated each other but at least home was quiet and free of arguments.' He ran his free hand across the back of his neck in a now familiar reaction to stress.

She'd lost her mother but her father and her brothers had given her a lot of happy times. Life on the station had been calm and supportive. 'Did either of your parents remarry?'

He cleared his throat. 'My mother married her university professor a year after the divorce. Cliff's OK. He tried too hard to be the "responsible" parent. Neither he nor Mum approved of Dad's post-divorce lifestyle.'

Intrigue drove her questions. 'Did you see much of your father, growing up?'

He nodded. 'I spent the school holidays with him. His business took off a year after the divorce and he became quite wealthy. Going to Dad's was like entering a different world, a world without boundaries or rules. I loved it. I got to meet all sorts of people, although the summer Dad dated a series of swimwear models is the year I remember most vividly.'

He laughed. 'I learned *very* quickly to only tell each parent the bare minium about my time in the ex-spouse's household. Mum and Cliff would have had a court order preventing me from going to Dad's if they'd known less than half of what went on.'

'What sort of things?'

'If I tell you, I might have to kill you.' His aura of melancholy evaporated and he gently kissed her fingertips, his mouth slowly moving along her hand and up her arm. 'You taste absolutely wonderful. I could kiss you all night.'

She hugged his words close. This was what she'd dreamed of on all those long and lonely nights.

Go slowly, remember Nathan. The faint voice gained

volume but Linton's mouth reached her jaw, sapping her concentration.

Each touch of his lips fired her blood, each touch stoking her response, tightening her breasts into tingling swirls and fanning out liquid heat between her legs, urging her to lie back and savour the ministrations of the man she adored.

He groaned and slid his hand along her leg, avoiding the entanglement of the tulle. 'Seeing you tonight was like finding hidden treasure.'

His thick voice couldn't hide his desire. He kissed the edge of her mouth and her body moved toward his, needing his touch like it needed air.

You're not treasure, you're not a possession. The uncooperative part of her brain stayed focused and forced her to stay on track with the conversation. 'Did your dad remarry?'

Linton paused, his lips resting warm and firm on her jaw. 'Hell, no.'

His emphatic response drove a stake of unease into her.

He trailed butterfly kisses across her cheek but she refused to be distracted. 'Why "Hell, no"?'

His hand caressed her hair. 'He's having far too much fun to ever tie himself down to marriage.'

Just like his son. The words exploded in her head with the deafening boom of a bomb.

The playboy doctor.

The man who never dated a woman more than once. The man who in the past year had never dated her, never even looked twice at her.

Seeing you tonight was like finding hidden treasure.

She drew in a ragged breath. He'd noticed her tonight when she'd met his dare and dressed up especially for him. Had his dare been more about what he wanted than about helping her?

A bitter taste filled her mouth. Oh, what had she done?

Like a balloon snagging on a thorn, her wonderful evening popped and her euphoria cascaded over her, clawing at her mouth and nose, suffocating her. Why did she make such appalling choices with men? She'd been so dumb. So stupid.

She'd trusted Linton. She'd thought he understood her. But he didn't because right now he only had eyes for a body that caused her grief, whether it was hidden or on display.

Nathan had forced her to cover up. Linton had pushed her to uncover. Both had pushed for what *they'd* wanted.

And she'd let herself be pushed. The realisation rocked her. Neither of them really knew her or what made her tick.

Do you know yourself?

The hard truth sent her blood plummeting to her feet. She'd always been so scared she'd disappoint that she recreated herself for those around her. Just like she'd done with Nathan. Just like she'd done tonight.

Linton had accused her of hiding and she still was—it was just that the costume was different.

How could she expect anyone to consider what she wanted when she didn't know herself? The thought acted like a steel support running the length of her spine. She needed to take stock and work out what she wanted, who she really was.

But in the confusing mess of this realisation, there was one thing she knew for sure. Linton didn't really want *her*. He didn't care what was inside the package; he just wanted to play with the sparkly gift-wrap. He was bewitched by her body—a fake façade.

Well, she didn't want to be plundered treasure and she refused to be fool's gold.

She deserved better than that.

CHAPTER SEVEN

LINTON bounced into A and E remarkably full of energy despite little sleep. At two a.m. Emily had reminded him that she had to be on duty at eight so he'd reluctantly relinquished her from his arms and headed home.

He should have slept well.

Instead, he'd tossed and turned and he couldn't blame stifling summer heat or concern about a patient. He really should have slept well. But every time he'd closed his eyes, his arms had ached for a petite redhead with audacious, sparkling eyes.

So he'd given up trying to sleep. Not that he'd admit that to anyone, especially Baden Tremont. For some inexplicable reason his brain had kept returning to Emily's mouth and every single kiss.

And there'd been many.

He hadn't kissed like that since… Come to think of it, he'd never kissed like that before. Usually the kiss, although very enjoyable, was a perfunctory preamble to further exploration. But Emily's lush mouth had captivated him from the first moment and he couldn't get enough of it.

The whole evening had felt surreal. Emily had a siren's body made for lusty tumbles and her mouth had intoxicated him with her brand of kisses—a mixture of innocence and growing confidence. From the first touch he'd been lost in the wonder of her mouth and the craziest thing had happened. He'd been possessed by this overwhelming need to protect her and it had controlled him all night.

Even now, six hours later, he couldn't quite fathom how that had happened. So, instead of suggesting she come and have coffee at his place, he'd taken her back to her father's house and spent an hour necking on the porch, stealing kisses like a seventeen-year-old. Hell, he'd been far more restrained than a seventeen-year-old. He'd only got as far as running his hand up the back of her leg before she'd reminded him of the time.

He couldn't wait to go on from where he'd left off and he had the perfect plan. Emily would be off at two and they could picnic at Ledger's Gorge. It might even be warm enough to swim. An image of what Emily would look like in a bikini thudded through him and sweat broke out on his top lip.

Emily's not like Penelope. The thought quickly skated across his brain, fading away as he caught sight of Jodie.

'Morning, Linton.' Jodie looked up from her end-of-shift reports, the only nurse at the desk.

'Morning.' He found himself glancing around, looking for Emily, but she was nowhere to be seen. Disappointment rammed him hard. He pulled on his white coat and glanced at the clear board. 'Busy night and you've moved everyone on?'

Jodie shook her head. 'Really quiet. I think Patti and I had a much quieter time than you did.' She grinned. 'I hear the ball was fabulous.'

His lips curved up in a broad smile. It was probably a ridiculously silly grin but he couldn't help himself. 'So Emily's given you all the lowdown on the frocks and the suits, all the girly gossip?'

'No, she's not in yet.'

Startled, he glanced at his watch while Jodie continued talking. It wasn't like Emily to be late.

'Jason and Daniel dropped in at three a.m. with coffee and some food they'd sneaked out for us. They regaled us with stories.' Jodie swept some paper plates and disposable coffee-cups off the desk and into the bin as the doors opened.

'Jodie, please grab an ophthalmology kit from the supply room.' Emily walked in, issuing orders and supporting Daryl Heath, the police sergeant. She glanced at Linton, her grey eyes flicking over him, their expression neutral. 'It's good that you're here, Linton, because Daryl needs a doctor.'

She walked past with their patient toward the resus room, her shimmering cobalt blue hair vivid against her regulation-issue green scrubs.

Linton stood bolted to the floor, staring after them and blinking rapidly. *Bright blue hair.* Subconsciously he'd known Emily wouldn't be in a figure-hugging ballgown at work but he hadn't expected this, not after last night. What was going on? He quickly picked up his stethoscope and followed them.

Emily had placed an eye patch over Daryl's eye and was taking his blood pressure, the stethoscope in her ears conveniently preventing any conversation. Not that he could talk to her about anything other than their patient, and from the defiant tilt of her chin she knew that.

'What brings you in to see us this early Sunday morning, Daryl? I thought after last night you'd be having a sleep-in.' Linton shook the well-respected officer's hand.

'The Red Cross know how to throw a good bash, don't

they? But I must have done something to my eye because this morning it's throbbing so hard it feels like it might pop out of my head.' His hand formed a fist by his side, as if he was trying hard not to rub his eye to soothe it.

'It got so sore so fast I thought I better come in and see you.' He glanced around at all the equipment and shivered. 'I don't think I'm so sick that I need to be in here, though.'

Linton grinned. 'We need a room that we can darken so we can examine your eye properly. That's why Emily sat you in this chair, rather than getting you up on the trolley.' He leaned forward and lifted the eye patch.

The area around the eye was puffy and the eyelid was swollen. Red lines criss-crossed the sclera, which should have been white. The whole area looked angry and sore.

He turned on his ophthalmoscope and peered through the small aperture, the tiny globe providing the light to examine the eye. The conjunctiva, the thin, transparent covering of the eye, was also swollen and red.

'He's got a slight temp of 37.8 Celsius.' Emily read out the digital display the moment the ear thermometer beeped, her voice professional and clipped. 'Other observations are within normal limits.'

He didn't miss the fact she'd given the observations information when he couldn't look at her, or that every action of hers seemed stiff and starchy this morning. Last night's Emily seemed a figment of his imagination in more ways than one.

Daryl's pupil, which should have contracted to a small black disc in reaction to the bright light, reacted sluggishly. A red flag waved in Linton's brain. He switched off the ophthalmoscope and put a new eye patch over the good eye. 'What line can you read on the chart?'

'Your glasses were so dirty that everything would have

been out of focus,' Emily gently chided as she passed Daryl his glasses, which she'd cleaned with a soft cloth.

The patient leaned forward, squinting. 'Hell, can I start at the third line?'

'Sure, start where you can.' Linton caught a sudden flash of blue out of the corner of his eye. He turned to see Emily nibbling her bottom lip in concern. The memory of the touch of those lips on his mouth blasted through him in a wave of heat.

Daryl's recitation of the third line of the chart grounded him and he fished his pen out of his top pocket. 'I want you to follow the pen for me with your eye, not your head.' He held it in the midline of vision and slowly moved it to the left.

Daryl's eye started to move but he suddenly raised his palm to cover it. 'Fair go, Doc, that doesn't tickle.'

Emily silently handed him a bottle of fluorescein, an eye dye to expose a damaged cornea.

'Thanks.' He smiled at her and caught a shadow darken her eyes to a cloudy grey before she turned to pick up a bottle of solution.

'Daryl, I need you to tip your head back and as soon as I've put these drops in I need you to blink to distribute the dye.' He carefully administered the single drop to the lower conjunctival sac.

Daryl blinked rapidly.

Emily leaned forward and tucked a towel around Daryl's shoulders. 'Now I'm going to squirt some saline in your eye to remove the excess dye and see if something has gone into your eye and caused some damage.'

'It's a bit of a rigmarole, isn't it?' Daryl obediently tilted his head back and held the edge of the towel to his face.

'Now I need you to rest your chin here.' Emily pointed

to the chin rest on the slit lamp and helped their patient get into position.

Linton explained the procedure. 'I'm looking for blue dye. There's quite a bit of it about today and not all of it is in your eye.'

Emily smiled sweetly and ignored him. 'Daryl, what Linton is trying to say is that if you've done any damage to your cornea the dye will stick to it and show up as blue.'

Linton leaned into the slit lamp, putting his eye against the aperture and muttered, 'Pretty much like the damage Emily's done to her hair.'

He heard her sharp intake of breath. Good. At least he'd got a reaction rather than the cool, distant nurse persona.

'All set.' Linton leaned into position, his eye up against the aperture.

Emily flicked off the lights, plunging the room into darkness.

Using the blue light filter, Linton examined the eye but he couldn't detect any blue dye at all. He sighed. Seeing the dye would have been a nice easy diagnosis but that wasn't going to happen. Meanwhile, he had a patient whose vision was less than normal, had a pain on eye movement and a sluggish pupil response. It wasn't looking good. 'You can turn the lights on again, please, Emily.'

He moved the slit lamp out of the way and sat again, facing Daryl. 'The good news is the cornea isn't damaged.'

'And the bad news?' the sergeant responded instantly. He obviously knew the 'good news, bad news' scenario, as he had probably used it himself in his job.

'I'm working on a diagnosis.' Linton's brain whirred, delving into stored knowledge. 'Have you had a cold lately?' He gently tapped Daryl's face around the sinuses. 'Any pain here over the last week?'

'Yeah, I had a few headaches last week. I was taking horse-radish and garlic tablets and Nance had me on eucalyptus in-halations. I even tried the cold tablets—you know the ones that dry you up.'

The blurred edges around the symptoms suddenly sharp-ened into crystal-clear focus. 'I'm pretty sure you've got orbital cellulitis.'

'What's that?' Daryl's brow creased at the unfamiliar words.

Linton translated. 'The infection from your sinuses has gone across to your eye.'

'Is it serious?'

'It is if we don't treat it. Orbital cellulitis is one of those things that comes under the heading of "Act fast". I'm afraid you're going to be spending a few days with us while we put in a drip and give you IV antibiotics. The visiting ophthalmolo-gist is due in next week so he can see you then, but meanwhile I'll talk to him by teleconference to confirm my diagnosis.'

Emily patted Daryl's arm reassuringly. 'You did the right thing coming in and in a few days you'll be feeling a lot better.' She slid a tourniquet up his arm, tightening it against his biceps. She glanced at Linton. 'If you write up the order now, I'll set up the antibiotics and give him some analgesia.'

A spark of irritation skated through Linton as he clicked his pen and picked up the chart. What she really meant was, *I've got it covered, you can leave.* Well, he wasn't leaving until he was good and ready. And not until he'd talked to Emily on her own.

'Are you allergic to penicillin, Daryl?'

'Nope, had it before with no side effects.'

'Great.' He put the authorised drug chart on the trolley, giving Emily a long questioning look.

She busied herself inserting the IV.

Linton swallowed a sigh. 'Daryl, I'll ring Nancy and tell her to pack you a bag and then you can give her a ring when you get settled up on the ward.'

The sergeant nodded. 'Thanks, Doc. She'll get a surprise that I'm here. She was still asleep so I sneaked out when the pain got a bit much.'

'You probably shouldn't have driven with your eye like that,' he gently rebuked the experienced police officer.

A chastened expression merged with one of affection. 'I didn't want to wake her.'

Linton marvelled at the care and consideration Daryl had shown his wife, despite the pain he must have been in. He couldn't remember a single moment when his parents had shown any sort of thoughtfulness toward each other.

'Emily, give the first dose of antibiotics now, and then Daryl can go upstairs. Get Jason to transfer him when you're ready.'

She nodded her understanding. 'Yes, Doctor. You can make your call now. Daryl and I are just fine.'

In other words, *you can leave now*. Well, two could play at that game. 'Catch you later, Daryl.'

He strode out of the room, his steps purposeful and determined. Emily might think he was leaving but he had another plan entirely.

He made the call to the ophthalmologist in Sydney, confirming his diagnosis and treatment plan, and then he walked out the front door of the hospital.

Town was still very quiet. The only people joining the keen cyclists were parents of young children who were out walking slowly and closely examining every insect, flower, tree and cat they came across. How did they do it? It would take an hour to walk the length of the street. Being a parent wasn't something he spent any time thinking about. His parents' botched job hadn't made him want to have a long-term relationship, let alone be a parent.

He passed a couple who stood holding hands while they indulgently watched their toddler pointing excitedly to a butterfly. Their exchanged glances, so full of devotion and love, punched him unexpectedly in the gut, making him stagger.

He needed coffee.

He went to the bakery, which had just installed a brand-new coffee-machine imported from Italy, along with an Italian cousin, who at twenty-five had the local girls flocking to watch him *barista* with flair and drool over his accent. Cosmopolitan Milan had collided with Warragurra.

'*Buon giorno.*'

'Morning, Paolo. I need a decaf latte—'

'No, *Dottore*, it is Sunday morning. You do not want decaf.'

Linton laughed. 'Very true, Paolo, I want an espresso but Emily usually has a decaf, doesn't she?'

'Not on a Sunday. On Sunday mornings I only serve strong coffee, and especially this Sunday after the ball. You take one sugar for Emily. I see she has an accident with her hair. She needs sugar.'

'She needs something,' Linton muttered to himself as he grabbed the Sunday paper and some freshly baked Danish pastries. With the paper under his arm, his coffee-cups stacked and his free hand clutching the brown bag of pastries, he headed back to A and E.

By the time he arrived, Daryl had been transferred to the ward, Jodie had gone home, the board was empty again and he found Emily furiously cleaning the pan room, her blue hair almost neon under the fluorescent light.

He deliberately stood in the doorway. 'I've got coffee.'

She stopped and turned, her smile losing a tug of war with the rest of the muscles in her face. 'Thanks. I'll be there in a minute.'

'I meant *real* coffee, from Tatti's. Paolo's made it for you just how you like it. Come now or it will be cold and he'll never forgive you.' He stayed still until she peeled off her gloves with a resigned shrug.

He moved back to allow her though the door, unable to stop himself from breathing deeply, wanting to catch a waft of the perfume that he now associated so strongly with Emily. He followed her back to the desk, admiring the way her scrubs moved across her bottom as her hips swayed.

You're pathetic.

Shut up.

The war of words spun in his head but he felt strangely disconnected from them, his attention fully on Emily. He popped the top off her coffee and passed it to her. There was no point beating about the bush. 'What have you done to your hair?'

Her cup stalled at her cherry-red lips. 'I told you, I never liked red hair.' She put the cup down and rummaged through the filing cabinet. 'What have you done with the roster?'

'What have you done with the woman I danced with last night?' The question he'd wanted to ask since she'd walked into work this morning shot out of his mouth uncensored.

Her busy hands froze on top of the files, her shoulders rigid. She turned around and faced him, her face working hard to be free of expression, but her flashing eyes gave everything away.

'Cinderella's gone and now you're left with the real me. Last night wasn't real, Linton. Last night was a bit of fairy dust and make-believe. Granted, it lasted two hours past midnight but then life went back to normal.' She pointed to her head and plucked at the V of her top. 'This *is* me.'

The confusion he'd battled with since her arrival won out. 'No, I don't think it is you. I don't understand. I thought you enjoyed coming out of your chrysalis and emerging into the light.'

Grey eyes the colour of a summer storm flashed at him. 'Don't presume to know me, Linton, because you don't have a clue who I really am.' She took a long slug of her coffee and then breathed in deeply, her breasts straining against her top.

His gaze immediately fell to her chest, seeking the image of creamy breasts from last night, which burned so brightly in his mind. Seeing an imagined image of her in a bikini top. Clearing his mind of everything except that. 'Come to Ledger's Gorge this afternoon and I can get to know you. We can swim up under the waterfall and—'

'No, thanks.' She pulled out the roster and slammed the filing-cabinet drawer closed.

The coolness of her voice whipped him. He shook his head, not quite believing he'd heard correctly. 'We don't have to swim. What about a walk?'

'No, thank you.'

Obviously he was missing something. Perhaps she wanted to have a say in the destination. 'What would you like to do?'

She tilted her pert chin upwards, as if slicing the air around it. 'Linton, I don't want to do anything with you except work.'

An alien emotion circled him. 'You're dumping me?'

Incredulity creased her brow. 'How can I be dumping you? We weren't even on a date. Besides, you're not known for a follow-up call and you're especially not known for a follow-up date, so you should be relieved.'

The barb hit him in a place usually so well protected that nothing penetrated. He ignored her comment, focusing on his need. He smiled a knowing smile. 'But you have to admit we had a great time together, especially on your veranda.' His voice deepened of its own accord. 'Don't you want to explore that further?'

Her eyes darkened to the colour of polished iron ore.

He knew that colour. A self-indulgent thought warmed him. Whatever was going on behind that blue hair, she couldn't deny the attraction that simmered between them.

Silver immediately glinted in the grey depths, flashing at him like the light from a welder's torch. The abrupt change, so unexpected, startled him.

She drew herself up onto the balls of her feet, her body almost vibrating. 'You've known me for a year, Linton. In all that time you've never seen me as anyone other than a reliable nurse who made your life easier. The *one* time I put on a slinky dress, you suddenly see me.'

Her voice trembled. 'Except that wasn't really me. I showed you what you wanted to see. You obviously prefer to see me that way but the problem is, I don't agree.' She hugged her arms around herself. 'I thought you understood me but I got that so wrong. Last night was all about *you* and nothing to do with me. You are so...so shallow. Everything I've every heard about you and wanted to ignore is true. You really are the playboy doctor. Well, sorry, I don't want to play.'

Her words cut and ripped, the truth stark and unrelenting. *I showed you what you wanted to see.* Anger surged in to soothe the pain. 'I have never pretended to be anything other than what I am. I have never made a promise I haven't kept.'

A flush of colour stained her cheeks. 'That doesn't make

you honourable.' She picked up the roster and, hugging it close to her chest, walked away from him.

His anger staggered under the weight of her accusation. He wanted to yell at her to come back, that she was wrong, that she knew nothing about him, but he kept hearing the same words over and over. *You are so shallow.*

He wasn't shallow. He was nothing like the man that had destroyed her confidence, telling her she was unattractive, telling her what to wear.

You told her what to wear.

No! His rage stampeded over the ugly thought. What he'd done had been totally different. It had been concern for her that had made him encourage her to come out from behind her baggy clothes and wear that dress. It had been the action of a friend.

But the memory of her taste, the touch of her lips against his, the feel of her head against his chest, the vision of her curvaceous body in that dress—all of it whipped him like a cat-o'-nine-tails.

Hell, a friend didn't kiss another friend to the point of exhaustion.

You've known me for a year, Linton.

What had he done? His head pounded and he rubbed his neck as he tried to make sense of it all.

The unpalatable truth trickled through him. Emily was right. He'd admired her as a nurse, he'd seen her as a mate and nothing more. Last night he'd let raging, unchecked hormones turn a friendship on its head. He'd let lust for her body ride roughshod over their camaraderie, totally ignoring the woman inside the gorgeous body. A woman who was still hurting and emotionally raw from the abuse she'd had levelled at her by her ex-boyfriend.

A sigh shuddered from his lungs. He'd been a total fool. Seducing a friend wasn't part of the friendship code.

With a startling clarity that made him sway, he realised he'd never had a female friend before.

Tamara?

No! Tamara hadn't been a friend. Tamara had been a self-serving schemer. He'd thought he'd married a partner for life but she hadn't actually wanted him. No, Tamara had never been a friend.

He thought of this morning, working with a cool and starchy Emily. A vision of that sort of relationship sent a shudder of loss through him. He missed her friendship already.

He jammed his hands in his coat pockets, his heart pounding hard. He'd messed this up because he had no idea how to be friends with a woman. He knew how to date, how to charm, how to get his own way, but he didn't have a clue about platonic friendship. That wasn't a lesson his father had taught him.

You are so shallow.

A metallic taste burned the back of his throat at her words, which had pierced with deadly accuracy.

He wanted Emily's friendship back. He wanted the companionship she'd offered, the teasing when he took himself too seriously, the shared laughs. He wanted all of it.

He'd just have to show her he was nothing like that man she'd left and he was a lot deeper than she thought he was.

CHAPTER EIGHT

THE pages in the book blurred and Emily's wrist ached from the copious notes she'd written. Five cold cups of tea cluttered the desk and she could see right through the clear bottom of the glass bowl holding bright-coloured chocolate lollies. She had to keep focused to have all the required course work for her Master's done by the time her residential week arrived. And it was scarily close.

'Em, it's five o'clock.' Jim banged on the Woollara Station's office door before opening it and poking his head around. 'I think you've done enough for the day. The sun's setting, it's officially Saturday night, the lamb's roasting in the oven and Hayden just rang. He, Nadine and the kids are coming over.'

'Thanks, Dad. I'll come and set the table for you.'

'I've done that. You can shell the peas and talk to me while I make the gravy.' He gave her a fatherly smile.

'Deal. I'll be there in five.' Emily closed her books. She'd been working all day on her Master's, retreating to the office for peace and quiet, but now she was ready to stop.

She hadn't seen her middle brother and his family for a few weeks and baby Alby would have changed so much.

Anticipating an enjoyable evening, she hummed to herself as she returned her father's desk to its usual neat state.

Family dinners were always fun. She and Mark were the only siblings still living at home. Stuart and Eric shared bachelor quarters down by the shearing shed and Hayden and Nadine's house was one hundred kilometres away on the northern boundary.

But when word got out that Jim was cooking a roast, it was amazing how many of her brothers appeared in the kitchen, and they usually brought a few mates with them. Still, it *was* Saturday night and Eric and Stuart had gone into Warragurra to the rugby match so she didn't expect them to be coming.

That meant more time with Hayden and Nadine and more cuddles with her nephews. After the week she'd had she could do with a bit of family time. It would be a lot less complicated than work. Last Sunday morning had changed everything between her and Linton. Actually, the ball had changed everything between her and Linton.

A sigh shuddered through her. She still hated that she'd let stars in her eyes dazzle and blind her, affecting her judgement. When she'd seen the way Linton had gazed at her on Sunday morning, as if he could see through her clothes, she had known that the decision she'd made in the early hours of that morning had been the right one.

A hard one, but the right one.

At the moment she didn't know which was worse—the blatant desire in Linton's eyes or memories of the bitter derision of Nathan's words. Both of them had wanted to mould her into something that wasn't her.

She acknowledged that in a way she'd let both men try and change her, but all of that was over now. She wasn't going to think about Linton any more, because when she did her heart pounded in anger and then beat quietly in sadness, leaving her totally confused.

She straightened her shoulders as she switched off the office light. She was older and wiser now. She and men didn't match. Right now she needed to focus on herself, work, her Master's and enjoy her extended family.

She made her way across the yard with a dog for company, and the low bellow of cattle competing with the raucous screech of the yellow-crested cockatoos nesting for the night. Two kangaroos bounded near the far fence, the fading light sending them to the shelter of the trees down by the river, the twinkling light of the evening star guiding their way.

As she drew level with the house, a four-wheel-drive pulled up, the tyres crunching on the gravel. A three-year-old boy tumbled out and raced toward her, his blond hair flying. 'Emily!'

'Tyler!' She swooped him up in her arms and spun him around.

Squeals of delight showered over her.

'Hey, sis, you're looking good.' Hayden gave her a kiss on the cheek and a questioning look. 'Been shopping?'

Experimenting with new clothes was part of working out her very own style, one she was choosing for herself. Not too revealing but not sacks either, she'd been enjoying the process.

She put a squirming Tyler down and watched him run toward the house, ignoring her brother's gaze. 'I might have.'

'About time.' Hayden spoke matter-of-factly. 'You should burn those horrible baggy shirts.'

'Shut up.' She playfully elbowed her brother in the ribs. Of all her brothers, Hayden knew her best.

Hayden caught her in a headlock.

'Play nice, you two.' Nadine's gentle voice interrupted their horseplay.

'Oh, can I cuddle Alby?' Emily put out her arms for the baby.

His mother smiled a tired smile. 'You can cuddle him for as long as you like.'

The bang of the wire door made them look up. Tyler stood on the back veranda with his hands on his hips, looking as self-important as a pre-schooler could look. 'Granddad says peas need shelling and I can help 'cos I'm a fwee-year-old.'

'That you are, mate.' Hayden bounded up the steps and raced him into the house.

The aroma of roasting lamb and garlic wafted over Emily as soon as she entered the kitchen. A big metal bowl sat in the middle of the table filled with pea pods, freshly picked from the home-paddock garden. Tyler climbed up onto a stool and Hayden sat next to him, demonstrating how to shell the peas.

'Hey, do you remember the time we ate so many peas while we were picking them that there were none for dinner?' Hayden grinned at Emily.

She laughed. 'Mum was furious because the circuit magistrate was coming to dinner that night and there were no green vegetables.'

Jim poured a generous slurp of red wine into the gravy, his deep, rumbling voice joining the laughter. 'Your mother was trying to outcook Mrs Sanderson, who'd fed him the night before. You two put her reputation as the district's best cook on the line.'

The laughter and warmth of the kitchen encircled them, relaxing Emily. She cuddled the baby, breathing in the sweet milky smell. A long-held dream of a baby of her own hovered briefly before she dismissed it as nonsense. She wanted a child but not without a husband. Right now the chances of that ever happening were zero to nothing. She really had to learn how to pick the right guy.

She glanced up and watched Nadine and Hayden teaching their son how to shell peas while Jim poured drinks and stirred the gravy. Everyone devoured the pre-dinner pesto dip and almost all of Tyler's chips, much to his chagrin.

'Granddad said they were for me.' He mutinously moved the bowl to the side.

His father moved it back. 'Sharing the chips is the right thing to do, mate.'

Tyler's bottom lip wobbled.

'Right, then. I'm almost ready to carve and dish up.' Jim clapped his hands.

The wire door banged. 'That's perfect timing, Dad. Hope you've cooked the usual big one.' Stuart strode into the kitchen, his cheeks ruddy from the evening chill.

'What happened to the post-match celebrations?' Emily raised her head from admiring the perfect shape of Alby's tiny ears.

Stuart grinned. 'Dad's cooking a lamb roast, sis. I never miss that.'

'How much did Warragurra lose by?' Jim clapped his hand on his youngest son's shoulder.

A sheepish expression crossed Stuart's face. 'We're missing Ben McCreedy. We came in for a drubbing, fifty-seven ten. Combine that woeful score with the rain and the crush at the Royal, and Eric and I thought we'd come home for some family fun.'

'Hey, Dad.' Eric's stocky bulk crossed the threshold and he immediately moved away from the door. A tall man stood in the shadow of the dark veranda. 'You remember Linton. We thought he looked like he could do with a feed.'

Emily's knees buckled as she clutched Alby tightly against her. Linton stood tall and solid, filling the doorway, a smile on his handsome face, a Warragurra Roosters' scarf around his neck, his brown hair ruffled by the wind and his long legs clad in tight blue denim.

Casual, gorgeous and all male.

She swallowed a groan as a traitorous swirl of heat wound through her. Of all the men her brothers could have run into at the match and invited home, why did it have to be Linton?

Her vision of a relaxed family evening vaporised before her eyes.

'Come in, Linton.' Jim's voice boomed. 'Dinner's almost on the table. Choose yourself a seat.'

Linton shook Emily's father's hand. 'Are you sure?'

'Absolutely. The boys are always bringing home extras and there's plenty.' He plunged a carving fork into the leg of lamb. 'Emily, Linton hasn't met Hayden and Nadine.'

Linton caught the ripple of tension across her shoulders. He'd spied Emily the moment Eric had moved away from the door. If the truth be told, he'd been searching for her the moment he'd looked into the room. His blood warmed at the sight of her, even though once again he hardly recognised her.

Her hair was no longer blue but a warm honey blonde. The soft curls brushed her shoulders, tickling the fine wool of her chocolate-brown V-necked sweater, which contrasted with a finely striped shirt with white collar and cuffs. Low-rise cords, the grey-brown colour of the bush wallaby, hugged her hips.

Country chic.

Totally gorgeous. His gut kicked as desire rolled it over. He immediately stomped on it. *Think friend.* Emily was his colleague and hopefully soon-to-be-again friend. He'd only accepted Eric's invitation to dinner because he'd thought it would be an opportunity to show Emily a completely different side of him.

A and E had been frantic lately and there hadn't been any time to talk to her about anything other than patients. He doubted she would have accepted an invitation for coffee, lunch or dinner, even if he had offered.

All week at work she'd had bright blue hair and a pale face. She'd been steely professional, only seeking him out about work-related issues. Yet now, surrounded by her family, the prickly woman was gone and she glowed in the warm earthy colours that suited her so well. He hardly recognised her but it wasn't just the clothes or the hair. Something about her was different, he just couldn't quite pin down what.

She held his gaze for an infinitesimal moment, her expression questioning, before she laid the baby in the pram. Straightening up, she spoke briskly, as if she was at work. 'Linton, I'd like you to meet my middle brother, Hayden, his wife Nadine—'

'And me!' A little boy tugged at her sweater.

The starchy Emily evaporated, her face creasing in laughter lines as she bobbed down and picked up the child. 'And Tyler.'

Tyler leaned out of her arms toward the pram. 'And that's my baby brother.' The pride in his voice was unmistakable.

A strange sensation washed over Linton. He didn't want to call it loneliness. He moved forward, his arm extended as Hayden rose to his feet. 'Great to meet you. Emily didn't mention she was an auntie.'

'She's probably too busy bossing you around at work.' Hayden grinned as he shook Linton's hand.

The welcome in Hayden's grip relaxed him. 'She's been known to have an organising moment or two.'

'I do *not* boss.' Emily sat Tyler on his chair.

Her brother gave a snort and turned toward his sister. 'Yeah, right, and pigs might fly. You've been bossy since the moment you were born.' He turned back to Linton, rolling his eyes. 'When she gets a bee in her bonnet, she's legendary. Once she turned this kitchen into a production line. She had all of us boys preserving fruit and baking cakes to enter in the Warragurra Show. Eric in an apron was a sight to behold.'

'I publicly thanked you for your contribution when I won first prize.' Emily slid onto her chair.

'And I'm still wearing *that* down at the clubrooms.' Hayden tied a bib around Tyler's neck.

'I was just helping you get in touch with your feminine side, so you should be thanking me because, if I remember, it was after that show that Nadine noticed you.' Emily shot Hayden a triumphant look, her chin tilted skyward.

'Nadine noticed me because of my spectacular riding skills at the rodeo.'

'The time the bull bucked you and you went to hospital?'

Nadine patted a chair with her hand. 'Sit down, Linton, and just ignore them. This is what they do.'

Linton sat down and put his serviette on his knee. 'So was it the cooking or the riding of the bull that made you notice Hayden?'

The young wife smiled a knowing smile. 'Actually, it was his enthusiasm and total commitment to whatever he takes on. This family has that in spades.'

Linton surreptitiously glanced at Emily, immediately recognising what Nadine meant.

Eric and Stuart joined them, adding their stories about

Emily bossing them around, the loving banter obvious in their voices.

Jim carved the meat and plates were passed down the long table. Outstretched arms reached and received the dishes of roast vegetables and peas, and mint jelly was generously dobbed on top of the thick gravy. Glasses clinked, cutlery scraped against the blue and white china, and the satisfied sounds of a group of people eating good food echoed around the kitchen.

'I think we should send a hundred head of cattle down to the sale yards next week.' Hayden reached for the salt.

'Mark, have you met the new kindergarten teacher?' Nadine casually picked up the pepper grinder.

The bachelor shifted uncomfortably in his seat and looked at Hayden. 'So are you going to muster on Tuesday?'

Eric waved his fork. 'You should ask her out, bro.'

'Linton, I was reading in the *New Scientist* about surgeons using scorpion toxin to highlight malignant cells.' Jim's blue eyes burned with intelligence and hospitality.

Linton opened his mouth to reply.

'I made these peas, Granddad.'

'And you did a great job, buddy.' Jim handed the preschooler a spoon. 'But how about using this, rather than your fingers?'

'Did anyone read about the latest report on salinity?' Emily voiced the question into the congested air.

Mark attempted to stick to one topic. 'Dad, will you be mustering with us on Tuesday?'

'Mark can you fix the pump on the boundary dam sooner rather than later?' Stuart scooped more potatoes onto his plate.

'And when you've done that, you can call into the kinder

and fix the pump on the rainwater tank. I tried but you're better at that sort of thing.' Hayden shot his brother a wicked grin. 'Hey, Tyler, you'd like Uncle Mark to come and visit you at kinder, wouldn't you?'

The little boy's blue eyes widened in delight. 'I can show him the walking fish.'

Linton's brain whirled as he tried to grab onto a conversation but found it had immediately morphed into something different. He caught Emily's twinkling gaze, her eyes dancing with laughter at what he knew must be a completely bewildered expression on his face.

He mouthed, 'Is it always like this?'

She nodded and asked her question about the salinity report again.

This time Jim replied, and Linton realised that in conversations at this table it was survival of the fittest. Whoever talked loudest and more often got heard. The memory of dinners past in his childhood homes floated through his mind.

The quiet meals with his mother and Cliff, often focused on earnest political discussions, which had contrasted dramatically with meals at his father's house. The large modern glass and granite table had often been filled with strangers—women who had been trying to impress his father by mothering Linton. Women his father had had no plan on seeing a second or third time.

Once he'd left home, many meals had been spent at the hospital talking shop, or cooking for one at his own place, and more recently out at restaurants on dates, having the usual 'getting to know you' conversations.

All of those meals had lacked the warmth, vitality, competitiveness and camaraderie of this table. He had a sense of having missed out on something special in his family homes. His bewilderment suddenly vanished and everything became clear. He wanted to be part of it, he wanted to be in on this chaotic conversation, and at the same time he could show Emily that he wasn't the shallow womaniser she'd tagged him as.

He projected his voice into the melee. 'Scorpion toxin is fluorescent so it outlines the boundary of the malignant tumour.'

Jim nodded. 'Nature's amazing, isn't it?'

Eric spluttered. 'Amazing? It's a right pain. Those kangaroos knocked over the river paddock fence *again*.'

Emily squirted green liquid detergent into the sink and started to attack the large pile of dishes now that everyone had consumed more sticky toffee pudding than was probably good for them. It felt good to be doing *something*, rather than just sitting and wondering why Linton was here. Why was he casually leaning back in a chair at her father's table, looking for the entire world like he belonged there?

He even sounded liked he belonged. He'd matched her brothers in their verbal sparring debates that were synonymous with family meals, as well as taking a genuine interest in everyone, actively drawing them out, seeking their opinions.

And he did it with such casual ease, looking completely and utterly, devastatingly gorgeous. The "shallow man" accusation she'd hurled at him almost a week ago seemed grossly unfair today.

She silently screamed as confusion encircled her. She wanted to run to the woolshed, just like when she'd been a little girl. Home was supposed to be a sanctuary from the world—a Linton-free zone.

Instead, her heart had been skipping beats all night, making her feel giddy. It had completely ignored every reasonable request she'd made of it to beat normally and treat Linton like any other guest. Every nerve pulled taut, ready to snap, and she just wished Linton would go home so she could find her equilibrium again.

Not that he'd really talked to her. He'd been busy chatting with everyone else. He'd even made an effort with Tyler. It rankled that she felt ignored. She shouldn't care.

Voices from the table drifted over to her and she heard snatches of conversation and her father discussing the Warragurra Rodeo, which was going to be held the following weekend.

'Where are the teatowels kept?' Linton's deep voice unexpectedly rumbled behind her.

A strong tingling wave washed through her. Angry with herself, she snapped, asking the question that had bugged her all night. 'Why are you here?'

His green eyes flickered with darker shards of green, giving her a look that made her feel small and mean. 'Your brothers invited me.'

He reached around her and grabbed a teatowel, his heat slamming into her. He dropped his voice so only she could hear. 'You look great, by the way.'

She plunged a bowl under the white suds and vigorously scrubbed it with the brush, trying to stop the sensation of lightness sweeping through her. She didn't want to enjoy the compliment. She was furious with him. She breathed out a strained but polite 'Thanks'.

'Your dad reads pretty widely.' His strong, tanned hands dextrously wiped a plate dry.

'What, for a farmer?' Suds sprayed her in disapproval.

He raised his brows in question. 'Emily, do you have a problem with me being here?'

Yes! Yes, I do. But she couldn't say that. He was the guest of her brothers, although why he'd want to be here after she'd called him shallow she had no idea.

Anger meshed with longing, need duelled with frustration. He had no right to look so at home in her family kitchen! Not when he'd hurt her so much. She paused, her gloved hands resting on the sink, and pulled in a deep breath. 'I'm sorry, that was rude. I've been studying all day and I'm tired and scratchy.'

'Study does that.' He gave a nod of understanding. 'I've been thinking about what you said the other day.' He pushed the teatowel deep into the glass and looked thoughtful. 'You were right. I was pretty shallow and I hurt your feelings and abused your friendship. Our friendship.' He caught her gaze, his eyes serious. 'Sorry.'

Had she been holding a plate, it would have slipped from her fingers. She gripped the edge of the sink for support as her knees sagged. So that was why he was here—he'd come to apologise. She hadn't expected that at all. Nathan had *never* apologised, he'd only blamed.

'You want to be friends?' She couldn't hide the disbelief in her voice.

Contrition interplayed with hesitancy. 'I do. I think we can do that, don't you?'

'Colleagues and friends?' She must sound completely vacant, repeating everything he'd said, but her mind continued to be blank, unable to absorb this astonishing turnaround.

He nodded. 'Friends and colleagues.'

She rolled the idea around in her head. This meant they could start afresh with no confusion. The crazy desire that had simmered between them would disappear now they had ground rules. They were workmates and friends, pure and simple. They'd never socialised together before the ball so there was no reason to expect that to change.

Everything was moving forward to a new and improved working relationship. She couldn't stop herself from smiling broadly. 'Apology accepted. Here's to the new order.' And she handed him a dripping pile of cutlery.

'Hey, Linton.' Stuart and Mark pushed their chairs back from the table. 'You ever been to a rodeo?'

Linton opened the drawer and dropped the cutlery into the slots as he dried each item. 'No, no yet.'

'Mate, you can't go back to Sydney before you've experienced a rodeo.' Eric appealed to Emily. 'Can he, sis?'

Three sets of eyes stared at her as her heart leapt into her mouth. What Eric was really saying was that the Tippett family would take Linton as their guest. And as all her brothers and her father would be involved in riding horses and roping bulls, that meant she would be the host. She would be the one spending all of Saturday with Linton.

Linton away from work was a totally different proposition. Dread danced with a sensation she refused to name.

She stared back at her brothers' questioning eyes. They had her on toast.

She gulped in a breath, playing the only card she had. 'Linton's pretty busy. I doubt he'd want to spend a day in the dust, watching you guys play around trying to prove you're men.' She turned back to the sink.

Linton flicked his teatowel like a whip. 'I'd love to go.'

Four small words sealed her fate.

CHAPTER NINE

EMILY checked the message on her phone for the third time. *Meet you by the stables. Linton.* But she couldn't see him anywhere.

She scanned the crowd again. Cowboys and cowgirls promenaded in their best jeans. Fitted button-down shirts in every colour of the rainbow were tucked neatly behind ornate belt buckles, which sparkled in the sunshine, and showed off a wide variety of waistlines. A hat graced every head, some tipped forward, some tipped back and some hung against their owners' backs, flicked off by the occasional gust of wind that sent dust and leaves swirling into the air.

Linton should have stood out in the crowd because he didn't own any western gear. He was a city boy through and through. A city boy with a penchant for all things Italian.

'There you are. I thought I must have missed you.' Linton's hand caught her arm.

She spun around, his touch making her dizzy, the rich timbre of his voice making her heart skip. She gazed up at him, blinking rapidly. 'Linton?'

He flicked his thumbs into the belt hooks of his moleskins and threw his shoulders back, standing tall, his chest straining the fabric of his jade-coloured shirt.

She forgot to breathe.

Then he grinned, his eyes flashing, and he tipped his hat. 'Ma'am.'

A giggle bubbled up, escaping through her lips.

'Hey, the salesman at Country Outfitters said this was the gear I needed.' Indignation clung to his words. 'I thought I looked like a pretty good cowboy.'

You look sensational. Good enough to eat. 'You look like a stockman.'

'Why not a cowboy?' He sounded like a little boy who had lost the costume competition.

'Denim is the cowboy code and you're in moleskins, which is the fabric of choice for drovers, stockmen, graziers and shearers. You'd better watch out—Dad might offer you a job. How are your roping skills?'

'I lassoed a pretty good nurse for the afternoon.' He slipped his hand against hers, his lean fingers closing around her finer ones. 'So, this is a rodeo. Busy, isn't it? Your brothers told me all about the camp drafting, which is on at four, so can you take me there?'

His wide palm engulfed her small hand, stealing all coherent thought. She stole a glance at him but his expression gave nothing much away. Smile lines creased the edges of his eyes and he looked happy, interested and laid-back.

All week at work he'd been affable and relaxed. She'd noticed little things like how he'd brought her a drink when he'd made one, how he'd asked if Mark had gone to kinder to see Tyler's Mexican walking fish and if she'd finished her first assignment for uni.

And, unlike with Nathan, none of it had come with a condition.

Instead, all of it had been the action of a friend doing the sorts of things that friends did for each other. And they'd

talked about all sorts of things and laughed about nonsense.
They'd become friends. Good friends. She believed he really
did enjoy her company—in fact, at times he sought her out
just to talk. Their friendship seemed to be working well for
both of them.

It's harder than you thought.

She ignored the voice. Friendship was what they both
wanted and it would be perfect if she could only ditch these
irrational shimmers of sensation whenever he came near. They
were supposed to have gone, banished by their friendship
pact.

But they kept popping up to haunt her, like right now. She
hauled in a deep breath, trying to settle her somersaulting
stomach. The only reason he was holding her hand was so he
didn't lose her in the crowd. She took a step and tugged his
hand. 'If we go to the arena now, you can see some bull riding.'

Linton stood still, frowning. 'Please, tell me none of your
brothers do that.'

'They all tried it once, Hayden even twice, but fortunately
their skills lie on the back of a horse and camp drafting is a
lot safer.' She tugged on his hand again. 'Come on, you need
to get some red dust on those boots of yours so you don't look
like such a city slicker.'

He counter-tugged, managing to move her slightly behind
him as he strode off, his long legs quickly eating up the
distance. 'I've been here for over a year, you know.'

She jogged to keep up. 'Mate, even if you married a local
girl, settled down and had children and grandchildren…'

A horrified look streaked across his face at her words.

Half of her wanted to laugh and half of her wanted to cry.
She forced herself to continue, 'You'd still be a city bloke,
but your great-grandchildren would be locals.'

'That's never going to happen.'

His emphatic words pierced her like tiny arrows. 'What? Having grandchildren or marrying a local girl?' She worked hard to keep her tone light.

'Neither.' He took a sharp left, following the sign to the arena.

She stopped walking, dismay for him thundering through her. Even though she knew that they would never work as a couple, she'd assumed that at some point in the future he would marry. 'So even when you're back in Sydney, on track with your career plan of being in charge of a city hospital A and E, you still have no plans to marry?'

'No.' Determined, clear green eyes stared down at her. 'I tried it once.'

She stared at him, speechless, her brain refusing to work. 'You...you've been married?' She couldn't hide the shock in her voice.

He shrugged. 'We all make mistakes.'

She tugged him over to one side, out of the main thoroughfare. 'You've never said anything about being married.' She blurted out the words, stunned at his casual mention of such a big issue. Didn't friends tell each other things like that?

Tension radiated along his jaw. 'I was young and stupid. I'm divorced now.' The words rushed out stilted and defiant.

She stared at him, seeing a steely resentment she'd never really glimpsed before. Was this tied up with the playboy doctor? The need to know burned inside her but she wasn't certain he'd tell her. She gave it a shot. 'With my disastrous attempt at an adult relationship, I'm hardly in a position to judge you.'

His gaze wavered for a moment and then he spoke, his voice flat and devoid of emotion, as if he was telling a tale he'd told too many times before. 'From the age of twelve my father told me how much his life had improved once he'd divorced my mother. I hated hearing that and I used to daydream about happy families, and how I would fall in love and get married one day and *stay* married.'

'That sounds pretty normal.' She'd daydreamed the same sort of thing. In weaker moments she still did.

He snorted. 'Yeah, well, it's not normal for the Gregory men.' He ran his hand across the back of his neck. 'I met Tamara at a party when I was a fifth-year med student. She was majoring in literature and her student life was very different from mine. She went to plays, parties and poetry readings, and enjoyed campus life, while I was strapped to a horrendous study load. She'd call by the residence and drag me out and for the first time in a long time I had fun.' A grimace crossed his face. 'I completely missed that she had an agenda.'

She nodded her understanding, thinking of Nathan. 'Looks like we share that in common.'

His mouth twitched into a half-smile. 'I guess so. Anyway, my father wasn't happy about the amount of time I was spending with Tamara and he had her sussed much better than I did. But I was twenty-three, not a kid, and the more he pushed for us to break up, the more I pulled the other way. Tamara was keen to get married and I was determined to show Dad he was completely wrong about marriage.'

She thought of her parents, and of Nadine and Hayden. 'There's every chance he's wrong.'

Contempt instantly filled his face. 'No, Dad was spot on. Tamara and I lasted less than six months. Turns out she desperately wanted to be married to a doctor, only she'd picked the wrong one to suit her purposes. She didn't want the lifestyle that goes with an intern working sixty-plus hours a week, so she conveniently found herself another doctor—older, richer and further up the career ladder.'

The hurt in his voice was like a knife in her chest and her hand briefly stroked his arm, wanting to lessen his pain. 'She walked away from a good man.'

He shrugged off her words. 'It taught me a valuable lesson and now I listen to my father. I don't do long-term relationships and I won't ever let another woman put me in that position. I will never get married again.'

His matter-of-fact tone tinged with bitterness crashed down on her like a lead weight. *I will never get married again.* His words bellowed in her head and crazily part of her heart ripped slightly as her stomach unexpectedly tipped upside down.

Nausea rose upwards, almost making her gag.

His hand touched her arm. 'Are you OK? You look a bit white.'

She stepped back slightly, breaking the contact. 'I don't think I should have had that fried chicken from the snack bar.'

Instantly concern etched his face. 'Are you up to this rodeo?'

She gave herself a shake and plastered a smile on her lips. 'Absolutely. We can't have you going back to Sydney next year without experiencing the quintessential outback event.'

She marched toward the arena, wishing she could ride on a bucking bull. It would be a hell of a lot safer than dealing with Linton's personal bombshells.

Linton flinched every time a cowboy hit the dirt, bucked off a raging bull within seconds of being released from the pen. Emily had doggedly pushed through the crowd and she stood on the third rung of the blue temporary railing, while he stood slightly below her, his feet firmly on the ground. They were so close to the action that dust clogged his nostrils.

She called down to him. 'The cowboy needs to sit over his hand. If he leans back he can be whipped forward as the bull bucks. He doesn't want to do that because he can collide with the horns.' Emily pointed to the current rider who stayed seated using his posture and the power of his thighs to grip the beast.

Even through the dust and the aroma of the animals, her perfume taunted him. He should be transfixed by the skill of the cowboys on the bulls, but he kept sneaking peeks at her. He hadn't expected her to be wearing a skirt today but the layered denim flared out around her knees every time she moved, flashing a hint of skin—the only bit of her skin visible before the rest of her shapely legs disappeared under the decorative leather of her knee-high boots. The floral motif in cream, pink and green hugged her calves before merging into stitched pink leather.

He'd never seen pink cowgirl boots before—they were distinctively Emily. She could wear the most unusual things with flair.

He flexed his fingers against the urge to rest his palm against the area of soft skin behind her knee. He closed his eyes against the image of creamy thighs.

Being friends with Emily was supposed to have flattened out his response to her. Lusting after friends wasn't acceptable and yet every time he slotted her into a safe hole, every time he pegged her down, she surprised him. She had more facets than crystal and every one of them intrigued him.

Bright, intelligent, funny and prosaic, he enjoyed every moment he spent with her. Since he'd apologised she'd seemed more relaxed around him and the last seven days had been one of the best weeks he'd spent in Warragurra.

One of the best weeks you've had anywhere.

He refused to acknowledge the thought. *She's just a friend.*

'No!' Emily's voice speared through him.

Surely he hadn't spoken his thoughts out loud?

A flash of blue and large expanse of pink suddenly pushed past him as Emily flung her leg over the railing.

He grabbed her, stalling her flight. 'What are you doing?' Irrational fear for her gripped his chest.

Her look of incredulity threw him and he quickly scanned the arena. A cowboy lay eerily still in the red dirt as the bull charged frantically round the ring.

He'd been so busy gazing at Emily he'd missed the moment the cowboy had been thrown.

His grip tightened around her thigh. 'You're not going in there until the bull has been penned, and then I'm coming with you.'

Her mouth flattened into a mulish line but she stayed still. 'The moment the first-aiders arrive we can go in.'

Seconds ticked by, lengthened by the impotence of not being able to act until the scene was safe and secured. Finally, the bull disappeared into the pen, the gate closing firmly behind it.

'Now.' Emily shook off Linton's hand and jumped down, a plume of red dust rising behind her.

He hurdled the railing and quickly followed.

They crossed the wide arena, arriving at the cowboy just as the first-aid workers arrived.

'Good to see you, Doc.' Ash, one of the first-aiders, immediately handed over his kit, relief clear on his face.

'Troy, where does it hurt?' Emily's hands started to open the cowboy's shirt, looking for injury.

'I thought I was free, I thought I was clear, but then he

tossed me and caught me on the leg.' Troy struggled, trying to sit up, but fell back in pain.

'I need the scissors.'

Ash handed her a pair of shears and with precision born of experience she quickly cut the cowboy's jeans straight up the front.

Linton's gut heaved as he registered the extent of the injury on Troy's leg. The bull's horn had entered his leg, piercing the skin, with an entry and an exit wound. The leg lay at a strange angle to its partner, a sure sign of a fracture. 'Did it trample you?'

'Nah, I managed to roll away.'

'You're damn lucky.'

He caught Emily's relieved expression and nodded. If the hoof or horn of a five-hundred-kilogram bull had connected with Troy's chest or abdomen, there was every chance the cowboy would now be dead.

He turned his attention back to the leg while Emily wrapped a tourniquet around Troy's arm. 'The anterior tibia artery and the peroneal artery run pretty close to this puncture wound. What's his BP like?'

'One hundred on sixty.' Emily chewed her bottom lip. 'Is he bleeding into his leg?'

Linton pressed his fingers on the top of Troy's foot, feeling for the pedal pulse, which was weak and thready. 'He's lucky Warragurra Base is only a ten-minute ambulance ride away or I would have to make a fasciotomy incision to release the trapped blood and relieve the pressure.'

'Will my leg be OK?' Troy's voice wobbled.

Linton sighed. 'I'm pretty certain you've fractured your fibula, one of the bones in your lower leg. I'm worried about nerve damage and infection so the sooner we get you to

Warragurra Base and under the care of Jeremy Fallon, the better.'

'Em, I'm really thirsty.' The young man's face was covered in dirt.

Emily swiftly inserted the IV. 'Troy, you'll be going to the operating theatre so I can't give you anything to drink, but you can rinse your mouth.'

Ash handed her a water bottle and together they helped Troy rinse and spit.

Using sterile gauze and saline, Linton cleaned and covered the puncture wounds before sliding an inflatable splint onto Troy's lower leg. 'As soon as you're at the hospital we'll give you a tetanus shot and a huge amount of antibiotics.'

The dazed cowboy nodded vaguely, shock starting to catch up with him.

The piercing siren of the ambulance heralded its arrival. Andrew and fellow paramedic Pete jumped out and opened the back door.

Emily jogged over to assist.

Linton looked up just as Andrew's arm slid around her waist for an instant as he leaned in to greet her.

Green rage stabbed him in the chest so hard he gasped. His legs tensed as if to propel him up from his squatting position like a runner in the blocks, to project him over to place himself firmly between Andrew and Emily.

His hands shook on the splint. He breathed deeply, focusing on the job like it was a lifeline. None of this made any sense. If he'd learned one thing in the last two weeks it was that he wouldn't let anything compromise his friendship with Emily.

Especially lust. He'd almost messed things up once and he wouldn't risk that happening again. Emily was his nurse, his friend and his good mate.

Besides, Emily was a country girl who deserved to marry a guy who wanted a rural life and a tribe of kids. He didn't want any of that.

Friendship was what they both wanted, what they had agreed on.

She called his name and he looked up into silver-grey eyes full of concern for their patient but backlit with a simmering heat. A heat he instantly recognised. A heat he knew he matched.

A fireball of lust exploded in his chest, matching the heat of desire and naked need in her eyes.

A need they had for each other. A need their friendship hadn't diminished one tiny bit. If anything, it had increased it, ramping it up to a raging inferno.

Emily cleared her throat and tossed her head, forcing down the thunderous wave of molten craving for Linton that had suddenly exploded inside her when he'd caught her gaze. He'd stared so deeply into her eyes she could have sworn he'd seen her soul. 'Um, Andrew and Pete want to know if you're riding back to the hospital with Troy?'

Linton stood up. 'If Jeremy can meet the ambulance at the hospital, I won't have to go back. Troy's vital signs are stable for travel, Pete and Andrew are the most experienced paramedics and Daniel is more than capable of doing the pre-op stuff. I'll talk to Jeremy now.' He punched a number into his phone and then hailed Andrew to bring the stretcher.

Andrew dropped down next to their patient. 'Right, Troy, we're going to transfer you now. Can you lift yourself up on your arms? Pete and I will help you.' He put his arms under Troy's.

Emily controlled Troy's legs.

'On my count. One, two, three…' Andrew grunted.

A moment later Troy was lying on the stretcher, his face pale and sweaty. 'I'd rather be riding the bull.'

'You'll be feeling a lot better in a few hours.' Emily patted his arm.

Troy grabbed her hand. 'Eric's kept pretty quiet about his stunning sister. How about a date?'

'Get in line,' Andrew quipped, but his expression stayed serious.

Emily laughed and extricated her hand from Troy's. 'Ask me when you can dance on both legs, cowboy.' She waved, floating on the compliments as Andrew and Pete started to push the stretcher toward the rig.

'Ask you what?' Linton's breath caressed her ear, his brown hair brushing hers as he leaned in close.

She gave a self-conscious laugh to cover her hammering heart. 'Troy's high on painkillers and wants to ask me out on a date.'

Linton grunted as his arm snaked around her waist. 'Come on, we have to get out of the arena.' He ushered her across to the nearest gate.

She fully expected his arm to drop away the moment they were on the spectators' side of the gate but he left it there, the touch casually light but, oh, so wonderful. 'I gather Jeremy is at the hospital.'

'Yep, which means you can continue with showing me the rodeo.'

A crazy feeling of relief ricocheted through her. She shouldn't care so much that he was staying, but she did.

'Emmie! Emmie!'

Emily looked around but couldn't see who was calling her name. Suddenly, a pair of arms wrapped themselves around her knees. 'Tyler.' She tousled his hair. 'Where's Mummy?'

Linton moved away and Emily saw him relieve Nadine of the pram.

Her sister-in-law gave a weary smile. 'I hear you've both had a bit of excitement.'

'I saw the ambulance's red flashing lights,' Tyler announced proudly. 'Now I'm going to watch Daddy get the heifer to run around like the number eight.'

'If we can ever get close enough.' Nadine sighed as the crowd surged around them.

'I think I can help with that.' Linton bent down to Tyler's height. 'Would you like a ride on my shoulders so you can see?'

Tyler glanced at Nadine, who nodded.

'Yes, please!'

Linton hoisted the almost four-year-old up onto his shoulders.

Tyler yelled out, 'Yee-hah' and pretended to crack a whip.

Linton attempted to whinny.

Emily bit her lip as she caught the enthusiastic grins on both the big boy's and the little boy's faces. Yet this was the man who didn't want to marry and have children. Did he have any clue what he was going to miss out on by not being a father?

'Having fun?' Nadine asked softly, her brown eyes seeing far too much.

'More fun than Troy.' She quickly followed Linton, making way for the pram and avoiding a conversation she didn't want to have with her sister-in-law.

Nadine found a place to sit so she could feed Alby, and Emily and Linton safely flanked the enthusiastic Tyler on the rails. Cheering, they watched closely as all the Tippett men manoeuvred their horses through their paces.

'They're so fast.' Admiration vibrated through Linton's voice.

She smiled at his interest. 'They need to be. I know a lot of mustering gets done by helicopter these days but a good stockman and his horse are invaluable. There are plenty of times when you have to cut a beast out from the mob and send it into the stockyard.'

'They don't seem to like being separated.' Linton pointed to Hayden as he wielded his horse around to drive the heifer away from the mob.

'It's a natural instinct to return to the safety of the mob. Bit like humans really. What you know seems safest, but it's not what is necessarily best for you.'

He tilted his head and studied her for a moment. 'Like how for the last few years you've been trying to be the person you think people want you to be rather than being true to yourself?' His gaze shot precise darts. 'Like dyeing your hair when everything gets too much for you?'

Air whooshed out of her lungs as if they'd been punctured. She gripped the railing, her head spinning. He'd worked it out—the connection between how she was feeling and her hair. His intuition scared her. It was like being stripped naked in front of him and being completely on show.

She defiantly lifted her chin, grappling to regain her composure. 'Actually, I was thinking more of you. How you're scared of letting yourself get close to anyone again so you date and move on. It sounds lonely to me, and doesn't it get tiring?'

'I'm close to plenty of people.' Emerald eyes flashed angrily and deep furrows creased his brow. 'I know what works for me and relationships don't. I have the right to make that choice.'

'Look!' Tyler pulled on Linton's sleeve, breaking the moment as Eric rode in on his new horse, rider and beast moving almost in unison. He jumped on the rails in excitement. 'Uncle Eric said he's going to win.'

Emily studied the horse's reactions to her brother's touch, part of her thankful, part of her frustrated, that the difficult conversation had just been cut short. 'I think he needs a bit more time to get to know his horse and then he could be un-beatable.'

Linton slid his hand on the little boy's back, pushing him gently against the rails to keep him safe. 'I think it would be great if a Tippett won. Maybe one day you'll be out there.'

'Of course I will be.'

Linton grinned. 'Good to see a man who knows his mind.'

They watched the rest of the competition and then all the Tippett men joined them, Hayden victorious with the winner's cup and Eric agreeably accepting second place.

'But watch your back, bro. Next year that cup is mine.'

Laughter and banter carried in the air as dusk fell quickly. The stars rose and twinkled in the night sky and the carnival part of the rodeo kicked off. Country and western music floated across the showgrounds; squeals and screams rent the air as heart-stopping, body-jolting, adrenaline-rushing rides spun and twirled, their lights merging into bright lines of red, green and blue.

The sideshow alley quickly filled with strolling couples and excited children. Cowboys showed off their skill with popguns, mowing down the moving metal ducks and claiming prizes for their girls. Children, sticky with fairy floss, fell asleep on their fathers' shoulders, the wonder of the day catching up with them. Nadine and Hayden gathered their children and headed off to the babysitter's, planning to return and enjoy an evening of grown-up fun, while the other Tippett men drifted off to the band tent.

Suddenly Linton's hand caught Emily's. 'Come on. Stuart tells me that if I want to be a cowboy, apart from being able to rope and tie, sit on a horse for twelve hours a day and wrestle a steer, I need to take a girl line-dancing.' He winked at her. 'And those pink boots of yours look like they can teach my boring brown ones to dance.'

Laughter threatened to tumble from her lips. Urbane Linton line-dancing was an impossible image. But she glimpsed the same sense of purpose in his eyes that he always wore at work, whether it was in the middle of an emergency or teaching the medical students.

Luxurious warmth flooded her. He was offering to go line-dancing because he thought it was what she wanted to do. He was a sincere, caring man, the polar opposite of Nathan. She didn't even want to compare the two of them because it was no contest at all.

When she'd lashed out at him after the ball it had been because she'd wanted him to see her for who she truly was, and today on the railings he'd told her with pinpoint accuracy that had seen and knew the real Emily. He was a great friend.

Sure, but he still wants you.

The heat and lust that had passed between them in the arena had left her in no doubt that he still desired her. Only this time it was different. This time she knew she meant more to him than just a curvaceous body.

And you want him.

She accepted the words without argument. Her defences against the overwhelming attraction she had for him had now crumbled to dust. Every time he stood near her she quivered with need. She wanted to be in his arms, she wanted his touch on every part of her body, she wanted…him. All of him.

And for the first time in her life she really knew what she wanted. She wanted what he was prepared to give—one night.

The acknowledgement of that truth sent a glorious sense of freedom through her. She was finally being true to herself. She didn't care what people would think, she didn't have to hide behind clothes or other people's opinions. She was no longer scared of disappointing someone, and if she did, well, it didn't matter.

Linton had looked at her today like no man had ever looked at her—with naked and consuming need.

And she wanted him with every part of herself.

He doesn't want a wife or family. You can't have sex and still be friends. The rational thoughts tried valiantly to implant themselves into her euphoria.

But she closed her mind to them. She was done with being sensible and cautious. She'd worry about all of that tomorrow. Right now she wanted to see that look in his eyes again. The look that said, 'I want you now.'

But she knew he wouldn't act on it because of the way she'd rejected his last attempt at seduction.

No, this time she would have to be the one to ask.

The idea thrilled and terrified her all at the same time.

CHAPTER TEN

'UM, ISN'T the line-dancing tent in the opposite direction?' Linton glanced around as Emily firmly dragged him away from sideshow alley, the sounds of the night receding into the distance.

Her left hand rested on her hip, her expression cheeky. 'No self-respecting cowboy learns to dance in public.' She turned toward the stables. 'I'll run you through the basic steps first, before unleashing you on an unsuspecting crowd.'

'Hey, I'm not that uncoordinated.' But his comment was lost in the noise of the old wooden door sliding open.

The sweet smell of hay wafted out to meet them, the aroma released by cool air meeting warm. Emily flicked on a light. The naked bulb struggled to emit a weak yellow glow. A horse neighed.

'Hey, Blossom, it's just me.'

She moved inside and stroked the horse's head as three other familiar-looking horses stirred from their rest, inquisitively looking to see who had entered their domain.

Linton followed, his eyes quickly adjusting to the gloom. 'Isn't that Eric's horse?' He recognised the distinctive patterned coat.

Emily smiled. 'Well spotted, Doctor. We might just make

a cowboy out of you yet. Welcome to the Tippett barn. We use this stable at rodeo time and during the agricultural show. During the show, we basically live here for a week.'

He took in the fairly primitive surroundings. 'Where do you sleep?'

'There's a loft upstairs.' She pointed to a ladder. 'It's luxury compared to a swag on hard ground.' She clapped her hands together. 'Right, let's see what you're made of, and if you can impress the girls.' She circled her arm, indicating the interested horses.

He growled in indignation. 'I always impress the girls.'

She arched her brows and wrinkled her button nose. 'Is that so?'

The challenge fizzed in her eyes, socking him in the chest. It was the first sign of blatant flirting he'd ever seen from her.

'So, you stand legs apart.' She adopted a wide stance. 'Put your weight on your left foot and then step your right diagonally forward like this.'

He copied her actions.

'Then you lock your left foot behind and step your right foot to the right. This is called wizard or Dorothy steps.'

'As in the Wizard of Oz?' He executed the basic steps.

'I suppose so. Now we do it all to the left and then again to the right.'

He danced the steps both left and right. 'This is pretty simple, and it's all to the count of eight?'

'You catch on fast, cowboy.' She flashed a wide smile, her white teeth gleaming in the low light.

His gut kicked over. 'What about the promenade?'

She quickly moved in front of him, her back pressing firmly against his front as she placed his right hand on her waist and held his left hand up above her shoulder.

Her heat instantly invaded his body, darting in deep and rippling out, before settling in his groin. He swallowed a groan.

She moved forward and he moved with her, and together they walked in a circle between the horse stalls. 'This is a square dancing position.' She twirled in his arms and came to face him, her hands resting palms down on his chest, her fingers splayed in proprietorial firmness.

Silver eyes gazed up at him from under thick brown lashes. 'Line-dancing is pretty much all about no-touch technique.'

The words washed over him, their sultry tone leaving little to be interpreted.

He met her gaze full on. 'Square dancing sounds like much more fun.'

'So why am I teaching you line-dancing?' Her arms snaked around his neck as she rose on the tips of her pink leather boots and kissed him.

Soft, luxurious lips closed over his, nipping at his bottom lip, firmly giving and demanding at the same time. White lights fired in his head.

He'd memorised the touch of her mouth but the reality of it outshone the memory, dimming it to a dull, flat grey.

For a few blissful moments he passively accepted the caresses, the kisses and the wonder of the sexiest mouth he'd ever known. But with each stroke of her tongue, with each nip of her teeth, his desire raged against his self-imposed restraint until it spilled over, hot and demanding.

He kissed her right back.

He tasted the spice of her perfume, the musk of desire and the simplicity of need.

He recognised that need. He knew it intimately.

With one gentle tug the pearl snap buttons on her blouse

opened and he gave thanks for the ease of western clothing. His hand touched fiery hot skin. As he nuzzled her neck, his fingers dealt with the more complicated issue of her bra fastening. The frothy lace finally gave way and ripe, heavy flesh rested where it belonged, in the curve of his hand.

It felt so right. His thumb caressed her breast, teasing her nipple to rise against his skin.

She gasped.

Pulling back slightly, she ripped open his shirt, pressing her lips against his chest, her tongue abrading his nipples.

He locked his knees for support as his blood pounded away from his head.

He gently gripped her head, raising her mouth back to his and then his hands caressed her breasts, kneading and stroking, until she sank against him, her moans of pleasure threatening his control.

Suddenly she pulled away, panting, her lips glistening and swollen and her eyes large black discs of pure lust. She'd never looked so beautiful.

The cool evening air rushed in against his bare chest, bringing his surroundings back into focus, and some sanity along with it.

This was Emily. His friend. His hand rubbed the back of his neck. 'What are we doing?' Somehow his voice managed to croak out the words.

She grabbed his hand. 'What we both want.'

He pulled her against him, staring hard into her eyes. 'This isn't a good idea.' He tried to make the words sound convincing as his body screamed in protest.

Her hand cupped his cheek. 'I think it's a perfect idea.'

He tugged at his hair. 'Are you sure this is what you want. I can't prom—'

She put her forefinger against his lips. 'Shh. It's all right. This time I know what I'm doing. I want this. One night is all I'm asking.'

'Em—'

Her mouth crushed his, filling him with her flavour of innocence and arousal.

Step back now! But the faint voice struggled to make itself heard against the pounding of his blood and the raging power of his desire for this incredibly sexy woman who stood in front of him.

As hard as it had been, he'd stepped back once before when she hadn't wanted him.

But this time she was offering.

Just one night.

This time he couldn't step back.

Somehow, on boneless legs they made it up the ladder to a mattress bedded down on hay. Emily knelt in front of him, her chin tilted, her shoulders back as she shrugged off her already open shirt and bra. The white soft glow of moonlight shone through the cracks of the corrugated iron, highlighting her alabaster skin, shadowing the curves of her body and making her look like a Florentine statue.

He gazed, mesmerised by the gift he had in front of him.

Then she smiled and reached for his belt.

In an instant he had her on her back. 'Sweetheart if you want this cowboy to perform at his best, he shucks his own pants.'

She laughed, her eyes dancing with wicked intent.

A sudden realisation of practicalities sounded through the fog of Linton's desire. 'I wasn't planning this. I don't have a condom.'

She stroked a finger down his chest, her voice suddenly serious. 'It's OK. I've been on the Pill for a very long time.'

Take her, she's yours. The last barrier of sense fell away and he lowered his head to hers, losing himself in her mouth, in the softness of her breasts, in the generosity of her body, which welcomed him like no other ever had.

Emily's hands gripped Linton's head as his mouth grazed across her body, lighting a fire of sensation that built in intensity with every stroke of his tongue. Nothing had prepared her for this. Not any of her fantasies, certainly not the controlling sex she'd known with Nathan. Nothing at all.

Pleasure morphed with pain. Her breasts ached with need, her legs quivered with longing, and a desperate emptiness inside her pleaded to be filled.

He paused for a moment, lifting his head, his eyes dark with arousal. He gently swept her hands up above her head. 'Sweetheart, I can't move if you immobilise my head. Lie back and enjoy, I want to give you this.'

'But I want you, I need you.' She whimpered the words on a ragged breath. She didn't care that she was pleading—nothing mattered except her need of him.

'Oh, my darling, you'll have me, don't worry about that.' He flashed a wicked grin and dropped his head between her legs.

She shattered at his touch, crying out his name as her body called for his.

He cradled her close, his whispered words promising her longed-for fulfilment. Then he eased inside her slowly, her muscles straining, and she felt his hesitation.

'No, don't stop.' Her hands clawed at his buttocks.

His eyes, full of caring, gazed down at her and then she moved against him, taking him, accepting all of him, driving them both to a place way beyond the stars.

She came back to earth piece by piece, completely reconfigured, a new Emily.

She lay snuggled in his arms, languorous and sated, but at the same time feeling more energised than she'd ever felt in her life.

She loved resting her head on his chest, hearing his heart beat strongly and rhythmically beneath her ear. Loved the way a trail of pale brown hair arrowed down his washboard flat abdomen, hinting at the power that lay at its destination.

And what a mighty power it was.

Linton was the most amazing lover. Not that she had vast experience to draw on, but from what he'd just shown her, she knew he was the man for her.

The *only* man for her.

Her stomach suddenly rolled.

Oh, God, she loved him.

No, this couldn't be happening. This was a one-night stand, a physical thing, pure lust, pure insanity. It was supposed to be the answer to her moving on—make love and get him out of her system.

But instead she'd fallen in love with a kind and generous man who had set her on the path of realising she could be whoever she wanted to be. A man who listened to her, took a great interest in her life and actively encouraged her to take risks, and at the same time acted as her safety net.

A man who only ever wanted one night. A man who didn't believe in for ever.

Leave now.

Shock drowned her. Nausea pulled at her and she breathed deeply, trying to settle her stomach. She couldn't be sick. Not here. Every part of her screamed to get away. She rolled from his side, sat up and pulled her shirt on.

He stirred and reached for her, his voice thick with post-coital relaxation. 'Hey, where are you going?'

She tugged on her boots before another spasm hit her, making her double over. 'Bathroom. Dodgy rodeo food.'

'Wait, I'll come with you.' He pushed a muscular arm through his shirtsleeve.

Her foot hit the top rung of the ladder, bile scalding her throat. 'Can't wait.'

'Emily!'

But she ignored his call, ignored the incredulity in his voice and she ran out of the stable and straight to the toilet block, her stomach surging.

Slamming the cubicle door behind her, she promptly vomited into the bowl.

The security guard outside the bank of women's portable toilets gave Linton a severe look. 'Can I help you, sir?'

Linton silently groaned. He'd been looking for Emily for ten minutes, quietly saying her name outside a few of the cubicles, trying not to draw attention to himself. What did you say to a security guard when you'd lost the woman you'd just had sex with?

'I'm waiting for someone.'

His brain spun. He'd just experienced some of the most amazing sex of his life and now Emily had disappeared. Part of him thought he must have imagined the whole thing. But he could still smell her perfume on his skin, and feel her hands on his body, taste her on his lips. It hadn't been a dream. It had been a glorious reality.

And lying with Emily for those few precious minutes with her warm body snuggled against his had been… He reached for a word but all he could come up with was 'perfect'. He frowned. That couldn't be the right word at all.

And then she'd rushed off.

Usually that's your role.

He stiffened against the thought and ran his hands through his hair. He needed to see her, needed to talk to her. Check she was OK, not just from food poisoning but also in other ways.

He started pacing. What had he just done? He'd let desire overrule every aspect of common sense. Emily wasn't a one-night sort of a girl. If he could just talk to her, check she was OK.

Make sure she has no expectations. The cynical voice pulled no punches.

He kicked the dirt, trying to kick the acrid thought away. No, he would take her out to dinner on a real date so they could firm up their friendship. Make sure it would survive tonight's madness.

A squeaky door opened and he spun around. A white-faced Emily appeared.

He instantly put his arm around her, worried she was about to fall over. 'You look shocking.'

She mustered a wry smile. 'Gee, you sure know how to make a girl feel good.'

He tucked stray curls hair behind her ear and whispered, 'I've never made a girl sick before.'

She patted his arm. 'No need to worry, your reputation is intact. I brought this on myself. I stupidly let that aroma of salt and deep-fried fat tempt me, and it makes me sick every time.' She sighed as contrition filled her face. 'Sorry. It wasn't the best way to end something that was pretty spectacular.'

'It was spectacular, wasn't it?' He grinned despite himself.

'But completely insane.' She wobbled against him.

He tilted her chin with his fingers, forcing her to look at him. 'Do you regret it?'

Shadows darkened her eyes before she quickly blinked several times. 'No, of course not.' Her words rushed out, tumbling over each other, almost too definite. 'It was my idea, remember? Just one night and this was it.'

The firmness of her voice should have reassured him. Instead, disquiet wove through him that he had trouble shrugging off.

She cleared her throat. 'I really need to go home to bed.'

'I'll take you.'

She pulled away from his touch. 'Dad's going to take me. I texted him.'

Her dismissal of him rankled. 'I would have happily taken you.'

She shrugged. 'You don't need a forty-minute drive in both directions.'

He should be relieved that she wasn't clingy, that she had no expectations of him. Instead, he had this crazy sensation of being discarded 'So…you'll be OK?'

She folded her arms across her chest. 'I'll be fine after some ginger tea and a long sleep.'

His skin prickled with frustration. 'I'll see you next week, then.'

She waved to her father and Stuart, who had just appeared in the distance. 'No, on Monday I leave for Sydney.'

Her soft words hit with the force of a punch. 'What do you mean, you'll be in Sydney?'

'I'm taking some annual leave to finish two assignments, as well as doing my residential week for my Master's. I'll be gone almost three weeks.'

All control seemed to be streaming away from him. 'Hang on, you can't just leave.'

She sighed and shook her head. 'Do you *ever* read your

memos, Linton? Cathy and Michael are back from their honeymoon so you'll have your old team back. You'll have a great time and you won't even miss me.'

She turned and greeted her father. 'Sorry, Dad.'

Jim rolled his eyes. 'Honestly, Emily, you know you shouldn't eat rodeo food. Come on, I'll take you home.' He put his arm around his daughter's shoulder. 'Night all.'

''Night.' Linton watched them walk away with an inexplicable feeling of isolation.

Stuart clapped him on the shoulder. 'You any good at pool?'

The question startled him. 'Fair, although your sister's whipped me at it twice. Why?'

'Mark's off romancing the kinder teacher so the Tippett team is one short. And I wouldn't worry about Em, she whips most of us.'

He should say no. He should go home. This wasn't his family. But his family had never offered him anything like this sense of belonging. The feel-good flush at being included overrode the amber caution light that started flashing in his brain, telling him his inclusion in this family's life was getting way too deep.

CHAPTER ELEVEN

SYDNEY'S unseasonably warm winter sun sparkled off the blue water of the harbour. Emily sat in the park at Circular Quay, admiring the architectural brilliance of the Opera House, the distinctive sails glowing white in the sunshine. Street theatre drew crowds, with young English and American backpackers doing feats of brilliance with fire and chainsaws, their engaging banter filling the air.

There was colour and movement, cosmopolitan sophistication, big city verve but, as much as she enjoyed it all, she was counting down the days until she returned to Warragurra.

Her mobile phone rang, the display unreadable in the bright sunlight. 'Hello, Emily Tippett.'

'Why aren't you in lectures?'

A deep voice tinged with mock seriousness rumbled down the line, warming her in places sunshine never could. She instantly smiled. 'Why are you ringing me if you think I won't answer?'

Linton had been calling and texting with increasing frequency during her time in Sydney. It had been the last thing she'd expected and it totally confused her. But she refused to dwell on that confusion. Instead, she lost herself in the sound of his voice.

He laughed. 'Good point. I should have texted you but I had a few minutes spare after a frantic morning.'

She heard the warbling of magpies over the phone and a wave of homesickness hit her. 'Where are you?'

'Down by the river.'

She pictured the gnarly river red gums lining the ancient watercourse, casting their much-needed shade over the often dry and dusty park.

'Where are *you*?'

His welcome voice broke into her thoughts. 'Outside the Museum of Contemporary Art.'

'Exactly what course are you studying?' His teasing warmth radiated down the phone. 'So will patients now be getting a dissertation on modernism in Australia as well as an ECG?'

She laughed, loving the buzz that vibrated inside her when they had these silly conversations. 'That's right. And I was thinking we need fluorescent gel for the ultrasound so we can create works of art on abdomens.'

'It has interesting possibilities. Of course, I think the professional approach would be to workshop it first.' His voice became husky. 'I'd happily donate my abdomen to the cause.'

The image of his flat, toned stomach flooded her mind. Her fingers tingled as if they could still feel the strength of it and her mouth recalled the salty taste. Puffs of heat spiralled through her and she had to force her voice to sound normal, rather than breathless, which it so wanted to be. 'I'll keep that in mind.'

His flirting was killing her but, tragic case that she was, she lived for his daily phone calls and his supportive texts, which seemed to pop up just when she thought her head would explode from too much academic jargon. He made her laugh and that in turn made her put her studies into perspective.

She dusted lint off her fine corduroy skirt. 'I just needed some air. I'm completely over having to apply theory to everyday things which are as much a part of me as breathing. I can't wait to come home.' *I can't wait to see you in person, even though it will only be at work.*

'Well, not long now. You're flying back on Saturday afternoon, right?'

'Yep, right in the middle of the grand final match.' She could hear her brothers groaning from here. 'Somehow I don't think familial devotion is so strong that the lads will abandon the match to collect me, so I'll bring my book and wait until half-time, when a taxi might take the chance at a fare.'

'I'll pick you up.'

The offer came instantly, shocking her, sending her blood to her feet. But at the same time buoying her up. 'Really? Are you sure? I wasn't dropping a hint.'

'Emily.' The stern doctor's voice had materialised.

She could imagine him rolling his eyes and shaking his head.

'It would be my pleasure to pick you up. It will be great to see you and, besides, I owe you dinner.'

'You do?'

'I do.' His voice was firm. 'I'll see you on Saturday, then. Bye.'

'Bye.' *I love you.* The unspoken words boomed in her head.

Suddenly a blast of energy whipped through her, urging her to deal with the final outstanding assignments required by the end of her residential week. Then she could head home. Home to Linton.

Hugging the thought close, she grabbed her backpack and jumped to her feet. The Opera House tilted sideways, the green grass at her feet spun upwards and her stomach flipped over and over before surging up to scald the back of her throat. She sat down heavily on the seat and waited for the spinning to stop.

She slowly blew out a breath to steady herself. That had been weird. Perhaps she was hungry? She rummaged through her bag, looking for a lolly or a muesli bar, something that would give her an instant sugar fix. Her fingers grasped a foil packet and she pulled it out, but it was only her contraceptive pill. She almost dropped it back in the bag but her fingers gripped it harder as she noticed she was about to start the hormone tablets again.

A rogue thought struck her. She should have had her period by now.

Her heart pounded hard against her ribs. She slowly counted backwards, her mind trying to race against her imposed thoroughness. She *always* started her period on the second day of the placebo tablets and she'd taken the seventh placebo last night.

Her roiling stomach plummeted to her feet. *No.* She couldn't be pregnant. She couldn't. She'd never missed a pill—she'd taken it every day at the same time for the three years since she'd gone on it to lessen period pain.

But you'd never had sex while on this brand of pill.

Her head fell into her hands as realisation slugged her. The night they'd made love she'd been sick, so even though she'd taken the pill, it hadn't stayed in her system long enough to do the job it had been designed to do.

It was a classic mistake. One she'd seen women make over and over.

Only she was a health professional. She knew better. She straightened up, holding onto that thought like a lifeline. The problem here was that she knew too much and she was jumping to silly conclusions. She wouldn't be pregnant— there would be some other much more reasonable explanation.

She threw her backpack over her shoulder and walked to the closest chemist, ignoring the wobbly sensation that had transferred from her stomach to her legs. On auto pilot she purchased a pregnancy test.

Five minutes later, in the spartan confines of a public toilet, she worried her bottom lip, her eyes glued to the stick in the little plastic cup.

Nothing was happening. She blew out a long-held breath. She'd just panicked and caused herself a heap of stress for nothing.

The timer on her watch sounded and she picked up the stick and cup, ready to dispose of them in the bin.

A faint blue colour slowly emerged, darkening before her eyes.

Pregnant.

She slumped against the cubicle wall. Oh, God, how had her life come to this?

Gulping in air, she tried to think clearly as a thousand thoughts charged around her head. She was going to be a mother. She was going to have a baby.

Linton's baby.

Sheer joy and abject fear collided in her chest.

It will be great to see you. I owe you dinner. Linton's deep, sexy voice bounced around her head. On the phone he'd sounded genuinely pleased that she was coming home.

Had he missed her? She delved in her pack and found her

phone. Flicking through her inbox, she counted and averaged that she'd received about two texts a day from him and she could only remember two or three days they hadn't spoken.

And he'd initiated all of it. Surely that meant something.

It *had* to mean something.

Perhaps all his talk about never marrying again, never having children, were now empty words. Perhaps the playboy doctor had decided his playing days were over and he was ready to settle down.

I don't do long-term relationships and I won't ever let another women put me in that position. I will never get married again. His bitter words peppered her brain.

Darkness closed in on her. She loved this man and carried his child. It should be a wonderful, wonderful thing. But would he see it that way?

Plans and ideas popped into her head, things she could do, things that would make it easier for him, how she could lessen the impact, how she could…

Stop it! The tumbling thoughts abruptly stopped.

That would be a backward step. No, she had to stay true to herself and she knew what she had to do. She would return to Warragurra and tell him that she loved him, and that they were going to be parents.

Then she would ask him to marry her.

Linton scanned the wide blue skies, his hand shielding his eyes from the glare of a Warragurra sun, which hinted at the extreme heat that would arrive in a few months. Winter was fast coming to a close and the brilliant red of the flowering gums in the main street declared spring could not be stopped.

The airport was extremely quiet as the entire town was at the grand final, the Roosters having managed to turn around their form late in the finals. Team flags fluttered in the breeze, the distinctive maroon and yellow decorating everything that stood still at the airport and in the town.

He leaned against the waist-high cyclone fence, enjoying being on his own. Work had been busy but with Michael and Cathy back it had, as Emily had predicted, been very smooth.

But he'd missed Emily. Her sharp wit, her friendly smiles, her total absence of obsequiousness…

You missed her body, too.

He ran his hand across the back of his neck. He couldn't deny it. He missed her lingering perfume, the way his hand fitted in the small of her back when she passed through a doorway before him, and he missed the way her eyes sparkled when she smiled.

It was crazy but he felt cheated by the fact she'd rushed off to Sydney. Their *one night* had left him feeling short-changed because it hadn't been one night. It had been an hour.

But at the same time part of him had been worried that she would regret having given herself to him, that everything between them would have changed. However, over the phone she seemed to be the same Emily as the one he'd known before they'd made love.

His good mate.

He usually only made love with experienced women, never totally trusting a naïve 'just tonight' because they usually wanted a hell of a lot more from him.

Like Tamara had.

And Emily, despite her previous relationship, wasn't experienced. Women like Emily wanted home and hearth and a happy ever after.

He couldn't promise that to anyone.

But hearing her voice each day had helped allay his fears and she certainly hadn't sounded like she had any regrets. She'd obviously meant what she said.

Just one night, and this was it. The space under his ribs ached and he pressed against it, wondering if he should have a liver-function test as that ache had been bothering him lately.

He glanced at his watch. Three-thirty. The plane should be here soon and he and Emily could spend the rest of the afternoon and evening together. He'd decided against dinner at the Royal as the grand final crowd would be in full swing.

Instead, he was really looking forward to taking Emily home to dinner and being able to sit across from her when he talked to her rather than imagining if her cute nose was wrinkling or if her hands were busy gesticulating, talking for her as much as her mouth.

He had so much to tell her. Jason had finally managed to master suturing and she'd appreciate what a momentous achievement that was, whereas Cathy had just looked bemused at the high-fives.

The buzz of the Beech Baron's propellers sounded before he sighted the white, five-seater plane. Five minutes later its wheels touched down and it taxied to a stop. The pilot jumped out of the cockpit, pulled down the steps and opened the plane's door.

Two men and a woman appeared and then Emily stood in the doorway, her flyaway curls fire-engine red.

His gut kicked in alarm. What the hell was wrong? But then she smiled and waved and he realised she'd probably just missed Warragurra. He was learning her hair was like an emotional universal indicator, going as many colours as the paper strips in the chemistry lab. The country girl must have tired of the city.

He strode out to meet her, his eyes only for her, when he heard a loud, familiar male voice sound from behind her.

'Linton, I thought I'd surprise you. Lucky for me this young lady seems to know you.' Bushy eyebrows rose in a lecherous look. 'I can see why you're enjoying small-town life.'

His father stood next to Emily, his hand on the small of her back, guiding her in front of him.

Linton's stomach fell to his feet. Of all the days his father could have chosen to have one of his frequent but unannounced visits, this wasn't his best choice. His quiet dinner with Emily evaporated before his eyes. 'Dad.' He extended his hand. 'Good to see you.'

'You're still welcome for dinner.' Linton hauled Emily's bag out of the boot of his car as the farm dogs barked in joyous glee at seeing Emily again.

Emily smiled a tired smile. 'We can do it another time. You head back to town and catch up with your dad.'

Linton slammed the boot closed. 'He does this. Just turns up unannounced for a few days. It's usually when he's between girlfriends.'

'He's probably lonely.' Grey shadows hovered under her eyes and exhaustion hung over her in complete contrast to her usual bubbly style. On the journey out to the station she'd been interested in his conversation but he'd sensed an unusual reserve. Something that hadn't been present in their phone calls.

'Dad's hardly lonely.' But he noticed she hadn't heard his words.

She stood gazing out across Woollara's home-paddock garden, out toward the shearing shed, breathing in deeply. 'It's great to be home.'

She took a tentative step forward, stopped and then gave a self-conscious laugh.

He grinned at the glimpse of a young girl in her face. 'What?'

Her eyes sparkled. 'It will sound silly but when I've been away I usually go and visit the river, and say, "Hello, I'm back."'

He extended his hand, not wanting to leave her just yet. 'Let's go together. I could do with a walk.'

'Thank you. That would be lovely.' Her face broke into a smile that encompassed her entire body, totally vanquishing the tiredness that clung to her.

It was like being showered in golden light, and heat spiralled through him, warming him at first before stoking into a fiery blaze.

Her hand touched his and he pulled her into his arms to placate muscles that had ached to hold her. His lips hungrily sought hers, desperate to taste her, desperate to brand her with his own taste.

She responded instantly, her arms wrapping themselves around his neck, her body moulding itself to his, her lips kissing him until his need for breath made him draw away regretfully.

She laughed as he regained his breath, her arm around his waist. 'I take it that you missed me.'

He slid his arm around her shoulders and started walking toward the river, dropping a light kiss on the top of her head. 'I did.'

The two sheepdogs raced in front of them, before quickly turning and racing away again.

She glanced up at him, her grey eyes serious. 'That's good, because I really missed you.'

A muscle in his neck tightened and he tried laughter to release it. 'So that's why your hair's scarlet.'

She stumbled against him before finding her footing again. 'Partly.'

The softness of her voice sent a streak of discomfort through him. He'd expected her to deny it; he'd expected her to say it was the agonies of having to study nursing theory, the stress of getting two large assignments completed in a short space of time.

They walked the last hundred metres to the riverbank in contemplative silence. She broke away from him and caught the swinging rope that hung from the large gumtree by the side of the waterhole. Her eyes took on a far-away stare. 'I loved swinging off this rope when I was a kid. We'd all come down here and Mum would cook sausages and Dad would be the biggest kid of us all, bombing us as he let go of the rope.' She turned toward him. 'Where did you swim?'

He put his hands gently on her shoulders, the need to touch her, to be connected to her paramount. 'Dad had a pool.' He thought of the times he'd swum there alone, in stark contrast to the scene she'd just depicted.

She stepped in close and unexpectedly dropped her head on his chest as a shudder trembled through her.

The shudder built on his own unease. He ran his hand down her cheek. 'Emily, what's going on?'

She bit her lip and dragged in a breath, tilting her head to look up at him, joy and hesitancy filling her gaze. 'Um, there's no easy way to say this so I just will. We're pregnant.'

Blood pounded loud in his ears as his breath stalled in his lungs. *Pregnant! A child, their child.* For an instant a fuzzy image of a child on his knee and Emily's arms around his neck played through his brain, bringing warmth and a sense of belonging.

Never let yourself get trapped, like I did, son. His father's mantra exploded in his head, driving away the fragile image. Confusion swamped him. He put his hands on her forearms, lifting her slightly away from him. 'How? How can you be pregnant?'

She smiled at him like he was a child himself. 'Three weeks ago we had a pretty intense moment in the loft at the stables.'

Irritation skated through him at her smile. 'I know how babies are made, Emily. But you said you were on the Pill. You said you were protected.'

An anguished look crossed her face. 'I told you the truth, Linton. But when I got sick it mucked up the hormone levels and I didn't even think because it had been such a long time since I'd…'

Made love. He needed to move, he needed to think. He dropped his hands from hers and raked them through his hair. 'Hell, what a mess. Two health professionals who should have known better, with an unwanted pregnancy.'

'It's not unwanted.' Her quiet words sliced deeply through him, like the blade of a surgeon's scalpel. 'I want to have *our* baby very much.'

His head snapped up to meet her gaze. Love shone from silver eyes, pure and all-encompassing. Like a fist to the gut, white pain winded him. His legs threatened to crumple underneath him.

She loves me.

Emily stood before him, loving him and pregnant with his child.

His worst nightmare encircled him, binding him with its tendrils of responsibility and commitment. He didn't want to get married again. He didn't want to be a father. He didn't want to be loved.

He started to pace, his brain slowly emerging from the fog of shock. 'This should never have happened. Getting married for the sake of the child doesn't work. I'm living proof of that. We'll share custody and I'll support you and the child financially.'

Her shoulders stiffened and suddenly she seemed taller. 'So just like that you'll deny your child a loving home.'

Her accusing words stung. 'No, I will not deny this child anything. He will have two loving homes. Yours and mine.' He stared her down. 'It worked for me.'

'Oh, yeah, right, and you're such an emotional rock.' Derision slashed across her face. 'Children need two parents in the same house.'

Memories of his early years pounded in his head and he heard himself yelling, 'Not if the parents are going to tear each other apart.'

'So you're not even prepared to try?'

It took every ounce of his willpower to ignore the disgust in her voice. 'I know it wouldn't work.'

She stepped in close, her scent encircling him, her hand resting gently on his arm. 'I know this is a shock and that you're scared. I'm scared too but sometimes the best things in life require a huge risk.'

Her soft voice continued, like balm to the chaos in his head. 'We're not your parents. We are not you and Tamara. We have a chance. We laugh together, we work together well, we're really good friends—we can do this. We can be a happy family.' Hope shone from her eyes, driven by love.

For the first time in weeks the space under his ribs stopped throbbing.

But then, like the roar of a cyclone, voices suddenly detonated in his head, exploding Emily's words. *Don't make the same mistake twice, son.* Tamara's whining voice chased his father's. *You've made my life miserable.*

He lifted Emily's hand from his arm. 'But friendship isn't love and without that we'll destroy each other. I watched my parents do that. I lived it with Tamara. My father's right. It's not a risk I'm prepared to take again.'

Her shocked gasp sounded as painful as if he'd struck her across the face. He hated it that he'd hurt her but one of them had to be rational. One of them had to see sense, skirt the emotional minefield that would inevitably blow up in their faces.

She slumped against the tree but then she jutted her chin out, eyes blazing. 'You told me that Tamara didn't love you so of course your marriage failed, how could it not? And did it ever occur to you that your father is wrong? That by listening to his jaundiced view you can't recognise love when it's staring you in the face.' She threw her arms up, her face suddenly hard and determined.

'So go live in your safe little controlled world where you don't have to risk a thing,' she said. You once told me that I was never true to myself. Well, I've grown up. You obviously don't want this child but I do. He'll have four uncles and a grandfather that will love him to bits, and that will have to be enough.'

She stepped away from the tree. 'Go back to Sydney and take your financial support with you. I don't want it.' Spinning on her heel, she ran up the bank, back toward the homestead, back toward her home.

'Emily!' He called her name but she didn't stop.

And what would he say if she did stop? He couldn't offer her what she wanted. He couldn't accept what she offered. It was a no-win situation.

A sigh shuddered out of him, generated from the depths of his soul. As hard as it seemed right now, she'd come to see he was right.

And he knew he was right.

He inhaled sharply as the space under his ribs burned hot and raw.

CHAPTER TWELVE

LINTON longed to go home. He'd even settle for a medical emergency to pull him back to the hospital, not that he'd wish ill health on anyone. Since his father's arrival twenty-four hours ago they'd been to the huge grand final party at the Royal, played golf that morning and now he was saddle sore from playing polo. His father had seen Penelope's invitation and had insisted they attend.

This was his father's modus operandi every time he visited—socialising non-stop.

Warragurra was too small to avoid running into Emily's family but so far he'd managed a distant wave in the crush at the Royal and the same today with Nadine and Hayden. Dealing with that uncomfortable reality would come soon enough. Sadness settled over him. He'd enjoyed the friendship of the brothers.

'You played well.' Penelope's voice purred as she handed him a glass of champagne.

He clinked her glass. 'Thanks. I'm a bit rusty.'

She stared at him brazenly, her eyes hungry. 'You looked pretty good to me.'

He ignored the comment and took another sip of champagne. Any other time he would have taken the flirting bait.

He would have linked his arm with hers, told her she looked stunning, complimented her on her natty new handbag and strolled with her toward an evening that would have finished with the two of them in bed.

She raised her perfectly waxed eyebrows. 'Where have you been hiding yourself lately?'

Emily's face washed through his mind. He steeled himself against the sensation of loss that seemed to grow inside him every time he thought about her. 'Work's been busy.'

'Too much work makes Linton a dull boy.' The pout of her mouth closed around the fine glass flute.

Exasperation flared inside him. He was a doctor, for heaven's sake. Doctors by the nature of their jobs worked hard. He'd never had to explain that to Emily, she just knew. She understood.

'That's what I've been telling him.' Peter Gregory's voice boomed beside him as he stepped up next to Penelope.

'But sons never listen to their fathers.' Pen appraised his father's expensive casual clothes, his hand-made Italian shoes, his trendy Sydney haircut and his designer watch. 'You look too young to be Linton's father.'

Peter's chest puffed out and Linton braced himself for the line he'd heard all his life.

'Well, I'm more like an older brother than a father.'

Peter extended his hand toward Penelope. 'Peter Gregory, seeing as Linton's a little slow on the introductions.'

She seized his hand. 'Penelope Grainger. Lovely to meet you.'

'And you. I must say that shade of pink suits you perfectly, but, then, I'm sure you could model any designer's clothes to their advantage.'

Linton cringed and quickly downed the last mouthful of

his champagne. What was his father thinking? Penelope was too young for him.

Penelope's hand fluttered at her throat. 'Peter, would you like to watch the next chukka with me?'

Peter slipped his arm through hers. 'That sounds delightful.'

As they strolled off, Peter turned back toward Linton and winked.

Linton knew that wink. It meant the game was on and he thought he was in with a chance.

His blood suddenly dropped to his feet and white noise buzzed loudly in his head as reality hit him. He was his father. Hell, he even acted like his father, using the same lines, the same mannerisms.

His stomach churned, the champagne burning and fizzing as his future rolled out before him and he hated the way it looked.

Did it ever occur to you that your father is wrong? Emily's pointed question hit him between the eyes. He sagged against the pole of the marquee, needing the support it offered.

For the first time in his life he'd just seen his father for who he truly was.

A very lonely, emotionally shallow, fifty-two-year-old man.

A man who'd never enjoyed a successful adult relationship because he rejected every woman before they'd got close to him. A man who had never known a soulmate.

He forced air down into his lungs against the tightness constricting his chest. He didn't want to end up like his father. He wanted more out of life than that.

We have a chance. Emily's voice sounded through the swirling mess that was his mind. All this time he'd thought that, by committing to Emily and the baby, he was being trapped.

But, in fact, he was being rescued.

Oh, God. What had he done? Yesterday he'd sent away the best thing that had ever happened to him. He'd rejected Emily's love and he'd rejected his one chance at real happiness.

He loved her. She was his soulmate.

The realisation slugged into him so hard his legs trembled.

'Are you all right, sir?' An anxious waiter hovered.

The words cut through his shock and bewilderment. 'I'm fine. There's just something I have to do.'

He ran from the marquee straight to his car. He'd drive direct to Woollara, straight to Emily.

He only hoped she would forgive him.

Emily had finished the rosters, completed the stock order for the supply room, scrubbed the pan room and now she'd run out of things to do. Sunday afternoon in A and E could be frantic but today, when she needed to be busy, it had failed to deliver.

Technically, she wasn't even due back until Monday but she'd reworked the rosters, making sure she worked most weekends and afternoon shifts. That way she would see a lot less of Linton and work more with Daniel and Michael.

Mostly she just wanted to run back to the Flying Doctors but she had an obligation to work out a two-week resignation period and she wasn't going to leave abruptly and end up looking petty.

Once she was back working with the Flying Doctors, she wouldn't run into Linton very much at all. And then he'd be gone, back to Sydney, where he belonged.

The aching sadness inside her grew with every passing minute. She pulled the calendar off the wall, counting how many weeks Linton still had left in Warragurra. She closed her eyes against the evidence. It was months. He'd leave around the time she'd commence maternity leave.

Maternity leave. It all seemed so surreal. She was going to be a mother. She hadn't mentioned the pregnancy to her family yet—it was all too new, too raw. Emotionally she wasn't ready to tell them because her brothers would probably go ballistic. She grimaced. Linton might decide it would be safer to leave Warragurra early after all.

And her dad? How would he react when he found out his little girl had got herself knocked up? She hoped he'd do what he often did when faced with big dilemmas. He'd hug her briefly and then get practical.

Well, she needed practical. Juggling a baby and full-time shift work would be…impossible? She shook herself. It had to be possible, she had no choice.

'Em.'

She turned to see her father gripping the edge of the nurses' station, his face a deathly grey.

'Dad?' She shot to her feet, terror gripping her. She grabbed a wheelchair, and pushed it behind him.

He fell into it, groaning. 'Hurts.' He gripped his chest and his lower abdomen with both arms.

'Jason.' She called the medical student, who'd been studying in the staffroom.

He appeared immediately. 'What's wrong?'

'Ring Michael now! Tell him it's my father.' She pushed the wheelchair quickly into the resus room. 'Dad, can you get up onto the trolley if I help you?'

Beads of sweat lined Jim's forehead as he gasped for breath. 'I…drove…here so…I…can…do that.'

She locked the chair and, putting one foot between her

father's and one on the outside of his leg, placed her arms under his armpits and heaved.

Jim stumbled to his feet and together they shuffled around until his bottom touched the trolley.

She swung his legs up on the trolley and pulled off his boots, terrified by how her usually stoic and in-control father was dwarfed by this pain.

'Where does it hurt, Dad?' She fitted him with nasal oxygen.

'Everywhere.' He slumped against the pillows, sweaty and ashen, his face streaked with fear. 'I'm dying, aren't I?'

'Not today.' Her words sounded more confident than she felt. She flicked on the ECG machine, her fingers fumbling with the packaging that held the dots. She applied the dots with shaking fingers. *Where was Michael?* She calculated the amount of time it should take him to arrive at the hospital from his house.

Hurry up! She needed her dad. Her baby needed his granddad. She couldn't do motherhood without him.

Jason walked through the door. 'Doctor's on his way.' He gently took the leads from her numb fingers and connected them. Staring past her at the screen, he confidently announced, 'Sinus rhythm, elevated rate.'

Relief rushed through her. It wasn't a heart attack.

The door swung open. 'Jim, you look lousy.' Linton strode into the room, his mud-splattered polo whites outlining his long, strong legs. He tossed his quilted leather vest onto a chair and rolled up his royal-blue sleeves. 'Where does it hurt?'

Emily struggled to breathe. Fear for her father tripped over her shock at seeing Linton. Every painful moment of their conversation twenty-four hours ago reverberated in her head. He'd rejected her and in doing so he'd rejected her family.

'Michael is my father's doctor.' The words whipped out of her mouth, harsh and uncompromising.

His jaw stiffened, as if he'd been punched, but he reached for a stethoscope as he barked at Jason, 'Obs?'

She turned on the hapless Jason. 'I specifically told you to ring Michael.'

Jason blushed bright red. 'I—'

'I don't care who the hell looks after me—just take the pain away.'

Her father's anguished voice grounded her. 'Sorry, Dad.' She shot Linton a blistering look but the expected satisfaction from such an act didn't come.

Instead, he met her gaze, his eyes flickering with something akin to an apology. She quickly looked away and assisted her father into a gown so he could be examined.

'When did the pain start?' Linton's focus was one hundred per cent on Jim as he tapped the man's abdomen.

'I got a twinge a couple of hours ago just after I'd arrived in town for the historical society's meeting.' He flinched as he leaned forward. 'I think I'm going…to be…'

Jason thrust a bowl under Jim's chin as the grazier vomited into the bowl.

'He needs fluids.'

Linton's concerned voice tore at the fragile scab on Emily's heart. How could he come in here and act all worried and caring for her father when he couldn't love her or their baby?

Emily hung up the primed IV that Jason had prepared and then slipped a tourniquet around her father's arm. 'I'm just going to put in a drip, Dad.'

'I'll do it for you.' Linton ripped open an alcohol swab, his face stern and unyielding.

'That won't be necessary. I can do it.' She spoke through gritted teeth, the cannula box in her hand. She didn't want his help.

Jim glanced between the two of them and tilted his head toward Jason. 'I want the lad to do it.'

Jason hesitantly stepped forward, putting his hand out for the equipment.

'If that's what you want, Jim.' Linton gave a rueful smile and passed the swab to Jason.

Surprise rocked her. She hadn't expected him to capitulate to her father's request. Or let Jason execute the task.

'We'll give you morphine for the pain, Dad.' She clipped a drug chart under the clip of the chart board and handed it to Linton.

'Are you allergic to anything, Jim?' Linton pulled out his pen. 'Can you take pethidine?'

'Both are opiates, aren't they?' His face contorted in agony. 'Either one will do as long as it…stops…the…pain.' He closed his eyes, clearly exhausted. 'Do you always contradict each other?'

'I just want what's best for you, Dad.' Emily's frustration pumped though her as she checked the dose of pethidine with Jason. It was bad enough that her father was so ill, without having to deal with Linton.

'Linton will do that. Go wait outside.' Her father patted her arm.

'Ah, Jim, I need Emily here, so if you can go back to being the patient, that would really help.' Linton winked at Emily as he listened to Jim's chest.

Her heart bled a little more. Her father was treating her like a child, and Linton should be behaving like the low-life he was, but instead he was completely understanding and being kind.

None of it made any sense.

She injected the pethidine into the rubber bung on the IV line, knowing that within a minute it would act, easing her father's pain.

Jim suddenly gripped his lower back. 'Here. The pain's here but it goes all the way around the front and down here.' He pressed his groin area.

'He's got a temperature of 39.2.' Jason read the display on the ear thermometer.

'Renal colic.'

She spoke at the very same moment as Linton.

He smiled at her and nodded, his eyes full of warmth and adoration.

She staggered under the gaze. How could he look at her like that and yet tell her he couldn't love her?

'Well, it's good to see you two finally working together.' Jim's opiate-induced, glassy eyes stared at them both. He turned to Jason. 'Do they normally misbehave?'

Jason's mouth opened and shut, stunned at the question, unsure if he should answer it. 'Um, usually they're a team, Mr Tippett.'

'Well, of course they are.' Jim relaxed against the pillow. 'Had a lovers' tiff, did you?'

'Dad!' Emily's face burned with embarrassment and indignation pounded through her, despite the fact she knew it was the drug talking.

Jim grinned at Linton. 'I always found it worked best to say sorry, son. Oh, and flowers and chocolates never go astray either.'

Jason's eyes enlarged, incredulous at the conversation.

Linton seemed to choke on laughter. 'I'll keep that in mind, Jim. Meanwhile, hopefully, with the analgesia relaxing you,

you'll pass the kidney stone that has been giving you so much grief. I'll start you on antibiotics and we'll monitor your urine output, but right now the best thing for you to do is sleep.'

He turned to the stunned Jason. 'Mr Tippett is your patient, Jason. Do half-hourly observations, strain all urine and call us if there is any change.'

'Yes, Dr Gregory.' Jason stood a little taller.

'Emily, I need to talk to you.'

The supplication in Linton's voice battered at all her defences but she needed to stand firm. 'I need to stay with Dad.'

'No, you don't. I've got Jason looking after me.' Jim mumbled, 'Go and sort out whatever it is you need to sort out. Your mother and I never let the sun set on an argument.'

Emily sighed. Her father had *no idea* that the argument that lay between Linton and herself was insoluable. When two people wanted opposite things, resolution was unreachable.

She wasn't sure she had the strength to rehash the same arguments. But her father wasn't going to let her stay so she kissed him on the cheek and left the room.

She marched straight to the desk, opened her father's history and started to write up the nursing notes.

'That can wait.' Linton's quiet words sounded behind her. 'Come and have a cup of coffee.'

She spun around. 'Coffee makes me nauseous.'

'Ginger tea, then.'

She expected him to smile, the way he always did when he aimed to get his own way. Instead, his expression looked almost sad.

'Please, Emily.'

She could have resisted his smile. She could have stood resolute against the charm. But his complete lack of artifice disarmed her.

'All right.' She walked to the staffroom, each step filling her with dread.

He filled two cups with boiling water from the rapid-boil urn and jiggled a ginger teabag through one and regular tea though the other. He sat down on the couch next to her, handing her the cup.

'Thank you.'

'You're welcome.'

Stifling politeness expanded between them like a bubble. It was hard to believe that they had once reached for each other with such passionate need that everything else had faded to insignificance.

He cleared his throat. 'Michael rang me because his car wouldn't start.'

She nodded, resignation sliding through her. Was this their future? One of excessive politeness and treading with extreme caution?

'But I would have wanted to be here anyway. I have enormous respect for your father, he's a good man.' He delivered the words to the opposite wall.

She put down her tea, the drink far too hot at the moment. 'Well, that's good to know.' She couldn't hide the sarcasm from her voice. 'I'm not sure he's going to feel quite the same way about you.'

She wanted the barb to sting, to wound, to hurt him as much as he'd hurt her.

He flinched. 'I deserved that.' Putting his cup down on the side table, he turned to face her, his eyes dark with indecipherable emotions. 'Yesterday I behaved abysmally and I'm sorry.'

Exhaustion hit her as she realised why he wanted to talk to her. To give her a hollow apology. 'Are you here for absolution? Because if you are, I don't think I'm the right person to give it to you.'

He ran his hand across the back of his neck. 'I've been the biggest fool on earth.'

She didn't want to recognise the penitence on his face or hear the sorrow in his voice. 'You won't get an argument from me.'

He struggled to smile. 'You never let me get away with anything, Emily, and that is one of the many reasons why I love you.'

Her ears heard the words but her brain struggled to compute them. 'You love me?' The disbelief in her voice roared in her ears.

He reached for her hands, his palm closing over her knuckles with a touch so gentle it was as if he thought she might break. 'I love you. I'm sorry it took me so long to work it out.'

'But…but yesterday you told me you couldn't love me.' Her heart pounded so hard she could hear it in her head. Incredulity fought with want and need as she searched his face, looking for clues to solve this abrupt turnaround.

Pain slashed his face. 'If I could take back yesterday, take back all the hurtful things I said, then I would. You were right. I had no idea what love really is.'

'But you do now?' A bubble of hope slowly rose from her pit of despair. She wanted to believe him but she couldn't, not yet.

'I do now.' His deep voice vibrated with feeling. 'I love you so much it hurts.'

Hope sped through her. 'I know how that feels.' She bit her lip, trying to understand. 'But what happened to change your mind?'

He leaned in close. 'Dad.'

'Your father told you to marry me?' She couldn't stop the incredulity in her voice.

He shook his head. 'No. Dad doesn't know anything about you and me. Yet. But he soon will.' He rested his head on her forehead. 'This afternoon at the polo, it was like the scales fell from my eyes.'

His breath caressed her face. 'You were right, totally and utterly correct. My father is wrong about relationships. They don't trap people—they release love.'

Her heart tumbled over with joy. 'You really do love me?'

'I really do love you.'

He pulled her into his arms, kissing her hard and fast, making her feel giddy with wonder and bliss.

Then he cuddled her close. 'I'm so sorry it took me so long to realize that. All my life my father told me that marriage was a nightmare. I'd lived with my parents long enough to believe it and I hadn't managed to make a success of it with Tamara.'

He gripped her hands more firmly. 'Believing Dad absolved me of my ever risking my heart again. Except I lost it to you without even knowing.'

She cupped his cheek with her hand. 'I think I lost my heart to you the first day I met you.'

His eyes sparkled with elation. 'You've taken me on a wondrous journey, shown me how amazing a loving family can be and completed me in every way. You're my best friend. I didn't recognise that our friendship was love.'

'It's love of the strongest kind.'

He nodded his agreement. 'And our baby will grow up basking in our love and the love of your family. A grandchild might even soften up the old man.' He hesitated. 'That is, if you'll marry me.'

Sheer joy and happiness exploded inside her and she smiled a wide smile. 'Are you asking me?'

He slid off the couch, kneeling on a muddy knee. 'Emily Tippett, love of my life, mother of my child and future children, will you marry me?'

She looked into his earnest face, full of love, tinged with a sliver of doubt, and threw herself into his arms. Her lips touched his and she knew she was home.

She's forgiven me. Relief surged through Linton, quickly overtaken by all-encompassing happiness. She tasted so good he never wanted to let her go. 'I take it that's a yes.'

She nodded, her eyes dancing.

He pulled her to her feet. 'Let's go and tell your dad.'

She laughed. 'What, you think in his pethidine haze he'll give you permission to marry his only daughter?'

He slipped his arm around her waist and grinned. 'That's my plan.'

They walked along the corridor, her fingers snaking inside the gaps between the buttons on his shirt. 'You do realise he'll ask you how you're going to provide for me and where we're going to live.'

He paused outside the resus room door, twirling one of her crazy red curls around his finger. 'I guess we need to talk about that. I've always seen Sydney as the place I'd return to.'

Her commitment to him shone in her eyes. 'I'll come to Sydney if that's what you want, as long as I have a month at Woollara a couple of times a year so the baby knows his country heritage.'

The strength of her love made him dizzy. 'Or her heritage.'

'Either way.'

He gazed into her eyes, amazed at how long-held plans

could change without a murmur of regret. 'Except that I think our children deserve to grow up with their granddad teaching them to ride horses and their cousins teaching them to shell peas and climb trees.'

Her gasp of delight was reflected in the joy on her face. 'So you'd settle here in Warragurra?'

'I think you and I belong in Warragurra.' He lowered his lips to hers and kissed her.

Time stood still. Nothing existed but his lips on hers, the comfort of her arms, the wondrous touch of her body pressed hard against his and the promise of a future together.

'Hey, sis, there are sick people in this joint. Do you want to make them feel worse?'

He looked up to see Eric leading the rest of the Tippett family into the department. Holding Emily close to his side, all he could do was grin.

Emily giggled.

'It's about time.' Hayden, with Tyler on his shoulders, thumped Linton on the back before exchanging a knowing look with Nadine.

Mark smiled quietly at both of them, his face full of approval.

Stuart grinned. 'We've got a back-up member for the Tippett pool team.'

'You'd have to be desperate,' Emily teased. 'But he's got other skills.' She laid her hand possessively on his chest.

'So the flowers did the trick, Linton?' Jim's voice called as everyone walked into the room.

Emily reached up on tiptoe and pulled Linton's head down close to hers, her eyes sparkling with joy. 'Are you sure about this, about living in Warragurra? My family can be pretty full on.'

He glanced around, feeling all the love in the room. 'I wouldn't have it any other way.'

And he kissed her all over again.

THE NEW GIRL
IN TOWN

BY
BRENDA HARLEN

Brenda Harlen grew up in a small town surrounded by books and imaginary friends. Although she always dreamed of being a writer, she chose to follow a more traditional career path first. After two years of practicing as an attorney, including an appearance in front of the Supreme Court of Canada, she gave up her "real" job to be a mom and to try her hand at writing books. Three years, five manuscripts and another baby later, she sold her first book—an RWA Golden Heart Winner—to Mills & Boon.

Brenda lives in southern Ontario with her real-life husband/hero, two heroes-in-training and two neurotic dogs. She is still surrounded by books ("too many books," according to her children) and imaginary friends, but she also enjoys communicating with real people. Readers can contact Brenda by e-mail at brendaharlen@yahoo.com.

This book is dedicated to everyone
who has fought the fight against breast cancer
with courage and strength—you are an inspiration.
And to the memory of those who ultimately lost
the battle—you are not forgotten.

With thanks to the researchers, doctors and other
health-care professionals who offer direction and hope.

Chapter One

Zoe Kozlowski definitely wasn't in Manhattan anymore.

Years of living in the city had acclimated her to the sounds of traffic—the squeal of tires, the blare of horns, the scream of sirens. She would no doubt have slept through the pounding of a jackhammer six stories below her open bedroom window or the wail of a fire truck speeding past her apartment building, but the gentle trilling of sparrows shattered the cocoon of her slumber.

In time, she was certain she would get used to these sounds, too, but for now, they were new and enchanting enough that she didn't mind being awakened at such an early hour. As she carried her cup of decaf chai tea out onto the back porch, she could hear not just the birds but the gentle breeze rustling the leaves and, in the distance, the barking of a dog.

She stepped over a broken board and settled onto the top step to survey her surroundings in the morning light. The colors were so vivid and bright it almost hurt to look at them—the brilliantly polished sapphire of the sky broken only by the occasional fluffy white cloud. And the trees—there were so many kinds, so many shades of green around the perimeter of the yard. Evergreens whose sweeping branches ranged in hue from deep emerald to silvery sage. Oaks and maples and poplars with leaves of various shapes and sizes and colors of yellow-green and dark green and every tone in between.

She found herself wondering how it would look in the fall—what glorious shades of gold and orange and rust and red would appear. And then in the winter, when the leaves had fallen to the ground and the trees were bare, the long branches glistening with frost or dusted with snow. And in the early spring, when the first buds began to unfurl and herald the arrival of the new season.

But now, edging toward the first days of summer, everything was green and fresh and beautiful. And while she appreciated the natural beauty of the present, she was already anticipating the changing of the seasons. Not wishing her life away, but looking to her future here and planning to enjoy every minute of it.

She knew the yard was in as serious need of work as the old house in which she'd spent the night, but as she took another look around, she was filled with a deep sense of peace and satisfaction that everything she saw was hers.

She'd get a porch swing, she decided suddenly, impulsively. Where she could sit to enjoy her first cup of tea every morning. She would put down roots here, just like those trees, dig deep into the soil and make this place her home.

It was strange that she'd lived in New York for almost ten years and never felt the same compelling need to put down roots there. Or maybe it just hadn't occurred to her to do so in a city made up of mostly concrete and steel. Not that she hadn't loved Manhattan. There was an aura about the city that still appealed to her, an excitement she'd never felt anywhere else. For a young photographer, it had been *the* place to be, and when Scott had suggested moving there after they were married, she'd jumped at the opportunity. They'd started out at a tiny little studio apartment in Brooklyn Heights, moved to a one-bedroom walk-up in Soho, then, finally, only four years ago, to a classic six on Park Avenue.

She'd never imagined leaving there, never imagined wanting to be anywhere else. Until a routine doctor's appointment had turned out to be not-so-routine after all.

In the eighteen months that had passed since then, her life had taken a lot of unexpected turns. The most recent of which had brought her here, to Pinehurst, New York, to visit her friend Claire and—

Oomph!

The breath rushed out of her lungs and her mug went flying from her fingers as she was knocked onto her back by a furry beast that settled on her chest.

She would have gasped if she'd had any air left to expel. Instead, she struggled to draw in enough oxygen to scream. As she opened her mouth, a big wet tongue swept over her face.

Ugh!

She wasn't sure if the hairy creature was licking her in a harmless show of affection or sampling her before it sank its teeth in. She sputtered and tried to push it away.

A shrill whistle sounded in the distance and the dog—at least, she thought it was a dog, although it didn't look like any kind she'd ever seen before—lifted its head in response to the sound. Then the tongue was back, slobbering over her again.

"Rosie!"

The animal withdrew, just far enough to plant its substantial behind on top of her thighs, trapping them beneath its impressive weight.

Zoe eyed it warily as she pushed herself up onto her elbows, bracing herself for another attack. A movement at the edge of the woods caught her attention, and she turned her head to see a tall, broad-shouldered figure moving with long-legged strides across the yard.

She shoved at the beast again, ineffectually, and blew out a frustrated breath. "Can you get this darn thing off me?" she asked through gritted teeth.

"Sorry." The man reached down to grab the animal by its collar. Zoe's irritation was forgotten as her gaze swept over her rescuer.

His hair was dark, almost black, and cut short around a face that seemed to be chiseled out of granite. His forehead was broad, his cheekbones sharp, and his nose had a slight bump on the bridge as if it had been broken once or twice before. His jaw was dark with stubble, and his eyes—she couldn't be sure of the color because his face was in shadow, but she could tell that they were dark—were narrowed on the beast. He wore an old Cornell University T-shirt over a pair of jeans that molded to the lean muscles of his long legs and a scuffed pair of sneakers.

"Are you alright?" he asked, his voice as warm and smooth as premium-aged whiskey.

"I'm fine. Or I will be when you get this thing away from me."

"Rosie, off." He spoke to her attacker now, the words accompanied by a sharp tug on the collar. The four-legged beast immediately removed its weight from her legs and plopped down on its butt beside the man, tongue hanging out of its mouth as it gazed at him adoringly.

Zoe figured the beast was female. She also figured the man was used to that kind of reaction from the women he met. She might have been inclined to drool herself except that a half-dozen years as a fashion photographer had immunized her against the impact of beautiful faces. Well, mostly, anyway. Because she couldn't deny there was something about this man's rugged good looks she found appealing enough to almost wish she had her camera in hand.

The unexpectedness of that urge was something she would think about later, Zoe decided as she pulled herself to her feet, then rubbed a hand over her face to wipe away the dog drool. She tugged at the frayed hem of the cut-off shorts she'd pulled on when she'd rolled out of bed, conscious of the fact that they fell only a couple of inches below the curve of her butt.

"What the heck is that thing?" she asked, taking a deliberate step back from man and beast.

"He's a dog," the man responded in the same whiskey-smooth tone. "And although he's overly affectionate at times, he doesn't usually take to strangers."

"Obviously it's a dog." At least it had four paws and wagging tail. "But what kind? I've never seen anything so—" *ugly* was the description that immediately came to mind, but she didn't want to insult the man or his best friend, so she decided upon "—big."

His smile was wry. "He's of indeterminate pedigree—part deerhound, part Old English sheepdog, with a lot of other parts mixed in."

She glanced at the handsome stranger again, saw that he was giving her the same critical study she'd given his pet. She was suddenly aware that her hair needed to be combed, her teeth needed to be brushed and her T-shirt was covered in muddy paw prints. Then his gaze lifted to hers, and she forgot everything else in the realization that his eyes were as startlingly blue as the sapphire sky overhead.

"Did you ever consider putting your dog in obedience classes?" she asked. "Preferably before it—he—knocks somebody unconscious."

"As a matter of fact, Rosie graduated top of his class. He can heel, sit, lay down, roll over and speak." He shrugged and smiled again. "He just hasn't learned to curb his enthusiasm."

"No kidding," she said dryly. Then she frowned. "Did you call *him* 'Rosie'?"

"It's short for Rosencrantz."

"Rosencrantz," Zoe echoed, wondering what kind of person would inflict such torture on a helpless animal. Not that this one was helpless, but the name still seemed cruel.

"As in Rosencrantz and Guildenstern," he told her. "From *Hamlet*."

She was admittedly surprised—and more intrigued than she wanted to be by this sexy, blue-eyed, Shake-speare-reading stranger.

"Where is Guildenstern?" she asked apprehensively.

"With my brother," the man answered. "My business partner found the two puppies abandoned by the creek in his backyard. He and his wife wanted to keep them, but they already have a cat and a baby on the way, so I got one and my brother took the other."

She noticed that he spoke of his partner having a wife but didn't mention one of his own. Not that it really mattered, of course. She had a lot of reasons for moving to Pinehurst, but looking for romance was definitely not one of them—especially when the wounds of her failed marriage had barely begun to heal.

"Well, you need to keep that thing on a leash," she said, forcing her thoughts to refocus on the conversation.

The animal in question immediately dropped to its belly and whined plaintively.

Zoe frowned. "What's wrong with him?"

"You said the *L*-word," he told her.

She looked at him blankly.

"*L-E-A-S-H.*"

"You've got to be kidding."

He shook his head. "Rosie hates being tied up."

"Well, he'll have to get used to it because I don't appreciate being attacked in my own yard by your mongrel pet."

"Your yard?" He seemed surprised by her statement. "You bought this place?"

She nodded.

"Are you rich and bored? Or just plain crazy?"

She bristled at that. "You're not the first person to question my sanity," she admitted. "But you're the first who's had the nerve to do so while standing on my property."

"I'm just…surprised," he said. "The house has been on the market a long time, and I hadn't heard anything around town recently about a potential buyer."

"The final papers were signed yesterday. This is my house, my land, my space."

"If this is your house, your land, and your space, then that would mean—"

He paused to smile, and she cursed her traitorous heart for beating faster.

"—you're my neighbor."

Mason watched as her pale cheeks flushed with color, making him think she might be attractive if she cleaned herself up. Right now, however, she was a mess. Her long blond hair was tangled around her face, her brow—above incredibly gorgeous eyes the color of dark chocolate—was creased with a scowl, and her skimpy little T-shirt was covered in mud. But he couldn't help but notice that the shirt clung to curves that looked soft and round in all the right places, and he felt the stir of arousal.

He gave himself a mental shake, acknowledging that he'd definitely been too long without a woman if the sight of this disheveled little spitfire was turning him on.

His current hiatus from dating had been a matter of choice as much as necessity, since his break-up with Erica had coincided with a flurry of big jobs that had required all of his attention and focus. Recently, however, things at the office had started to slow down a little. Enough at least that he could catch a decent amount of sleep at night and maybe even consider getting out socially again. If he did, maybe he'd meet a woman who was more his usual type.

But it was this woman who had his attention now. Because she was, if not his type, at least his neighbor, which made him naturally curious about her.

"Tell me something," he said.

"What's that?" she asked warily.

"What possessed a city girl like you to buy an abandoned old house like this?"

"What makes you think I'm a city girl?"

He allowed his gaze to move over her again, lingering, appraising. "The designer clothes and fancy watch, for starters. But mostly it's the casual self-confidence layered over restless energy that says to hell with the rest of the world and somehow fits you as perfectly as those snug little denim shorts."

She tilted her chin. "That's quite an assumption to make after a five-minute conversation."

He smiled. "I enjoy studying people—and women are a particular interest of mine."

"I don't doubt that's true," she said dryly.

He wasn't dissuaded by the comment or her tone. "You never did answer my question about why you bought this house."

"It's a beautiful house."

"It might have been a dozen years ago," he allowed. "Before Mrs. Hadfield got too old and too tight-fisted to pay for the repairs."

"What happened to Mrs. Hadfield?" she asked, in what seemed to him a blatant attempt to change the subject.

"She passed away about eighteen months ago, left the house to a grandson who lives in California. He put it on the market right away, but there was only one early offer on the property and he refused to sell to a developer, insisting his grandmother wouldn't have wanted the house torn down and the land divided."

After that deal had fallen through, Mason had learned from the real estate agent that the grandson had some specific ideas about the type of person Beatrice Hadfield wanted living in her house after she was gone. But he'd refused to elaborate on the criteria, even to the agent, and she'd mostly given up on selling the house—until now, apparently.

"And you know about this unsuccessful sale because…" she prompted.

"Because there are no secrets in a small town."

"Great," she muttered. "And I hated feeling like my neighbors were on top of me in the city."

She really wasn't his type, but she was female and kind of cute, and he couldn't resist teasing, "I'll only be on top if that's where you want me, darlin'."

Her chocolate eyes narrowed as she drew herself up to her full height—which was about a foot shorter than his six feet two inches. "It won't be," she said coolly. "And don't call me 'darling.'"

He held up his hands in mock surrender. "I didn't mean to offend you…" He paused, giving her the chance to offer her name.

"My name is Zoe," she finally told him. "Zoe Koz-lowski."

It was an unusual name but pretty, and somehow it suited her. "Mason Sullivan."

She eyed his outstretched hand for a moment before shaking it.

Rosie barked and held up a paw.

His new neighbor glanced down, the hint of a smile tugging at the corners of her mouth. He found himself staring at that mouth, wondering if her lips were as soft and kissable as they looked.

Way too long without a woman.

"You didn't tell me he could shake," she said, removing her hand from his to take the paw Rosie offered.

"Another of his many talents," he said, oddly perturbed that she seemed more interested in his dog than in him. Not that *he* was interested in *her,* but he did have a reputation in town for his success with the ladies, and never before had one thrown him over for an animal.

"Now if only you could teach him to respect the boundary line between our properties."

"That might take some time," he warned, as she released Rosie's paw and straightened again. "He's become accustomed to running through these woods over the past several months."

"It won't take any time at all if you keep him tied up," she said.

Rosie whimpered as though he understood the threat, compelling Mason to protest on the animal's behalf.

"He's a free spirit," he said, then smiled. "Like me."

She tilted her head, studying him like she would a worrisome crack in a basement foundation. "Do the women in this town actually fall for such tired lines?"

It was an effort to keep the smile in place, but he wouldn't give her the satisfaction of letting it fade. "I haven't had any complaints."

"I worked at *Images* in New York City for six years," she said, citing one of the industry's leading fashion magazines. "I spent most of my days surrounded by men who made their living playing a part for the camera, so it's going to take more than a smile to make me melt."

Okay, so she was tougher than he'd expected. But he hadn't yet met a woman who was immune to his charm—it was only a matter of finding the right buttons to push. "That sounds like a challenge."

"Just a statement of fact," she told him, bending to pick up a mug that he guessed Rosie had knocked from her hand with the exuberance of his greeting. "Now if you'll excuse me, I have things to do today."

He stepped down off the porch, his hand still holding onto the dog's collar, his eyes still on his new neighbor. "It was nice meeting you, Zoe."

"It was certainly interesting," she said, but with a half smile that allowed him to hope she wasn't still annoyed at Rosie's manner of introduction.

And as he turned toward his own home, he found himself already looking forward to his next encounter with his new neighbor.

Zoe walked into the house with a smile on her face and a positive outlook for the day despite—or maybe because of—the unexpected events of the morning. Though she couldn't have anticipated meeting one of her neighbors in the backyard, and so early, she thought she'd handled the situation. She'd even managed to engage in a casual conversation without worrying too much about where he was looking or what he was thinking. It was a gloriously liberating experience.

Mason Sullivan was a stranger who knew nothing of her or her past, a dog owner simply apologizing for the affectionate nature of his pet. He was a man who'd looked at her like she was a woman—a completely normal interaction that followed a year and a half of wondering if anything would ever seem normal again.

In the past eighteen months, she'd lost everything that mattered: her husband, her job, her home, and—most devastating of all—her sense of self. She'd packed most of what she had left into a tiny storage unit, loaded a dozen boxes in the back of her car, then driven out of the city, determined to start her life over again somewhere new. What she really wanted was to go someplace where no one knew who she was, where no one would look at her with pitying glances or talk to her in sympathetic murmurs. Someplace where she could pretend she was still the woman she used to be.

What she'd found—on a visit to Claire, her best friend and confidante—was a charming Victorian house that caught her attention so completely she actually stopped her car right in the middle of the road to stare.

It was an impressive three stories of turrets and towers despite having been badly neglected and in desperate need of repair. The roof on the wraparound porch was sagging, the chimneys were crumbling, paint was peeling, and several of the windows were boarded up.

As Zoe studied the broken parts of the whole, she had to fight back tears. There was no doubt the house had once been strong and proud and beautiful. Now it was little more than a shadow of its former self—abandoned, neglected and alone.

Just as she was.

She almost didn't see the For Sale sign that was mostly hidden by the weeds that had taken over the front garden, but when she did, she knew that it was meant to be hers. She'd pulled her car off the road and into a gravel driveway as overgrown with weeds as the yard, then picked up her cell phone and dialed the number on the sign.

For the past year and a half, she'd been looking for some direction and purpose, and here, at last, she'd found it.

Or maybe she really was crazy.

She acknowledged that possibility as she set her mug in the sink. But even if she was, she was committed now. The house was hers—along with the weighty mortgage she'd secured for the purchase and improvements. And though there was a part of her that was terrified to think she'd made a huge mistake, another—bigger—part of her was excited by the challenges and opportunities that lay ahead.

She was going to fix up this broken-down house and turn it into a successful bed-and-breakfast. Although there were several such establishments already in town, none were as majestic as the building that was now her home. Or as majestic as she knew it would be when she was finished with it.

She glanced at her watch, noted that it was almost eight o'clock. The architect—who happened to be the husband of the lawyer who'd helped her purchase the property—was due to arrive in a little more than half an hour.

She was excited about meeting him, anxious to get started. But she also felt the first niggle of doubt, a twinge of uncertainty. It was one thing to spin elaborate dreams inside her mind, and something else entirely to share these hopes with someone who could help her realize them—or destroy them.

As she made her way across the dusty floor, questions and doubts dogged her every step.

What *was* she doing?

It was what her friends and colleagues had asked when she'd walked away from her job at the magazine. They'd expressed sympathy for what she'd been through but on the whole agreed that the best thing for Zoe was to maintain the status quo as much as possible. She thought it ironic—and more than a little irritating—that so many people who hadn't been through what she had could have so much advice about how to cope.

It was only Claire who really understood. And it was Claire who agreed Zoe should live the life she wanted to live rather than the one she had; Claire who knew that sometimes a person needed a new beginning in order to continue. And Claire had been thrilled when her friend had chosen Pinehurst for that fresh start. Admittedly, her excitement had been tempered by apprehension when she'd seen the house Zoe intended to buy, but her support had never wavered.

As Zoe batted away a cobweb, she wondered what her former colleagues in Manhattan would think now. Then she shook her head, refusing to let her mind continue along that path. She didn't have time for doubts or recriminations—she needed to get ready for her appointment with the architect.

The taps creaked and the pipes groaned, but Zoe managed to coax water out of the shower head in the main-floor bathroom. It wasn't very warm or clear, but it was enough to wet a washcloth to scrub over her face and her body. Trying to rinse the shampoo out of her hair was a different story, and she wondered if she should have spent the money on a motel room last night—at least then she could have had a hot shower with good water pressure. But she knew the renovations on the house would be costly, and what was left in her bank account after medical expenses and the down payment wasn't exactly extravagant.

She banished the negative thoughts. Although the real

estate agent had warned her that the house needed a lot of work, Zoe wasn't afraid of rolling up her sleeves and getting her hands dirty. In fact, she looked forward to it and even believed the work might be therapeutic for her. What worried her was the work she couldn't do herself— the cost of hiring electricians and plumbers and whatever other tradespeople she might require. Hopefully, Jessica's husband would be able to tell her exactly what she needed and maybe make some recommendations.

Another quick glance at her watch warned that she had less than ten minutes before he was expected to arrive. She felt the twist of anxiety in her belly as she pulled on a pair of jeans and a plain white T-shirt. She didn't know what to expect, what the architect would suggest, what the cost would be.

She glanced around with a more critical eye. Was it a pipe dream to believe she could turn this run-down old home into the proud beauty she knew it had once been?

Well, pipe dream or not, it was hers now—and she was determined to give it her best shot.

The phone was ringing when Mason walked through the front door with Rosie. The dog ran across the room to his water dish and began slurping noisily; Mason picked up the receiver. "Sullivan."

"You're there. Good." Nick Armstrong sounded frazzled, which wasn't at all like the man Mason had known since college and worked with for almost fifteen years.

"What's up?" he asked.

"I need you to cover an appointment for me this

morning." Then his voice dropped a little as he said, "Hang in, honey. We're almost there."

After a brief moment of confusion, Mason realized the second part of his friend's comment wasn't directed at him. He also noticed that despite the soothing words, there was a note of panic in Nick's tone.

"What's wrong with Jess?" he asked, immediately concerned.

"Her water broke. Only about half an hour ago, but her contractions are already coming hard and strong and way too close together."

Now Mason understood the panic.

Nick and Jess had both waited a long time for the baby they were finally having, and the thought that anything might go wrong at this stage was too horrific to even contemplate.

"Breathe, honey," Nick murmured to his wife.

Mason heard Jess's response—sharp and succinct and completely unlike the cool, poised woman she usually was. That's what having a baby did to normally calm and rational people, he guessed, and was grateful that parenthood wasn't looming anywhere in his future.

Marriage and babies? He shuddered at the thought. Hell, just the suggestion of commitment was enough to make him break out in hives. He'd learned a long time ago how completely love could tear apart a person's life, and he wanted no part of any of it.

His best friend had chosen a different path, however, and Mason was willing to help in any way he could. "Concentrate on your wife," he said. "I'll take care of the business."

"Thanks, Mason."

"Don't worry about it." He winced in automatic sympathy as he heard Jess swear again in the background. "Tell Jess I'll bring her a pint of strawberry ice cream from Walton's later."

"She'll love that," his friend said. "I gotta go now—we're pulling up at the hospital."

"Wait!" Mason said before his friend could disconnect.

"What?"

"When and where is this appointment?"

He took the information from his friend and smiled as he hung up the phone.

This day, he thought, just keeps getting better and better.

Chapter Two

Zoe recognized Mason as soon as she responded to his knock at her front door.

He'd shaved and changed into khaki pants with a shirt and tie rather than the jeans and T-shirt he'd had on earlier, and he didn't have the mammoth beast with him, but the deep blue eyes and sexy smile left her in no doubt that it was her neighbor.

"What are you doing here?" she asked.

"We have an appointment," Mason said, unfazed by the lack of welcome in her question.

"You're Jessica's husband?"

"No." His quick response was confirmed by an emphatic shake of his head. "I'm his business partner. Nick sent me along with his apologies for not being able to meet with you personally. He was on his way to the hospital—it looks like Jessica is going to have the baby today."

It had been apparent to Zoe when she'd been introduced to Jessica Armstrong that the other woman was nearing the end of a pregnancy, but she hadn't realized she was quite that far along.

"I know you were expecting Nick," Mason continued. "But I'm sure you understand that he needed to be with his wife right now."

"Of course," she agreed immediately. But she couldn't help remembering when she'd been in the hospital, without her husband by her side. It hadn't been a happy occasion but the beginning of the end of their marriage.

"Zoe?"

Her attention snapped back to the present.

"Sorry," she apologized automatically. "My thoughts were just wandering."

"Would you rather reschedule when Nick is available?"

"No," she said. "I don't want to reschedule. I just want to know what has to be done to fix this house."

"How much time do you have?"

She narrowed her eyes. "What's that supposed to mean?"

"I'm just suggesting you take a good, hard look around you," Mason said.

She did, and she saw the beauty that had been neglected. The gleam of the hardwood under the layers of dust, the sparkle of the leaded-glass windows beneath the grime, the intricate details of the trims and moldings behind the spider webs. She saw history that needed to be preserved and promise waiting to be fulfilled. But she wasn't comfortable telling him any of those things, so all she said was, "The real estate agent assured me that the building is structurally sound."

"The foundation looks solid," he admitted. "But the roof needs to be replaced, the chimneys need to be reconstructed and the porch rebuilt. And that's just what I could see from the outside. If you really want a home here, it would probably be easier and cheaper to tear this building down and start over again."

It might be easier and cheaper, but it wasn't what she wanted to do. She needed to fix the house—to prove it was valuable and worthwhile despite the damaged parts.

"I'm not interested in easy, and I don't have any illusions that it will be cheap, but I want to restore this house," she told him.

He shrugged. "I just wanted to make sure you considered all of the options."

She nodded stiffly, although in her heart she knew she couldn't consider demolition as one of the options. Destroying what was left of this fabulous old building would break her heart all over again.

As they moved through the house, Mason took measurements and made notes with brisk efficiency, but he never failed to point out various flaws and defects as they moved from one room to the next through the house. She was frustrated by his incessant negativity and on the verge of telling him she would find another architect when she noticed the inherent contradiction between his actions and his words.

He warned her that the ceiling had sustained some obvious water damage, but his gaze lingered on the pressed tin squares. He claimed that all of the plumbing was horribly outdated, but she'd seen his eyes light up when he'd spotted the old clawfoot tub. And while he was complaining that someone had painted over the mantle of the fireplace, his fingers caressed the hand-carved wood.

"The frames on all of these windows are starting to rot," he said. "They'll have to be replaced."

She sighed, and when she spoke, her words were infused with reluctant resignation. "Maybe you're right. Maybe I should just tear this place down."

His head swiveled toward her, as she'd known it would. His eyes narrowed suspiciously. "Is that what you want to do?"

"I'm starting to believe it's the most logical course of action."

"It is," he said again, after a brief hesitation.

She smiled. "I hope you're a better architect than you are an actor."

"What are you talking about?"

"You can't stand the thought of this beautiful building being destroyed."

"This building is a far cry from beautiful," he told her dryly.

"But it was once, and it can be again, can't it?"

He was silent for a moment before finally conceding, "Maybe."

After so much verbal disparagement, Zoe wasn't willing to let it go at that. "You can see it, can't you?"

she pressed. "You can picture in your mind the way it used to be—the way it should be again?"

"Maybe," he said again. "I've always thought it was a shame that someone didn't step in and do something to save this house before it completely fell apart."

"Why didn't *you?*"

He gave her one of those wry half smiles. "Because as much as I can admire the graceful lines and detailed workmanship, I'm also aware of the time and money needed to fix this place."

"I would think a successful architect would have the necessary resources for the job."

"What I don't have," he warned her, "and anyone in town will tell you the same thing—is the ability to commit to any kind of long-term project."

"Is that why you were baiting me—to determine if I was committed?"

"You had to have dropped a bundle of money already to buy this place," he said. "I'm guessing that's proof of your commitment. I only hope you have a bundle more, because you're going to need it to restore this house properly."

Anxiety twisted knots in her belly. "I'm hoping to do some of the simpler jobs myself. Patching, sanding, painting."

"This house needs a lot more than patching, sanding and painting," he warned.

"I know." And she'd budgeted—hopefully enough— for the other work she knew would be required. "But I want to be involved with the project, not just writing the checks."

His gaze skimmed over her, assessing. "You said you worked at *Images* magazine?"

She nodded. "As a photographer."

"Have you ever done any home renovating before?"

"No," she admitted reluctantly.

"Why did you leave that job to come here?"

"I don't think that's relevant."

"Of course it is," he disagreed.

"I'm committed to this restoration," she said. "That's all that matters."

He studied her for another few seconds before saying, "There are a couple of good general contractors I can recommend. They're local and fair."

She opened her mouth to protest, then decided it wasn't worth arguing with him—she'd rather save her energy for the work that needed to be done. "You can give me their names and numbers after we take a look at the attic."

Mason followed Zoe up the narrow and steep flight of steps that led to the attic. He tried to keep his focus on the job, but he couldn't tear his gaze from the shapely denim-clad butt in front of him. He'd been right about one thing—Zoe Kozlowski cleaned up good.

The blond hair that had been tangled around her face this morning was now tamed into a ponytail, with just the tiniest wisps escaping to frame her oval face. She'd put on a hint of makeup, mascara to darken her lashes, something that added shine to her soft, full lips. Not enough to look done up, but enough to highlight her features.

She was an attractive woman. A lot more attractive than he'd originally thought. Still not his usual type, although he enjoyed women too much to be picky about specifics. And though he enjoyed a lot of women, he never got too close to any one of them except in a strictly physical and always temporary sense.

She turned at the top of the stairs and stepped through an arched doorway and into darkness. He heard the click of a light being switched on, illuminating her slender figure standing in the middle of the attic. He felt the familiar tug of desire any unattached man would feel in the company of a pretty young woman. Emphasis on young, he thought, guessing her age to be somewhere between early- to mid-twenties. Which meant she was too many years younger than he to consider acting on the attraction he felt.

And yet there were shadows in her eyes that hinted she had experienced things beyond her years, a stubborn tilt to her chin that suggested she'd faced some tough challenges—and won. He figured she was a woman with a lot more baggage than the suitcase he'd seen tucked beside the antique couch in the living room, and that was just one more reason not to get involved. While he could respect her strength and determination, Mason didn't do long-term, and he definitely didn't do issues.

He liked women who laughed frequently and easily, women who wanted a good time with no expectations of anything more. He'd thought Erica was such a woman. Until, after less than three months of on-and-off dating that was more "off" than "on," she'd told him it was time he stopped playing around and made a commitment. The night she'd said that was the last time he'd seen her.

He didn't regret ending things with Erica. He couldn't imagine himself in a committed relationship with any woman, and he had no intention of ever falling in love.

But he couldn't deny there were times—times when he was with Nick and Jessica—that he wondered what it would be like to love and be loved so completely. Usually the longing only lasted a moment or two, then he'd remember his father and how losing the woman he loved had started a slow but steady downward spiral that had eventually destroyed him. No, Mason didn't ever want to love like that.

"What do you think?" Zoe asked.

Her question jolted him out of his reverie. He glanced around the enormous room illuminated by a couple of bare bulbs hanging from the steeply sloped ceiling. There were old trunks covered in dust and cobwebs hanging from the rafters. "I think it's dark and dreary."

Some of the light in her eyes faded, making the small space seem darker and drearier still.

"It is now. But if there was a window put in there—" she gestured to the far end "—the room would fill with morning sunlight. It would be perfect for a bedroom and office combined. And there's a bathroom immediately below, so it would be easy enough to bring up the plumbing for an ensuite." She gazed at him hopefully. "Wouldn't it?"

"I'm not sure it would be easy," he warned her. "But, yes, it could be done."

She smiled at him, and he felt as if his breath had backed up in his lungs. He hadn't seen her smile like that before, was unprepared for how positively beautiful she was when her eyes shone, her cheeks glowed. And her mouth—his gaze lingered there, tempted by the sexy curve of those full lips.

He stuffed his hands in his pockets to resist the sudden urge to reach for her, to taste those lips, to test her response. He wondered how it would feel to have a woman look at him like that, to know her smile was intended only for him, the sparkle in her eyes because she was thinking about him.

He gave himself a mental shake, forced himself to focus on what she was saying rather than his imaginative fantasies.

"This will be my space," she decided. "With gleaming hardwood floors, walls painted a cheery yellow, a four-poster bed and—"

Not wanting to think about Zoe tucked away in her bed, he interrupted quickly, "You'll never get a four-poster bed up here. Not the way those stairs curve."

She considered, then sighed. "You're right. Well, the furniture is only details."

"If you're going to tuck yourself away up here, what do you plan to do with the rest of the house?"

"I'm going to open a bed-and-breakfast." She smiled again, her eyes lit up with hope for her grandiose plan.

He hated to dim the sparkle in her eyes again, but someone needed to ground this woman in reality. "There are already a half-dozen bed-and-breakfasts in town," he pointed out. "And even in the height of summer, they're never booked to capacity."

"I'm not looking for busloads of tourists," she said. "But creative marketing and effective advertising will bring enough people here to make the business succeed."

"You never did tell me what brought you here from the big city," he said.

"Obviously I was looking to make some changes in my life."

"Why?"

She narrowed her gaze on him. "Are you this nosy with all of your clients?"

"You're not just a client, you're also my neighbor," he reminded her.

"That's just geography."

"Okay—we'll hold off on the personal revelations until you consider me a friend."

"Friend?" she said, with obvious skepticism.

"Does that seem so impossible to you?"

"Not impossible," she said. "Just surprising."

"Because most men want to skip that part and head straight to the bedroom?"

"Maybe," she admitted hesitantly.

He grinned. "But I'm already in your bedroom."

"So you are." Now she smiled, and again he felt the punch of attraction low in his gut. "But only because you have a really impressive…tape measure."

Zoe left Mason to take his measurements of the attic, heading downstairs on the pretext of needing to dust off the dining room table and a couple of chairs so they could talk about her ideas for the renovations when he was finished. The reality was that she needed some space. The oversized attic that she envisioned as her living quarters seemed far too small when he stood so close to her.

If her purchase of this house had been irrational, her attraction to Mason Sullivan was even more so. He was obviously educated and intelligent, and he was undeniably handsome, but he was also heartache waiting to happen. He was the type of man to whom flirting came as naturally as breathing.

Yeah, she knew the type. And while she couldn't deny she was attracted, she could—and would—refuse to let it lead to anything more. She'd lost too much in the past year-and-a-half, taken too many emotional hits to risk another. And yet, there was something in the way he looked at her that made her feel young and carefree again, that made her want to be the woman she used to be—if only for a little while.

A fantasy, she knew, and a foolish one at that. And when she heard the sound of footsteps at the top of the stairs, she pushed it out of her mind and hastily finished wiping the table.

"I can't even offer you a cup of coffee because I haven't had a chance to get out for groceries yet," she said apologetically.

"That's okay," he said, taking the seat across from her.

She linked her fingers together on top of the table, tried not to let her nervousness show. This was the moment of truth—the moment when she found out if her dreams for this house could be realized or if she'd made a colossal mistake in clearing out most of her savings for the down payment.

He opened his notebook, turned the pages until he found a blank one. His hands were wide, his fingers long, the nails neatly cut. They were strong hands, she imagined, and capable. Hands that would handle any task competently and efficiently, whether sketching a house plan or stroking over a woman's body—

Zoe felt heat infuse her cheeks even as she chastised herself for that incongruous thought.

"You want the attic divided into three separate rooms—a bedroom, bathroom and office," he said, reviewing the instructions she'd given him. "Four bedrooms and two bathrooms on the second level, with each bedroom having access to one of the bathrooms."

She nodded.

"What about this floor?"

"I'm not sure," she admitted. "I don't know that it needs any major changes, but the layout doesn't feel right."

"Because it's been renovated and modernized," he told her. "The space is too open."

"What do you mean?"

"This room—" he gestured to the open flow between the dining and living areas "—is too contemporary for this style of house. You need to break it into individual rooms more appropriate to the era."

As soon as he explained what he meant, she realized he was right. "What do you suggest?"

"A traditional center hall plan with a large foyer as

you come through the front door. With this whole side as the dining area so that you can set up several smaller tables for your guests, connecting doors to the kitchen, and, on the other side, a parlor in the front, maybe a library behind it."

The possibility hadn't occurred to her, but now that he'd mentioned it, she was intrigued by the idea.

"You could build bookcases into the walls on either side of the fireplace, add a few comfortable chairs for guests to relax and read."

She could picture it exactly as he described and smiled at the cozy image that formed in her mind. "You're really good at this."

"It's my job."

She shook her head. "I'd say it's a passion."

He glanced away, as if her insight made him uncomfortable, and shrugged. "I've always loved old houses."

"Why?" she asked, genuinely curious.

"Because of the history and uniqueness of each structure. Don't tell Nick, or he might start looking for a new partner, but I actually enjoy renovating old buildings more than designing new ones. It's an incredible experience—revealing what has been hidden, uncovering the beauty so often unseen."

She didn't want to like him. It was awkward enough that she was attracted to him, even though she was determined to ignore the attraction. But listening to him talk, knowing he felt the same way she did about this old house, she felt herself softening toward him. "It must be enormously satisfying to love what you do."

"The key is to do what you love," he told her.

She nodded, understanding, because there had been a time not so very long ago that she'd done just that. But somewhere along the road that love had faded, too.

"Isn't there anything you're passionate about?" he asked.

She expected the question to be accompanied by a flirtatious wink or suggestive grin, but his expression was serious, almost intense. As if he really wanted to know, as if he was interested in what mattered to her.

"This house," she answered automatically.

"That's obvious," he said. "But what fired your passion before you came to Pinehurst?"

She shook her head, refusing to look back, to think about everything she'd left behind. "Can we focus on the house right now?"

"Okay."

But the depth of his scrutiny belied his easy response, and she didn't relax until he'd turned his attention back to his notebook.

"Where did you want to put your darkroom?" he asked.

The question made her realize she'd relaxed too soon.

"I don't need a darkroom," she said.

"There's plenty of room in the basement," he continued as if she hadn't spoken. "And it's certainly dark down there. Or you could convert the laundry room.

"I designed a home for Warren Crenshaw and his wife, Nancy. They're both nature photographers—not professionally, but it's a hobby they share. We put a darkroom right off their bedroom."

"I don't need a darkroom," she repeated tightly. "I'm not a photographer anymore."

"Whether or not you have a camera in your hand, you're still a photographer. It's the kind of thing that's in your blood—like designing houses is in mine."

She shook her head, swallowed around the lump in her throat. "I left that part of my life in Manhattan."

He hesitated, as if there was something more he wanted to say, but then her cell phone rang.

"Excuse me," she said, pushing her chair away from the table.

She dug the phone out of her purse, connecting the call before it patched through to her voice mail. "Hello."

"Where are you?" Scott asked without preamble.

The unexpected sound of his voice gave her a jolt, and made her heart ache just a little. The question, on the other hand, and the tone, annoyed her. "Why are you calling?"

"I just wanted to check in, see how you were doing."

She walked toward the window, away from where Mason was still seated at the table. "I'm fine."

"I'd be more likely to believe that if you were where you said you'd be."

"I *am* in Pinehurst," she told him.

"You said you'd be staying with Claire."

"Not forever."

He sighed. "She told me you were thinking about buying a house."

She frowned at that, wondering why her friend would have told Scott anything. But she couldn't blame Claire because she knew, better than anyone, how charming and persuasive he could be. "And?"

"Buying a house is a major decision," he said gently. "And you've had a tough year."

"Too late."

She heard his groan, fought back a smile.

"It was completely irrational and impulsive," she admitted. "I saw the sign on the lawn, contacted the agent and made an offer."

"Please tell me you at least had a home inspection done."

Now she did smile. Reasonable, practical Scott Cowan would never understand the need deep within her heart that had compelled her to buy this house. "A home inspector would have told me it needed a lot of work," she said, not admitting that she'd been given a copy of the report from an inspection done on the property just a few months earlier. "I already know that."

"Christ, Zoe. Have you gone completely off the deep end?"

"That seems to be the general consensus," she agreed.

"Let me contact my lawyers," he said. "Maybe there's a way to undo the transaction."

"No," she said quickly.

"What do you mean 'no'?"

She sighed. "I mean, I don't want it undone. I want this house."

"You could be making a very big mistake," he warned.

She knew he was right. But she'd spent the better part of her twenty-nine years doing the smart thing, the safe thing—and she'd still been unprepared for the curves that life had thrown her way. Even if buying this house turned out to be a mistake, it would be *her* mistake.

"Why should you care?" she challenged. "You walked out on me, remember?"

"You kicked me out."

He was right, she had to admit. But only because she couldn't continue to live with him the way things had been.

"Does it matter?" she asked wearily. "The end result is the same."

"I'll always care about you, Zoe."

And that might have been enough to hold them together if other obstacles hadn't got in the way. She rubbed her hand over her chest, trying to assuage an ache she wasn't sure would ever go away. "Was that the only reason you called?"

"When's your next appointment with Dr. Allison?"

She felt the sting of tears. If he'd been half as concerned about her twelve or even six months ago, what had been left of their relationship might not have fallen apart.

"I have to go, Scott."

Before he could say anything else, she disconnected the call. She heard the telltale scrape of chair legs against the hardwood floor and blinked the moisture from her eyes.

She felt Mason's hand on her shoulder, gently but firmly turning her to face him. "Zoe?"

She didn't—couldn't—look at him. She just needed half a minute to pull herself together, to find the cloak of feigned confidence and false courage that she'd learned to wrap around herself so no one would see how shaky and scared she was feeling inside.

"Who was that on the phone?" he asked.

She took a deep, steadying breath and prepared to dodge the question. After all, it was none of his business. She hardly knew this man; she certainly didn't owe him any explanations.

But when she looked up at him, she realized he wasn't trying to pry or interfere. He'd asked the question because he knew she was upset, and he was concerned. In the past eighteen months, she'd withdrawn into herself. She'd been let down by people she'd counted on, disappointed by friends who hadn't been there for her. Except for her almost daily phone calls to Claire, she'd been on her own. She'd learned to rely on herself, to need no one else.

After only a few days in this small town, she knew that was one of the reasons she'd come here—because she didn't want to live the rest of her life alone. She wanted—needed—friends to care about and who would care about her.

So she took what she hoped was the first step in that direction and answered his question honestly.

"That was my husband."

Chapter Three

*H*usband?

Mason's head reeled. Zoe's announcement had caught him completely unaware. And delivered as it was, in that soft, sexy voice, the punch was even more unexpected.

It took a minute for his brain to absorb this startling bit of information that—at least for him—changed the whole equation.

Zoe was married.

He couldn't have said why her revelation surprised him so much, or why it left him feeling oddly disappointed. He only knew that he needed to stop thinking of this woman as his sexy new neighbor and focus on the fact that she was someone's wife.

Damn.

Zoe might not be his usual type, but he found himself drawn to her regardless. There was just something about her that intrigued him—enough so that, in the brief time between their first meeting that morning and his return for their scheduled appointment, he'd found himself looking forward to spending time with her, getting to know her. And maybe, eventually, moving toward a more intimate and personal relationship with her.

Of course, that was all before he'd learned she was married.

It was his own fault for letting his fantasies get ahead of him, and he silently cursed himself for that now. His hand dropped away and he took a step back.

She gazed at him uncertainly as she folded her arms over her chest. Her cell phone was still clutched in her hand—her left hand. He noted that fact along with the absence of any rings on her fingers.

"You don't wear a wedding band," he noted.

Of course he knew that not everyone did. But he sensed that she was the type who would, that if she'd made a commitment to someone, she would display the evidence of that commitment. Then again, he'd been wrong about assuming she was uninvolved, so maybe he was wrong about this, too.

She shook her head and moved back to the dining room, returning to the chair she'd vacated to answer the call. "No, I don't wear a ring. Not anymore. Not since…that is, I'm—I mean we're—getting a divorce."

"Oh," he said, as he absorbed this second unexpected—but more welcome—revelation. And then he felt like a heel, because he was relieved to know that her marriage had fallen apart so that he didn't need to feel guilty for fantasizing about a married woman.

"We're just waiting for the final papers to come through," she admitted.

"I'm sorry," he said lamely.

She shrugged. "It happens."

Yeah, he knew that it did. He also knew that a break-up was never as easy as she implied, even if it was the right choice.

"How long were you married?" he asked.

"Almost nine years."

He stared at the woman who didn't look like she was twenty-five. "Did you get married while you were still in high school?"

She smiled at that. "Fresh out of college."

"How old were you when you went to college?"

"I'm twenty-nine," she told him.

And he was thirty-seven—which meant there weren't as many years between them as he'd originally suspected, but there was still the barrier of her marriage. And even if her divorce papers came through tomorrow, she was obviously still hung up on her husband. Her evident distress over his phone call was proof of that.

"What did your soon-to-be-ex-husband want?" he asked. "Did you take off with his coffeemaker or something like that?"

"No, nothing like that. We actually had a very civilized settlement."

"Then why was he calling you now?"

"He heard from a friend of mine that I bought a house and wanted to tell me he thought it was a mistake."

"Did you tell him it was none of his business?"

"Yes," she said. "But after nine years of marriage— and not just living together, but working together, too— some habits are hard to break."

"Is he a photographer, too?"

"No. He's the senior fashion editor at *Images*."

"Is that why you left Manhattan?"

She shook her head. "It's a big enough city that I could have stayed, found a new apartment, a new job, and probably have never seen him again if I didn't want to. But everything just seemed so inexplicably woven together there. I needed to get away from all of it, to make a fresh start somewhere else."

"Well, you picked a good place for that."

"Speaking from experience?"

His surprise must have shown, because she smiled.

"Maybe I didn't peg you quite as quickly as you did me," she said, "but the more I listen to you talk, the more I hear just the subtlest hint of a drawl."

"You can take a boy out of the south, but you can't take the south out of the boy," he mused.

"How far south?"

"Beaufort, South Carolina."

"What brought you up here?"

"I came north to go to college, met Nick Armstrong there, came to Pinehurst for a visit one summer and decided to stay up here to go into business with him."

"Do you go home very often?"

"This is my home now."

"Don't you have any family left in Beaufort?"

He shook his head again. "There's just me and my brother, Tyler, and he's living up here now, too."

"No wife or ex-wife?" she wondered.

He shuddered at the thought. "No."

"Well, that was definite enough."

"Not that I'm opposed to the institution of marriage. In fact, I was the best man when Nick got married." He grinned. "Both times."

"He was married to someone before Jessica?"

"To your real estate agent actually."

Now *that* came as a surprise to Zoe.

"I don't know Jessica very well, obviously," she said. "But the way she talked about Nick, I got the impression they'd been together forever."

"They've been in love forever," he agreed. "Had a brief romance when they were younger, then went their separate ways and found each other again only last year."

"Doesn't that seem strange to you?"

"It's a small town," he reminded her. "And Nick's ex was remarried long before Jess ever came back to town."

Zoe thought about the possibility of Scott marrying again, and wondered if she could ever bring herself to be friends with her ex-husband's new wife. Then she decided it was a moot point. He was out of her life; she'd moved away; they'd both moved on.

She felt the familiar ache of loss, but it wasn't as

sharp or as strong as it once had been. She'd finally accepted that he couldn't be what she'd needed him to be any more than she could be what he'd wanted. And while her body would always carry the scars of what had finally broken their marriage, she realized that her heart was finally starting to heal.

Mason didn't know anything about babies, but he couldn't deny that the pink bundle in Jessica's arms was kind of cute. Elizabeth Theresa Armstrong had soft blond fuzz on her head, tiny ears and an even tinier nose. She yawned, revealing toothless gums, then blinked and looked at her mother through the biggest, bluest eyes he'd ever seen.

"She's a beauty, Jess."

The new mother beamed. "She really is, isn't she?"

"Absolutely," he agreed. "Just like her mother."

Jess chuckled. "Actually, she looks exactly like Nick's baby pictures."

"No kidding?" He glanced at the proud father standing by the window. "Let's hope she has better luck as she grows up."

His partner chose to ignore the comment, asking instead, "How was your appointment with Ms. Kozlowski?"

"It was…interesting," he said, unconsciously echoing Zoe's description of their initial meeting. He carried the vase of flowers he'd brought for Jessica over to the windowsill to join the other arrangements that were already there. "The house needs a lot of work."

"What did you think of the owner?" Jess asked.

"I think she needs her head examined," he said. "And so do you, for not trying to talk her out of buying that place."

"No one could have talked her out of it."

Mason had caught only a glimpse of Zoe's steely determination and guessed Jess was probably right.

"You still should have tried," he said, setting the pint of promised ice cream and a plastic spoon on the table beside her bed.

"If she hadn't bought it, we wouldn't have got the referral," Nick pointed out. "And it would've killed you to watch another architect put his hands all over that house."

"So long as you keep your hands on the *house*," Jess said.

Nick lifted an eyebrow in silent question.

Mason shook his head. "She's not my type."

"Is she female?" his friend asked dryly.

"A very attractive female," Jess interjected. "Who's new in town and doesn't need to be hit on by the first guy she meets."

"I was the consummate professional," Mason assured her, and it was true—even if he'd had some very personal and inappropriate thoughts about her.

The baby squirmed, and when Jess started to shift her to the other arm, Nick swooped in and picked her up.

"Do you want to hold her?" he asked his friend.

Mason took an instinctive step in retreat. "No, um, thanks, but, um…"

Jess took advantage of having her hands free to reach for the container of ice cream. As she pried open the lid, she commented, "I've never seen you back away from a woman before, Mason."

"My experience is with babes, not babies." He felt a quick spurt of panic as his friend deposited the infant in his arms and stepped away, leaving the tiny fragile bundle in his awkward grasp. Then he gazed at the angelic face again and his heart simply melted.

He reminded himself that he didn't want what his friends had. Marriage, children, family—they were the kind of ties he didn't dare risk. Yet somehow, these friends had become his extended family.

He'd had a family once, a long time ago. Parents who had loved one another and doted on their two sons. He'd been fourteen years old when his mother got sick; Tyler had been only ten. Elaine Sullivan had valiantly fought the disease for almost two years, but everyone had known it was only a matter of time. The ravages of the illness had been obvious in her sunken cheeks, dull eyes and pasty skin.

Gord Sullivan had fallen apart when he'd realized the woman he loved was dying. Unable to deal with the ravages of her illness, he'd looked for solace in whiskey—and other women. Mason had never figured out if it was denial or some kind of coping mechanism. He only knew that his father's abandonment had hurt his mother more than the disease that had eaten away at her body.

Four years after they'd lowered Elaine's coffin into the ground, her husband was laid to rest beside her. The doctors blamed his death on cirrhosis of the liver. Mason knew his father had really died of a broken heart.

It was a hard but unforgettable lesson, and when

he'd buried his father, Mason had promised himself he wouldn't ever let himself love that deeply or be that vulnerable. He refused to risk that kind of loss again.

And yet, when he looked at Nick and Jess and their new baby, the obvious love they felt for one another evident in every look that passed between them, he found himself wanting to believe that happy endings were possible. He wanted to believe his friends would be luckier than his parents.

One of the drawbacks of buying the house and its contents, Zoe realized, was having to *clean* the house *and* its contents. After Beatrice Hadfield died, her grandson hadn't removed anything from the house, which meant there was a lot of cleaning *up* to do before she could even begin to tackle the dust and cobwebs that had taken up residence in the vacant house over the past couple of years.

She took down all the curtains and stripped the beds, then spent half a day and a couple rolls of quarters at The Laundry Basket in town. She emptied out closets and dressers and shelves and cupboards and packed up dozens of boxes for charity. She sorted through cabinets full of china and stemware, tossing out anything that was cracked or chipped. When she was done, she still had enough pieces left to serve a five-course meal to twenty guests.

It took her three days to get through the rooms on the first two floors, then three more days to sort through everything in the attic. There were trunks of old clothes, shelves of old books and boxes and boxes of papers and photos. She was tempted to just toss everything—it would certainly be the quickest and easiest solution—but her conscience wouldn't let her throw out anything without first knowing what it was.

She found letters and journals and lost a whole day reading through them. She felt guilty when she opened the cover of what she quickly realized was a personal journal of Beatrice Hadfield's from some fifty years back, but the remorse was eclipsed by curiosity as the woman's bold writing style and recitation of details quickly drew Zoe into the world in which she'd lived back then—and the passionate affair the woman had had with a writer who had rented a room in the house for several months one summer. A writer who had gone on to win several awards for plays, more than one of which Zoe had seen on Broadway.

On the morning of the seventh day in her new home, there was still cleaning to be done and she'd run out of supplies. So she grabbed her keys and purse and headed into town for what was intended as a quick stop at Anderson's Hardware. She didn't anticipate that being a newcomer in a town where almost everyone knew everyone else would make her a curiosity.

She'd barely managed to put the first items—a bucket and mop—in her cart when a tall, white-haired man approached.

"I'm Harry Anderson," he said. "You must be the young lady who bought the Hadfield place."

She nodded. "Zoe Kozlowski."

"Welcome to Pinehurst, Zoe." He smiled. "Is there anything I can help you find?"

"I just needed to pick up a few cleaning supplies."

She thought she was capable of browsing and making her own selections, but Harry Anderson clearly had other ideas. Instead of leaving her to her shopping, he guided her around the store, asking questions and making suggestions along the way.

Other customers came and went, each one exchanging greetings with the store owner who, in turn, insisted on introducing her. While he was occupied with Sue Walton—"her family owns the ice-cream parlor down the street"—she steered her cart toward the checkout.

She wasn't sure she had everything she'd need, but she had at least enough to get started and she really wanted to get back home and do just that. She was paying for her purchases when Tina Stilwell, her real estate agent, came into the store.

"I thought that was your car outside," Tina said to Zoe, then she stood on tiptoes to kiss the cheek of the man beside her, "Hello, Uncle Harry."

"Hello, darling."

"Did you forget about our lunch plans?" she asked Zoe.

Zoe glanced at her watch, as surprised to see that it was almost lunchtime as she was by the other woman's reference to plans she knew they'd never made. "I guess I did."

"Well, you girls go on, then," Harry said. "I don't want to keep you any longer."

"Thanks for your help, Mr. Anderson," Zoe said.

The old man smiled at her. "It was real nice meeting you, Zoe. Good luck with that house."

"Thanks," she said.

Then, to Tina, as they walked out of the store, "And thank *you*."

Tina smiled. "My uncle Harry is a darling man with far too much time on his hands."

"I can't believe I was in there an hour," Zoe said. "I've never spent an hour in a hardware store in my entire life."

"You've never lived in Pinehurst before. This town operates on a whole different schedule than the rest of the world."

"I miss Manhattan already," she muttered, unlocking the trunk of her car to deposit her purchases inside.

The other woman chuckled. "What do you miss? The crowds, the noise or the chaos?"

"All of the above." She closed the trunk. "But I think what I miss most is the anonymity."

"I felt the same way when I first moved here from Boston."

Zoe smiled. "Is there anyone living in this town who actually grew up here?"

"Of course," Tina said. "I'll fill you in on all the local characters over lunch."

She glanced at her watch again. "I really have a ton of things to do at the house."

"Have you eaten?"

"No," she admitted, belatedly realizing that she also needed to restock her dwindling food supply.

"Then let's go," Tina said. "Because if we don't show up at Freda's, Uncle Harry will know before the end of the day that I lied to him."

And so she ended up having lunch with Tina at the

popular little café. And she enjoyed it, far more than she expected to. It had been a long time since she'd shared a simple meal and easy conversation with a friend. And though she didn't know Tina very well, she already considered her a friend—one of the first she'd made in Pinehurst.

Then she thought of Mason, and wondered whether he might be another. She'd been thinking about him a lot since their initial meeting a week earlier—probably too much—so she put those thoughts aside and dug into her spinach salad.

When Zoe finally got home after lunch and grocery shopping, she felt as though she'd already put in a full day and hadn't even begun to tackle the dust and dirt. She shoved a bucket under the kitchen tap and turned on the water, thinking that it would have been nice to hire a cleaning service to come in and scrub the place from top to bottom. But that was a luxury she couldn't afford—especially not when she had time on her hands and nothing else to do.

Still, it was almost nine o'clock before she decided to hang up her mop for the night. Although she was physically exhausted, her mind was unsettled, her thoughts preoccupied with everything yet to be done. She decided a nice cup of tea would help her relax and get some sleep.

After the kettle had boiled, she carried her mug out to the porch and settled into an old weathered Adirondack chair. She lifted her feet to prop them on the railing, then dropped them quickly when the wood creaked and swayed. Instead, she folded her legs beneath her on the chair and cradled her mug between her palms.

The darkness of the nights still surprised her, with no streetlights or neon signs to illuminate the blackness of night. There was only the moon, about three-quarters full tonight, and an array of stars unlike anything she'd ever seen. She breathed deeply, filling her lungs with the cool, fresh air, and smiled. It was beautiful, peaceful, and exactly what she needed.

At least until she heard a thump on the porch and registered the bump against her arm half a second before she felt the shock of hot tea spilling down the front of her shirt and a disgustingly familiar wet tongue sweeping across her mouth.

She sputtered and pushed the hairy beast aside.

"Rosie, down."

He sat, panting happily beside her chair.

Zoe resisted the urge to scream, asking instead, in a carefully controlled voice, "Where is your master?"

The beast tilted his head, as if trying to understand the question, but—of course—made no response to it.

"Maybe you're smarter than he is," she said. "Do you understand the word *by-law?*"

The beast merely cocked his head from one side to the next.

"Or *dog pound?*"

He barked, but then he licked her hand, clearly proving his ignorance.

"How about *leash?*" she asked in a deliberately friendly tone.

The beast dropped to his belly on the porch, covered his ears with his paws and whimpered.

Zoe exhaled a frustrated breath and untangled her

legs. She set the now half-empty cup of tea on the arm of the chair and stood up. "Let's go," she said.

Rosie danced in ecstatic circles around her, nearly tripping her on the stairs.

It was the start of the ninth inning in a tie game when Mason heard knocking. He scowled at the door, his eyes still glued to the television. It was early in the season, but his commitment to his Yankees was resolute. Unfortunately, so was the pounding.

He swore under his breath as he pushed himself off the couch. The lead-off batter singled to right field and Mason pulled open the door. The sight of the woman on the other side was so unexpected—and so unexpectedly appealing in a pair of yoga-style pants that sat low on her hips and a skimpy white tank top—he actually forgot about the ballgame playing out on the fifty-two-inch screen behind him.

"This beast is a menace," Zoe said tightly.

He winced and glanced at the animal sitting obediently at her side. "What did he do now?"

"What did he do?" she echoed indignantly. "Look at me."

He took her words as an invitation, allowing his eyes to move over her—from the slightly lopsided ponytail on top of her head to the pink-painted toenails on her feet—lingering momentarily at some of the more interesting places in between.

"This—" she gestured to the stain on the front of her shirt that he'd thought was a flower "—was a cup of very hot tea."

"It's…pink."

Her cheeks seemed to take on the same color.

"It's herbal tea," she said. "Raspberry. But that's not the point."

"Of course not," he agreed solemnly.

Her eyes narrowed. "The point is that you were going to keep him on a leash."

Rosie tucked her paws over her ears and whimpered.

Zoe rolled her eyes in disbelief. "You've obviously taught him to react whenever he hears that word. Why can't you teach him to stay off my property?"

"I think he has a crush on you."

She sent him a look of patent disbelief.

"I'm not kidding," he told her. "He's never wandered away from the backyard without me before."

"I find that hard to believe."

"It's true. And I really am sorry about—" his gaze fell to the pink stain on the front of her shirt and the tempting feminine curves beneath it "—your tea."

She crossed her arms over her chest. "I'm hopeful it will wash out."

"Then will we be forgiven?"

"Maybe the dog," she said. "Not you. You should know better than to let him roam free."

He scratched the top of Rosie's head. "He's just very affectionate."

"His affection is wreaking havoc on my wardrobe."

"You're welcome to come over anytime to use my washer and dryer, if you want."

"Thanks," she said. "But I'll stick with The Laundry Basket."

"That's right," he said. "You don't like to be on top of your neighbors."

Her eyes narrowed on him.

He grinned. "Or was it that you didn't like your neighbors on top?"

"Maybe it's just some neighbors in particular that I have a problem with."

"You'll get over it," he said confidently. "Pinehurst is too small a town to hold a grudge against anyone for long."

"I'll give it my best shot," she told him.

He couldn't help but chuckle. "I think I'm going to enjoy getting to know you, Zoe Kozlowski."

"Maybe another time," she said. "Right now, I want to get home. I have a ton of things to do in the morning."

"Wait," he said, as she turned away.

She hesitated with obvious reluctance.

"Let me walk you back."

"I don't need an escort."

"I know you don't," he agreed, sliding his feet into his shoes. "But it's a nice night for a walk and I don't want you going home mad."

"I wouldn't count on your company changing my disposition," she warned him.

He grinned. "I'll chance it."

"What about the beast?"

He glanced regretfully at the animal by his feet. Rosie was looking up at him and thumping his tail in eager anticipation. As much as Mason regretted having to punish him, the dog had to learn that there were consequences to his actions. "Stay."

The bundle of fur immediately sprawled on the floor,

settling his chin on his front paws and looking up at his master with sorrow-filled eyes.

Mason ignored the guilt that tugged at him as he closed the door.

"Why do you call him that?" he asked.

"What?"

"The beast."

"Because he is one."

"You're going to hurt his feelings," he warned.

She turned, a reluctant smile tugging at the corners of her mouth. "His or yours?"

"You have a beautiful smile, Zoe."

He was disappointed, although not surprised, that his comment succeeded in erasing any trace of it.

"Flattery is not going to get you or your dog off the hook."

"Why are you assuming that I have an ulterior motive?"

"Because everyone does."

He took her hand, rubbed his thumb over the back of her knuckles. She didn't tug away, but he could tell by the wariness in her eyes that she wanted to.

"Have dinner with me," he said impulsively.

"I already ate."

"I didn't mean tonight."

She hesitated. "I'm going to be busy with the house for quite a while."

"You still have to eat," he pointed out.

"I know but—"

"Tomorrow night," he interrupted what he was sure would be a refusal. "We'll barbecue some steaks, open a bottle of wine—"

"I really don't—"

"—and talk about the plans for your house," he continued.

The rest of her protest died on her lips. "My house?"

He couldn't help but smile. Every woman had a weakness—he'd just never before met one whose soft spot was a pile of crumbling bricks.

"I had some concerns about the kitchen renovation I thought we should discuss before I draw up the plans."

"So this would be a…business meeting?"

"We can call it whatever you want."

She frowned at that. "I'm not ready to start dating again."

"And I don't date married women," he told her.

"Okay." She smiled now, clearly relieved. "In that case, yes—I'd like to have dinner with you tomorrow night."

"Good." He released her hand when they reached her back porch. "Seven o'clock?"

She nodded. "Sounds good."

He watched her walk up the steps, appreciating the toned length of her legs, the round curve of her butt, the gentle sway of her hips. Yeah, she had some nice moves and an appealing look, and it occurred to him that though he was sorry she was going through a divorce, he was glad she wouldn't be married for very much longer.

Chapter Four

There were times that Zoe really missed her morning cup of coffee. Saturday morning was one of those times.

After her evening visit from Rosie and her confrontation with Mason, she'd had a lot on her mind and found sleep eluded her for most of the night. Some of her preoccupation was caused by worries about the house, about the concerns stirred up by her recent conversation with her ex-husband. She hadn't expected that he would accept her plans or understand her choices. Somewhere along the line, their lives had started to take different paths, until—at the end—she'd wondered how they'd ever believed they would be together forever.

Still, his doubts nagged at her, his implication that

she was in over her head worried her. There had been a time when she would have laughed at such naysayers, because she was strong and determined and invincible. Now she knew differently.

But she'd managed to put those concerns aside fairly easily. A lot more easily than her thoughts about Mason Sullivan.

He was, she knew, the real reason she'd been awake through so much of the night. Because she'd been thinking about him, and worrying about the long-dormant feelings he stirred inside her.

She was attracted to him—there was no denying that. There was something about those blue eyes and the easy smile that warmed her blood in a way that made her realize she'd been cold for too long. If the sudden attraction she felt surprised her, it worried her even more. She hadn't anticipated experiencing those kind of feelings again, and she didn't know what to do about them.

But she did know that daydreaming about Mason wasn't going to get her work done. In fact, fantasizing about the sexy architect could only complicate her life at a time when she was trying to keep things simple—at least on a personal level. And so she resolved to put everyone and everything out of her mind, crank up the radio and get the house cleaned.

She'd just plugged in her boom box when the doorbell rang. She wasn't expecting any company, but her heart skipped a beat at the thought that it might be her closest neighbor stopping by. She was surprised—but not disappointed—to find her best friend on the porch.

She threw open the door to give Claire a hug before asking, "What are you doing here?"

"What kind of a greeting is that?" her friend chided.

"The greeting of someone who thought you would be on your way to Pennsylvania this weekend for your son's baseball tournament."

"That's what I thought, too," Claire admitted. "But the Hawks lost two of their first three games so they didn't advance to the finals. Instead of Laurel and I heading to Scranton today, Rob and Jason came home last night."

"He must be so disappointed."

"Who?" Her friend's lips curved. "Jason or Rob?"

Zoe smiled back. "I meant Jason, although I imagine it was a blow to the coach, too."

"It was," Claire agreed. "But considering that they went undefeated all the way to the playoffs last year, they were overdue to lose a game—or two."

"Well, I'm sorry for Jason—and Rob—but I'm happy for me," Zoe said. "I've been so anxious for you to see inside this place."

"I'm sorry I couldn't get over last week when you got the keys, but things have been crazy at school and Laurel's had extra music lessons to prep for her upcoming recital and—"

"You don't have to apologize for having a life," Zoe said.

"You mean for having children who have lives," her friend corrected. "I'm just the cook and chauffeur."

She smiled again. "I'm just glad you're here now and with—" she eyed the take-out tray in Claire's hand "—dare I hope that's coffee?"

"It is. I know you mostly gave up caffeine—"

"*Mostly* being the key word. And I was sorely regretting not having any on hand this morning."

"Then you can take this," Claire said, passing her the tray, "while I go get the rest of the stuff from the car."

"The rest of the stuff" turned out to be two armloads of housewarming gifts. There was a ficus plant in a brass pot with a big red bow around it, a bottle of Zoe's favorite chardonnay, a handful of glossy magazines featuring Victorian home designs and renovations and a Tupperware container filled with homemade chocolate chip cookies.

"Oh—and one more thing," Claire said, pulling a camera and several canisters of film out of her purse. "Rob finally bought a digital, so this one was just sitting around. It's one of those point-and-shoot models designed for amateurs like me, but I thought it would serve the purpose."

"What purpose might that be?" Zoe asked in a deliberately casual tone.

"Before and after pictures," her friend said, sliding the camera across the countertop toward her. "So that you can show people what it used to look like after the renovations are complete."

"That's a good idea," she acknowledged, but reached for one of the paper cups instead of the Canon.

Claire took the other cup, indicating a willingness to let the subject drop—at least for now.

"Let's go into the dining room," Zoe suggested, leading the way. "You can tell me if the table and chairs are real antiques."

"You got the furniture with the house?"

"I got *everything* with the house, and I've spent the past week trying to figure out what to do with it all. But I'm glad for the furniture because without it, we'd be sitting on the floor."

"Well, knowing how old Beatrice Hadfield was when she passed away, I'd bet you did get honest-to-goodness antiques," Claire said.

"You knew Mrs. Hadfield?"

"She was my math teacher in high school. And my mother's math teacher when she was in high school." Claire frowned. "Maybe my grandmother's, too."

Zoe laughed. "She wasn't *that* old."

"Close enough." Her friend smiled. "It's so good to hear you laugh, Zoe. And to see you looking so happy."

"I'm feeling pretty happy. And a little overwhelmed when I let myself think too hard about everything that needs to be done around here," she admitted. "But mostly happy."

"I'm happy that you've decided to stay in Pinehurst."

"But?" Zoe prompted.

"But I'm worried that you've rushed into this. That six months from now, you'll regret walking away—not just from the magazine, but from your whole life in New York City."

She shook her head. "I don't have a life in New York City anymore."

Claire hesitated a moment before asking, "Have you talked to Scott since you've been here?"

"He called last week."

"I thought he might." Claire winced. "I didn't realize

you hadn't told him about the house, and when I mentioned it, he seemed a little, uh, concerned."

Zoe smiled. "You mean he went ballistic?"

"Something like that."

"Funny how much he cares so much about what I'm doing now that we're almost divorced."

"Are you doing okay with that?" Claire asked gently.

"I am," she assured her friend. "I'm sad, of course, that our marriage ended the way it did, but I have no doubts that it was over. And, for the first time in a long time, I'm looking forward to the future. I'm excited about this project, thrilled to finally have a sense of direction and a purpose."

"And your purpose now is to operate a bed-and-breakfast?"

She nodded. "Are you going to try to talk me out of this—tell me I'm crazy to even consider it?"

"Nope. Because you're one of the smartest, strongest, gutsiest women I know, and I don't believe there's anything you can't do."

Her friend spoke so sincerely that the words brought tears to Zoe's eyes.

Then Claire, understanding that something needed to be done to lighten the mood before they both ending up bawling, added, "Although I'd suggest you at least run a dusting cloth and vacuum around here before you open the door to guests."

Zoe managed to smile at that. "I think it will be a while before I open the door to anyone but my closest friends."

"That's what I figured—and the reason I'm dressed like this." She indicated her T-shirt and leggings.

"You brought me coffee and you came to help me clean? You really are a true friend."

"My motives aren't completely altruistic," Claire admitted. "I was in desperate need of an excuse to get out of the house after Rob's mother showed up this morning for an unexpected visit."

"Then I'll have to thank Rob's mother if I ever meet her, because I'm really glad you're here."

"Me, too." Claire finished off her coffee, set her empty cup aside and stood up. "Now let's tackle some dirt."

"I can't believe how horribly neglected this place was," Zoe said when they finally decided to take a break for lunch.

"It's been vacant for almost two years," Claire reminded her. "And Mrs. Hadfield probably hadn't managed to do a thorough cleaning for several years prior to that."

Zoe spread butter on bread for sandwiches. "It's sad to think that she lived in this big old house all by herself for so long. And died alone."

"Her grandson tried to get her to move out to California," Claire told her. "But she refused to move away from the only home she'd ever known, especially to some godforsaken place so overrun with hippies and movie stars it would only be fitting for it to fall into the ocean."

Zoe chuckled at that as she layered slices of turkey and Havarti. "Sounds like she was quite a character."

"That she was. And always sticking her nose into all her neighbors' business." She smiled her thanks as she took the plate and bottle of water that Zoe passed to her.

"Speaking of neighbors," she continued on her way into the dining room. "Have you met Mason Sullivan yet?"

Zoe put down the sandwich she'd just picked up and stared across the table in disbelief. "You know him?"

Her friend smiled. "Honey, I'd bet there isn't a single woman in this town who doesn't know Mason Sullivan."

"You're not single."

Claire's smile widened. "I used to be."

Zoe decided she wasn't going to ask—she really didn't want to know. Instead, she said, "Yes, I've met Mason. He's going to draft some renovation plans for me."

"Hmm." Claire chewed on her sandwich. "Has he hit on you yet?"

"Well, he seemed extremely interested in my plumbing and wiring."

Her friend laughed. "And did you check out his…structure?"

She couldn't lie. Nor could she prevent the smile that curved her lips. "I can confidently state that there were no obvious flaws."

Claire studied her across the table for a long moment, smiling smugly until Zoe couldn't stand it anymore.

"What?" she finally demanded.

"I was just noticing the intriguing color in your cheeks. In fact, if I didn't know better, I might almost suspect that you were blushing," her friend teased.

Zoe scowled. "I'm too old and jaded for that."

"You're not even thirty yet."

"Getting close," she said, remembering a time when

she'd dreaded the milestone, hated the thought of growing older. Now she looked forward to it and intended to cherish every day on the journey.

"Which means you should be old enough and wise enough to appreciate that you've been given a second chance—not just at life, but for love."

"Right now, I'm just taking things one step at a time," Zoe said lightly.

"Buying this house was a good first step. Getting to know your neighbor a little better could be the second."

"One step at a time," she said again.

"Okay," Claire relented. "If you don't want to talk about Mason, let's talk about dinner."

"We've just finished lunch."

"I know, but Rob said he would throw together a broccoli and chicken casserole tonight and asked if you wanted to join us."

She was touched by the offer, pleased that her friend's husband would think to include her in their family plans and apprehensive about declining the invitation.

"Thanks," she said, picking up her plate and empty bottle to take them back into the kitchen. "But, um, actually, I have other plans."

She heard the scrape of chair legs on the floor as Claire followed her. "You moved into town just over a week ago and you already have plans with someone other than me?"

"I thought you were going to be away all weekend," Zoe reminded her. "But I can cancel and—"

"You absolutely will *not* cancel," Claire said firmly. "But you will tell me what your plans are."

"I'm having dinner with Mason," she admitted, accepting that there was no way to keep that information from her friend.

"The man moves even faster than I remembered."

"It's not a date," Zoe told her.

"According to whom?"

"Both of us."

"You discussed the fact that you were having dinner together and agreed that it wasn't a date?"

She nodded.

Her friend chuckled. "One of you was lying."

"It's a business meeting, to discuss ideas for renovating my house."

"Uh-huh. And where is this…business meeting… taking place?"

Zoe sighed. "At Mason's."

"Uh-huh," Claire said again, her eyes twinkling.

"You're making a big deal out of something that really isn't."

"Maybe we should wait until tomorrow to discuss which one of us doesn't have a clear picture of what this business-meeting-at-Mason's-house really means."

"Now I'm definitely going to cancel."

"Don't," her friend said quickly. "Please. Give him a chance. Give *yourself* a chance."

Zoe shook her head. "I'm not ready."

Claire laid a gentle hand on her arm. "I don't mean to push. And you shouldn't let yourself be pushed if you're really not ready. But I worry that you're using everything that's happened in the past year-and-a-half as an excuse to put your life on hold. You need to start living again."

"I want to," she admitted softly. "But I'm scared. Not of Mason, but of the way I feel when I'm around him."

"Which means that you're feeling something," her friend pointed out smugly.

It had been a long time since she'd felt anything other than disappointment and despair, sorrow and regret. When she'd found Hadfield House, she felt the first stirrings of hope and joy and excitement and anticipation. And then she'd met Mason, and suddenly she was feeling all kinds of things she wasn't prepared for.

"Lust," she admitted on a wistful sigh. "Pure unadulterated lust."

Claire's smile came back in full force. "A very good sign."

Zoe shook her head. "Except that my sexual experience is extremely limited, and although my hormones are showing definite signs of life again, my heart isn't ready. I can't face that kind of rejection again."

"I'm not suggesting you fall in love with the man. Just spend some time with him, see where things go."

"They might not go anywhere," Zoe said.

"You never know." Her friend's smile turned to a frown when her watch beeped. "I didn't realize what time it was getting to be. I have to run or I'll be late getting Laurel to gymnastics."

Zoe followed her to the door. "Thanks—for the housewarming gifts and especially for all of your help. The house looks a thousand times better already."

"I think we made enough progress that you won't

need to feel guilty about taking a few hours for your dinner-with-Mason-that-isn't-a-date."

"It isn't a date," Zoe said again.

"Of course not."

Her eyes narrowed in suspicion of her friend's easy agreement.

"Just one last piece of advice before I go," Claire said.

"What's that?"

"Take the chardonnay."

After Claire had gone, Zoe continued to work. But with every minute that passed, bringing her another minute closer to her scheduled dinner meeting with Mason, her trepidation grew.

Last night she hadn't thought twice about marching over there, propelled by anger and indignation that his dog had been trespassing again. Tonight, she was an invited guest, and for some inexplicable reason, that left her a jumble of tangled nerves.

It's just dinner, she reminded herself. It wasn't a date—Mason had said so himself.

So why was she so nervous just thinking about it?

Why did she feel as if she would be crossing some kind of line she wasn't ready to cross?

She tried to find reassurance in Mason's assertion that he didn't date married women. Except that he knew she was just waiting for her divorce to be final, and she wondered if he was waiting, too.

It didn't seem to occur to him that the interest he'd expressed might not be reciprocated. Probably because he was built like a statue of a god and had a smile that would melt any woman's reservations at ten paces. As it might have melted hers had her personal circumstances been different.

But the truth was, she had a lot of things to work out on her own before she considered getting involved with anyone again. She'd meant it when she'd told him she wasn't ready to start dating, and she wasn't going to change her mind because a simple look from Mason Sullivan made her heart race. Her heart was still too battered and bruised from everything she'd been through over the past year-and-a-half to want to open it up again.

Even before she had met her husband, she hadn't been the type to engage in casual relationships. She'd had very definite plans for her life that didn't leave much time for meaningless flirtations or recreational sex. She'd wanted a home and a family—but mostly she'd wanted the stability she hadn't had growing up.

She'd thought she was getting everything she wanted when she had married Scott, that her dreams were finally within her grasp. And for the first few years of their marriage, she had continued to believe it. They'd discussed their plans for a family, talked excitedly about having a baby, and Zoe had believed he'd wanted a child as much as she had. But whenever she'd pressed, he had balked. *Maybe next year.* Except that next year had never come.

She'd finally gone in for a checkup, wanting her doctor's okay before she brought up the subject again. But the doctor hadn't given her the okay. Instead, he'd scheduled a follow-up exam, which had led to additional tests, and somewhere along the way Zoe had started wanting the normalcy of her life back even more than she wanted a baby.

She'd heard people say it about other couples who had separated—well, at least they didn't have children. As if that was supposed to be some sort of consolation. She knew the same thing had been said when her marriage had fallen apart, but Zoe wasn't grateful for the fact. More than anything, she'd wanted a baby, a family, a home. And now, only months away from her thirtieth birthday, she was painfully aware of being alone.

When she and Scott had exchanged vows, she'd thought that was something she would never have to worry about again. Now that their divorce was almost final, she realized she'd been alone for a lot longer than the period of their separation. They'd been living separate lives under the same roof without even realizing it, until that roof had caved in and the foundation of everything had crumbled.

Her husband was the first man she'd ever loved, the only man she'd thought she would ever love, and it had broken her heart to acknowledge the end of their marriage. When she'd packed up her belongings and walked out of their apartment for the last time, she couldn't have imagined ever wanting to get involved in a relationship that would risk her heart again.

Yet despite all that painful history, she couldn't deny that she was attracted to her new neighbor, and that was what unnerved her the most. It was easy enough to discount what he said or did—obviously flirting came as naturally to Mason Sullivan as breathing. But what was she supposed to do about these feelings he stirred inside her?

Embrace them, Claire had said. *You've been numb for far too long.*

But Claire was stronger than she was, braver than she was.

Zoe wanted only to ignore the feelings. She wasn't ready to do anything else.

So she dropped the cloth back into the bucket of soapy water and dried her hands. Then she picked up her cell phone and called Mason to decline his dinner invitation.

She wasn't sure if she was relieved or disappointed when his voice mail clicked in after the third ring. She listened to the low, sexy voice that carried just the slightest hint of the south and wondered, as she was advised to leave a message, if it was in bad taste to cancel plans electronically. Then she decided she didn't care—it was a matter of self-preservation. Besides, it was a Saturday, and she had no doubt that Mason Sullivan wouldn't have any trouble making alternative plans for his evening. And she had enough work to do to keep busy until she fell into an exhausted—and hopefully dreamless—slumber.

Mason spent most of Saturday at the office, catching up on some work and figuring out a schedule for new projects then, when Nick had popped in, filling his partner in on the latest business developments. After Nick had gone home to his wife and new baby girl,

Mason headed to the grocery story to pick up a couple of steaks and a few other things for his dinner with Zoe.

He was whistling as he loaded up his grocery cart, looking forward to spending a few hours in the company of an interesting and attractive woman. Not a date but a dinner meeting, he reminded himself, although he wasn't convinced the distinction was anything more than semantics.

But he understood Zoe's reluctance to jump back into the dating pool before her divorce was final. There were a lot of piranhas in that pool and an unsuspecting swimmer could get eaten alive. It was natural that she would be hesitant, maybe even wary. Heck, recent experience had made *him* wary.

Until meeting Zoe had piqued his curiosity enough to make him want to test the waters again. Except the thought of getting back out there didn't entice him as much as the thought of being with her. Which might prove to be something of a dilemma since she'd been clear that she wasn't looking for any kind of personal relationship. But Mason was confident that, with a little time and some gentle persuasion, he could change her mind. In fact, it was a challenge he looked forward to.

His confidence took a serious hit when he got home from the grocery store and heard the message Zoe had left on his voice mail.

He was disappointed by the change of plans—then annoyed with himself for letting it matter enough that he could be disappointed.

He shoved the steaks into the refrigerator and

reached for the phone to call for pizza. He had no intention of sitting around and thinking about a canceled business meeting that wasn't even a date.

But he hesitated before punching in the number that he knew from memory because he really didn't want to spend yet another Saturday night sitting at home alone.

He tried calling his brother but got his machine. Then he sat and stared at the phone as he considered his other options. It was disheartening to realize how limited those options were.

He wasn't so desperate for company that he would intrude on Nick and Jessica while they were still settling in with their new baby. And though he had other friends, most of them had families or wives or at least significant others with whom they would be spending their evening.

His attention shifted when Rosie propped his chin on Mason's thigh. He ruffled the thick fur on the top of the dog's head. "Looks like it's just you and me tonight," he said. "You want pepperoni or sausage on that pizza?"

Rosie gave one short bark and went straight to the door.

"Okay—walk and then pizza."

He went to the back door, sighing when the animal streaked past him and immediately tore off through the woods toward Zoe's house.

Okay, maybe he'd suspected that Rosie would head in that direction. The dog's infatuation with their new neighbor had been immediate and enthusiastic—and obviously one-sided. And maybe, Mason mused wryly as he made his way through the woods, he and the dog had more in common than he wanted to admit.

He could hear the music before he stepped out of the

trees—Bruce Springsteen singing about "Glory Days." As he crossed the sloped lawn, the gravelly voice grew louder and was joined by another voice—this one decidedly feminine and definitely off-key. He smiled as he listened to her sing at the top of her lungs, thinking that she was trying to compensate with enthusiasm for what she lacked in talent.

He stepped onto the porch and knocked, but of course, she didn't hear the rap of his knuckles on the wood door. She probably couldn't hear anything over the pulsing beat of the music. He tried again, banging harder this time. Then gave up and tried the handle, surprised to find it unlocked.

He hesitated, because he knew she'd be annoyed if he just walked in. On the other hand, she was the one who'd left the door unlocked—which wasn't so unusual in a town like Pinehurst but unexpected of someone recently moved from the big city.

The dog had his big head halfway through the door before Mason had eased it open even a few inches.

"You have to stay here," he said.

Rosie's head tipped back, and he stared beseechingly at his owner through dark liquid eyes.

"I don't understand it, either," Mason assured him. "But for some reason, you're not her favorite animal right now, especially since you're not on an *l-e-a-s-h*, so it would be best if you just waited out here for a while."

The dog reluctantly backed out of the door and settled onto the porch, though he was clearly none too happy about being relegated to the outside.

Although he felt another tug of guilt, Mason none-theless closed the door tightly to ensure that Rosie stayed out before following the music up the stairs.

He found Zoe in one of the bedrooms on the second level.

She was on a ladder, about halfway up, and putting all the muscle she had in her slender arms into scrub-bing the walls. Her hair was tied back in a loose ponytail from which several strands had escaped and were clinging damply to her neck. She was wearing a tiny little tank top that didn't quite meet the top of her cut-off shorts, and when she reached up, several inches of pale skin were exposed. Her legs were toned and tanned, her feet tucked into battered sneakers.

There was a square fan in the window, but it seemed only to circulate rather than cool the air. The portable CD player blasted out another Springsteen song. She wasn't singing along anymore, but the volume of the music still prohibited any attempt at conversation so he crossed over to the boom box and pressed the stop button.

The abrupt quiet obviously startled Zoe, because she pivoted quickly. Too quickly considering her precarious perch on the narrow step.

The ladder wobbled; she wobbled.

Mason instinctively reached up to steady her.

But as his hands caught her around the waist, his palms came into contact with the smooth warm skin of her exposed midriff.

He heard her inhale sharply, saw her eyes widen and felt the air fairly crackle around them.

The moment seemed to spin out between them, reflected in the emotions that swirled through the depths of her dark eyes.

Surprise.

Confusion.

Awareness.

Desire.

Apparently the needs that were churning inside of him were churning inside of her, too, and wasn't that a lucky coincidence?

But along with the desire he could see in her eyes, there was wariness, too. It was the wariness that had her leaning back, away from the pull of whatever was drawing them together.

As she did, her elbow hit the bucket that was perched on the top step of the ladder.

He watched helplessly as the pail tipped forward.

Chapter Five

Zoe let out a startled squeal as the sudsy water splashed over her.

Without thinking about the fact that she was still perched on the ladder, she launched herself out of the way of the waterfall—and into Mason's arms.

He stumbled back a step but held on, gathering her against his chest so she wouldn't fall.

The shock of the surprise shower made her stiffen; the warm, solid strength of his body made her melt.

Oh my, was all she could think, as she absorbed the unexpected and thrilling sensation of being held tightly against him.

Their bodies were aligned intimately from shoulders to knees, her breasts crushed against the hard wall of his chest, her thighs trapped between his. And he was hot and hard and gloriously male everywhere she touched.

He was also, she reminded herself, her neighbor. And her heart was too fragile to risk the consequences of lusting after any man.

His arms remained locked firmly on her waist as he lowered her to the ground.

Slowly.

Inch by inch.

And with every inch, she was achingly aware of her body sliding against his, of the rising heat generated by that friction. So much heat, intense and unexpected, that she wondered that she didn't spontaneously combust.

She finally felt the floor beneath her feet, but it seemed to be shifting and tilting, keeping her off-balance. And the hands that had automatically grabbed hold of him when she'd fallen continued to grip the muscles of his arms as the world spun around her.

She exhaled a slow, unsteady breath and tried to shake off the fuzzy cloud of sensation that was fogging her brain.

She tipped her head back, to tell him that he could let her go. But the dark intensity of his gaze took her breath away, and the unspoken words tumbled silently out of her mind and into oblivion.

His lips curved in a slow, sexy smile that made her mouth go dry and her heart beat so hard against her ribs she worried that he could feel it.

"Well, this is unexpected," he said. "And very, very nice."

She wasn't sure *nice* was the word she would have

chosen. It was far too tame to describe the wild currents that were suddenly ricocheting through her system.

"I have to admit, I've wondered about this," he said huskily.

She had to moisten her lips before she could ask, "About what?"

"How you would feel in my arms."

"Oh."

"You feel good, Zoe." His hands skimmed up her back, then down again.

She tried to focus, to think of the thousand and one reasons that this shouldn't be happening, but her mind was fuzzy, and reason was a misty cloud rapidly dissipating in the heat being generated between them.

"I'm wet," was the only response she could manage.

His lightning-quick grin made her cheeks flush.

"You still feel good," he said. "Although I wouldn't object if you wanted to take off those clothes."

She managed to pull herself out of his arms, to somehow support herself on rubbery legs.

She suspected that he was the type of man who would press if he knew he had the advantage. Zoe had no intention of letting him know that those long, steady looks made her stomach muscles quiver and his slow, easy smiles turned her knees to jelly.

Eight days, she reminded herself. She'd met this man only eight days ago, and she knew that if she wasn't careful, she'd find herself in bed with him before another eight days were up.

She took a step back, away from the heat of his touch and the reach of temptation.

"I need to, uh, mop this up."

But Mason had already reached the mop that was propped against the wall. "It looks like you've made strides toward getting this place into shape already."

Zoe tugged her sodden T-shirt away from her body and squeezed some of the water out of it. "Other than the lake on the floor, you mean?"

He smiled. "Yeah, other than that."

"A friend of mine stopped by this morning to give me a hand."

"I didn't know you knew anyone in town." He dragged the mop through the puddle.

"No one except Claire. At least, not until I bought this place. Now people seem to be coming out of the woodwork.

"I met Harry Anderson at the hardware store yesterday, had lunch with my real estate agent, and today Doug Metler—the local mailman—knocked on the door to say 'hi.'"

"I know who Doug is."

"I should have figured you would. But I've never known the name of any of my mail carriers before. Anyway, after Doug went on his way, Tess Richmond from across the street came over to welcome me to the neighborhood, and Ron Griffiths from down the street brought over some blueberry muffins that his wife had baked."

"Irene makes great muffins, doesn't she?"

She blew out a breath as she reached for the mop to finish the cleanup, but he shook his head and continued to soak up the spill.

"Yes, they were great muffins," she said. "But that's hardly the point."

His smile widened. "I warned you that you'd find living in Pinehurst quite an adjustment after the big city. And though most people are genuinely friendly and helpful, you will meet some who are just plain nosy."

"I'm still trying to figure out which category you fit into," she admitted.

"I would think the fact that I'm holding a mop should answer that question."

"Maybe. But you still haven't told me why you're really here, and, as much as I appreciate the effort, I don't think it's to wash my floors."

"You're right," he admitted. "I came over to take another look at the attic, talk about the renovations and find out how you like your pizza."

"It's Saturday night," she reminded him. "Don't you have anything better to do?"

"I did have plans," he said. "But my date called at the eleventh hour to cancel. Left a message on my voice mail, if you can believe that."

"It wasn't the eleventh hour," she said. "It was several hours before the scheduled meeting time that you said *wasn't* a date."

He shrugged. "Whether it was or not, you still bailed on me."

She had, and because she still felt a little guilty about that, she couldn't meet his gaze when she said, "Because I have too much to do around here."

"Yeah, I can see why you wouldn't want to take a break for something as trivial as a meal."

"I took a break for lunch."

"What time was that?" he challenged.

"I don't know." But the low rumble in her stomach betrayed the fact that it had been several hours before.

And Mason's quick grin told her that the sound had not gone unnoticed. "So what do you like on your pizza?"

She sighed. "Just cheese."

He finished mopping up the spill and put the mop inside the bucket. "Not very adventurous, are you?"

"Is there something wrong with enjoying the simple things in life?"

"Not at all." He smiled. "Just as there's nothing wrong with a little variety—or spicing things up every once in a while."

She was no longer certain they were talking about pizza, so she remained silent.

"Why don't I order while you're changing your clothes?"

"I never said I wanted pizza."

"No, but your stomach did."

She couldn't argue with that. Instead she said, "My cell phone's on the table in the dining room."

Mason was just hanging up the phone when Zoe came down the stairs.

She was wearing a pair of well-worn jeans and an oversized T-shirt now, but her feet were bare and her hair had been brushed out of its ponytail and hung loose to her shoulders.

"I liked the shorts better," he told her.

"The shorts are now in a rapidly growing pile of dirty laundry," she told him.

"At least you can't blame Rosie for *this* wardrobe mishap."

"No," she agreed, then narrowed her eyes. "But speaking of the beast, where is he?"

"On your porch."

"You left him outside?" she asked incredulously. "Alone?"

"I didn't figure you wanted dog hair all over the house you've been working so hard to get clean."

"I don't," she agreed. "But you can't just leave him alone outside. What if he ran away? Or somebody tried to take him?"

He chuckled at that. "The only place Rosie has ever run is here. And can you imagine anyone wanting to steal that animal?"

"Probably not," she admitted, her mouth turning up at the corners. "But maybe you should let him in, anyway, so he doesn't scare off the pizza delivery boy."

"Are you sure?"

"I don't dislike your dog," she said, moving into the kitchen. "I just don't like his habit of pouncing on me from out of nowhere."

Mason opened the front door, grabbing hold of Rosie's collar before he went tearing through the house in search of Zoe. "Down," he said, then released his hold.

Rosie didn't jump, but his whole body quivered with the effort of restraining himself. And when he reached Zoe's side, he rubbed his head affectionately against her thigh, leaving a smear of white dog hair on her jeans.

Zoe sighed as she patted his head. "You really are a beast."

The dog just stared at her adoringly.

She shook her head and turned her attention to Mason. "Can I get you something to drink?"

"What have you got?"

She scanned the contents of her refrigerator. "7UP, orange juice, water and white wine."

"Red wine goes better with pizza," he told her.

"Well, white is all I've got. Do you want a glass or not?"

"Sure."

She dug through a box of unpacked utensils on the counter until she found a corkscrew, then adeptly uncorked the bottle and poured wine into two juice glasses.

"I haven't got around to washing any of the stemware yet," she explained, handing him one of the glasses.

"I remember chugging back wine from the bottle on one or two occasions when I was in college," he said. "This is definitely a step up."

Her lips curved, and he was struck again by how truly beautiful she was when she smiled.

"To clean floors," she said, holding up her drink.

"And to pizza in thirty minutes or less," he added, touching the rim of his glass to hers.

Rosie barked, clearly insulted that he'd been left out of the toast.

Zoe looked down at him. "Are you thirsty, too?"

She took a bottle of water from the fridge and emptied it into a bowl for the dog.

Rosie barked again, in appreciation this time, and immediately began slurping.

"Tap water would have been fine," Mason told her.

"The tap water still looks a little rusty—I don't even like to shower in it, never mind drink it."

"Rosie wouldn't care. He'll drink out of the toilet if I forget to put the lid down."

She shuddered at the thought as she pulled out the stool on the opposite side of the breakfast bar and sat down across from him.

"What's with the camera?" he asked.

She froze with her glass halfway to her lips, her eyes sliding across the counter to the item in question as if she'd never seen it before. "Oh. That. It's, um, Claire's. She thought I should take pictures of the house to document the work in progress."

"That's a good idea," he agreed. "Though I would have expected a photographer would have her own camera."

She took a long swallow of her drink. "I have several, but I put all of my equipment in storage when— before—I moved."

Before he could press, the doorbell rang. Rosie raced for the front door, barking and dancing in circles on the way.

"Must be the pizza," he said. "He goes nuts for pizza."

"I think he's just nuts—period," Zoe muttered as she pushed back her chair. "Can you get the door while I run up to get some money?"

Mason started to tell her that he'd put the order on his account, but she was already halfway up the stairs.

He shrugged and went to answer the door.

And found it wasn't the usual delivery kid but a gorgeous—and familiar—woman standing on the porch.

"Claire?"

The surprise that flashed in her eyes turned to pleasure, and the quick and easy smile that curved her lips took him back fifteen years. "Hello, Mason."

"You're Zoe's friend," he suddenly realized.

She nodded. "Is she here?"

"Yeah. Uh, come in." He stood back so that she could enter. "I didn't realize—she mentioned a friend named Claire, but I never suspected it might be Claire Kennedy."

"It's been Lamontagne for eleven years now," she told him.

Before he could say anything else, the doorbell rang again and Zoe was coming back down the stairs.

"*That* will be the delivery boy," Mason said, as Rosie started dancing and barking again.

"Do you want to stay for a slice of pizza?" he heard Zoe ask Claire when he turned around with the box in hand.

"No, thanks. Rob and the kids are waiting in the car. We're on our way out to a movie, but when I saw the lights on here, I thought you might have cancelled your—" she paused to smile "—date, and I was going to ask you to join us."

"Mason just stopped by to discuss the renovations," Zoe said.

"Because you did cancel our date," he felt compelled to add.

Claire smiled again as she sent her friend a look as if to say "I told you so."

"Have fun at the movies," Zoe said to Claire. Then to Mason, "I'll go get plates and napkins."

His eyes followed her progress across the floor, enjoying the gentle sway of her hips as she disappeared into the kitchen. When he turned his attention back to Claire, he saw her gaze narrowed on him, considering.

"Are you going to ask me to stay away from your friend?"

"No. Partly because Zoe wouldn't appreciate my interference, and partly because I think you could be good for her."

"So much for my reputation as the type of guy mothers warn their daughters about."

Claire smiled. "Your reputation is still intact," she assured him. "Believe me, I am a mother, though I hope I won't have to be warning my daughter about men like you for a lot of years yet. But I'm also a woman, so I can appreciate that a woman sometimes needs a man her mother wouldn't approve of."

"Thank you, I think."

She chuckled. "I won't ask you to stay away from Zoe, but I will ask you to be careful, though."

"I'm not in the habit of being anything else," he told her.

Claire hesitated, as if she wanted to say more, but then she only nodded as she reached for the door. "Enjoy your pizza."

Zoe took the plates and wine into the dining room. It was less cluttered than the kitchen, she reasoned, and wasn't at all motivated by her curiosity to know what

Claire and Mason were discussing. Which was just as well, since she couldn't hear them, anyway.

It had surprised her to learn that her friend had dated the architect. Maybe because she knew how happy Claire was in her marriage, and Rob—although truly a fabulous man who was devoted to his wife—had nothing on Mason Sullivan. But what did she know? She was basing her assumptions on the contrast of her warm, cordial feelings toward Rob and the hot jolt of awareness that zinged through her system whenever she was near Mason.

And when she thought about it, she realized that although her friend was privy to all of her deepest secrets, she really hadn't known Claire for very long. Not even two years—though those years sometimes felt like a lifetime.

As she settled into a chair to wait for Mason to bring in the pizza, her mind drifted back to the day she had met Claire.

It was a day that had irrevocably changed the direction of her life, setting her on the path that had brought her to the time and place she was at right now.

She remembered that Scott had offered to go with her to the hospital the day of her mastectomy. Just as she remembered thinking, even then, that he'd made the offer as a courtesy rather than out of any real desire to be with her. Instead, she'd taken a taxi, insisting that she wanted to be alone. She'd checked in, then changed into her surgical gown, climbed onto the gurney and prepared to wait and battle alone against the panic escalating inside of her.

Then Claire had walked in.

Prior to that day, Zoe had communicated with her only via e-mail and, less frequently, by telephone. She'd never seen her before, would never have guessed who she was until she'd said, *Hi, Zoe. I'm Claire.*

And for some inexplicable reason, Zoe's eyes had filled with tears and her throat had tightened. She wanted to ask why the other woman was there, but she suddenly hadn't been able to speak and knew that if she tried, she'd fall apart.

Claire, unfazed by Zoe's silence, had sat down beside the bed and taken her hand. *I'm here for you. Because I've been where you are, and no one should ever have to go through this alone.*

She'd stayed when they'd taken Zoe down to surgery and was waiting in the same spot when they'd brought her back up again.

She was the one person Zoe had truly felt she could count on, the one person who had been there for her when no one else had been, the one person who had really seemed to know who she was and what she'd wanted.

Which brought her full circle back to the question: Did she want Mason Sullivan?

I'm not suggesting you fall in love with him. Claire's voice echoed in the back of her mind. *Just spend some time with him, see where things go.*

When Mason walked into the room, she felt that hot jolt again and decided that she just might follow her friend's advice after all.

It wasn't quite how Mason had planned to spend his Saturday night, but he couldn't complain about the fact that he was seated across from a beautiful and intriguing woman, sharing a bottle of good wine and a Marco's extra-large. Candlelight and soft music might have added some ambience, but he thought it just as likely such overtly romantic touches would make Zoe even more wary.

He wasn't a patient man by nature. If given the choice, he would always choose instant gratification over long-term gains. He preferred the rush of playing the stock market to the security of government bonds. On the other hand, he had a clear understanding of the differences between a woman and a financial investment, and he appreciated that a more cautious approach sometimes reaped greater rewards.

He knew he would need to be very cautious with Zoe. He was equally certain the rewards would make it worthwhile.

As he transferred a slice of pizza to his plate, he thought they were off to a pretty good start. A casual meal and some light conversation should help her warm up to him a little.

The bump against his thigh had him tacking an addendum onto that thought: so long as Rosie didn't blow it for him. Again.

"This is good," Zoe said.

"It's even better with sausage," he told her, discreetly sneaking a piece of crust under the table to Rosie.

"I'll take your word for it."

"You really don't like sausage on pizza?"

"No."

"Pepperoni?"

"I really like just cheese."

"What's your favorite color?"

She licked a smear of pizza sauce from her thumb and frowned at the unexpected question. "I don't have one."

"Favorite baseball team?"

"I don't watch baseball."

"Basketball?"

She shook her head.

"Football? Soccer? Hockey?"

"None of the above."

"Okay—who's your favorite Stooge?"

"*The Three Stooges* are the only thing more tedious than professional sports."

He frowned and nibbled on a piece of sausage.

"James Bond?" he asked cautiously.

Her lips curved. "Sean Connery."

"Favorite movie?"

"Why all the questions?"

"I'm curious about you." He picked up the bottle of wine, topped up both of their glasses. "And all I've managed to learn through observation and inference is that you like cheese pizza, Australian wine, and you sing along with the radio—or at least with Springsteen."

She paused with her glass halfway to her lips. "You heard that?"

He grinned. "I'll never be able to listen to The Boss again without thinking of you."

"I'll never be able to sing 'Glory Days' again

without remembering the humiliation of this moment."

He decided not to state the obvious—that she really wasn't able to sing it before.

"Now you have to share something you've done that is just as embarrassing," she told him.

He grinned. "I've never done anything *that* embarrassing."

At her narrowed stare, he chuckled.

"And why am I supposed to tell you a story that reveals my humiliation?"

"So that I won't have to move out of the neighborhood to maintain my dignity."

"Alright," he relented. "In second grade I insisted on wearing my Batman pajamas to school."

She just stared across the table at him, waiting.

"Every day for a whole week," he continued.

The roll of her eyes suggested that she still wasn't impressed.

"Because I thought I really was Batman."

Her gaze narrowed. "Really?"

He shrugged. "I was seven and had a vivid imagination."

"Okay, that might have been embarrassing," she allowed. "But I was thinking about something that might have happened in the past decade or so."

"Well, my most recent source of embarrassment would have to be my dog, who suddenly seems to have developed an obsession with my new neighbor."

"An obsession?"

He nodded. "She only moved in about a week ago,

but every time I turn around, he's escaping from my backyard to visit her—and usually wreaking some kind of havoc in the process."

"Are you afraid that she'll call animal control?"

"Nah. I'm more worried that she won't look past the menace that my dog has become to see what a great guy I am."

"Why does that worry you?"

"Because I like her."

Her brow furrowed as she lifted a second slice of pizza from the box. "If she only moved in a week ago, you can't know her very well."

"Yeah, but I'm working on that."

She took her time wiping her fingers with a paper napkin. "You might find, once you get to know her, that you don't really like her after all."

"What worries you, Zoe—that I won't? or that I will?"

She lifted her head to meet his gaze. "You don't worry me."

Oh, yes, I do, he thought, pleased to realize that he did. Pleased to know that he could shake her cool confidence with just a word, a look, a touch. And curious about how she would respond when he really did touch her.

"Then tell me," he said, "what made you wake up one morning and decide you wanted to stop taking pictures and start making pancakes instead?"

"Actually, a bed-and-breakfast never even occurred to me until the real estate agent mentioned the possibility. I just wanted the house."

"And you took the idea and ran with it?"

She shrugged. "Seemed like a good idea."

There was still something she wasn't telling him. He didn't know why he was so certain, only that he was.

"Well, I was able to get copies of the original blueprints for the house," he told her. "Which makes my job a lot easier. I should have the plans for your renovations drafted by the end of next week, so you can start looking for a contractor to oversee the work."

"You said you would give me some names," she reminded him.

He nodded. "There are several companies in town that do good work. Barclay Builders, Carson Construction, Pinehurst Rehab & Renovation."

"Who would you recommend?"

"Any of those would—"

"If you needed work done," she interrupted. "Who would you call?"

"Pinehurst Rehab. But that might be because it's my brother's company."

"If I mention your name, will he cut me a deal—or double his rates?"

Mason laughed. "Hard to say, although I'd guess on the deal because he has a soft spot for pretty women."

"Something that runs in the family?"

"Wherever would you get that idea?"

"Claire," she told him. "She warned me about you."

"What did she say?" he asked, more curious than insulted.

"That you'd probably hit on me before you finished drawing up the plans for my renovations."

"Well, proper planning takes time. And a beautiful

woman is hard to resist." He emptied what was left of the wine into her glass. "Even when that beautiful woman is technically still married to someone else."

"Are you hitting on me?"

"I don't hit on married women." But he reached over to tuck a strand of hair behind her ear, smiled when she went still. "Usually."

Her eyes darkened, her breath caught, confirming his suspicion that she wasn't as unaffected as she pretended to be. He let his fingertips trail down her throat, felt the flutter of her pulse and wondered how she would react if he pressed his lips there. The wondering made him want; the wanting made him worry.

He dropped his hand and sat back.

"I should go," he said. "Before I forget that there are rules to the game."

"I was married for nine years," she reminded him. "I don't even know the game, never mind how to play it."

His gaze locked with hers, held. "Are you trying to warn me or tempt me?"

"I'm trying to be honest. I'm not looking for a relationship or a fling or anything in between."

"Then I'll be honest, too," he said, "and tell you that I'm going to do my darnedest to change your mind."

Chapter Six

It took Zoe a full two weeks to get the house thoroughly cleaned, and when that was done, she turned her attention to the jungle that had taken over the yard outside. She considered hiring a landscaper to get rid of the weeds and cut back everything that had grown wild over the past couple of years, but although she'd never been much of a gardener, it somehow seemed like cheating. This was her rehab project, and although she knew she couldn't handle every aspect of it on her own, she wanted to make the effort to do as much as she could.

Claire was a lot more knowledgeable than she was about flowers and stuff, and she'd promised that the beds would fill with colorful blooms if she got rid of the weeds that were choking the flowers. Zoe was making a valiant effort while keeping her fingers crossed that she was actually pulling out the weeds and not the flowers.

On her second day in the garden, Zoe was tackling the perimeter on the east side of the property when she heard an unfamiliar chirping sound. Not that she was yet able to identify any of the birdsongs that normally serenaded her in the morning, but there was something about this impatient, almost frantic, peeping sound that urged her to leave her trowel in the dirt and explore.

As she made her way toward a trio of evergreen trees, the sound grew louder. She knelt on the damp ground and carefully lifted the low-lying branches of the widest tree. There was a nest on the ground, and she immediately feared that it had fallen. But on closer inspection, she saw that it was upright and intact and the baby birds inside appeared unharmed. Noisy—but unharmed.

She shuffled a little closer for a better view. There were four babies, recently hatched, she figured, as they were still mostly bald with their eyes closed and their open beaks thrust into the air.

She was so awed by the discovery that she didn't stop to think but hurried into the house for the camera that Claire had left when she came to visit that first time. She was on her belly on the ground, propped up on her elbows and snapping pictures when a louder, more frantic call drew her gaze to the sky.

The mother bird, she guessed, as it swooped toward her, screaming and flapping. Zoe didn't know if the bird would really attack, but she wasn't taking any chances. She made a quick retreat, the camera clutched tightly in her hand.

She kept her distance after that, using the zoom function to capture images of the mother ducking under the cover of the tree to feed her babies, then backing out again to hunt down more food. She didn't know how long she'd been watching when she heard the sharp, familiar bark then saw Rosie tearing across the lawn. The beast was making a beeline for her when it fell into the mother bird's radar. Obviously concerned for her babies, she dove toward Rosie.

Zoe held her breath, worried that the dog might somehow get hold of the mother, then let it out on a laugh when Rosie cowered in response to the bird's cries. When the bird flew away again, Rosie jumped up, dancing around and barking like a lunatic. Zoe lifted the camera again, snapping pictures until she'd finished off the first roll of film and was well into another.

The strange bird-dog dance ended only when Rosie was distracted by another of his favorite people—the mailman. Zoe scrambled to her feet to rescue him from Rosie's slobbering affection.

Thankfully, Doug didn't appear to be annoyed or intimidated by the beast.

"Looks like you're settling in and making friends with the neighbors," he commented.

"Yeah, I can see how it would look like that."

He grinned at her dry tone as he passed her a handful of letters. "I've got mail for Mason, too. Do you want me to take Rosie back?"

"No, it's alright. He'll wander back on his own when I go inside."

"Alright then." Doug lifted his hand in a wave as he headed back down the long gravel drive. "Have a good day."

"You, too," she said, smiling over the brief conversation with her mailman.

The smile faded when she flipped through her mail and saw the seal on the corner of the largest envelope. She carried it to the step and sat down, lifting the flap with trembling fingers.

In the Petition for Divorce that had been filed with the court, she was listed as petitioner and Scott Cowan was the respondent. While they'd both agreed that there were irreconcilable differences, Zoe was the one who'd wanted to formalize the break—she needed to clean the slate in order to start her life over again.

So it was ridiculous to experience a jolt of surprise when she opened that envelope and found her decree of divorce, signed by the judge and stamped by the court. It was just an official document confirming the legal fact of what she'd known for months—her marriage was over.

But she was surprised, and she was saddened to know that a union forged with so much pomp and circumstance could conclude with a routine mail delivery. That the hopes and dreams she and Scott had taken with them into their marriage had somehow been lost in their journey together.

Zoe tucked the decree back into the envelope, shoving the memories and regrets alongside it.

* * *

Mason wasn't sure what it was about Zoe that had gotten under his skin, but he found himself thinking about her at the oddest times during the day—and dreaming about her at night. No other woman had intruded on his thoughts the way she seemed to do, and that realization baffled as much as it annoyed him.

He wasn't entirely sure what it was about her that appealed to him. She was closer to skinny than slender and might have been described as having a boyish figure if not for the subtle swell of her breasts and the gentle curve of her hips. And yet, despite his usual preference for curvier women, he found that willow build alluring.

But it was the eyes, he decided, that really drew him in. There was something about those dark fathomless depths that seemed to reflect so much of what she was feeling and still hint at secrets. Or maybe it was her mouth—with its delicate shape and lush lips that were quick to curve. Or the soft, throaty laugh that sometimes spilled out so unexpectedly and never failed to punch him in the gut.

Not since his crush on Holly James in seventh grade had Mason allowed himself to be so distracted by a woman.

He'd had relationships, of course. Some people would say more than his fair share. But Mason approached dating the same way he approached fishing—for the sheer pleasure of it and never with the intention of hanging on to anything he caught. Not for very long, anyway, he thought with a grin.

But he made sure that the women he dated enjoyed the experience as much as he did. He was always honest about what he wanted—a good time—and clear about what he didn't—anything even remotely hinting at a commitment. If a lover was shocked when their involvement ended, it was because she obviously hadn't been paying attention to what he'd been saying.

There had, admittedly, been a few of those over the years. And more than usual in recent experience. It was as if there was something in the genetic makeup of women that allowed them to believe a twenty-five- or thirty-year-old guy just wanted a good time, but as soon as he passed the threshold of his thirty-fifth birthday, they assumed he was looking for the right woman to settle down with despite all assurances to the contrary. And when he finally managed to convince a woman that he did *not* want to live together or get married or whatever else she was set on, she stormed out, as if he'd misled her all along.

Maybe that was why he liked Zoe. He figured a woman just emerging from one failed marriage wouldn't be looking to jump into another one again.

But whatever the reasons for his attraction to his new neighbor, he genuinely enjoyed spending time with her. And he'd found frequent occasions and excuses to do so, even if it was only a half hour conversation in her backyard during one of his habitual walks with Rosie. Though Zoe still eyed the dog with wariness and trepidation, she'd stopped threatening to buy rope so that he could tie the animal up. In fact, when she'd told him about Rosie and the birds, she'd sounded amused rather than annoyed by the dog's antics. He liked to think that she was warming up to him as well as his pet, and he was fairly certain the sparks of attraction were zinging in both directions when they were together.

But aside from the attraction, she was easy to be with and interesting to talk to. She had her own opinions about things and didn't seem to care if those opinions butted up against his own—as they frequently did. She had some good ideas for her house, if not the slightest clue as to the work that would be required to implement them.

She wanted the interior of the house to reflect the exterior and had thrown herself into researching the Victorian era, studying color schemes and wall coverings and window treatments from the period. She was tackling the rehab with a focused intensity and enthusiasm he couldn't help but admire even as he wondered why it seemed to take precedence over everything else—and how long she could continue before she burned herself out.

Not his problem, he reminded himself, and whistled for Rosie so they could take their afternoon walk.

But as he tromped through the woods behind the dog, he found himself wondering again about Zoe's reasons for coming to Pinehurst. He knew about restlessness and could believe it was discontent that made her leave Manhattan in search of something different. And he understood the lure of history and the hope that had persuaded her to embark on her renovation project. But he couldn't help wondering what would happen, where she would go, when it was done.

Though he was content in the town that had been his home for more than a dozen years, he knew it was a world away from New York City. A lot of people moved from smaller towns to larger cities, looking for something bigger and better. It was less common for big-city dwellers to abandon the bright lights for quiet nights.

Jessica had, he suddenly remembered. Though she hadn't abandoned her career so much as shifted both her location and focus. Besides, she'd grown up in Pinehurst—and she'd been in love with Nick forever.

That they shared a deep and powerful bond was obvious to anyone after even only a few minutes in their company. It was apparent in the way their eyes would meet and hold, even from opposite sides of a crowded room. In the way Nick touched her, frequently, casually, easily. And in the way she smiled at him, as if there wasn't anyone else in the world.

He was genuinely happy for his friends, even if he'd never wanted what they had together.

At least, he'd never wanted it before. But lately, well, he'd found himself looking at Nick, seeing the contentment on his face, his excitement over the new baby, and wondering if it was so impossible to believe that he could someday meet a woman with whom he might want to share a future—or if he already had.

Even with that disquieting thought echoing in his mind, he could hear the music pumping out through the open windows before he followed Rosie out of the woods.

It was hip-hop now, and it made him smile.

Her taste in music was like so many other things

about her—unexpected and unpredictable. And just part of what intrigued him.

The door was unlocked again, and he found her in the smallest bedroom on the second level. He walked in just as she hefted a sledgehammer off the ground and, with obvious effort, swung it at the wall. The heavy tool punched into the plaster—and stayed there. With a wriggle of her hips and a groan of frustration, she struggled to pull it out again.

"What the hell—"

Of course, she couldn't hear the roar of his voice over the blare of the music.

Clamping down on his fury, he twisted the volume control to a more reasonable level. This time, when he spoke, his voice was quiet and carefully controlled.

"What do you think you're doing with that?"

She turned, still gripping the handle of the hammer with one hand as she brushed her bangs away from her face with the back of the other. "What does it look like I'm doing?"

"It looks like you're trying to kill yourself," he said, removing the sledgehammer from her grip. "Christ, this thing almost weighs as much as you do."

She shot him a look of annoyance. "Hardly."

"Pretty close, I'd wager."

"Wager elsewhere," she suggested. "I'm busy here."

"Not with this," he told her.

She folded her arms over her chest and huffed out a breath. "You were the one who said this wall needed to come down."

"And you said you would call my brother about taking it down."

"I did. His secretary said he was tied up on another job this week, and I didn't see the point in paying someone else to do what I'm perfectly capable of doing myself," she told him.

"Are you?" he challenged.

"I'm doing it, aren't I?"

He looked at the pitiful hole in the wall. "How long have you been at it? Are your arms screaming in pain yet? Are your shoulders burning? Because they will," he promised her. "You'll break down long before that wall."

She tilted her chin. "I'm a lot tougher than I look."

"I don't doubt that for a minute, honey. But you're not cut out for this kind of physical labor."

"I can do it," she insisted.

"Why?" he asked gently.

"Because it needs to come down and—"

He cut off her explanation with a shake of his head. "Not the wall—the whole house. Whatever possessed you to want to tackle such an enormous project on your own?"

Zoe couldn't tell him the truth—he already thought she was crazy for buying this place. And suggesting that she felt some kind of kinship to this broken and damaged old home, well, even she thought that was a little crazy.

Instead, she sank down onto the edge of the bed she'd covered with old sheets to protect it from dust and debris and considered her response to his question. "Let's just say I was at a crossroads in my life."

He leaned against the dresser, facing her. "Because of the divorce?"

"Among other things."

"What other things?"

"Nosy neighbors," she said. "Now will you please let me get back to work?"

He appeared unfazed by her flippant remark but when she reached for the sledgehammer, he held it away from her.

"Find something else to do."

She blew out a breath. "I appreciate your concern, but—"

"No, you don't. You wish I'd go away and stop interfering in your life."

Her lips curved reluctantly. "That, too."

"Well, it's not going to happen. Not today, anyway." He nodded toward the doorway. "Why don't you go empty out the kitchen cupboards or something?"

The dismissal stung her pride, had her chin lifting. "I think you're forgetting that this is my house."

"Not for a minute." He sent her one of those slow, lazy grins that made everything inside her melt. "I would never have been crazy enough to sink my life savings into buying it."

"And yet, you seem to be here, at every possible opportunity, wanting to put your hands all over it," she retorted, wondering how her blood could pulse with want even when he irritated her—as he frequently seemed to do.

"You should have realized by now that the house isn't all that I want to put my hands on," he said.

She took an instinctive step back, her cheeks flooding with heat as the implication of his words finally sank in.

"Does that really come as a surprise?"

"Yes. No. I don't know."

He grinned at her again. "Just something for you to think about."

She shook her head. "I can't."

"Can't think?"

"I certainly can't think about getting involved with anyone right now. I'm not ready—"

He took a step toward her, pressed a finger against her lips, halting the flow of words. It was a gentle touch, the contact fleeting, yet her skin tingled, burned.

"You've already been thinking about it," he said.

She opened her mouth to deny it, closed it again without saying a word.

"I've been thinking about it, too," he admitted. "A lot."

"I can't—it's not—" She swallowed, a difficult task when her throat was suddenly bone dry.

That cocky grin flashed again. "You can. It is. And you will stutter a lot more before we're done."

Retreat, she decided, was less humiliating than stuttering again.

She turned to leave the room, conscious of his eyes watching her every step.

Zoe emptied out the cupboards. Not because Mason had deigned to delegate the task to her, but because it was a job that needed to be done.

If she had the money, she'd rip out everything and

rebuild the kitchen from scratch. Since she was keeping a close eye on her budget to ensure she didn't deplete her funds before all the work was done, she'd opted to refinish the cabinets instead of replace them. Fresh paint and new hardware would give the tired wood a much needed facelift.

The countertop, however, needed to go. It was the ugliest faux marble surface she'd ever seen, and chipped and stained on top of that. Granite, although pricey, would give her the solid durable surface she wanted.

The vinyl floor was yellowed with age and coming apart at the seams, and though she'd considered other options, she really wanted natural wood. She'd been thrilled to find a local supplier who was willing to give her a deal on reclaimed pine. She'd also found a rack to put over the island and she could already picture it there with copper pots hanging down.

She was so caught up in her vision of the kitchen that she forgot to stay angry with Mason for kicking her out of the upstairs bedroom that would become a second guest bathroom.

In fact, not only was she no longer angry, she was touched by his concern. Not that she needed anyone to look out for her, and ordinarily she wouldn't appreciate anyone trying to tell her what to do, but just this once, it was nice to think he cared enough to worry about her.

Scott hadn't worried about her, that was for certain. He'd had too many responsibilities at the magazine to be concerned about what she was doing. And she'd been too strong and independent to let it bother her. In fact, she probably hadn't even been aware of it—until the phone call had come from her doctor's office and she'd desperately wanted not to have to face it alone.

Well, she wasn't alone right now—as the noise emanating from upstairs reminded her. It sounded like Mason was making more progress than she had, and though she hadn't asked for his help, she was grateful for it.

She folded the top of the box she'd finished packing and pushed it aside. Then she poured a tall glass of lemonade and carried it up the stairs, curious to see how he was doing. When she got to the bedroom where he was working, she stopped in her tracks.

There was a huge hole where the wall had been, but that wasn't what caught her attention.

No—her gaze was focused on the man prying away chunks of plaster with a crowbar. He'd taken off his sweatshirt, leaving him in only a T-shirt that was damp with sweat and clinging to muscles that rippled with his every movement. Her mouth actually watered as she watched him work, noting the bunch and flex of tight muscles in his arms, his shoulders, his back.

Oh, my.

She could only stare, breathless and weak, her heart pounding, her hormones clamoring.

She wasn't sure how long she stood there, just watching and—oh, yes—wanting, before he turned his head and saw her.

"I, uh, thought you might be thirsty."

She somehow managed to make her legs move so she could carry the glass across the room to him.

"I am." He let the crowbar dangle from one hand as he reached for the drink with the other. "Thanks."

She watched his throat work as he drained the glass and felt her own go dry. His skin was slick with perspiration, and his jaw was dark with stubble. He didn't look like a man who designed houses right now, but one who built them. A man, she would bet, who was as knowledgeable and skilled about pleasuring a woman as he was drawing up a plan or tearing down a wall.

"You seem to be, uh, making good progress."

"It's coming along," he agreed. "I worked in construction through high school and college, but I forgot how much I enjoyed it."

"Well, then, I'm glad I could help you rediscover the pleasure."

"It shouldn't take me too long to finish up in here," he said. "Then we could rediscover other pleasures."

"As tempting as that sounds…no."

Mason couldn't help but smile as Zoe turned away.

Despite the prim tone, he knew that she was tempted. And that, at least for now, was enough.

As she started toward the door, the sound of a sharp bark from outside, followed by a frenzy of barking, had her changing direction and heading over to the window.

"I don't believe it," she said. "There really are two of them."

He didn't need to peer over her shoulder to see what she was talking about—the barking had been a dead giveaway. But he crossed the room anyway, because it gave him an excuse to get closer to her and to watch the way her pulse skipped when she realized he was close.

"I warned you," he said.

Her lips curved. "Is his name really Guildenstern?"

"Yes, it is. And where there's Guildenstern, there's Tyler. C'mon," he said. "I'll introduce you."

He followed Zoe outside in time to see that his brother was just finishing up a phone call. Tyler tucked the cell into his pocket and crossed the yard in a few quick steps, an easy smile on his face.

"Tyler Sullivan," he said, ignoring his brother to offer his hand to Zoe.

She took his hand and gave him a smile. "Zoe Kozlowski."

"I was going to return your call today," he told her. "But since I had to come this way from another job, I thought I'd stop by." He continued to hold her hand as he lifted speculative blue eyes to meet the narrowed gaze of his brother hovering behind her. "I hope this isn't a bad time."

"Not at all," she said, finally extracting her fingers from his grasp. "I'm eager for you to take a look around, let me know if you're interested in the job."

"I'm definitely interested," Tyler said, and grinned in response to his brother's dark scowl.

"Keep looking at her like that and I'm going to have to pound on you," Mason warned, as he fell into step beside him.

The grin widened. "I'm thinking she would be worth it."

He cuffed his brother in the back of the head, just on principle.

It didn't take Mason long after Tyler had gone to finish tearing down the wall—at least what he could do with the rudimentary tools Zoe had on hand. But the open space seemed to open up endless possibilities, and he was pleased with the results when he carried his glass into the kitchen for a refill of the lemonade.

Zoe had been busy emptying out the cupboards, as attested by the pile of boxes stacked in the corner.

"I think you got the easier job," she grumbled as she rolled yet another piece of china in yet another sheet of newspaper.

"The less tedious one, anyway," he agreed.

He took the pitcher of lemonade out of the refrigerator.

"Did you want a drink?" he asked.

"Sure." She rolled her shoulders back then pointed to the cabinet over the sink. "There are still a couple of glasses in there. It occurred to me that I'd need to keep some dishes out if I actually wanted to eat."

"Good thinking." As he reached for a glass, a large manila envelope slid out of the cupboard and onto the counter.

Zoe sprang to her feet and grabbed the envelope, but not before he spotted the official emblem in the corner.

He poured her lemonade without saying a word.

She accepted the glass with murmured thanks.

"Well," he said after a long awkward moment had passed. "I think I understand now why you were trying to bash through that wall."

"Because it needed to be done," she said.

"You mean you weren't pretending to hammer your now ex-husband?"

She shook her head. "I told you before, it was an amicable split."

"Amicable doesn't mean painless."

"No." She set her glass on the counter and went back to wrapping and packing.

Obviously she didn't want to talk about it, and he considered just letting it go. But he saw defeat in the slump of her shoulders and sadness in her eyes.

Not his problem, he thought again. Except that it would take a stronger man than he was to walk away from a woman who was so obviously hurting. Instead of walking away, he laid his hands over hers, halting their quick, nervous movements.

"Are you okay?" he asked gently.

Zoe stared at Mason's hands—so strong and warm on hers—and nodded. It was the only response she could manage; the only one that was acceptable to her. She couldn't tell him that she was yearning for something new even while aching over the loss of what had been. She couldn't explain that her heart was pounding with anticipation while weeping with regrets.

"I am okay," she finally said. "I guess it's just harder to let go than it is to hold on sometimes, even when what you're holding on to isn't what you need anymore."

She pulled her hands away from his to reach for her glass and take a long drink.

"Our marriage started to fall apart a couple of years ago," she confided. "But I didn't want to admit it—I didn't want to fail. My mother's been married four times and in love more times than you can imagine. Each time, she swears he's the one—the final one, the only one. And he is—until the next one comes along.

"I didn't want to live my life like that. I promised myself I would only ever get married once and that it would be forever."

"It takes two people to make a marriage work," he pointed out. "Or fail."

She nodded. "I know. And I really believe we both wanted it to work—we just didn't know how. I guess I'm just sad that we failed, that the love we both felt so strongly in the beginning just faded away."

"So now you move on," he said, not unkindly. "You live the life you want to live and don't worry about pleasing anyone else."

"Sounds like a philosophy that would work really well on a desert island."

"Personal relationships do tend to complicate things," he admitted. "That's why I've never wanted to tie my life to someone else's, why I've been so careful to avoid any kind of entanglements. I refuse to depend on anyone else for my happiness."

"That sounds like the kind of absolute conviction that comes from having your heart broken."

"Or seeing what a broken heart can do to someone else," he said. "My parents were married for eighteen years, completely and indisputably in love with one another."

It was the bitterness in his tone that warned her the story didn't have a happy ending.

"Then my mother died," he said. "And my father was so overcome by grief, he eventually drank himself to death. He just couldn't bear to live without her."

"How old were you?"

"Sixteen when my mom died—almost twenty when my father was buried. Tyler's four years younger, so my grandmother—my mother's mom—moved in until he graduated high school. Then she married an RV salesman and moved down to Florida."

She smiled at that. "Is she still there?"

"Yeah. She's eighty-one now, her husband's eighty-four, and they recently celebrated their tenth anniversary."

There was both affection and amusement in his tone now, and it told her more than his words about the depth of his feelings for his grandmother.

"That's a nice story."

He brushed her bangs away from her face, his touch gentle. "You okay now?"

She nodded, and this time she meant it.

"Then I should be going."

The surprise must have shown on her face, because he smiled.

"Did you think I'd be all over you the minute your divorce was final?"

"No."

"Are you disappointed?"

"Of course not," she said, blushing.

He quirked an eyebrow. "Not even a little?"

"No," she lied.

He grinned. "You have been thinking about it, though."

"Thinking that it would be a bad idea," she told him.

"Which is why I'm willing to give you a little more time to accept the inevitability of it before I kiss you the way I've been thinking about doing."

Zoe didn't know how to respond to that without stuttering again, so she saved herself the embarrassment by remaining silent.

"Spending some time together away from the house might be a good start," he continued. "What do you think?"

"Are you asking me to go on a date?"

"*Date* is too formal a word for what I had in mind."

"What did you have in mind?"

"Fishing."

She shook her head. "No."

"Why not?"

"Because."

"That's not a reason," he chided. "Do you have other plans for tomorrow?"

"No, but—"

"I'll pick you up at six, we can grab breakfast on the way."

"Six o'clock? In the morning?" She stared at him. "Are you insane?"

"It's a bit of a drive to the lake, so we might as well get an early start."

"I don't want to get an early start or a late start or any kind of start," she said. "Because I don't want to go fishing."

He touched a hand to her cheek. "I'd like to spend the day with you."

And that easily, he obliterated all of her protests.

Chapter Seven

"I don't get this fishing thing," Zoe said as she followed Mason through the long grass toward what he'd promised was a prime location on the lake.

"What's not to get?"

"Well, you admitted that the number of fish in the lake has been dwindling over the past few years and that you don't usually keep the ones you catch, anyway. So what's the point?"

"The point is to relax," he said with exaggerated patience as he continued down the overgrown path.

"Relax? I have flower beds to weed, a porch to sand, a gazebo to paint—and those are only the jobs at the top of the list."

"Which is all the more reason that you need to do

something like this," he pointed out. "You've been working almost nonstop since you moved in."

"I still can't believe I let you talk me into this," she muttered.

"You couldn't resist the opportunity to be with me," he teased.

She shook her head as the beast, who had raced ahead as soon as Mason opened the door of the SUV, let out a sharp bark.

"And Rosie, of course," he added, and grinned.

"I know why you invited me, though," she said. "So that I could carry all the gear."

"I've got our lunch."

And she knew the cooler he was lugging was a lot heavier than the rods and tackle box in her hands. But the long poles were awkward to handle and kept whacking against low-hanging branches or, when she shifted her hold so they weren't sticking up into the air, getting tangled in the long weeds.

At last they came to the clearing, and Zoe had to admit it was a pretty spot. There was a grassy bank dotted with wildflowers that sloped down toward the rocky shore of a clear blue lake.

"The lake's quite deep here, so we can drop our lines right from the shore."

"Did I mention that I don't know how to fish?"

"The look on your face when I mentioned fishing was a pretty good hint." He set the cooler under the shade of a tree, then came over to take the poles and tackle box from her. "That's why I brought you a closed-face reel—it's easy to cast and unlikely to tangle.

You just hold down the button as you draw your arm back, then release it when you cast toward the water."

"Piece of cake," she said.

He smiled. "You'll get the hang of it quickly—I promise."

She had to give him credit for patience. He took his time explaining every step of the process, though a lot of what he said was lost on Zoe when he held her close, her back against his front, to demonstrate the proper casting procedure.

But after several unsuccessful attempts, she finally managed to land the baited hook in the water rather than on the grassy bank.

"Good," he said, then set about preparing his own gear.

"Why don't you have one of those little ball things on yours?" she asked after he'd cast his line.

"Because I don't need one."

She frowned at that. "Why do I need one?"

"Because you've never done this before so you might not realize what's happening when a fish is tugging on your line. The bobber being pulled into the water will let you know."

"And what do I do when the bobber goes in the water?"

"You tug on the pole to make sure the fish is hooked, then you reel it in."

"Okay. The bobber goes down, I pull up, then reel in."

"That's right." He finished reeling his own line back in, then tossed it out again.

"How long does it usually take to catch a fish?"

"There's no 'usual,'" he said. "Sometimes you catch one, sometimes you don't."

"You mean I might not catch a fish today?"

"You definitely won't if you don't stop talking and starting fishing."

"My line's in the water," she pointed out.

"Then sit down and get comfortable."

"You're not sitting. And you keep reeling in and casting out again. How come?"

"Because some fish are more likely to take bait that's moving."

"Then why did you tell me to leave mine in the water?"

"Because I thought it would be easier for you to relax that way."

She sat down, braced her forearms on her bent knees, the end of the pole cradled between her hands. "Where's Rosie gone?"

"Exploring."

"You don't worry that he'll take off?"

"He never has before."

She stared at the red-and-white ball floating on the water. "I think it moved."

"What moved?"

"The bobber thing."

He shook his head. "Could you maybe signal before you change direction in a conversation?"

"Do I pull up now?" she wanted to know.

He shook his head. "It's just drifting along with the movement of the water. It needs to be pulled under the surface."

"Oh." She continued to watch the floating ball. "How is this supposed to be relaxing?"

She thought his sigh sounded a little less patient

now. "You know, I think I liked you better an hour ago when you were still half-asleep and not talking."

"I had coffee at the diner."

"And?"

"Caffeine revs me."

"Now I understand the pink tea," he muttered.

"Anyway, I thought you invited me to come fishing with you so we could talk."

"I distinctly remember saying 'fishing' not 'talking.'"

"Why do the two have to be mutually exclusive?"

"Do you even know how to sit back and clear your mind?"

"Clear my mind?"

"Yeah. Do you think you can handle that?"

She frowned. "No. Because now I'm thinking that I'm supposed to be relaxing and…"

The words trailed off as he dropped to the ground beside her. He put his pole aside, then took the one from her hands and set it down, too.

"What are you doing?"

"Helping to clear your mind."

And then his mouth was on hers.

She didn't have time to think or prepare or defend. She didn't have time to do anything but absorb the lovely shock that sparked at the first touch, then yield to the mastery of the kiss as those skilled and hungry lips moved over hers.

Later, she would think about how fast he'd moved—and how he'd taken his time. How his mouth cruised over hers, his exploration patient, unhurried—and very,

very thorough. How he traced the shape of her mouth with the tip of his tongue and nibbled gently on the full curve of her bottom lip. How she could do nothing but sigh—and surrender to the pleasure.

Her blood heated. Her head spun.

Her body yearned.

He cradled her face in his hands, his touch gentle but unyielding as he held her captive to the onslaught of his mouth. She lifted her hands, curled them around his wrists and felt the rapid beat of his pulse, echoing her own heartbeat. Everything else faded away into dreamy layers of mist and fog.

She didn't know how long he kissed her, just that it seemed like forever but not nearly long enough. And when his lips finally eased way, she nearly whimpered in protest.

"What are you thinking about now, Zoe?" The question was a whisper against her lips.

"Huh?" She blinked, tried to focus, but everything was as soft and nebulous as a dream. "What?"

His lips curved slowly, smugly.

"Good answer," he said, and kissed her again until her mind was spinning like a fishing reel when the line was being cast.

Then he turned away from her, picked up his pole again and tossed his line into the lake as if the kiss had never happened.

Mason wished the kiss had never happened.

As he shifted his rod from one hand to the other, he cursed himself for including a woman in what had always before been a solitary venture. She'd been on his mind a lot lately—which was one of the reasons he'd planned to come fishing today, to get away, empty his head and relax. Now he was more tightly wound than his line—and aching to release some of the tension.

He glanced sideways at Zoe. She was sitting cross-legged on the grass now, the reel of her fishing pole cupped loosely between her palms, her gaze focused intently on the water. She was also, he noted, quiet.

He wondered if he should apologize for kissing her, then decided it was ridiculous to apologize for something he already wanted to do again. He had yet to decide whether or not he would give in to that urge.

He might wish it had never happened, but he wasn't sorry he'd kissed her. He was only sorry that he'd pushed after promising to give her time. He hadn't intended to move so fast. He knew she needed to mourn and accept the loss of her marriage before she'd be ready to move on. Wasn't that why he'd invited her to come with him today? Because he knew she was hurting and needed a distraction.

Instead, she'd turned out to *be* a hell of a distraction.

Because though he might have moved faster than he'd intended, she sure didn't seem to have any problem keeping pace. From the moment his lips had touched hers, it had been like setting a match to dry tinder—immediate flame and intense heat.

He was surprised by how out-of-control he felt. Even as a teenager, he'd never wanted anyone as much as he wanted Zoe right now. Then again, there had been a lot of other stuff going on in his life when he was a teenager, and he hadn't had much time for dating. He'd spent too many months watching his mother die, pleading and praying that she wouldn't, then too many years after she was gone trying to hold his father back from the brink of self-destruction. He'd failed on all accounts.

He didn't blame himself. He knew he wasn't responsible for either the disease that had eaten away at his mother or the sorrow that had consumed his father, but he was undeniably affected by the loss of both of his parents in such a short period of time. Though Gord Sullivan had held on for four more years after his wife's death, for all intents and purposes, he was gone from his family as soon as he buried his beloved Elaine. Mason saw how his father's grief had slowly but inexorably destroyed not just the quality of his life but his will to live, and he had vowed that he would never let himself feel that kind of devastation. He would never be that vulnerable. He would never love so wholly and completely.

But somehow Zoe made him forget all of his resolutions. She made him forget logic and reason. Hell, he couldn't even seem to think when she was around— except about how much he wanted her.

Part of it was sexual attraction—pure and simple. But the rest of it wasn't so simple. He didn't just want her, he wanted to be *with* her. He wanted to spend time with her, talking to her, laughing with her or even just sitting quietly with her.

She was just a woman, like so many other women he'd known. And yet, she was somehow different.

Because no other woman had got under his skin the way she'd done. No other woman had plagued his mind during the day or haunted his dreams at night. He'd always managed to maintain an emotional distance, but it seemed to be a losing battle with Zoe. Maybe for the first time in his life, he was truly falling for a woman, and he didn't know how to handle it—or even if he wanted to.

At their initial meeting, Zoe's first impression of Tyler Sullivan had been that he bore a striking resemblance to his brother—not just in the color of his hair and his eyes or the wide shoulders and long, lean build, but in the way his mouth curved just a little bit higher on one side than the other when he smiled, and in the way his eyes sparked with interest or humor. He was undeniably good-looking, irresistibly charming and outrageously flirtatious.

Her second thought was that he seemed young to be running a successful building company. But a few discreet inquiries had confirmed the reputation of Pinehurst Rehab and so she'd hired him.

In the two weeks since he'd started the renovations on Hadfield House, she'd had no cause to regret that decision. In fact, with each day that passed and each job that was completed, she'd only been more impressed with his work ethic. He came early, stayed late, and could frequently be found working right alongside his crew. He didn't seem to mind when she peeked in to see how things were coming along, and he answered her questions patiently and thoroughly.

If he occasionally lingered to flirt with her after the other men were gone—as he sometimes did—she couldn't help but feel flattered even if she knew better than to take him too seriously.

"What's the scoop with you and my brother?" Tyler asked, leaning against the kitchen counter with a can of soda in his hand.

Zoe passed him a plate with two sandwiches and a pile of potato chips. It was a Sunday and while the rest of his crew had been given the day off, Tyler had come by to install a couple of replacement windows. She figured the least she could do was to make him lunch.

"I'm not sure I understand the question."

"Do you have a relationship with my brother?"

"He's my neighbor, obviously," she said. "But I like to think that he's also become a friend."

"Friend?" Tyler laughed.

She frowned and munched on a chip. "Why is that funny?"

"Because when I told him I was coming over to put in your windows, my brother made it very clear I wasn't to touch anything else."

Zoe felt her cheeks flush. "I'm sure you misunderstood."

"Then you're not sleeping with him?"

"Tyler!"

He grinned. "You don't have to answer that question."

He was completely outrageous and somehow disarmingly charming. "You're way off base on this. Your brother's interested in the house—not me."

"The house has great bones," he said. "But you have much nicer curves."

She laughed. "And you have even more in common with your brother than I originally thought."

"If you mean we have great taste in women, I'd have to agree."

"I mean that you're arrogant, charming and outrageous."

Tyler grinned. "We do have a lot in common—which is how I know he's interested. Because you can bet that if I'd seen you first, I'd be making a move."

"Well, I don't know what seeing me first has to do with it, but I can assure you that he hasn't made a move." She thought of the kiss at the lake, the kiss that had made everything inside her melt into a gooey puddle of need, and dismissed it. Because that kiss— as knock-your-socks-off fabulous as it had been for Zoe—had obviously meant nothing to Mason because he hadn't even attempted a repeat performance.

Tyler narrowed his gaze on her, as if he knew she was holding something back. "He hasn't?"

"He kissed me once," she admitted. "But that was a few weeks ago now, so I have to assume that if he was interested, he isn't anymore."

"Then maybe he's not as smart as I thought." He carried his empty plate to the sink, then turned, sandwiching her between the counter at her back and his body at her front. "And maybe I was wrong to worry that I would be poaching."

"Poaching?" she queried.

He lifted a shoulder.

"He means trespassing." Mason's voice—tinged with annoyance—interrupted from the doorway. "And yes, you are."

Tyler winked at her before turning around. In that moment, Zoe knew that he'd known Mason was in the doorway when he'd asked about her relationship with his brother.

"It looks like you finished the windows," Mason told him.

"Sure did."

"Then beat it."

"I'll see you tomorrow, Zoe," Tyler said, unfazed by his brother's rudeness. "Thanks for lunch."

"Thanks for giving up your day off to put the windows in."

"Not a problem," he said, and sauntered unhurriedly out the door.

Zoe waited until she heard Tyler's truck start up before she spoke to Mason. "You were rude."

"He was poaching," he said simply.

"Poaching?" she echoed again, then shook her head. "I know what it means, I'm just having a little trouble understanding it in this context."

"It means that you were wrong in assuming I was no longer interested." He slid his hands around her waist and drew her into the circle of his arms.

"I haven't seen much of you over the past couple of weeks."

"Miss me?"

"No," she lied weakly.

"I missed you," he said, and settled his mouth over hers.

She was prepared for his kiss this time, but still unprepared for the slow burning need that spread through her body in response to the kiss.

She'd dated casually and infrequently in college, then she'd married Scott right after graduation. In the past nine years, she'd only been kissed by her husband. When the marriage had fallen apart, or maybe for the reasons it had fallen apart, she'd never expected to want like this again. But as his lips continued to move over hers, she couldn't deny that she wanted Mason.

She wanted to touch and be touched, to give and to take, to once again feel the pleasure of passion. What made her want even more was that she'd dreamed about it—about making love with Mason. Frequently and in glorious, mind-numbing detail. And she'd been haunted by those dreams as much awake as asleep.

But in her dreams, everything was soft and misty and perfect. In her dreams, her body was warm and soft and responsive. In her dreams, she was happy, almost giddy, free of any inhibitions and all physical and emotional scars.

Unfortunately, her reality was different.

He said he wanted her. He kissed her as if he would never stop, touched her as if he'd never get enough. But he didn't know what she'd been through; he couldn't understand what he was getting into if they were to become physically involved.

She'd left Manhattan because her life had been irrevocably altered and, in making that decision, she'd acknowledged that some of her goals would have to change, some of her dreams had been lost. She certainly hadn't ever expected to want to open up her heart to a man again.

Then Mason Sullivan had stormed into her life and through the barriers she'd so carefully erected. He tempted her with warm eyes and hot kisses. He made her want things she had no business wanting, made her long for things she knew she could never have.

But now, as she felt the evidence of his arousal against her and the answering aching heat of her own desire, she wondered. He made her weak with wanting and empowered her with the knowledge that he wanted her, too. To be desired now, by this man, was a heady experience and she wanted to glory in it. Except that he didn't really want her—he wanted the woman he thought she was, and she hadn't been that woman for a long time.

Though her body protested at even the thought of ending this intimacy, she forced herself to pull away.

"That's why I've been trying to stay away," Mason told her, catching his breath. "Because when I'm with you, I can't help wanting you. And when I touch you, I don't want to stop."

"I'm really not ready for this."

He stroked a hand over her hair. "We'll take it slow."

She shook her head again. "I can't—I don't—" she let out an exasperated breath as her brain scrambled for an explanation he would accept—anything but the truth. At last she said, "I want us to be friends."

"We are friends."

"*Just* friends."

He smiled, then he touched his mouth to hers again in a kiss that was both unhurried and unrelenting, and she was helpless to do anything but respond.

This time *he* stepped back. "We'll take it slow," he said again.

Before she could say anything else, he was gone.

Outside of Pinehurst, miles beyond the wide rolling fields of farmland that bordered the easternmost edge of the town, there was an enormous old barn that was referred to by locals simply as "the old barn." It was sometimes used as an auction house, occasionally as a community gathering space, but had gained notoriety for the flea market that was held there every Sunday. And every Sunday, seemingly regardless of the time of year or the weather, it was packed to bursting with vendors hawking their wares and customers looking for bargains.

Zoe and Claire eased their way through the crowd, from stalls set up with orderly rows of homemade jellies and jams to makeshift tables heaped with knock-off Rolex watches, through towering shelves filled with old and new books past booths of glossy handcrafted furniture, between glass showcases of exquisite antique jewelry and freestanding displays offering the latest in household gadgets.

The air was rich with the scents of damp earth, musty hay and fresh caramel corn.

Zoe was munching on a handful of the sweet, salty treat as she followed her friend through the maze of chaos to a table displaying handmade linens. She'd been looking forward to this outing since Claire had called to suggest it a few days before, not just because she loved the atmosphere of the market but also because she wanted to talk to her friend about something that had been tugging at her mind. She hadn't counted on the noise and the crowd making conversation so difficult, and she took advantage of the relative quiet of the corner to finally say, "I'm thinking of having an affair."

Claire traced the edging of a Battenburg lace table-cloth and nodded approvingly. "Good for you."

Zoe frowned.

Her friend sent her a sidelong glance. "Did you think I'd be shocked?"

"*I'm* shocked," she admitted. "I've never considered anything like this before."

"You've been married for the past nine years," Claire reminded her.

Zoe nodded. Scott was the first man she'd ever been with. She'd never imagined being with anyone else, had certainly never had sexual fantasies about any other man.

Until Mason.

She could ignore it, deny it, pretend the attraction she felt didn't exist, but she couldn't will it away. The heart-pounding, mind-numbing passion she felt when he kissed her was new and unfamiliar. If she'd ever felt the same dizzying rush of excitement and anticipation with Scott—and she wanted to believe that she had—it had been a long time ago, so far back in her memory that what she felt with Mason now seemed enticingly new, completely unfamiliar and dangerously tempting.

"I think part of what makes this so strange," she

said, "is that I've never been really attracted to anyone but Scott."

"That is strange," Claire agreed. "Were you in a marriage or a convent? Because I love my husband, but a wink or a smile from a good-looking man can still make my heart go pitter-patter."

"My heart doesn't go pitter-patter," she admitted. "It pounds so hard inside my chest I wonder that my ribs don't crack."

Her friend smiled. "Yeah, I can see how Mason Sullivan could have that effect on a woman."

"I never said it was Mason."

"The only other man whose name I've heard you mention is Harry Anderson, and he's a little old for you, not to mention married with four kids and a grandchild on the way."

"Okay—it is Mason." She hesitated a moment before asking, "Did he have that effect on you?"

Her friend checked the price tag, sighed with obvious regret and carefully refolded the item.

"Hmm?" Claire moved on to a set of doilies.

"When you were dating Mason? Did your heart pound like that?"

"No. For me it was nothing more than the pitter-patter." She frowned as they moved away from the doilies. "Come to think of it, the only man who ever made me feel that kind of pulse-racing excitement was Rob."

"Why are you saying that as if it's a bad thing?"

"It's not—for me. But it makes me worry that you might be falling in love with Mason instead of just falling into bed with him."

She shook her head. "I won't—one heartbreak in this lifetime is enough."

Claire turned to study her closely, then sighed. "Honey, that dreamy look in your eyes tells me that you're already halfway there."

Zoe sifted through a bin of ceramic knobs, searching for something that would work with the new bathroom cabinets she'd picked out. "We came here last weekend," she said. "To look for lamps for what is going to be the library."

"He went shopping with you? Without any bribes or threats involved?"

"It was actually his idea."

"Oh. Well." Claire smiled now. "Maybe you're not the only one who's halfway there."

"We were shopping for lighting, not diamonds," she pointed out dryly.

"Rob hates coming here," her friend mused, almost to herself. "The parking is terrible, the crowds drive him insane. He'll come—if I ask. But he'd certainly never suggest it himself."

She shrugged. "I think Mason just knew what I was looking for and thought we might be able to find it here."

"Did you?"

"I got a couple of brass lamps with beaded shades. They're fabulous." She found a gorgeous cut-glass doorknob she couldn't resist even though she didn't know where she would use it. "Oh, and Mason picked up a turn-of-the-century mantle clock."

"I think maybe you found something else, too," Claire said.

"What's that?" Zoe asked, taking some bills from her wallet to pay for her purchase.

Her friend grinned. "A man who just might be worth the risk of falling in love again."

Chapter Eight

Zoe turned down Mason's invitation to celebrate the Fourth of July with friends at his home. Not because she didn't want to spend the day with him, but because she was afraid of how much she *did* want to. They'd been spending a lot of time together lately, shared more than a few sizzling kisses, and though there was a part of her that very much wanted to take that next step, there was another part that just wasn't ready.

He'd been surprised by her refusal, maybe even disappointed, but he hadn't tried to persuade her otherwise. Not really. He'd just shrugged and told her to stop by if she changed her mind.

She changed her mind more than a dozen times over the next couple of days, but in the end resolved to take a step back until she knew for sure what she wanted—and that she could give him what she knew he wanted. So when Claire called and invited her to spend the day with her family, Zoe jumped at the opportunity. Anything to get her away from the house and the temptation of Mason's invitation.

She didn't realize, until Rob pulled his van into the driveway just down the street from her own, that her best friend had conspired to thwart her plans.

It would be simple enough to climb out of the vehicle, walk right back down the driveway and go home. But as quickly as the thought crossed her mind, it was discarded. Doing so would be both childish and unappreciative of the effort Mason had made to get her here.

Instead, she picked up the bowl of potato salad she'd made and carried it toward the house.

Mason opened the door in response to her knock. His quick smile of greeting faded when he heard the pounding of paws behind him.

Zoe gripped the bowl in her hands tighter, bracing herself for the attack.

"Rosie, down."

At Mason's sharp command, the dog immediately dropped to the ground, his belly on the floor, his tongue hanging out of his mouth as he whined plaintively.

"Now that's a well-trained dog," Rob commented.

Zoe snorted, though she bent to pat Rosie's head, acknowledging his obedience.

"We're working on it," Mason said, and held out his hand. "You must be Claire's husband."

As introductions were made, she moved into the kitchen to put the salad in the refrigerator.

She heard Mason ask Claire and Rob and the kids what they wanted to drink, then sent them out to the backyard. "Down the hall, through the patio doors. Basically, just follow the noise," he told them.

Zoe turned as she closed the refrigerator door and bumped into Mason's chest. He caught her around the waist before she could back away.

"I thought you had other plans for today," he said.

"So did I, not realizing when I accepted Claire's invitation to join her family for a barbecue at a friend's house that you were the friend."

"Would it have made a difference?"

"Yes," she admitted. "Because most of the people here are *your* friends, and I didn't want to give them the wrong impression about us."

"What is the wrong impression, Zoe?"

"That we're...together."

He slid his arms up her back. "And why is that wrong?"

"Because we're not," she insisted, aware of how ridiculous her argument sounded when she was still in the circle of his arms. "And you need to let me go before someone walks in."

"I will," he said, but drew her nearer. "As soon as I say a proper hello."

"Hello," he whispered the word against her lips.

"Hi."

Then he was kissing her softly, slowly and very thoroughly.

"I'm glad you decided to come, Zoe."

"I didn't seem to have much choice."

He cupped her face between his palms. "You always have a choice, Zoe."

She knew he was referring to more than her decision to stay for the barbecue. She also knew that it wasn't true.

Because her feelings for him were already stronger than she would have chosen. She'd been thinking about having an affair, not falling in love. But Claire was right—she was already halfway there and dangerously close to tumbling the rest of the way.

It was a good turnout, Mason thought, as he surveyed the collection of people around the backyard.

Nick and Jessica were there, with baby Libby, who was now six weeks old and, impossible as it seemed, even cuter than the last time he'd seen her. Nick's sister, Kristin, her husband, Brian, and Caleb, the youngest of their three children, had also come out. Then there was the Lamontagne family: Claire and Rob and their children, Jason and Laurel. It turned out that Jason played on the same baseball team as Caleb, so the boys were already acquainted, and Laurel, though nearly three years younger than the two boys, didn't have any trouble keeping up.

Tyler had been the last to arrive, and he'd come without a date this year, which was unusual. He had, however, brought Stern to play with Rosie, and the two dogs were tearing through the yard like they were being chased by the hounds of hell instead of three screaming children.

But it was Zoe to whom Mason's attention was drawn throughout the day.

He was pleased to have her here, with all of his friends. But he was already looking forward to later, when those friends would be gone and he could be alone with her.

Right now she was playing volleyball in the pool with the kids—and Tyler, of course. Ty had been hovering around Zoe for most of the day, but in a protective brotherly way that didn't worry Mason in the least. Though Tyler was a lot closer to Zoe's age than he was, Mason could tell by the easy way they interacted that their relationship was strictly platonic. Zoe wasn't nearly as comfortable around him, and he realized he didn't want her to be. He wanted her aware and interested, and he knew she was both, even if she continued to fight the attraction that flared whenever they were together.

A round of high-fives among the members of the winning team—not Zoe's—indicated that the game was over. Mason watched her swim to the stairs at the edge of the pool and climb out. He watched as she rubbed a towel over her body, over her arms, her legs, her bare midriff. The red halter-style bikini top cradled her breasts and displayed just a shadowy hint of cleavage. The low-rise bottoms dipped a couple of inches below her belly button and highlighted the sweet curve of her buttocks.

He was pleased when she came over to the patio where he'd dropped into a lounge chair to take a break from the various activities going on. She took a can of 7UP from the cooler, popped the top.

"Who won at horseshoes?" she asked.

"Me and Rob."

She sat down across from him and smiled. "Did I thank you for inviting them today?"

"No," he said. "But there's no need to. I thought you'd be more comfortable with some of your own friends here."

"And you're not uncomfortable with one of your ex-girlfriends here?"

"Are you uncomfortable with the fact that I dated Claire?"

"No." But she didn't meet his gaze. "Not really. I mean, I know it was a long time ago, before I knew either of you. It's just…weird."

"I never slept with her, Zoe."

"I didn't ask."

He smiled. "But you were wondering."

"Maybe," she allowed after a moment's pause.

"In fact, if I remember correctly, we didn't go beyond the holding-hands-kiss-good-night stage."

"Oh."

"Does that make it a little less weird?"

She shrugged. "It's really none of my business."

"Sure it is," he told her. "Because I *am* going to sleep with you."

"That's still undecided."

He leaned forward to tip her chin up with his finger and had the pleasure of watching her eyes go dark, wary.

"Only the 'when' is undecided," he promised her, and brushed his lips over hers, light and easy.

Her eyes remained open, wary, though the hitch in her breath gave her away.

Keeping it easy, he tapped a finger to the end of her nose. "You should have a hat on. Your skin's turning pink."

"I, uh—" she blinked, drew away. "I have sunscreen on. I didn't bring a hat."

"There's a baseball cap on the top shelf of the hall closet," he told her. "Go get it so your pretty skin doesn't burn."

Zoe went to get the hat. Partly because it wasn't something that she figured was worth standing on the patio and arguing with him about. And partly because it seemed like a good excuse to make a strategic retreat from any discussion about their relationship.

He was so confident about the direction in which they were headed, and she was still so uncertain—and feeling guilty about being uncertain. But she didn't know what she wanted. Or maybe she did know, but knew that what she wanted most—a family like Claire and Rob's or Kristin and Brian's or Jessica and Nick's—she couldn't have.

She shook off the thought and ignored the yearning as she moved through the house. She paused when she saw Jessica curled up at one end of the sofa in the living room with her baby. In the soft glow of the afternoon sun, she looked like a Madonna with child—beautiful, peaceful, ethereal.

Zoe didn't mean to stare, but she couldn't seem to look away. And as the baby suckled hungrily at her mother's breast, she felt a phantom tug in her own breasts, and a sharp pang of longing deep in her heart.

But she felt something else, too. Something she hadn't felt in a very long time—the desire for a camera in her hand, the need to capture a beautiful, timeless moment that would never exist precisely like this again.

Then she glanced down and it was there, and her fingers reached instinctively toward it.

She'd had legitimate reasons for walking away from her career, although the decision hadn't been made without a certain amount of remorse and regret. She'd been saddened by everything she'd lost and, in her determination to start her life over, she'd cut out the good parts with the bad.

Maybe, she thought now, it was time to re-evaluate.

She set the camera down again and ducked back out of the doorway, making her way to the closet to get the hat Mason had sent her inside to find...and to dry the tears that were on her cheeks.

When Zoe walked past the barbecue where he'd started to cook dinner, Mason couldn't resist yanking on the ponytail that was pulled through the keyhole at the back of his Carolina Hurricanes baseball cap.

"Hey," she protested when he tugged on her hair.

"You look so cute, I couldn't resist."

She wrinkled her nose. "Cute?"

"The hat's a good look for you," Rob said, stepping into the conversation. "Except for your choice of teams."

"It's my hat," Mason told them.

"I'm a Rangers fan from way back, but I have to admit it was an exciting finish when the Canes took the Stanley Cup in oh-six," Brian said.

"The Stanley Cup?" Zoe's brows drew together. "Isn't that hockey?"

Mason didn't miss the looks of shock and horror that passed between the other men in response to Zoe's question.

"She doesn't watch sports," he explained. Then, to Zoe, "Yes, it's the ultimate prize in hockey."

"So how could a baseball team win the Stanley Cup?"

Tyler shook his head, choking back his laughter. "The Carolina Hurricanes are a hockey team, honey."

"Then why is their logo on a baseball cap?" she challenged.

And, without waiting for an answer, she turned and walked away.

Mason couldn't help but grin at her bizarre logic as he watched her make her way over to the pool.

"Well." Rob seemed at a loss for words.

"Not his usual type, that's for sure," Brian said.

"So what do you and Zoe talk about when you're together?" Nick wondered. "Because you're obviously not discussing the pennant race."

"All kinds of things," Mason said. "Books and movies, world news and current events."

"Whether the Belter rosewood sofa would work better in the front parlor or the library," Tyler interjected.

"The parlor," Mason said. "With the balloon-back side chairs."

"See?" Tyler said. "They spend all their time together moving furniture around, hanging wallpaper, shopping for window coverings."

"So I'm helping her out with some things," Mason said, aware that he sounded just a little bit defensive. "What's the big deal?"

"The big deal is that I was actually starting to think it would never happen," Nick said.

"Thought what would never happen?"

"You falling in love," Tyler said.

Mason choked on a mouthful of beer.

Brian thumped him on the back, a little harder than was really necessary.

"This his first time?" Rob asked, in obvious disbelief.

Mason watched his friends all nod; he scowled.

"It's not happening this time," he said firmly.

"I have to agree with your friends on this," Rob said. "All outward indications are that you're hooked."

He shook his head.

"You just don't have the experience to recognize it," Brian added. "But we do."

His friends all nodded their agreement.

"But don't worry." Nick clapped a hand on his shoulder. "Zoe doesn't seem to be looking for all of that happily-ever-after stuff most women want. I'm sure it's only a matter of time before she cuts you loose."

He wanted to insist that he wasn't hooked, and at the same time, he wanted to demand to know why—if he was hooked—Zoe would cut him loose.

"Besides," Rob added, "I can't imagine she wants to stay around here in the long term."

Somehow the suggestion was more alarming than re-assuring. "Has she said something about leaving?" Mason wanted to know.

"No, but it makes sense that she'd head back to Man-hattan after the renovations are complete."

Mason scowled and tipped his bottle to his lips.

Zoe hadn't said anything to him about leaving Pine-hurst. Then again, she hadn't said anything at all about her long-term plans. Of course, he hadn't asked because it wasn't any of his business. He didn't do long-term.

Still, he was pretty confident that if he put his mind to it, he could convince her to stay.

It wasn't too long after dinner that the crowd started to thin out.

Nick and Jessica begged off before the fireworks started, worried that the noise might be too much for Libby. Kristin, Brian and Caleb were the next to leave, after the display of lights and rockets was concluded. Then Claire and Rob and their kids headed out imme-diately afterward. And when Tyler disappeared on the pretext of having somewhere else to go, Zoe and Mason were alone.

"I seem to have, uh, lost my ride," she said.

He smiled. "I'll make sure you get home later."

"It's late already."

"Not so late." He poked a stick into the fire, adjust-ing the logs. "You have somewhere you need to be early in the morning?"

"No," she admitted.

"Then stay," he said. "For a while."

He couldn't know how tempted she was, how much she wanted to be with him in every way. But as fierce as the needs were inside of her, the nerves were just as strong.

If they became lovers, he would be the first since her husband had left. The first to see her naked. The first to see her scars. As much as her body yearned for the fulfillment of physical intimacy, her heart wasn't ready to risk it.

"We could go skinny-dipping under the stars," he said.

"Or we could keep our clothes on and roast marshmallows by the fire."

He shrugged. "It doesn't sound like as much fun as skinny-dipping, but okay."

"Do you have any more marshmallows?" she asked, noting that the package he'd opened for the kids was completely empty.

"Yeah." He rose to his feet. "Kristin brought a couple of bags."

While he went inside, she waited by the fire, staring at the flames and worrying that her agreement to stay—even for a little while—would result in her getting burned.

She was a rational woman—careful, organized, logical. She liked schedules and routines, certainty and predictability. At least, that's what she used to believe. Then she'd had an impulse—buy a house. Not just any house, but a beat-up Victorian mansion that she felt needed her as much as she needed a purpose.

It was one spontaneous act that seemed to have turned her whole world upside down. Not twenty-four hours after moving into that house, she'd met Mason Sullivan—and her world had been spinning out of control ever since.

She was scared—out of her league and over her head and so many other clichés. She wanted her life back on track and the ground solid beneath her feet. Mostly, she admitted on a sigh, she wanted Mason.

When she glanced up and saw him striding across the lawn, her heart did that funny little roll in her chest that was becoming all too familiar, and she sighed again.

As he drew nearer, she noticed that he carried not just the marshmallows but a couple bottles of beer. She shook her head when he offered one to her.

"Thanks, but my head is already fuzzy." Although she wasn't sure if it was the beer or Mason's presence that was responsible for that effect, she was erring on the side of caution.

He sank down to the ground beside her and grinned. "Are you worried that I'll get you drunk and try to seduce you?"

"No," she said. "Because we both know that if you really wanted me in your bed, I'd already be there."

"I really want you in my bed," he said, and the huskiness in his tone assured her it was true. "I'm just waiting until you're sure that you want to be there."

"It's not that simple," she said, sliding a marshmallow onto the end of her stick and carefully positioning it close to the glowing embers of the fire.

"It could be," he said, placing his stick directly into the fire.

She shook her head as the edges of the marshmallow quickly heated, bubbled, then burst into flames.

He pulled the stick back, blew out the fire, then plucked the charred remains from the point and popped it into his mouth.

She continued to turn her stick, evenly toasting her marshmallow all the way around.

Mason stuck a second marshmallow into the fire.

"You obviously don't believe that patience is a virtue," she noted.

He shrugged. "I just want what I want when I want it."

"And I like to take my time," she said, finally judging her marshmallow to be done. "To make sure that it's really what I want and not some passing fancy."

"But if you wait too long—" he said, stealing the lightly toasted marshmallow off the end of her stick "—you might find that someone else has already taken what you wanted."

"Hey."

He held it away from her. "You want this?"

She responded by snatching it back.

Mason grinned as she bit into the marshmallow.

The outside was crisp, the inside gooey—just the way she liked them. She closed her eyes and hummed with approval as the sugary taste exploded on her tongue.

"Good?" he asked.

She nodded and offered him the rest.

He took her hand and brought it to his mouth to nip the last bite, then licked the remaining traces of marshmallow from her fingers. His tongue swiped the pad of her finger, then her thumb, then he sucked it into his mouth.

Arrows of heat rocketed through her system, straight to her core, and everything inside her melted like the marshmallow she'd just eaten.

His lips closed over her thumb, then slid away.

"I think I need another taste," he said.

Then his mouth was on hers, hot and hungry. And her mouth was just as hot, just as hungry. When his tongue speared deep inside, she welcomed the thrust, absorbed the passion. He tasted hot and sweet from the marshmallows, and incredibly and temptingly male.

The fire was starting to burn down, but the heat between them continued to rise as he eased her back onto the grass. He was stretched out beside her, his hands skimming over her, from the curve of her shoulders to the slope of her breasts, to the dip in her waist to the flare of her hips.

She was burning everywhere he touched, aching. She wanted to press her body against his and wrap her legs around him. She wanted to touch and taste and take. She simply wanted.

If she'd been able to think, she might have been shocked by the fierceness of the desire, the rawness of the need. But she couldn't think, she could only feel, and it felt wonderful to have his hands on hers, to have hers on him.

With every pass of those wide palms, her pulse rocketed, her senses scrambled, her body yearned.

She was overwhelmed by the sensations he evoked. Heat and hunger. Desires and demands. Nerves and needs.

His hand was beneath the hem of her T-shirt now, his fingertips skimming over the bare skin of her tummy, teasing, testing. Then tracing over the ridges of her rib cage to the swell of her breast.

Her nipple puckered as his thumb brushed over the wisp of lace that covered it, and spears of fiery heat shot to her core. She gasped and arched toward him, wanting more, wanting everything. His searching fingers moved to the centre clasp of her bra, dipped into the hollow between her breasts.

Later, she would be grateful for the rocket that was set off somewhere down the street, for the sharp crack of the explosion that finally penetrated the haze of lust that clouded her brain.

She pushed herself up, her breath coming in unsteady gasps as she fought to clear her mind and silence the indignant protests of her body.

To her complete and utter bafflement, Mason didn't move closer or protest her withdrawal in any way. Instead, he stroked a hand over her hair.

"I'm sorry."

She almost laughed, but she was afraid it might somehow set free the tears she was trying so desperately to hold in check. "Why are you sorry?"

"Because I promised we could take it slow, and I keep forgetting that in my eagerness to get you naked."

His patience and understanding only made her feel worse, because she couldn't guarantee that she would ever be ready to take that next step—and she couldn't tell him what was holding her back.

She stood up, tugged her T-shirt into place and slipped her feet back into her sandals. "I have to go."

Of course, he insisted on walking her home, and she didn't bother to protest.

When they reached her door and he touched his lips to hers again, it was light and easy. And brief—for both their sakes.

"Good night, Zoe."

Chapter Nine

Zoe sat cross-legged on the rosewood sofa in the parlor, hip-deep in samples, trying to select ceramic tiles and grout colors for the upstairs bathrooms. Beside her were strewn catalogs offering fixtures and hardware for the cabinets, stacks of paint chips and wallpaper books. Overhead, everything was quiet, and the silence was distracting.

She'd grown used to the sounds of construction—the shuffle and stomp of the workers' boots across the floors, the harsh bark of their gruff voices, the buzz of saws, the hum of sanders, the pound of hammers. It was unbelievably noisy and incredibly chaotic, but she loved to listen to the sounds of work in progress and she was pleased with the progress that had been made.

Today, however, was Saturday, and Tyler's crew had the day off. Everyone except Tyler, of course, who had come by to finish taping and mudding the drywall in the attic.

She heard his footsteps on the stairs, then the slap of the screen door against its frame as he went back out to his truck for one thing or another. She turned her attention back to the samples and sighed.

When she heard the door again and glanced up to see Tyler coming into the room, she smiled. "How are things going upstairs?"

"I'm making progress," he told her, then raised an eyebrow as he took in the books and papers strewn around her. "How about you?"

"Not much," she admitted. "After a few hours staring at color samples, champagne and seashell are starting to look the same."

"Ready to throw in the towel and run off to Hawaii with me?" he asked. "We could dance around in grass skirts, drink rum punch out of coconut shells, make love on the beach with the waves lapping at our toes and sleep snuggled together under the stars."

She smiled. "As tempting as that sounds right now, I have to say 'no.'"

"I'd go—but only for the sleeping under the stars part," Jessica Armstrong piped in from behind him. "Heck, I'd do anything for a solid three hours of shut-eye."

"And I'd take you," Tyler said. "If I didn't think that your husband would hunt me down and kill me."

"I'm glad I found out about your fickle affections before I accepted your offer," Zoe told him.

"You'd already turned me down," he reminded her. "I was merely trying to mend my broken heart in the arms of another beautiful woman."

Zoe couldn't help but laugh at the ready response. "Smooth as glass—and just as slippery."

"Speaking of beautiful women…" Tyler scooped the baby from Jessica's arms, held her high. "Are you keeping Mommy up at night?"

Libby answered his question with a wide toothless smile.

"Day *and* night," Jess clarified.

"This little angel?" He grinned at Jess before turning his attention to Zoe. "By the way, I was supposed to let you know that Jessica and Libby are here."

"Thanks."

"We were just on our way home from Libby's checkup, and I thought we'd stop in to see how the house is coming along," Jessica said. "But if this is a bad time…"

She shook her head. "This is a great time."

"That's because Zoe likes to procrastinate," Tyler said.

"And what are you doing right now?"

"Doing what he does best," Jessica interjected. "Flirting with the ladies."

He shrugged, grinned. "We all have our strengths."

"Give me my baby and get back to work."

He touched his lips gently to Libby's forehead before passing her over. "We'll be ready to grout by the end of the week," he told Zoe. "Unless you change your mind about Hawaii."

"I'll have the colors picked by Wednesday."

He nodded, already on his way out the door.

Jessica shook her head as she watched him go. "If he wasn't so darn sweet, that charm of his could be dangerous."

"I imagine that charm *will* be dangerous if he ever focuses it on one woman."

"Like the way his brother focused on you?" Jessica teased.

Zoe decided to let that question pass as she untangled her legs and pushed herself to her feet. "Can I get you a drink? I've got iced tea or lemonade."

"Lemonade sounds great," Jess said. "I've been trying to cut down on my caffeine intake while I'm nursing—it seems like the smallest amount winds Libby up like that bunny in the battery commercials."

Zoe chuckled at the image. "Did you want to come into the kitchen or—"

"Yes, please," Jessica said quickly. "I heard Mason telling Nick about the kitchen renovation and I'd love to see it."

"Well, let's have that drink, then I'll give you the grand tour if you want."

"Sounds great."

While Jessica sipped her drink, Zoe stole a cuddle with the baby.

"She's so beautiful," she said, just a little wistfully.

"She is, isn't she? I know I'm probably biased because she's mine, but after wanting a baby for so long, I look at her and think she's just perfect."

"Even when she's screaming at 3:00 a.m.?"

Jessica laughed. "Even when I feel like screaming right along with her. I just remind myself that we waited more than eighteen years to experience midnight feedings and dirty diapers."

"Eighteen years?" Zoe asked, surprised.

"Yeah. It's a long story but one that finally has a happy ending—or happy beginning, as I like to think of it since our life together has really just begun."

"I like the idea of a happy beginning—and to think that's what I'm working toward here."

"In Pinehurst? Or specifically with the house?"

"Both," she admitted.

"And Mason?" Jessica asked. "Where does he fit into your plans?"

"He doesn't. Didn't. I mean, he wasn't supposed to. Now…I just don't know."

The other woman chuckled. "I actually think I know what you mean, because that's exactly how I felt when Nick came back into my life and turned everything upside down. It's a wonderfully terrifying feeling, isn't it?"

"More terrifying than wonderful sometimes," she said.

"He's a great guy," Jessica said.

"But?"

"But nothing. I just happen to think he's terrific."

"Oh. I thought that was your prelude to the same warning everyone else has given me—that he'll break my heart if I let him."

Jessica looked genuinely startled. "If anything, I was going to ask you to tread gently so you don't trample on his."

"I don't think there's any worry about that."

"Then you obviously haven't noticed the way he looks at you."

"There's...an attraction," Zoe admitted. "I'm aware of that."

"He's a lot more than attracted," Jessica said. "He's at least halfway in love with you."

She shook her head. "No. Neither one of us is looking for any kind of deep emotional involvement."

Jessica smiled. "One of the lessons I learned over the years is that life doesn't always follow the path we want it to. I also learned that the twists and turns can sometimes lead us in a direction we never knew we wanted to go."

"Speaking of direction," Zoe said, in a not-too-subtle attempt to change the topic. "We should head upstairs to start our tour of the house."

They chatted about the renovations as they moved from the attic back down to the kitchen, then continued their conversation while an enthusiastic Libby banged a spoon on the glass-tiled countertop Zoe had opted for over granite after seeing something similar on a home decorating show.

"You've certainly been busy in the past few months," Jessica noted.

"I've done a lot of cleaning, painting and gardening, but not much else," Zoe admitted. "Tyler and his crew have been doing the major renovating."

"I love these tiles," Jessica said. "You obviously have good instincts about what works—or maybe just really great taste."

"I've done a lot of research," Zoe admitted. "Trying

to balance the traditional style of the house with modern conveniences and contemporary designs."

"Your photography background must have helped, too, letting you see things from different angles, knowing what to focus on and what to fade out."

She shrugged. "I never really thought about that."

"It's probably so instinctive now that you wouldn't need to."

"Maybe."

"I really did want a tour of the house," Jessica said. "But that's not the only reason I stopped by."

Zoe went to the refrigerator for the pitcher of lemonade to refill their glasses. As she did so, the other woman reached into her diaper bag and pulled out an envelope of photographs.

"I finished off a roll of film at Mason's barbecue and finally got around to getting the pictures developed," she said. "But there were several photos that I don't remember taking—that I couldn't have taken."

Zoe felt her heart pounding in her chest as Jess opened the envelope, racing as she flipped through the photos until she got to the ones she'd been referring to. She spread a half-dozen shots on the countertop—two of Jessica smiling down at the baby latched onto her breast, two close-ups of the baby nursing, then one of Jessica holding the baby against her shoulder, and another of her pressing her lips to the baby's forehead.

They were good photos, Zoe thought objectively. The lighting and angle and composition confirming that the photographer had at least a certain amount of talent.

"Did you take them?" Jessica asked.

She nodded. "I didn't mean to intrude. I was walking past while you were feeding Libby, and it was such a beautiful image and the camera was right there. I just couldn't resist."

"Please don't apologize. The pictures are fabulous," Jessica said. "I remember Mason mentioning that you were a fashion photographer in New York, but I had no idea you were this good. I mean, Libby's pretty darn cute, but these pictures are phenomenal. So good, in fact, I was hoping you might be willing to take some more."

"I don't really take pictures anymore."

The other woman laughed. "Could have fooled me."

"I mean professionally," she said. "I haven't worked as a photographer in almost two years, and until a few weeks ago, I hadn't even picked up a camera in that time."

"I don't know why you gave up your career—and it's none of my business," Jessica said. "But if you've started taking pictures again, maybe it's because you want to."

It was something she'd wondered herself, and she'd realized that her willingness to pick up a camera again was a definite sign of healing.

"I'm not trying to pressure you. I'm just asking you to think about it."

"I will," she promised.

Over the next few days, Zoe thought about it a lot. And because the pictures of Jessica and Libby had turned out so well, she finally found the courage to take the four rolls of film from Claire's camera into the photo-finishing center at the drugstore. When she picked them up a couple hours later, she was pleasantly surprised by the quality of those pictures, too.

Just looking at the photos of the baby birds, she could hear those frantic peeps that had drawn her attention from her gardening to the discovery of the nest. There were pictures of Rosie, too—more than she remembered taking. But the images made her smile at the memory of the dog's crazy antics, the way he'd alternately barked at and cowered from the mother bird, who would swoop down at him to draw him away from the location of her nest and her babies.

And finally, pictures of the house. Most of the earlier shots had been taken by Claire, and she was grateful to her friend for that. Recently, she'd been so focused on all the work still to be done that she hadn't realized how much work had been accomplished until she looked at those "before" photos. Seeing them now, she finally understood how far she had come—not just with respect to the renovations of the house but in every aspect of her life.

She'd survived the break-up of her marriage, the loss of her job, the move out of Manhattan. She was building a new life now—a good life—and she wasn't going to let old fears and insecurities hold her back any longer.

When she got home from the drugstore, she called Jessica and told her she'd take the pictures of Libby.

Then she called Mason and invited him for dinner.

When Mason accepted Zoe's invitation, he was looking forward to a few hours in her company and a good meal.

When he showed up at her house at the appointed

hour, there was a red sauce simmering on the stove, the tangy scents of tomato and garlic in the air, an open bottle of merlot on the table and tall slender candles in fancy glass holders.

He was touched that she would go to so much trouble and, recognizing that the scene had been set for seduction, grateful that the wait was almost, finally, over.

"Smells good," he said, leaning close to sniff as she stirred the sauce.

"Thanks." She smiled, but he could see a hint of nerves around the edges.

He wanted to turn off the stove, take her in his arms and take her upstairs to bed, but he knew the nerves were evidence of both apprehension and anticipation. He took a step back, reminding himself that he'd waited two months already, another hour or so wouldn't make a difference—except to Zoe. And he very much wanted everything to be right for Zoe.

He knew she hadn't been with anyone since her husband, and after the end of a nine-year marriage, he could understand that she'd be a little nervous about being intimate with someone else. He was flattered that she'd chosen him to be that someone else—and determined that he wouldn't disappoint her.

"Can I pour the wine?" he asked.

"Yes. Please." She put the lid back on the sauce, then turned up the burner under the pot of water she'd set to boil.

He poured and offered her a glass.

Her hand was trembling, just a little, when she took it from him. He didn't mind that she was nervous—

heck, he was nervous, too—but he didn't want her to be afraid, and he wasn't convinced that she wasn't both.

She sipped the wine. Then sipped again, as if hoping the alcohol would help settle her nerves. As tightly as she was wound, he figured she'd be intoxicated before she was relaxed. So he took the glass from her fingers and set it on the counter.

"Let's try something else," he said.

She read the intent in his eyes—knew he was going to kiss her. She was ready for it, eager even. She wanted her heart to pound the way it always did when he kissed her, the echo of it so loud in her ears that she couldn't hear herself think. Or maybe it was that the touch of his mouth on hers rendered her unable to think.

In any case, she'd been thinking about this night for too long already, carefully planning every step, rehearsing every word and movement. She didn't want to think anymore—she just wanted him to kiss her.

And he did—but the kiss wasn't quite what she'd expected. It wasn't the hot, hungry demand that caused her blood to heat and her body to melt. It was the softest whisper of his lips at her temple that made her heart sigh. Then a gentle touch to her cheek, a feather-light caress along her jaw, and—finally—a slow brush of his mouth against hers.

"More," she said, and sliding a hand around the back of his neck, pulled his head down.

He gave her more. As his lips cruised over hers, his tongue dipped in and his hands slid up. Desire pulsed like blood through her veins, a wave that rushed through her and washed away all her worries and fears.

Yes, this was what she wanted—to be swept away, to let the attraction that had been building between them for so long follow its natural course. Why had she thought to complicate it with explanations about things that couldn't possibly matter here and now? Why was she worried about what had happened in the past when the present was filled with such glorious promise?

There would be plenty of time for talking later. Much later, she hoped. For now, she just wanted Mason. She wanted to be with him in every way, to touch him and be touched by him, to feel like a woman should feel when she's with a man without all kinds of history and baggage in the way.

But as much as she wished it was possible, she couldn't will that history and baggage away. As tempted as she was to remain silent and just let things happen, she knew that wouldn't be fair to either of them.

She made herself ease back.

"We should turn off that sauce," he said.

She nodded. "Yes. No." Then shook her head. "I mean, yes. But wait," she said, when he reached for her again.

"I think we've waited long enough, don't you?"

The blatant hunger in the depths of his eyes made her heart stutter, her knees quiver.

She swallowed. "I want to be with you, Mason, more than you can imagine but…"

His hands stroked up her back. "Tell me what you're afraid of."

She closed her eyes and leaned forward against his chest, for just a minute. "I'm afraid that you'll change your mind."

His laugh was strained. "Why the hell would I do that?"

"Because there's something I have to tell you."

He continued to rub her back, silently waiting for her to continue.

She'd known this moment was coming, that she would have to tell him. He meant too much for her to continue to withhold something so important from him. But she'd worried about it—finding the right words, choosing the right moment.

Except that the moment had chosen her, and now words seemed to elude her.

She pulled out of his arms and took a step back, needing to face him, to see him, when she spoke.

He was watching her—steadily, patiently. Waiting, as he'd been waiting for weeks already. He was her neighbor, her friend, and she hoped he might soon be her lover. But first she had to trust him with the truth she'd been hiding.

She drew in a deep breath, linked her hands together, and said the words she'd never spoken aloud to anyone before, "I'm a breast cancer survivor."

He stared at her, his face pale, his eyes blank—as if he didn't understand the words she'd said or didn't believe them.

"What—" he swallowed. "How—"

It wasn't quite the reaction she'd hoped for, though she'd known he would be surprised by her revelation. She'd never hinted at what she'd been through, had deliberately kept the details to herself. She'd never felt comfortable sporting pink ribbons or talking about her diagnosis or treatment. In fact, she could count on one hand the number of people she'd told about her experience because she believed it was no one else's business—until she decided to share her surgically altered body with someone else.

So she could understand why Mason was looking a little shell-shocked by her announcement.

"I was diagnosed in August, two years ago. I had a—" she drew in a breath "—a mastectomy. And reconstructive surgery. That was in September."

She was surprised she'd managed to summarize the angst and fear that had plagued her for so long in so few words, but she didn't want to rehash the details, didn't want to relive the terror. She didn't want Mason to think about what she'd been through except to help him understand that these events had brought her to where she was now.

"The follow-up tests and check-ups have been normal," she continued, in an effort to reassure both of them.

Mason still didn't say anything, and his continued silence made her uneasy.

But she covered her discomfort with a shrug. "Anyway, I thought you should know."

The words buzzed in Mason's head like swarming cicadas. Words he would never have anticipated, could never have guessed.

breastcancerbreastcancerbreastcancer

No—it couldn't be true. Fate couldn't be that cruel. Not to Zoe—beautiful, sweet, amazing Zoe.

He barely heard anything she said after those two words.

And she was looking at him now, watching him, waiting for him to say something.

He swallowed.

Jesus, what did she want him to say? How the hell was he supposed to respond to something like that?

All he could say was, "I'm sorry."

Blindly, he stumbled out the door.

Chapter Ten

Zoe knew there was no point in feeling hurt or angry, but her emotions were stronger than reason, and she was both. She was hurt that Mason had walked out without a backward glance, angry that the relationship they'd been building didn't mean enough to him to want to at least try to work it out, and angrier at herself for letting it matter.

Because she couldn't deny that it did matter—not when the tears were already spilling onto her cheeks.

And as she sank to the floor, her eyes fixed on the door through which he'd made his hasty escape, she felt as if her heart was splitting wide open.

She didn't know how long she sat there or how long she cried before the tears finally stopped. When they did, she wiped the wetness from her cheeks and pushed herself to her feet. Though her throat ached and her eyes burned, she refused to wallow in self-pity any longer. She would channel her energies in a more productive direction, she decided, and started to paint.

She was finishing up the trim in The Rose Room— the name she'd given to the room at the southwest corner of the second floor since it had a narrow balcony that overlooked the rose gardens—when the doorbell rang. A quick glance at her watch revealed that it was almost midnight, and she tried to remember if she'd locked the door after Mason had gone. And then she wondered if maybe he'd come back, and she nearly tripped down the stairs in her haste to get to the door.

But it wasn't Mason at the door—it was Claire.

And she cursed herself for the twinge of disappointment even as she forced a smile and opened the door. "Isn't it a little late for an I-was-in-the-neighborhood-and-thought-I'd-drop-by visit?"

"It's actually an I-was-on-my-way-home-from-night-class-and-saw-your-lights-blazing-and-wondered-what-the-heck-was-going-on visit."

"Well, it's kind of hard to paint in the dark," Zoe explained.

"I'm sure it is," her friend agreed. "But why are you painting at midnight?"

She shrugged. "I wasn't feeling very tired, so I thought I might as well do something productive."

"At midnight?" Claire said again.

"I've actually been at it a little while. And I should get back—before my brush dries out."

"Mind if I come up and take a look?"

"Of course not." Zoe headed toward the wide stairs in the middle of the foyer. "You'll be amazed by how much has changed since you were here last."

"You're pleased with the progress, then?"

"Yeah. Tyler knows I'm anxious to have everything ready so I can start advertising after Christmas for a spring opening, so he's had his crew putting in overtime whenever they can."

"What about Tyler's brother?"

Zoe carefully scraped the excess paint from the bristles. "Mason? What about him?"

"I just wondered how things were going there," Claire said.

She continued to paint, slowly, deliberately. "Things aren't going anywhere with Mason."

"Oh."

She didn't have to look at her friend to know that she was frowning—and waiting for more of an explanation than the one Zoe had just given her. But Zoe didn't know what else to say.

"When I saw the two of you together at the barbecue, it seemed like you were definitely moving forward."

"Well, that was before."

Though she'd been certain she'd already cried all of the tears she had in her, she felt the telltale sting as her eyes filled again and quickly averted her gaze so Claire wouldn't see this evidence of her distress.

"You told him about your cancer," her friend guessed.

"Yes, I told him. Tonight, in fact." She tried to sound

casual but couldn't hide the raw anguish in her voice. "Because I thought we were moving forward and that he had a right to know before we did."

"I'm sorry, Zoe."

She shrugged. "So am I, but I can't change the way he feels."

"Maybe not," Claire agreed. "But what about your feelings?"

"I'm hurt—and angry. And there's a part of me that just wants to sit down and cry." She managed a teary smile. "But the truth is, I've already done that, and it seems ridiculous to cry over something like this considering that, in the past two years I lost my breast, my career, and my husband. In comparison, the end of a relationship that had barely begun to a man I didn't even know a couple of months ago should be insignificant."

"Maybe it should be," Claire said gently. "But it's not."

"No, it's not," she agreed, her attention deliberately focused on the trim she was painting.

Her friend was silent for a long moment while Zoe finished around the door. When she dipped her brush into the paint again, she saw Claire watching her.

"I'm fine now, really." She spoke the assurance knowing it wasn't true, but hoping it would be.

While Zoe was painting, Mason was trying his damnedest not to think about what she'd told him. Trying not to admit that she'd finally given him the missing piece of the puzzle he'd been trying to put together over the past few months, the piece that made all the little things he'd wondered about suddenly make sense.

The way she'd been comfortable and easy in the beginning, the first hint of nerves only starting to show when he indicated a personal interest. The way she'd kissed him back with a passion that made him ache and yearn, but pulled away from any more intimate contact.

And yet, even while the knowledge solved one puzzle it created another because he couldn't reconcile the woman he knew, the woman he'd come to care for so deeply, with her condition. She seemed so young and beautiful, so strong and vibrant, so vitally alive. But he knew the cancer would take all of that from her. It would steal the glow from her cheeks, the sparkle from her eyes and, eventually, the last breath from her body. It would eat away at her spirit and devour her soul until she was nothing more than a shell of the woman he'd come to know and admire.

He knew only too well what cancer did to a body—and to the people left behind. And he wanted no part of any of it. He refused to let himself get caught up again in what had been his worst nightmare—refused to even think about it.

Instead of thinking, he got rip-roaring drunk.

Mason was awakened Sunday morning by a rough and impatient shake.

"What the hell happened to you?"

It was Tyler's voice.

He blinked and tried to focus bleary eyes on his

brother. His gaze landed instead on the half-empty bottle of Jack Daniel's and the single glass on the table in front of him. Well, that explained why his head was pounding as if there was a little man with a sledgehammer trying to break out from the inside.

"Here." Tyler shoved a mug of hot coffee into his hand and dropped a bottle of aspirin in his lap.

Mason put the coffee aside to pry open the lid on the aspirin. Damn childproof caps.

Tyler grabbed the bottle back, popped the top and shook out four tablets.

"Thanks." Mason swallowed them down with a mouthful of hot coffee.

"Private party last night?"

"Yeah."

"Wanna tell me why?"

"No."

"Then I'll guess," Tyler said, settling into a chair with his own mug of coffee. "Zoe."

"I said I don't want to talk about it."

"I stopped by her house this morning," his brother continued anyway. "It wasn't too early, but I got her out of bed. She didn't look half as rough as you do, but it was obvious she didn't sleep last night. What happened—you two have a disagreement about what color to paint the dining room?"

"Very funny."

"Well, give me a hint, because I can't imagine why you'd want to screw up the best thing that ever happened to you."

Mason finished his coffee and pushed himself off the

couch to go for a refill. "How about finding out that Zoe has breast cancer?"

"Oh, hell." Tyler followed him into the kitchen.

"Yeah—that about sums it up."

"When did she find out? What kind of treatment is she going to need?"

He took another long swallow of coffee. "She found out two years ago. She had a mastectomy."

His brother frowned. "Then she's okay now?"

"Mom thought she was going to be okay, too, remember?"

"Of course I remember. But that was twenty years ago, and if you're using the memory of what she went through as an excuse to let go of Zoe now, then you don't deserve her, anyway."

"The cancer didn't just kill her, Tyler—it killed Dad, too."

"Did it ever occur to you that it was guilt as much as grief that made him drown himself in the bottle? Yeah, I remember what Mom went through. And I remember who was there with her in the end—you and me and Grandma. Dad couldn't handle seeing her like that, knowing he was losing her, and he wasted the last six months they might have had together by mourning her before she was gone."

"He loved her too much to watch her die."

"Did we love her any less?"

Mason frowned at that.

"Of course not," Tyler answered his own question. "And that's why you've spent the past twenty years avoiding anything that might even resemble a relationship.

Then Zoe came along, and you seemed to be building not just a house but the foundation of a future together.

"Now you have to ask yourself—why are you running scared? Are you worried that Zoe's battle with cancer might not be over and you don't have what it takes to stand by her? Or are you afraid of losing her? Because if that's your concern, well, you've pretty much ensured that all by yourself."

Zoe knew it was inevitable that she would cross paths with Mason sooner or later. They were neighbors, after all, and it wouldn't have surprised her to run into him at DiMarco's Grocery or Anderson's Hardware or Walton's Ice Cream Parlor. It did surprise her to find him standing at her back door less than forty-eight hours after making a quick escape through that same entrance.

And it annoyed her to find that his appearance there made her heart skip and race after he'd so mercilessly trampled upon it. And if she felt a small measure of satisfaction because his eyes were bloodshot and shadowed with dark circles, his jaw was unshaven and he generally looked like hell, she figured she was entitled.

"If you're looking for the beast, I haven't seen him," she told him.

"I'm not," Mason said. "I came to see you, if you've got a few minutes."

She glanced at her watch, torn between wanting him to stay and wishing he would go. "My dinner's in the oven, so I've got about ten minutes," she finally said.

"Can I come in?"

She stepped away from the door to allow him entry, but she didn't invite him to sit down or offer him a drink. Whatever his reason for being there, she didn't see any point in dragging it out. Her pride was all that she had left now, and she wasn't going to risk losing that, too, by asking for something he couldn't give her.

Instead, she moved to the counter where she'd left the lettuce when she went to answer the door, and began tearing up the leaves for a salad. She heard his footsteps follow her into the room, felt the weight of his eyes on her, but she deliberately kept her own gaze focused on her task.

"I owe you an apology," he said at last.

"You don't owe me anything, Mason."

"Yes, I do," he insisted. "And I'd appreciate it if you'd at least hear me out."

She finished her task before pushing the bowl aside and turning to face him.

"I freaked out when you said *cancer,* and I'm sorry."

She heard the words, knew he meant them, but an apology couldn't ease the ache inside. Nothing could.

"It's not an uncommon reaction," she told him. "I know a lot of people who still whisper the word, as if speaking it out loud will somehow bring the curse of the disease into their own homes."

"It just caught me off guard," he said. "I mean, you're so young, and you seem so healthy."

"I *am* healthy," she said. "I might not be whole, but I'm healthy."

He winced at that. "What you've been through doesn't make you any less beautiful or any less of a woman, Zoe."

"Are you saying it doesn't matter that I've lost a breast?" she challenged.

He couldn't meet her gaze when he said, "I'm saying that it shouldn't."

"But it does, doesn't it?"

He was silent for a long moment, then he finally said, "Yes."

It was hard to appreciate his honesty when the single word scraped at open wounds that were already raw and bleeding.

"My mother—" he had to clear his throat. "My mother died of breast cancer."

The revelation didn't shock her. She was familiar with the statistics, knew that one in every eight women would be diagnosed with breast cancer at some point in their lives. And when she'd cleared her mind enough to think beyond the fact that he'd walked out on her to wonder why, she'd suspected that he'd been close to someone who'd battled the disease. Only now did she remember him telling her about his mother's death, and his father's a few years later. She'd never thought to ask how she'd died, and it had certainly never occurred to her that his mother might have succumbed to the same disease she'd battled herself.

"I don't know the details of when or how she found the lump," he continued, "but I know that she didn't tell anyone for a long time because I remember her and my dad arguing about that. He didn't have any medical coverage through his work, so she refused to make un-necessary trips to the doctor. By the time she went to have it checked out, the cancer had spread."

His voice was level, almost detached, but she noticed that his fingers had curled around the edge of the counter, gripping it so tightly his knuckles were white. "They cut off her breast, put her through chemo and then radiation.

"Slash, poison, burn." He shook his head. "It was supposed to make her better. All it did was make the last two years of her life a living hell."

Her heart ached for him—for the teenager who'd lost his mother, and for the man still suffering over that loss. "I'm so sorry, Mason."

"When I hear the word *cancer*—I can't help remembering. And I hate to think of you going through all of that."

"I didn't," she told him. "I chose to have a mastectomy instead of a lumpectomy to reduce the need for follow-up treatment."

"My mother had a mastectomy."

"But you said her cancer had already spread," she said gently. "My doctors were confident that mine was found early enough that I didn't need to worry about involvement of the lymph nodes, and they recommended—partly because I was so young, I think—that I have only the lump removed and save the breast."

"Why didn't you?" ... about this?"

"Do you really w~ I wish it was a completely irrele-
"N~ ~ out since it isn't, I want to know what you
~.ent through."

The timer buzzed, indicating that her dinner was ready. She turned it off and pulled her fish out of the oven. "I'm not sure that I want to talk about it."

"Maybe you should anyway," he said. "Because I'm guessing, now that I know about the cancer and when you were diagnosed, that there's a connection between everything you tried to dismiss as 'crossroads'—the breakdown of your marriage, your sudden change of career, the move to Pinehurst."

"You're right," she admitted. "My diagnosis created something of a domino effect on all areas of my life—and apparently some of the tiles are still tumbling." And if she was completely honest with herself, she'd admit that she'd lived with the secrets for so long, been so careful to keep the truth close, that she really hadn't acknowledged and accepted all of the consequences herself. Maybe telling him would be a mistake. Or maybe, in some ways, it might be cathartic.

So when he asked again why she'd chosen to have the mastectomy, she took a deep breath and answered.

"Because it seemed easier to cover up the loss of my breast than the loss of my hair." The wry smile didn't hint at the knots tangled in her belly. "I know that sounds bizarre and vain and, in retrospect, I should have considered the fact that my hair would have grown back by now—and my breast never will.

"But it was more than just losing my hair—it was the fear of being sick, of anyone knowing what I was going through. I didn't want anyone knowing what I was going through. I didn't wanna see that I had cancer because…" her voice faltered, "see that I had would have to admit that I had cancer."

"You didn't tell anyone?" he asked, obviously surprised.

"Not at first. It was hard enough telling Scott. I

thought breast cancer was something that afflicted older women. I was only twenty-seven years old. I felt ashamed—as if it was somehow my fault that my body was defective. I was angry and helpless and confused. And terrified that everyone would start treating me differently.

"I just wanted to pretend everything was normal." She shook her head as she swallowed around the tightness in her throat. "No, that's not true. I wanted everything to *be* normal.

"But it wasn't. And I had to face that fact every time I picked up my camera to take pictures of women who were beautiful and perfect and whole."

"Is that the real reason you left Manhattan?"

"One of the reasons," she admitted. "I thought I could have the surgery and reconstruction and get back to work as if nothing had changed.

"Except that everything had changed. I tried to go through the motions of taking pictures, but it was a disaster. I played with lenses, adjusted angles, checked lighting, clicked the shutter. By all outward appearances, I was doing the job as I'd always done the job. But when I looked at the contact sheets, I saw that I'd only been focusing on parts. I'd have a picture of a shoulder or a hand—not the whole model or the whole of anything I was supposed to be photographing.

"Scott tried to be understanding, but he was caught between his editorial responsibilities and his messed-up wife. The magazine had to bring in another photographer and redo the whole shoot, which threw off the entire production schedule, cost a ton of money and raised a lot of questions about my ability to fulfill the terms of my contract. So I left. It seemed like the best solution for everyone."

She pushed off the thoughts, the regrets.

It hadn't been an easy decision, but it was the decision she'd made and the one she'd live with—hopefully, for a very long time.

"Is that when your marriage fell apart?"

She shook her head. "My medical problems only made me realize how far apart we'd grown. We were two people sharing a home and a bed but essentially living separate lives. I'd always been strong and independent, and suddenly I was weak and needy—and the change scared both of us."

So many emotions coursed through him as he listened to her talk. Empathy and admiration. Concern and regret. Fear and anger.

It was the anger that seemed easiest to focus on, and he heard the evidence of it in his voice when he said, "I can't believe you're making excuses for him."

"Some people just can't cope with personal crises."

He frowned at that. "Are we still talking about your ex?"

"Yes," she said. "But I don't blame you for walking out, either. I shouldn't have let things go as far as they did without making you aware of the situation."

"And that's it?" he demanded, unaccountably annoyed by her easy capitulation. "You're just going to accept that I couldn't handle what you went through?"

She glanced away, but not before he caught a

glimpse of the tears that filled her eyes. "What do you think I should do—take off my clothes and make you look at my scars?"

"I don't know," he said, though there was a part of him that almost wished she would. He wanted her to force the issue, to push him for more than he was ready to give, because then he could blame her for things not working out.

"I'm pretty sure that display wouldn't make either one of us feel any better," she told him.

"I really am sorry…for everything you went through."

She shrugged. "Now you know the whole story."

"Except where we go from here," he said softly, surprising himself as much as he'd obviously surprised Zoe with the words.

When he'd come here tonight, he'd done so because he'd wanted to apologize. And because he'd needed her to understand why it was impossible for their relationship to develop any further. But as he opened up to her about his past and listened to her talk about her experience, he found himself wondering if a future with Zoe really was impossible.

The hope that flared briefly in her eyes in response to his statement was quickly eclipsed by wariness, as if she didn't dare let herself hope, as if she wouldn't risk trusting in him again. "Where do you want to go?"

He stared at her for a long moment, the same uncertainty he'd heard in her voice reflected in his own heart. Despite his doubts and fears, he still wanted Zoe. But there was so much at stake—more than he'd ever been willing to risk with anyone before, maybe more than he was ready to risk even now. He was trapped by his own indecision, unable to take the next step forward, yet unwilling to let her go.

"I don't know," he admitted.

She turned away to get a plate from the cupboard, clearly intent on moving ahead with her dinner plans and effectively dismissing him. "When you figure it out, you can let me know."

Chapter Eleven

Zoe was painting the gazebo when Tyler tracked her down Friday morning.

"You've been making yourself scarce this week," he noted.

"I've been up and out early every day, scouring antique stores within a hundred-mile radius in search of bookcases for the library."

"Since you're home today, I'd guess you either found what you wanted or you ran out of stores."

She smiled. "I found a gorgeous solid walnut Eastlake bookcase in three sections. It's going to be delivered this afternoon."

"What time?"

"Between two and four."

"Then we'll definitely be able to make the movie."

"What movie?"

"The one we're going to see tonight."

"Thanks, Ty, but I'm not—"

"Don't say 'no,'" he urged. "It's a new sci-fi flick that I really want to see, but I hate going to the theater by myself like some loser who can't get a date."

"I don't think you'd have any trouble getting a date if you really wanted one," she said.

"Seems to me I'm having trouble right now."

"Sci-fi movies aren't really my thing."

"It's got to be better than sitting at home and brooding about the idiocy of other men."

She sighed. "I know you think your brother broke my heart, but he didn't. And even if he did, it's not your job to pick up the pieces."

"This has nothing to do with my brother," he assured her. "It has to do with me wanting to see a movie with you."

She didn't believe him for a minute, but she appreciated his effort.

"Okay," she finally agreed. "But only if you let me buy the popcorn."

Despite her initial reluctance, Zoe did enjoy the movie. And she enjoyed Tyler's company. He was handsome and charming and fun to be with, and when he said he was hungry after the movie, they picked up pasta from Mama Leone's and took it back to her house.

"I really do love the new look of the kitchen," Tyler said as he unpacked the bag of food. "I would have thought you'd put in a whole new set of cabinets if I hadn't seen you painting them myself."

"I'm not sure it's a job I'd ever want to tackle again, but I'm pleased with the way they turned out. I'm even happier with the changes you can't see—the roll-outs and dividers that help keep everything in its proper place inside the cabinets."

"Yeah, I can see you like things organized," he said, looking through the spice rack that had been attached to the inside of a cupboard door for the chili peppers. "Your spices are actually alphabetized."

"It makes it easier to find whatever I'm looking for."

He picked up a bottle, frowned at the label before putting it back. "What do you use cumin for?"

"Chili."

"One of my all-time favorites." He'd found the peppers and sprinkled a generous amount on top of his rigatoni. "There's nothing like hot chili on a cold winter day. Now if you told me you made lamb stew, too, I'd have to marry you."

"Then you're safe." Zoe twirled her fork in her angel hair pasta. "I've never cooked lamb in any shape or form. I do, however, make a pretty decent Guinness stew."

"Good enough." He reached across the table for her hand. "Wanna get hitched?"

She smiled, shaking her head, and tugged her hand away. "Been there, done that."

He suddenly turned serious. "You don't think you'll ever get married again?"

"I don't know what will happen in the future, but

right now, I can't imagine ever opening up my heart to someone that completely again."

"Except that you did, didn't you? You fell in love with my brother."

"I don't know." She toyed with her pasta. "I think I was definitely headed that way, but then there was an unexpected fork in the road."

"And my brother veered off in the wrong direction."

"He took the one that was right for him."

"What about what's right for you?"

"I'm still figuring that out myself," she said. "But I do know that I don't want to be with someone who can't accept me for who I am. I deserve better than that."

"You do," he agreed. "You're an amazing woman, Zoe. And my brother's an idiot."

She pushed away from the table to take her half-empty plate to the counter—and nearly dumped her leftovers down her front when a shadow at the back door made her jump.

She pressed a hand to her pounding heart. "Go home," she spoke to Rosie through the screen.

The dog whined.

Tyler carried his empty plate to the sink. "How did he get here?"

"The same way he always does, I guess."

"Always?"

She shrugged as she scraped the rest of her pasta back into the take-out container to go into the fridge. "It seems like always. Every day this week, that's for sure.

Usually I just tell him to go home and he goes, but last night, I had to call your brother to come and get him."

"Maybe the dog's trying to get the two of you back together."

She rolled her eyes at that.

"So what happened when you called Mason?" he asked.

"He came and got the beast."

"And?"

"And nothing. There was no reason for me to go outside and no reason for him to come in."

Tyler sighed. "Have I mentioned that my brother's an idiot?"

She smiled. "He has to figure out what he wants on his own."

Outside, Rosie barked.

Zoe pushed open the door and stepped out onto the porch. "You know your own way," she said to the animal. "Now go."

Rosie barked again.

"I'll take him over," Tyler offered.

"You don't mind?"

"Of course not. It's probably time I was heading out anyway."

She walked around to the front of the house with him. When they got to the steps, he leaned down to drop a friendly kiss on Zoe's forehead, chuckling again when he heard Rosie's whine turn to a growl.

"I'm not making any moves on her," he assured the dog. "Just saying good night."

She smiled. "Good night, Tyler. And thanks again for the movie."

"Anytime." He started to step off the porch when the crunch of tires on gravel indicated another visitor coming up the driveway.

"Expecting company?"

She shook her head as she watched the other vehicle pull up alongside Tyler's truck. It was a sportscar of some type, she guessed, with distinctively shaped headlights low to the ground. Maybe a Porsche 911 like Scott drove.

Then the driver's side door opened and he stepped out.

"Someone you know?" Tyler asked.

"My ex-husband."

He frowned. "Do you want me to hang around?"

She smiled at that, touched by his protectiveness toward her. She was disappointed that things hadn't worked out with Mason, but she was pleased with the friendship she'd established with his brother and she'd always be grateful to Mason for that.

"Thank you." She gave him a quick hug. "But I can handle Scott."

"I'll see you tomorrow, then," he said, and led Rosie away.

Mason wasn't in the mood for company, so when he heard the brisk knock on the door, he ignored it. When the door opened and his brother walked in, he intended to ignore him, too. Until he saw that Rosie was with him.

"Where did you find him?" he asked reluctantly.

"On Zoe's porch."

The response didn't surprise him. It seemed like every time he turned around lately, the dog was at Zoe's. "Keep it up and I will put you on a leash."

Rosie growled.

"I think man's best friend has gone over to the other side," Tyler said, amusement evident in his tone. "He growled at me like that, too, when I kissed Zoe good-night."

Mason turned his scowl on his brother. "I expected that you, knowing what she's been through, would have enough sense not to play with her emotions."

Tyler arched an eyebrow, but all he said was, "I happen to care about Zoe. And, for some inexplicable reason, I care about you, too, even if you deserve to be kicked in the butt for letting her get away."

"I'm not getting into this with you again."

His brother shrugged. "Okay—I thought you might want to know that Zoe's ex-husband is back in the picture, but if you're happy with the way things are, it doesn't really matter."

"What do you mean, her ex is in the picture?"

"He showed up at her house while I was there."

"What did he want?"

"I didn't hang around to chat," Tyler said dryly.

"You left—and left Zoe alone with him?"

"He's not an escaped convict—he's her ex-husband," his brother pointed out reasonably.

But Mason wasn't in the mood to be reasonable. "Who bailed on her because he couldn't handle the consequences of her condition."

"You mean—like you did?"

Mason glowered at his brother. "It's hardly the same thing."

Tyler's only response was to raise his eyebrows.

It was Tuesday before Mason found out, again through Tyler, why Zoe's ex-husband had come to see her, and Wednesday when he agreed to try to re-open the lines of communication with her. Although he found himself second-guessing that decision every step of the way toward her house late Wednesday afternoon.

He couldn't believe he'd let his brother talk him into this ridiculous plan that Zoe would no doubt see right through. But even knowing that, he was grateful for the excuse—any excuse—to see her again. Because in the ten days that had passed since he'd walked out of her kitchen, he'd finally realized that the possibility of losing her at some unforeseeable time in the future was preferable to losing her now because he wasn't smart enough to hold on to her.

She was obviously surprised to see him, even more surprised when he revealed the reason for his visit.

"You want to borrow some cumin?"

"Two tablespoons," he said.

"Okay." But she was frowning as she pulled open the cupboard door. "What do you need it for?"

"Tyler's making chili."

"Your brother's cooking?"

Mason nodded. "He was chopping up peppers and onions and stuff, so he asked me to come over to see if you had the cumin."

Zoe handed him a bottle. "There you go."

"Thanks."

"Was there something else you needed?" she asked, when he made no move to leave.

"No." He turned away, then back again. "Yes."

She waited.

"Tyler told me that your ex-husband offered you a job."

"Not a permanent position," she said. "Just as a fill-in for one shoot."

"Are you going to do it?" he wanted to know.

"He's stuck—the photographer that he'd planned to use was double-booked, and it would be a logistical nightmare to reschedule the whole thing."

"And you believe that this other photographer was suddenly unavailable?"

"I can't imagine that Scott would have come to me otherwise."

"Maybe he wants you back and figures if he can get you taking pictures for the magazine again, you might realize you've missed it and decide to return to Manhattan."

"I have no reason to question his motives," she told him, wondering why Mason was doing so and why her decision even mattered to him. "And this is a good opportunity for me—not to mention a potentially lucrative one."

"And after the photo shoot is finished?"

"I'll come back."

"When will that be?"

She shrugged. "Probably in four or five days."

"Four or five days taking pictures?"

"The photo shoot should only take a day or two, depending on the weather, then add another day on each end to accommodate the travel."

"It doesn't take more than a couple of hours to drive to New York City."

"No," she agreed. "But it takes a little longer to get to Exuma."

"Exuma?" he echoed dubiously.

"That's where the photo shoot is scheduled."

He scowled. "You're going to the Bahamas with your ex-husband?"

"I'm going to the Bahamas with the magazine."

"Is your ex-husband going to be there?"

"Why are you doing this?" she asked wearily. "You were the one who decided you didn't want me, remember?"

"I never said I didn't want you."

"You're right—you never said those words." Her eyes glittered with tears. "I read between the lines when you ran out the door."

The sharpness in her tone wasn't unexpected—the tears were. He deserved her anger, was prepared to deal with that. It was the hurt underlying the temper that cut him at the knees. He'd never wanted to hurt her, had never realized how much damage he could do to her heart in trying to protect his own.

"You read wrong," he said.

"It doesn't matter," she told him. "You got what you came here for and I have to pack."

As he watched her turn away, panic reared up like a wild beast, kicking and clawing and tearing him up inside. He couldn't let her go—not with so much still unresolved between them.

"Dammit, Zoe." He grabbed her arm, spun her back toward him. "If I didn't want you, this would be easy."

Her eyes flashed fire as she opened her mouth to respond, no doubt to tell him it was too little too late. He didn't want to hear it. He didn't need her to tell him that he'd been an idiot. What he needed right now was Zoe.

He hauled her against him and covered her mouth with his.

Her eyes widened with shock, her body stiffened. But she didn't pull away. And as his lips moved over hers, he felt the tension slowly begin to seep away until, finally, her eyes closed, her lips softened and her body melted against his.

He wrapped his arms around her, drawing her close, closer.

Beautiful, sweet Zoe.

He didn't know if he murmured the words against her lips or just inside his head. It didn't matter, really. What mattered was her response. The soft moan that came from deep in her throat as she fisted her hands in his hair and parted her lips for the searching thrust of his tongue.

He could feel the pounding of her heart, the frantic beat that matched his own.

Want you. So much.

His hands slid down her back, over the sweet curve of her buttocks. Desire—hot and greedy—surged through him.

He wanted to touch and taste and take.

He wanted to make her tremble and sigh. He wanted to feel her shudder and hear her moan. He wanted her breathless and quivering, aching for him as he ached for her. Then he wanted to tear away her clothes and bury himself in the sweet heat of her body.

The fantasy of doing just that—right here and right now—was shockingly vivid in his mind, the ache in his body painfully real.

He fought to remember that as much as he wanted her, he didn't want it to be like this. Not with so many questions and doubts still between them.

So instead of tearing away her clothes, he tore his mouth from hers.

His kiss had surprised Zoe, which was why his withdrawal only infuriated her more. She'd been on an emotional roller coaster for the past week-and-a-half, and every time she thought things were starting to level out, he sent her flying again.

"Damn you, Mason." She slapped her hands against his chest as if to push him away. She *should* push him away—make it clear that she wasn't going to let him churn her up and then walk out on her again. But somehow, instead of pushing him away, her fingers curled into his shirt and pulled him closer.

This time, it was her mouth that found his. This time, it was her lips and teeth and tongue that snapped the tight rein on his passion.

With a growl of pent-up frustration, he pulled her close, banding his arms around her to hold her against his hot, hard and very aroused body.

She thought she'd resigned herself to the fact that she and Mason would never be lovers. She couldn't have imagined that their relationship would be able to move forward after he'd walked out on her. But somehow he was here, wanting her, and making her want him.

If she let herself think about it, she might find herself filled with doubts and fears and insecurities. So she refused to think about it. The how or why didn't matter—not right now. All that mattered was that she felt more alive in this moment, in his arms, than she'd felt in a very long time.

She wound her arms around his neck. "You're not walking out on me this time."

"No." His kiss was long and deep. "I'm not going anywhere."

She moaned with anticipation as those fast, eager hands traced her curves through the thin barrier of her clothing, then gasped with pleasure when they found the warm flesh beneath.

But she wanted to touch as much as be touched. Despite shaking fingers, she managed to unfasten the buttons that ran down the front of his shirt. She pushed the material aside and let her palms slide over all that smooth taut skin, her fingers tracing the contours of all those hard, rippling muscles.

She touched her lips to his chest and inhaled the tangy masculine scent that made her want to gobble him up in quick, greedy bites. The temptation was more than she could resist, and she nipped at his shoulder, the gentle bite earning a quick, startled oath that became a tortured groan when she soothed the spot with her tongue.

"Bedroom," he muttered, scooping her into his arms. "Before I forget where we are and take you on the kitchen floor."

He took the stairs two at a time and was kicking open the bedroom door before she could catch her breath.

"Now." He lowered her gently to her feet. "Where were we?"

"Right about here," she said, tugging open the button at the top of his jeans with a quick flick of her wrist. "And here." She rubbed her palm against the hard length of him through the denim.

"I, uh—"

She had the pleasure of watching his eyes start to glaze before he circled her wrist with his fingers and tugged her hand away.

"I think you're, uh, skipping ahead a little."

"You said you wanted me," she reminded him.

"I do." His eyes were dark, intense. "More than you could imagine."

She took his hand and drew him toward the bed. "Show me."

He captured her mouth in another kiss as he eased her down onto the mattress. She wrapped herself around him, glorying in the weight of his body pressing against hers, the hardness of his arousal between her thighs.

His hands were relentless now, teasing, testing, taking, as they raced over her skin. His lips were hot and wild, scorching everywhere they touched. Desire thrummed through her with every beat of her heart, every pulse of her blood. She couldn't move, couldn't think, she could only feel.

Heat.

Want.

Need.

His hands were under her skirt now, stripping away her panties. Then his fingers gliding over her skin. From ankles to knees, knees to thighs. Her muscles quivered, her breath caught.

Then he touched her, just a feather light stroke of his fingers over the dewy curls at her center. She gasped as those fingers dipped into her. He groaned in appreciation when he found her wet and ready.

"Now," she said, her body aching for the fulfillment of joining with his.

He left her only long enough to get rid of his jeans and briefs, then took another moment to protect her before lowering himself over her again.

"Now," he agreed, and filled her.

Her eyes widened with shocked surprise at the first thrust, then closed again in dreamy delirium as he started to move inside her.

She felt the thundering beat of his heart against hers, steady and strong, when she wrapped her arms around him. She tasted the salty flavor of his skin when she pressed her lips to his throat. And she smiled in pure feminine satisfaction when the light scrape of her nails over his skin made him shudder.

They rolled over the mattress, mouths mating, hands grasping, hearts pounding. She rose up over him, her knees tight against his hips as she rode him to that dark, dangerous edge—and over.

Everything inside her that had tightened and tensed

finally burst free. When her body quivered, shuddered and slid bonelessly against him, he flipped her onto her back and drove her on.

"More," he said.

She'd thought she was spent, that there couldn't possibly be any more than the pleasure he'd already given her. Even as her mind spun and her senses shattered, she was arching beneath him.

He yanked her hips high, drove hard, harder. She hooked her legs around his waist, pulled him deep, deeper. Then they were racing together, fast, faster.

The climax tore a scream from her throat as it ripped through her, leaving her shuddering helplessly beneath the weight of his body as he groaned and emptied himself into her.

As often as Mason had imagined making love with Zoe—and over the past couple of months, he'd imagined it often—he'd never suspected that the experience would leave him feeling simultaneously drained and energized. He wanted to tuck her close to his body and curl up to sleep for a week. And he wanted her all over again.

But she apparently had other plans, because she climbed out of the bed, straightened the skirt that had bunched around her waist and tugged down the hem of her shirt.

And while he'd never been accused of being particularly insightful when it came to the methods and moods of women, he knew that something was definitely wrong.

"Zo?"

She was tugging open the drawers of her dresser, pulling out items of clothing seemingly at random. "I have to catch a plane in a few hours," she explained, "and I haven't even packed."

Her casual response and easy dismissal of the intimacy they'd just shared hit him with the force of a physical blow.

"And that's it? You're just going to leave?"

"I told you that I had to go."

"Can you at least take a later flight?"

She shook her head. "Not if I'm going to make my connection in Miami."

With a sigh of combined resignation and frustration, he scooped his jeans off the floor and pulled them on. "We need to talk about this, Zoe."

"No, we don't." She smiled at him, but he could tell it was forced. "Really, it's not a big deal."

"Not a big deal?"

"I'm not one of those women who confuse sex with love or assume that physical intimacy equals a relationship, so you don't have to worry about anything like that."

"My mistake," he said coolly.

She shoved a handful of lacy undergarments into a duffel bag. "Save the wounded act. We both got exactly what we wanted—nothing more and nothing less."

"Is that all this was to you—an opportunity to release some pent-up sexual tension?"

"I'd be a fool to think it could be anything more after you made it clear you didn't want to get involved with me," she said.

"I don't know how it is with people from New York," he said. "But where I come from, getting naked with someone usually indicates a certain level of involvement."

"But we didn't get naked, did we?"

"What?"

She shook her head. "It's okay. Really. I know my medical history makes you uncomfortable."

And suddenly the reason for her hurt and anger hit him like a two-by-four between the eyes.

"You think I didn't take your clothes off because I didn't want to look at your body?"

"It's okay," she said again. "Scott had issues with the scars, too."

"I'm not your ex-husband," he snapped. "And the only reason I didn't take your clothes off was because I was in too damn much of a hurry to get inside you. And it seemed to me that you were just as eager for the same thing."

"I really don't want to argue about this," she told him. "I'm already running behind schedule."

"Or maybe you're just running."

Her only response was to pick up her duffel bag and sling it over her shoulder.

Chapter Twelve

It was love at first sight for Zoe.

She'd had the opportunity to travel to a lot of different places when she'd worked at *Images,* but this was her first trip to Exuma and she was immediately enamored of the lush green vegetation, the crystal-clear water and the powder-soft beaches. It was, she thought, the closest thing to paradise she'd ever seen.

But as exotic and beautiful as it was, it wasn't home. And by the third day, Zoe was missing her house and wondering what Tyler's crew was working on now. Was the third-floor suite—formerly the attic—done yet? Would she be able to decorate in preparation of moving up there when she got back? Were her flowers still in bloom? Or were they uprooted because Rosie had been chasing squirrels again? Of course, thinking about Rosie made her think about Mason. Or maybe the truth was that thoughts of Mason always lingered in her mind and maybe she was missing him most of all.

She pushed those thoughts aside as she wiped perspiration from her brow with the back of her arm and waited for the models to get into position. When everything was set, she refocused the camera and snapped away until she was confident she had all the shots she needed. When she finally signaled that they were done, Scott strolled over.

She accepted the bottle of cold water with a weary smile.

"Thanks." She tipped it to her lips and drank deeply.

"Thank *you,*" he said. "You really saved my skin by coming out here."

She smiled. "You haven't seen any of the pictures yet."

"I don't need to see them to know they're great. I've been watching you enough since you got here to know you're in top form." He stroked a hand down her arm. "How does it feel—to be behind the camera again?"

"It feels good," she admitted, no longer surprised that it was true. "Except for the fact that it's nine hundred degrees in the shade." She took another long swallow, pressed the bottle to her forehead. "Whose idea was it to shoot in the Caribbean in August anyway?"

"Mine." He grinned. "I like the way you look in a bikini."

"What if I hadn't agreed to do this?"

He shrugged. "Then I would have been stuck with Perry—and he isn't half as cute in a bathing suit."

"I thought Perry was stuck in France."

"He was—is. But he expects to finish up there in another few days."

"So you could have rescheduled this shoot for next week."

He shook his head. "We had everything—including the models—booked for this week. It would have put us behind schedule and cost a fortune to delay even a few days."

"You spent a small fortune to bring me out here without even knowing if I'd be able to do the job."

"I knew you could do it—and in spectacular fashion," he said with confidence.

She smiled at that. "You never did like to admit when you'd made a mistake."

"I only ever made one," he told her. "When I signed the divorce papers."

"Our marriage was over long before that."

"Was it? I've wondered so many times since then if we could have fixed it—if maybe we still can."

"It's kind of hard to fix something that doesn't exist anymore."

"Don't you believe in second chances?"

"Sure," she said. "But I don't believe in making the same mistake a second time."

"Ouch."

She smiled. "I have a lot of good memories of the time we spent together, but I've moved on. We both have."

"You don't honestly expect me to believe you're serious about that kid you were out with the night I came to Pinehurst."

She smiled, thinking that it would have been easy to fall for Tyler—he was handsome, charming and fun. Unfortunately, she'd met his much more frustrating and complicated brother first and fallen for him, instead.

"No," she finally answered Scott's question. "Tyler and I are just friends."

"Is there someone else, then?"

She took another sip of her water as her thoughts drifted automatically to Mason. Even when he'd been trying to back off and she'd been trying to stay mad, there was an undeniable "something" that continued to draw them together—an incomprehensible chemistry that had sparked between them almost from the first and continued to build over the past couple of months until it had finally exploded in a frenzy of passion that had somehow left her both sated and yearning, both scared and wanting.

"Obviously there is someone else," he said.

"Yes, there is."

"Are you happy with him?"

"I think I could be."

"Then I hope he's a smarter man than me."

"That remains to be seen," she said lightly.

"Although he's obviously not too bright," Scott continued. "Since he let you fly off to a tropical island paradise with your ex-husband."

"He's smart enough to know he couldn't stop me," Zoe said. "And to warn me that he thought you were interested in more than my camera."

He grinned unashamedly. "Can't blame a guy for trying."

She couldn't help but smile back. "Thank you."

"For what?"

"Not giving up on me."

"I'm not going to give up hoping that you'll come back to *Images*, either."

"I can't," she said. "I'm not that person anymore."

"I know," he admitted. "The wife I loved and the photographer I admired pale in comparison to the woman you are now."

She hoped that was true. When she'd first been diagnosed, she'd thought it would be enough to survive. Now she wanted more. And in order to get "more," she needed to be a smarter, braver and stronger woman than she'd been—smart enough to recognize what she really wanted, brave enough to go after it and strong enough to fight for it.

"Thanks again for this opportunity." She kissed his cheek and turned away.

"Where are you going?" Scott demanded.

She smiled. "Home."

Zoe was tired when she got on the plane—but it was a good tired, the kind of satisfied exhaustion that came from the knowledge that she'd done her job well. The pictures would be fabulous, she was as confident as Scott about that. And though she had no intention of going back to her job at *Images*, it was both flattering and reassuring to know that she hadn't lost her touch and that there were other career options available to her if the bed-and-breakfast didn't work out the way she hoped it would.

But whatever her future might bring, she had no intention of running back to New York City. She wasn't running anywhere anymore. The girl who had taken off to college to escape the chaos of her mother's marriages, then to New York in pursuit of her husband's dreams, then away from the city and her crumbling marriage, had finally found what she hadn't realized she'd always been looking for. Maybe not with Mason—whatever their relationship might or might not be remained to be seen, but she loved the town and being close to Claire and the new friends she'd made. For the first time in her life, she truly felt as if she was home.

She stepped into the house, dropped her suitcase on the floor and kicked off her shoes. Then stared into the dining room at the neatly pressed linen cloth draped over the table, the china, crystal and silver set out for two, the candles waiting to be lit, the bottle of chardonnay chilling in a bucket of ice.

A movement by the kitchen doorway caught her eye, and when she glanced over, she saw Mason was there.

"You weren't supposed to be home until after seven."

"I caught an earlier flight. What are you doing here?"

"Making dinner." He took a few steps toward her. "How was Exuma?"

"Breathtaking. Is your stove broken?"

He smiled at that. "No. But if I'd invited you to dinner at my place, you might have said 'no.'"

And probably would have, she admitted to herself. Because as much as he'd been in her thoughts throughout her journey and despite her resolution to get in touch with him, she'd planned to wait, at least until the next day, to do so. She'd wanted to be rested and showered, dressed in something that didn't look as if she'd slept in it and wearing at least a touch of makeup. Instead, she suspected that she looked as weary as she felt, and she felt completely unprepared to see him now—especially when just looking at him made her knees weak.

"How did you get in here?"

"I borrowed my brother's key. Actually, I had to bribe him," Mason admitted. "With tickets to a baseball game."

"You gave up a ballgame to get into my house and make me dinner?"

"Not just any ballgame—the Yankees and the Red Sox." He took her hands in his. "I missed you, Zoe."

Her heart skipped, then raced. "Oh."

His smile was wry. "An I-missed-you-too would have been nice, but at least you haven't kicked me out."

She wasn't ready to put her heart on the line just yet and refused to feel guilty about it. Instead, she said, "I'm hungry, and whatever you're cooking smells good."

"Chicken Parisian with basmati rice—but it's not quite ready yet. Do you want a glass of wine while you're waiting?"

"Actually, I'd love a quick shower, if there's time."

"You've got time for a soak in the tub and the wine, if you want," he told her. "I wasn't expecting you to be early and I haven't even put the rice on yet."

"That sounds good," she agreed.

She took her wine upstairs, grateful for a few minutes to gather her thoughts and settle her emotions.

She'd wanted to see him. She couldn't deny that. But she'd expected to have a chance to prepare—to be rational and logical. It worried her that her heart had leaped so joyously at the sight of him, that his smile still had the power to make her bones melt, that she was incapable of objectivity and reason whenever he was near.

As the scented bubbles worked to soak away her fatigue, she considered whether to take a step back—or jump in with both feet.

Obviously, they had to talk about what had happened before she left and where they would go from here. She knew he cared about her, but she also knew that he had reservations about getting any more deeply involved. She couldn't blame him for that. She'd had reservations of her own long before she knew what he'd gone through with his mother.

Her heart ached when she thought of the boy he'd been—how difficult it must have been for him to lose first one parent and then the other. She could understand his frustration and his anger, even his fear. But she couldn't understand and wouldn't tolerate any negativity. She'd chosen an aggressive course of treatment to deal with her cancer because she'd wanted to get on with her life, and if they were to have any kind of relationship, he had to understand that she wasn't a victim—she was a survivor.

She finished her glass of wine and stepped out of the tub, reaching for a towel. As she scrubbed it briskly over her body, she watched the bubbles drain away. When she realized what she was doing, she forced herself to pivot around, to face the mirror she'd automatically turned away from.

She'd been angry with Mason for not wanting to look at her, accused him of being afraid of what he might see. But the truth was, she hadn't really looked either. Not since the day the bandages had been removed after her surgery, almost two years earlier, had she dared to look at herself in a mirror. Then, she'd been so distressed by the raw red lines and dark slashing threads, she'd bawled like a baby. She'd thought she had been prepared for what it would look like—but all she could think was that it wasn't her breast, it didn't look anything like her. And in that moment, she'd regretted even having the reconstruction.

Dr. Allison had tried to talk to her about it, had assured her the swelling would go down, the scar would fade, but Zoe didn't care. She never intended for anyone to see her naked again.

In retrospect, she could admit it was unrealistic for a woman not even thirty—and not in a convent—to remain celibate for the rest of her life. But she'd been adamant at the time, determined to punish her body for its betrayal.

Later, of course, she'd been grateful for the reconstruction. Grateful she'd been able to present herself, at least to the outside world, like a whole normal woman. Now, however, she was preparing to face a man without the barriers of clothing or pretenses—to show him the woman she was, flaws and all, and ask him to accept her that way. But first, she had to accept herself.

So she drew in a deep breath and let the towel drop to the floor. Slowly her eyes tracked downward, and her breath released on a sigh. Dr. Allison had been right— the ugly red slash she remembered had faded so that it was now only a faint pink line.

As she looked at herself in the mirror, she realized that her reconstructed breast was a symbol of the woman she was—imperfect, but alive and healthy and determined to live her life to the fullest.

Mason's life hadn't changed in the four days that Zoe was gone. He had mostly kept to his usual routine—taking Rosie for walks every morning and night. If he'd lingered in front of Zoe's empty house on occasion, he was just being neighborly—keeping an eye on things while he knew she was away. But the heaviness in his heart had warned that it was more than that, and the ache of longing worried him.

Rosie had missed her, too. The animal would sit and stare longingly at the house, whimper forlornly, then look to Mason as if he blamed his master for Zoe's absence.

Mason suspected that he was to blame, that she wouldn't have accepted her ex-husband's offer to go the Caribbean if he hadn't screwed things up so completely. And the thought of her in the Caribbean with her ex-husband nearly drove him insane.

Although Zoe hadn't seemed to think Scott wanted anything more from her than the taking of some photographs, Mason hadn't been so sure. He'd tried to console himself with the fact that they were divorced, tried to assure himself that she would never have gotten involved with him on any level if she wasn't well and truly over her ex. But he'd known Zoe only three months and she'd been married to Scott for nine years, and she'd gone off to Exuma not just with her ex-husband but obviously ticked off at Mason. It was enough to make him wonder…and worry. Had he blown his chance with her completely? Would she come back?

It was on the third day of her absence that he'd finally acknowledged the truth that had been nudging at his subconscious for weeks—he'd fallen in love with her. He wasn't sure when or how it had happened, but he no longer doubted the depth of what he was feeling.

And he finally recognized the opportunity he'd been given when she walked into his life. Or maybe it was more accurate to say that he'd walked into hers. In any case, he knew it was an opportunity that he'd nearly squandered. He wouldn't make the same mistake again—not if he was given a second chance.

He'd paced a lot in the four days that she was gone, and tossed and turned in his bed. The house had seemed too silent somehow, too empty. The quiet had never bothered him before, the isolation had never worried him. He'd enjoyed his solitary existence, appreciated the freedom of doing what he wanted when he wanted.

Throughout his entire adult life, he'd been careful to keep his relationships with women simple, casual, easy. If the thought of falling in love had scared him, the idea of committing to one woman had terrified him. But that was before Zoe, before he'd realized that love could be a gift instead of a curse. Before he'd understood that an even scarier prospect than spending the rest of his life with one person was the possibility of spending the rest of his life without Zoe.

Yeah, she was only gone four days. But in those four days, he'd missed her. He'd missed her energy, her smile, the light that seemed to shine from within her. And he realized that he wanted her with him, every day, for the rest of his life.

Now, he only had to find a way to convince her to take a chance on him. Dinner, he hoped, would be the first step.

He'd never cooked for a woman before. Not anything more complicated than tossing some meat onto a barbecue, which he didn't figure really counted since he did the same thing whenever he had his buddies over for a meal. It wasn't that he couldn't cook, just that he'd never dated a woman for whom he wanted to make the effort. Until Zoe.

So many things had changed since she'd moved in next door. It was as if he could divide his life into two parts: "Before Zoe" and "After Zoe"—or, if he was lucky, "With Zoe."

He heard her moving around upstairs—getting dressed—and forced his thoughts away from *that* mental image to concentrate on dishing up the chicken and rice.

He was carrying the plates into the dining room when she came down the stairs. She was wearing a dress—it was short, sleeveless and scooped low in the front and the back. Her hair tumbled loose over her shoulders, the way he liked it best, and her skin was lightly tanned and glowing from the bath.

"I thought, since you went to so much trouble for dinner, I should dress up for the occasion."

"You looked great before. Now you look...a hell of a lot more tempting than dinner."

Her lips curved. "Dinner looks good to me."

It was only when she looked at the plates in his hand that he realized he was still holding them. He set them on the table, then held out her chair.

He kept the conversation casual during the meal. He could tell she was a little apprehensive, though he wasn't sure if her nerves were because she didn't know why he was there or because she did. He was experiencing some tension, too, because tonight he would either get everything he wanted—or lose the woman he loved.

"I was thinking about another alteration to the house plans," she said, after she'd finally pushed away her plate.

"You want to make changes now—when the renovations are almost finished?"

"Not a big change," she assured him.

"The client never thinks it's a big change."

She smiled, and the light in her eyes took his breath away. "I want a darkroom."

"A darkroom, huh? I seem to recall that we had a similar conversation once before and you claimed you didn't need one."

"I changed my mind."

"I'm glad."

"You are?"

"Yeah, because it means your trip was obviously a success."

"So much so that Scott offered me a job back at the magazine."

"And?" He didn't think she would need a darkroom

in her house in Pinehurst if she was planning to go back to New York City, but he wanted to be sure.

"And I turned him down. I don't want to be a fashion photographer anymore, but I've realized that I am still a photographer. That I still want to take pictures. Which means, of course, that I'll need somewhere to develop those pictures."

"I think we can work out something."

"Good." She smiled again.

He pushed away from the table, cleared their plates. Zoe followed him to the kitchen carrying the wineglasses and the half-empty bottle. They worked together loading the dishwasher and straightening the kitchen.

"Now are you going to tell me why you're really here?" she asked as she topped up their wineglasses.

"Because you told me to let you know when I figured out what I wanted…and I want you."

Her hand shook, splashing wine over the rim of the glass. She set the bottle down on the counter and concentrated on wiping up the spill with a towel. When she was finished, she folded the towel, hung it over the handle of the oven door, then—finally—faced him.

He laid his hands on her shoulders, then stroked them down her arms to her hands and linked their fingers together. "Now the question is—what do *you* want?"

"You," she admitted. "I think I've wanted you from the beginning. And when I came home and found you here, I started to hope, but I was afraid to hope and…"

The rest of the words faded away when he touched his lips to hers. Once, softly, briefly.

"I figured out something else, too," he told her.

"What's that?"

"That I love you."

He heard her soft intake of breath, saw the flicker of surprise, then wariness filled her deep brown eyes.

"Mason," she began.

"Shh." He brushed his mouth against hers again, silencing whatever she intended to say. "Don't say anything. Don't doubt it. Let me show you."

She couldn't refuse him something that she, too, wanted. Instead, she took his hand and led him up the stairs to her bedroom.

Her heart was pounding, her blood was pumping, and her stomach was a tangled knot of nerves and anticipation. She wanted this—it seemed as if she'd wanted this forever. But she was also terrified that despite the reassurance of his words, the tenderness of his touch and the passion in his kiss, he would decide she wasn't what he wanted after all.

He stroked a hand gently over her hair. "You're trembling."

"I'm scared," she admitted softly.

"Am I moving too fast? I don't want—"

"No. You're not moving too fast. I'm just worried that you'll be disappointed."

"Never," he promised. "Although I have to admit that I'm a little scared, too."

"What are you afraid of?"

"Touching you—or not touching you." His mouth curved in a wry smile. "Does that make any sense?"

She nodded, understanding completely. "So much for sex being simple, huh?"

"Sex *is* simple. What's between us is more than sex."

"It doesn't have to be. We don't have to complicate this."

"It's already complicated," he told her. "But I'm finding I don't mind that as much as I thought I would."

Then he kissed her again. And the touch of his mouth to hers, that slow, sensual glide of his lips, wiped her mind of everything except the here and now. As the kiss deepened, her desire escalated and the last vestiges of fear faded away.

His touch was as patient and unhurried as his kiss, his hands trailing down her back, slowly stroking up again. When he tugged down the zipper at the back of her dress, she didn't try to stop him. When he pushed the straps over her shoulders, she let the garment slither down to the floor, leaving her clad in only a lacy pink bra and matching bikini panties.

He lowered his head and kissed the curve of her breasts above the scalloped edge of her bra, first one breast, then the other. Then his tongue dipped into the valley between them, and she shuddered.

He scooped her off the floor and carried her to the bed, laying her down gently on the covers. She pulled him down with her and fused her mouth to his. Their kiss was hot and hungry now, as greedy and impatient as the hands that dragged at his shirt, seeking and finding hard, bare skin. Her palms slid over his belly, his chest, his shoulders, stroking the smooth, sleek muscles.

He drew away to yank the shirt over his head, toss it aside. She found the button at the front of his pants, urging him to discard those as well and revealing a pair of dark, sexy boxer briefs. Then he was kissing her again, his hands were on her again, and the glorious weight of his body was pressing hers into the mattress. She wrapped her arms around him, locked her legs around his, and gave herself over to the passion he'd reawakened.

He found the center clasp of her bra and with a quick flick, it was open. She stilled. It was an automatic response, an instinctive reaction, and one that she cursed herself for even knowing she couldn't prevent it.

But he didn't miss a beat. And as his hands and his lips continued their exquisite torture, she found herself relaxing again.

His mouth skimmed down her throat, lower. His hands were on her breasts, then sliding over her hips, down her thighs. His lips were on her breasts, first one, then the other. He lingered a moment at her nipple—and though she couldn't really feel anything there, she didn't dissuade him. He was clearly enjoying his exploration of her body, and the realization was exhilarating. Then he moved over to the other nipple, his tongue circling the base, his lips closing over the turgid peak.

"You are beautiful, Zoe. And perfect just the way you are."

She shook her head, but he ignored her wordless protest. His hands and his mouth continued their leisurely sensual exploration, exploring all of the dips and curves of her body with such devastating thoroughness she was breathless and quivering with wanting.

"Mason, please."

His hands skimmed down the outside of her thighs, then up the inside. "I'm not going to be rushed," he said. "Not this time."

It was exquisite torture, the slow, steady building of heat and tension deep inside. His knee slid between hers, nudging apart her thighs, and she thought, *finally*.

But still he didn't hurry. Still he teased and tormented until her nerves were stretched so taut she thought they might snap. His fingertips skated up the inside of her thigh, then down again. Each time, moving just a little higher, a little closer to where she was practically begging to be touched. When his thumb brushed over the moist curls at the apex of her thighs, she gasped. When it started to move in slow, gentle circles over the nub at her center, she actually whimpered. When he slid his finger between the slick folds and into her, she flew apart.

She barely had a chance to catch her breath before he was driving her up again. Only then did he finally sheath himself with a condom and rise over her.

In one smooth stroke, he slid into her—not just filling her, but fulfilling her. She let her eyes drift shut as she lost herself in the erotic pleasure of his body inside her. Their bodies moved together in perfect rhythm, as if they'd joined like this a thousand times instead of only once before. It was, in so many ways, like a homecoming.

"Look at me, Zoe."

She opened her eyes, found his fixed on her. The emotion in his gaze took her breath away.

"I want you to see that I'm looking at you," he

said. "I want you to know that I want only you—for now and forever."

Then he kissed her again.

As his lips moved over hers, his body moved inside of hers, she felt the tension building inside again.

His arms came around her, anchoring her, as she shuddered and sobbed through the waves of release that battered her into mindless, boneless submission, then finally dragged him under with her.

She was exhausted.

Wonderfully, fabulously, gloriously exhausted. And though she was pinned to the mattress beneath the weight of Mason's inert body, she didn't mind. In fact, she was a little disappointed when he finally lifted himself off her, landing face-first on the pillow. But then he shifted to his side and tucked her against him, holding her close.

"Remember what I said about taking things slow?" he asked.

She nodded against his shoulder.

"Well, I don't want to take it slow anymore."

"Since we're naked in my bed, I'd say that's a good thing."

"I wasn't just talking about making love with you— although I'm definitely glad we've moved ahead in that direction."

"Then what were you talking about?"

His hand stroked down her side, from her shoulder to her hip in a lazy caress that both soothed and aroused. "Building a future together."

"I thought we would just take things one day at a time."

"I want to marry you, Zoe."

She froze as both euphoria and terror filled her heart.

"Aren't you going to say something?" he asked after a long moment of silence.

Her head was spinning so that she couldn't think, never mind talk. I. Want. To. Marry. You. She sucked in a deep breath, blew it out again. "Why?"

He propped himself up on an elbow to look at her. "Because I love you and I want to share my life with you."

"You don't—you can't—"

He silenced her with a kiss. "I can and I do."

She shook her head. "It's too much, too soon."

"Is it?" His tone was deliberately casual. "Are there rules about this sort of thing?"

"You know what I mean."

"Actually, I don't. I've never been in love before, so I'm not familiar with the procedure or protocol. But I do know what I'm feeling, and everything just feels right when I'm with you.

"I've spent my entire adult life avoiding any kind of serious relationships without even realizing it. Tyler told me that any first-year psych student could figure out why—because the loss of first my mother then my father made me put shields up around my heart so it wouldn't ever take that kind of emotional hit again.

"Maybe there's some truth to that," he allowed. "Or maybe it's even simpler—maybe I just never found anyone that I wanted to get serious with. Until you."

He cradled her face in his hands, gently tipped her

head back so that she had no choice but to meet his gaze. "I love you, Zoe."

Her eyes filled with tears. "Damn you, Mason."

"That's not quite the reaction I was expecting."

"Well, I never expected to hear you say those three words."

"I've never said them before," he told her. "To anyone."

The tears spilled over. "You shouldn't have said them now—not to me."

He kissed away the tears, brushing his lips over the wet trail on one cheek, then the other, in a gesture so tender it caused more tears to spill over.

"Why not?" he asked gently.

She swallowed. "Because I already screwed up one marriage—the last thing I want is to jump into another."

"Do you love me, Zoe?"

"I don't think I could be here with you now if I didn't."

This time when he kissed her, it was harder, fiercer and somehow triumphant. "Then marry me," he said. "So that we can start building our life together."

She didn't know what to say, how to respond to the man who was offering her everything she'd wanted for so long. She was tempted and she was terrified, and, most of all, she was worried that regardless of whether she said "yes" or "no," she would somehow end up hurting him.

"What do you say, Zoe?"

He was the man who'd loved her with frenzied passion and exquisite tenderness, who'd touched not just her body but her heart and healed the wounds that went so much deeper than the physical scars on her body. The man she loved.

Though she couldn't deny her feelings for him, she had no intention of making a life-altering decision after knowing him only three months. It was ridiculous to even consider anything different.

But when she opened her mouth to tell him just that, she heard herself saying "yes" instead.

Chapter Thirteen

Zoe held out her hand.

Her friend stared, speechless, at the diamonds winking from her third finger. "You're getting married?"

"Tell me I'm not crazy."

"You're definitely crazy," Claire said, then grinned. "But I'm so happy for you."

"You don't think it's too soon?"

"Time doesn't have anything to do with it," her friend said. "The only thing that matters is how you feel about each other."

"I've only known him three months, but I already can't imagine my life without him," Zoe admitted. "He makes me feel—I can't even describe how I feel when

I'm with him. Except that I've never felt like this before. I feel happy and hopeful, as if our future together can be anything we want it to be."

"That's exactly how you should feel when you're starting a life with the person you love."

"I do love him," she said. "I thought, after my marriage to Scott fell apart, that I would never be able to love someone again. I know I didn't want to. But suddenly Mason was just there, in my heart, filling it full of feelings I didn't ever expect to have again."

"You deserve this," Claire said, hugging her tight. "Have you set a date yet?"

"October sixth."

"Not this October?"

Zoe nodded. "I know it's quick. But Mason said he doesn't want to wait any longer than absolutely necessary to start our life together. I told him I couldn't plan a wedding in less than four months—so we compromised on two."

"If you need any help, let me know," Claire said. "I'd love to—"

"Be my matron of honor?"

Claire stared at her. "Are you serious?"

Zoe nodded.

"But you must have friends you've known longer than me—"

"No one who knows me better," she interrupted. "Certainly no one who's been there for me the way you've been. And no one who means as much to me as you do."

Her friends soft grey eyes shimmered with moisture. "Okay then," she sniffled and blinked back the tears.

"Two months isn't very much time, we better start making plans."

"It's going to be a small wedding," Zoe said. "Probably outside at Hadfield House, if the weather's good."

"We can get a tent to have the reception there, too." Claire pulled open a drawer where she found a pad of paper and a pen to take notes. "I know a great caterer. Did you want a sit-down meal or just hors d'oeuvres? A band or a D.J.? Real flowers or silk?"

Zoe's head was spinning. Mason had proposed only the night before, and put the ring on her finger that morning. She hadn't had a chance to think about any of the details yet—or to panic about everything that needed to be done in such a short time.

Suddenly Claire looked up from the paper, her eyes wide as another thought occurred. "And who's going to take the pictures?"

Over the next six weeks, Zoe and Claire worked out all of the details. As the day of the wedding drew nearer, Zoe found herself really looking forward to the occasion—and especially to starting her life with Mason.

Until the morning, less than two weeks before their scheduled exchange of vows, that she found the lump.

Mason had left early for work—although he'd taken time to make love with her before rushing off to a job site—and she'd reluctantly forced herself out of the comfort of her bed to shower and start her own day.

She was rubbing shower gel over her skin and thinking that she should schedule a pedicure before the wedding when she felt something on the underside of her breast.

Despite the steam rising from the water, she felt an immediate chill—an icy-cold that encapsulated her whole body. Suddenly weak in the knees, she braced her forearms on the tile, leaned her head against them, and forced herself to breathe.

"It's not a lump." She spoke aloud, as if hearing the echo of the words might convince her that they were true. "Of course it's not a lump. The breast is gone— I'm just being paranoid, afraid to let myself be happy."

But her fingers moved automatically to the underside of her breast, hesitating just below where she'd felt the ridge. "There's nothing there," she said to herself, and slid her fingertips over the skin.

But it wasn't nothing. It was something—a definite thickening of tissue between the implant and the wall of her chest.

"It's not cancer."

She repeated those words over and over again, reminding herself that there were numerous other possible explanations for the strange bump under her skin. It could be a cyst or a fibroadenoma. And even if it was a tumor, it could be benign.

But even as she considered the various possibilities, the one that remained at the forefront of her mind was cancer.

She knew that there was a ten percent risk of a local recurrence after surgery, and that ninety percent of such recurrences happened within the first five years of the surgery. She also knew that better than eighty percent of women with an isolated local recurrence following mastectomy eventually developed distant metastases.

And even with all of the research being done, that was always a grim prognosis.

Yeah, she knew all of the numbers, all of the cold, hard facts, and they terrified her.

She sank to her knees in the shower, buried her face in her hands and sobbed until the water turned cold.

As Mason headed back to Zoe's after work on Monday, he couldn't shake the feeling that something was wrong with Zoe. For a few days now, she'd been quiet and withdrawn and he didn't have the slightest idea why. She'd been busy over the past couple of months, making plans for the wedding and final preparations for the bed-and-breakfast, which she would open to guests in the spring, but she hadn't seemed overly stressed or preoccupied with anything.

Not until Friday, he decided, thinking back. She'd been fine in the morning when he'd said good-bye, but definitely distracted when he got home. He wondered if her preoccupation had anything to do with the call he'd received earlier that day, and when he got home, he asked her about it.

"The caterer contacted me today," he said. "He said you haven't got back to him with the final numbers for the reception."

"Actually, I wanted to talk to you about that."

"The numbers?"

"The wedding." She took the tray of manicotti out of the oven, lifted the foil to check it. "I think we should postpone the wedding."

"What?"

"It's just too soon. Everything's happening too fast."

He stared at her—at the back of her head, actually, since she seemed more interested in the pasta than in discussing their wedding.

He strode over to the oven, pushed the foil back down on the tray and forced her to look at him. "We set the date two months ago—"

"I was obviously out of my mind to agree to plan a wedding in two months."

"Not only did you agree to do it," he pointed out, "You've done it. Everything is ready for our wedding in nine days, so why would you want to postpone it now?"

"It just seems like we're rushing into this," she said.

"I thought we agreed there wasn't any reason to wait."

She glanced away. "I think a spring wedding would be nice."

"What's wrong with a fall wedding?"

"I got married in the fall the first time and—"

"You got married in January."

She frowned.

"Obviously you don't remember telling me that."

"My point is that it would be nicer to get married in the garden when the flowers are blooming."

His eyes narrowed. "What's going on, Zoe?"

"I just think we should wait a few months."

"Why?"

"Please." Her eyes were suspiciously bright. "I just need some more time."

His heart sank. "I love you, Zoe."

She didn't say the words back. In fact, she didn't say anything at all, and her silence was like a knife through his heart.

From the moment he'd realized he'd fallen in love with Zoe, he'd been certain about what he wanted. He'd been so certain, in fact, that it hadn't occurred to him she might not want the same thing. He hadn't considered that she might have reservations about getting married. Sure, she'd been hesitant when he'd first proposed, but he'd assumed her reluctance had been simply because she'd been so recently divorced. He hadn't worried that he'd pushed her too far too fast, that she might not love him as completely and wholeheartedly as he loved her.

And considering that possibility now was almost more than he could stand, but he had to know. "Do you love me, Zoe?"

She didn't meet his gaze. "I need time to be sure about my feelings."

Zoe hadn't expected that he would come back, certainly not that same night. And she hadn't expected that when he did come back, it would be with steely determination in his eyes.

"No," he said.

"What?"

"We're not postponing the wedding."

She folded her arms over her chest. "You don't get to make that decision unilaterally."

"We set the date together," he reminded her.

"Fine—let's change it together."

"No."

"You're being unreasonable."

His only response was to haul her into his arms and kiss her. She tasted his fury and frustration and, beneath the surface of those emotions, hurt and need.

She tried to resist—she really did. She knew what he was doing, trying to make her respond to his touch, to prove her feelings for him. But even knowing it, she couldn't prevent it. She couldn't deny the way her lips softened beneath his or the way her body yielded to his anymore than she could hold back the silent tears that spilled onto her cheeks as she kissed him back.

His lips softened and his hands lifted to cradle her face, his thumbs gently brushing the tears away. "Tell me you don't love me."

"I don't love you."

But the tears were streaming now, the anguish in her eyes undeniable.

"Now tell me why," he said.

And finally she did. She told him about finding the lump in the shower and her appointment earlier that day with Dr. Allison, who had tried to be reassuring but had done a core needle biopsy to determine the exact nature of the problem.

He held her while she cried, and he cried right along with her. But he never turned away from her, he never tried to downplay her concerns or her emotions. He did give her hell for not telling him right away—and for not letting him go with her to the appointment—but mostly he was just there for her as no one but Claire had ever been before.

"When will your doctor have the results?"

"I have a three o'clock appointment on Thursday."

"I'm taking you."

"You don't have—"

"I love you, Zoe."

He said it softly but with such conviction, she couldn't deny him the expression of her own feelings. She took his hand and led him upstairs to the bedroom. And she told him not just in words, but with her body and her heart, how much she loved him. She loved him with everything she had, everything she was, as if it might be their last time together.

Claire was the first person Zoe had told about finding the irregularity in her breast—the only person, in fact, until Mason had managed to pry the information out of her. And she was the one person who was with Zoe when she got the phone call early Wednesday morning changing her scheduled appointment with Dr. Allison.

"Are you going to let your fiancé know about the new appointment?" Claire asked when Zoe got off the phone.

"No, because then he'll juggle his schedule to try to go with me, and it really isn't necessary."

"I know you're worried," Claire said gently. "You don't have to pretend you're not."

"Of course, I'm worried, but I'll handle it. I'm not so sure Mason can."

"How do you think he'll handle it if he finds out you went without him?"

"That's really not on the top of my list of concerns right now."

"Is the wedding on that list?" Claire wanted to know. "Because you're supposed to be getting married in three days."

Zoe sighed as she zipped up her overnight bag—she wasn't planning on staying in the city but, not knowing the results of her biopsy, thought it was best to be prepared.

"He loves you," Claire said gently.

She nodded. Over the past few weeks, Mason had proven that to her in more ways than she could count. Even when she'd finally told him about the lump, he'd stood firm, insisting that he loved her and wanted to marry her. And although Zoe loved him even more for his conviction, too much had changed since his original proposal for her to hold him to it.

"Enough to stand by you no matter what happens," her friend continued.

Zoe knew that was probably true. But she loved him too much to put him through the hell of a second diagnosis and everything that might entail.

She closed her eyes, her grip instinctively tightening on the handle of her bag. God, she didn't even want to think about what would come after. Since she'd found the suspicious thickening on the underside of her reconstructed breast—she was terrified to even call it a lump—she'd been concentrating only on the first step: get to the doctor. She hadn't wanted to think any further than that, had been terrified by the possibilities.

"Let me come with you," Claire said.

"You have your book club tonight, and I'm not sure what time I'll get back or if I'll have to stay."

"I can skip my book club for one week."

Zoe shook her head.

Claire sighed and excused herself to boil the kettle while Zoe threw some things in an overnight bag. When Claire returned with two cups of peppermint tea, she studied her friend closely.

Zoe sensed her scrutiny, and the question she hesitated to ask. But when she finished her tea and set the cup aside to pick up her bag, Claire finally said, "Are you coming back?"

She forced a smile. "I only packed two pairs of underwear."

"Then I'll expect to see you on Friday."

Claire folded her friend in her arms and hugged her tightly; Zoe's throat was constricted as she returned the embrace.

She didn't look back as she made her way down the stairs. If she did, she might break down, and she couldn't get through this if she broke down.

One step at a time, she reminded herself, reaching for the handle of the door.

She blinked against the brightness of the sunshine as she stepped out onto the porch—and came face-to-face with Mason.

Zoe blinked again, thinking that he might be just an illusion, but when she opened her eyes, he was still there.

And pissed off, if his narrowed gaze and set jaw were any indication.

Her heart bumped hard against her ribs.

She didn't have to ask how he'd known. No doubt Claire had called him when she'd gone downstairs to make the tea. And though Zoe wanted to be angry with her friend, she knew her actions had been motivated by love and concern for her.

Mason pried her fingers from the handle of her bag, then slung it over his shoulder.

"Let's go," he said tersely.

She wanted to refuse, to dig in her heels, but he was already tossing her bag into the back of the MDX.

He opened the passenger door, and waited. Despite his silence, she sensed his impatience, as obvious as the anger that showed in the stiffness of his posture and the flex of the muscle in his jaw.

"Mason—"

"Just get in the car."

She flinched at the fury in his tone, started toward the open door, then stopped. "You know, I didn't ask you to go with me and—"

"No, you didn't, did you?" he interrupted. "In fact, you didn't even tell me you had an appointment today."

And that was when she realized he wasn't just angry, he was hurt. She felt a pang of regret that she'd caused him pain—the last thing she'd wanted to do was hurt him. But she knew he would be hurt a lot more if the results of her biopsy weren't good.

"I thought it would be better if I handled this on my own," she said softly.

"You're wearing my ring on your finger," he reminded her. "That means you don't handle anything on your own."

She touched his arm. "I know how hard this is for you."

"I don't think you do."

"That's why I wanted to deal with this on my own."

He shook his head. "Do you know what's the worst thing about this whole situation? It's not that you're facing the possibility of another battle with cancer, because you've done that once already and proven that you can win. It's that you don't trust me enough to stick by you if you have to do it again."

"That's not true," she denied.

He stared at her hard. "Isn't it?"

And she realized that maybe he was right. Maybe she hadn't wanted to tell him about the appointment because she didn't trust that he would be there for her as she needed him to be there for her, and if she didn't have any expectations, she wouldn't be disappointed.

"I'm not your ex-husband," he said gently.

"I know," she said, and in that moment, she finally accepted that it was true. "I'm sorry."

"I don't want an apology, I want your trust. But obviously we need to work on that some more." He waited until she was in the SUV, then he closed the door and went around to the driver's side.

"Where are you going?" she asked, when he turned toward downtown instead of the highway.

"To the courthouse."

"Why?"

"To pick up our marriage license."

She didn't say anything. The last thing she wanted was to get into a discussion about their wedding when she still wasn't even sure if it would happen.

You're supposed to be getting married in three days.

Claire's statement echoed in her mind, as did the question implicit in it.

I'm not your ex-husband.

No, he wasn't. And he would stand by her. She didn't doubt that any longer. But it would break his heart to do so, and she couldn't do that to him.

He pulled into the parking lot of the courthouse.

"Come on," he said.

She didn't think they both needed to be there to pick up a piece of paper, but she got out of the vehicle anyway.

There was nothing she wanted more than to marry Mason and live happily-ever-after with him, but the harsh reality was that her visit to Dr. Allison today could bring her whole castle in the clouds tumbling down around her. She wanted to think positively. She was trying really hard to retain an optimistic outlook, but the doubts and fears kept crowding in.

"Couldn't we pick up our marriage license on the way back?" she finally asked.

"We probably could," he agreed. "But the JP could only squeeze us in this morning."

"Why do we need to see the JP?"

"To get married."

His words stopped her dead in her tracks. "You can't be serious."

He turned to face her. "Why not?"

"Because we have a wedding planned for Saturday afternoon—"

"A wedding that you have no intention of showing up for if the news you get from Dr. Allison isn't what you want to hear."

She couldn't deny it, so she said, "This is ridiculous. We have almost fifty people—"

"I don't give a damn about our guests or the cake or the caterer or any one of the thousand other details that I'm sure went into planning the event, and I don't believe you really do, either. The only thing that matters is the vows—the pledging of our hearts to one another, the promise to stick together no matter what the future might bring."

He sounded as if he really meant it, and when he kissed her, she knew that he did. She hadn't realized that she was crying until he kissed her tears away, his lips brushing over first one cheek, then the other.

"I've cried more in the past week than in the past ten years," she told him. "And it's usually on your shoulder."

"I'm not afraid of a few tears."

"It could get a lot worse before it gets better."

"I know—but we'll focus on the 'better' part. Whatever happens, we'll be together. We'll face the future together."

Two hours later, Zoe was standing in the back of an elevator, twisting her brand-new wedding band on her finger. She still wondered if she should have been stronger, somehow found the strength to hold firm in her conviction to wait. But it was done now—they were officially married. And though she still worried about their future, she was relieved to know that she didn't have to be strong all by herself anymore. Whatever happened, he would be there for her, as she would be there for him.

When the bell dinged to announce their arrival on the

sixteenth floor, Mason touched his hand to the small of her back, gently propelling her forward.

She moved ahead, because his strength gave her strength. If he was strong enough to face this with her, she would be strong enough, too.

She glanced up at him, saw that his jaw was set, his eyes hard and focused, and the pulse in his throat was racing. She loved him so much, but never more so than in that very moment, and she took his hand, linking their fingers together as much for reassurance as to reassure.

He paused outside the door with Dr. Allison's name on it.

"I love you," he said. "For now and for always."

She tried to smile, but her lips trembled rather than curved. She tried to speak, to tell him that she loved him, too, but her throat was too tight to allow the words to escape.

"I know," he said softly to her, and managed a smile. "You don't have to say anything, because I know. And that's all that matters."

And Zoe knew that no matter what Dr. Allison had to tell her today, she could handle it with Mason by her side.

Epilogue

Rain was pounding on the roof when Zoe woke up.

She snuggled deeper under the covers, and sighed contentedly when she felt Mason's arm curl around her before he tugged her back against the warmth of his body.

"It's raining," she told him.

"Just like the day we got married," her husband noted.

He wasn't talking about the day of their courthouse ceremony but the day they'd renewed their vows in front of their family—including her mother, who had come from Montana with potential husband number five, and his eighty-one-year-old grandmother and her husband, who had made the trip from Florida in their RV—and friends. The weather had been gray and drizzly and dreary, but Zoe hadn't cared. Everything was right in her world because three days earlier, she'd found out that the lump she'd so feared was only scar tissue.

Now, three *years* later, Zoe and Mason were celebrating not just their third anniversary but her fifth year cancer-free.

"What are we going to do today?" she asked.

"Whatever you want, so long as it doesn't involve a visit to Hadfield House or a camera."

She smiled at that.

For the first two years of their marriage, they'd lived in Hadfield House, where she'd juggled her responsibilities as manager of the bed-and-breakfast with the demands of her newly launched business as a special occasion photographer. But both ventures had proven to be incredibly successful, forcing Zoe to make a choice. Six months ago, she'd hired another manager for Hadfield House, and she and Mason had moved out and into their new home—designed by Mason and built by his brother.

"I had thought I would be sad to leave Hadfield House," she admitted. "But it was time to move on."

"You'd accomplished what you needed to there," he agreed.

Something in his tone suggested that he understood more about the connection she felt to the house than she'd ever told him.

"What do you mean?"

"I'm not so clueless that I couldn't figure out that you needed to make something of that old house in order to heal yourself."

"I never would have said you were clueless," she assured him. "Although I never would have guessed you were that insightful, either."

"I'm proud of you, Zoe. And grateful, every day, that you are in my life."

He kissed her then, and she sighed her pleasure as her eyes drifted shut and her body melted against his.

"I have some ideas about how we can spend our anniversary," he murmured the words against her lips. "And they don't require leaving this room."

She wriggled closer to him. "Sounds interesting."

As his hands slipped beneath her pajama top, there was an impatient scratch at the door.

He groaned; she giggled.

"That beast is a menace," he said, echoing the statement she'd made to him so long ago.

But the words were no sooner out of his mouth than a cry came through the baby monitor. The sound of their ten-month-old son, adopted only three months earlier, filled her heart to overflowing with joy and pride and fear.

Mason was already out of bed and reaching for his jeans. "I'll take care of the dog, you take care of Liam."

She tied her robe around her waist and padded across the hall to the nursery, where their little boy was fussing.

"Good morning, my baby." She scooped him into her arms and held him close, breathing in his sweet baby scent.

Liam squawked and wriggled.

"I know—diaper, then breakfast, then cuddles," she said, laying him on the change table to take care of the first task.

She heard Rosie barking outside, and when Liam had a dry diaper on his bottom, she carried him to the window to watch the crazy dog dancing around in the rain.

"Da!" Liam clapped his hands together, a mile-wide smile lighting up his face.

"Yeah, there's your daddy."

"Ro!"

"And Rosie," she confirmed, then turned the baby around in her arms. "You know, you really need to learn how to say 'Mama.'"

He just stared at her with his big blue eyes.

"Bu-ba."

"Alright—we'll go get your bottle."

Mason came in, damp from the rain, just as she was settling Liam into his high chair with his juice.

"Hey, big guy." He dropped a kiss on the top of his son's head. "What are you and Mama making for breakfast today?"

"Ma!"

She nearly dropped the carton of eggs she'd taken out of the fridge. "What did he just say?"

"'Ma'—he says it all the time."

She put the eggs on the counter and turned around. "I've never heard him say it before."

He just shrugged. "It's usually when you're not here—when he's looking around for you and just before he starts screaming because he can't find you."

She smiled at that. "He looks for me?"

"Of course he looks for you—you're the center of his world." He wrapped his arms around her, nuzzled her throat. "Just as you're the center of mine."

Rosie barked.

"And his, too, apparently," Mason noted.

Zoe laughed and linked her hands behind his neck. "You know, I think I really like this life we've built together."

"I think I do, too," he said, and kissed her.

Somewhere in the background she registered the sound of the dog barking, the baby banging his bottle on the tray of his high chair and the telephone ringing.

"And though I sometimes wish it was a little less chaotic," he admitted, "it is ours."

And the best part, she knew, was that their life together had only just begun.

MILLS & BOON®

Fancy some more Mills & Boon books?

Well, good news!

We're giving you

15% OFF

your next eBook or paperback book purchase
on the Mills & Boon website.

So hurry, visit the website today and type **GIFT15**
in at the checkout for your exclusive 15% discount.

www.millsandboon.co.uk/gift15

MILLS & BOON®

Why not subscribe?

Never miss a title and save money too!

Here's what's available to you if you join the exclusive **Mills & Boon Book Club** today:

✦ *Titles up to a month ahead of the shops*
✦ *Amazing discounts*
✦ *Free P&P*
✦ *Earn Bonus Book points that can be redeemed against other titles and gifts*
✦ *Choose from monthly or pre-paid plans*

Still want more?

Well, if you join today we'll even give you
50% OFF your first parcel!

So visit **www.millsandboon.co.uk/subs**
or call Customer Relations on **020 8288 2888**
to be a part of this exclusive Book Club!